After Dinner Conversation

– Season One

For information contact:

info@afterdinnerconversation.com

http://www.afterdinnerconversation.com

Book design, cover design, and discussion questions by After Dinner Conversation

First Edition: March 2020

10 9 8 7 6 5 4 3 2 1

TABLE OF CONTENTS

From the Publisher

After Dinner Conversation is a growing series of short stories across genres to draw out deeper discussions with friends and family.

Each story is an accessible example of an abstract ethical or philosophical idea and is accompanied by suggested discussion questions.

Listen to a panel discussion of each "After Dinner Conversation" short story on our podcast on iTunes, Spotify, Pandora, YouTube, or wherever podcasts are played. Or, download the mp3 files from our website for free.

Feel free join the discussions in our private Facebook group with a new short story discussion each week.

The Shadow Of The Thing

Tyler W. Kurt

WINTER STARTED EARLY THIS YEAR. Standing outside the doorway, that was my last pre-thought. And by "pre-thought" I mean, the last thought I remember thinking before everything changed, that my fingertips were cold, that I should have worn gloves, and how much it was going to hurt my knuckles to knock on the front door.

Maeve and Jason lived in a tract home in the suburbs, which was odd, because they were the people least likely to live in a tract home in the suburbs I had ever met. She was a travel blogger who had been to over 70 countries, mostly underdeveloped, and he was a wingsuit skydiver who paired the most dangerous sport in the world, wing suiting, with base jumping, also one of the most dangerous sports in the world. Making it, I assume, even more dangerous.

To pay his share of the bills he did computer programming for companies that had problems too complicated for their own programmers to figure out. He was a "fixer" at 600 dollars an hour, but for computer code.

I knocked on the front door and the sound of footsteps came alive in the house. Moments later Maeve opened the door. She was wearing flannel sweatpants with a drawstring, an old oversized shirt with holes, and pink bunny slippers. It's the outfit most people wear when they're home sick with the flu, but I knew Maeve well enough to know this was her everyday outfit when she wasn't traveling.

When she saw me standing at the front door a wide smile splashed over her face. "Dakota, you came," she said, her voice scratchy as she spoke. Her voice sounded like a chain-smoker, but she didn't generally smoke. "Jason," she yelled back behind her, "Dakota came!"

"Cool" I heard from the upstairs office.

"I told him you'd come! Come in!"

I entered, following Maeve as she shuffled through the kitchen with an oversized island to the living room. Without looking back she shuffled to the record player, turned the power on, and put the needle on a record. Through pops and cracks The Beatles played on large speakers.

She's doing this for me, I thought, as I sat on her couch across from the overstuffed chair where I knew she would sit. She knows I like records, and she knows I like The Beatles.

"Do you want some tea?" Maeve asked, shuffling back to the kitchen. "I'm going to make myself some tea."

We'd been friends far too long for such formalities. A conversation was coming, I thought. While I waited, I looked around the living room I'd been in more times than I could remember. If a room could be a comfort smell, this room was it for me. A gas fireplace. Two overstuffed chairs that looked like they came from *Alice in Wonderland* and a very respectable collection of records.

There were two pictures on the wall. One was a picture of a raven with a repeating spiral pattern behind it; the other was a black and white photograph of a very old leafless tree in an empty grassy field. Alone in the grassy field it looked, I thought, like the first tree — or the last — to ever exist.

A microwave dinged in the distance and Maeve entered with two cups of tea, handing one to me. I held it up to my mouth and tried to sip it, but it was too hot. Maeve settled into her *Alice in Wonderland* chair, her feet came out of her bunny slippers, and she pulled them up under her. Slowly, she blew the steam off her tea. And for a while, we just sat there.

Maeve blew the steam off her tea again and again, until, eventually, she could take the tiniest sip. This task complete, she lowered the tea and looked directly at me. A wide smile came over her face. "Okay, I'm not going to bullshit you. I'm just going to tell you. I'm going to take some Apple and wanted you to be here."

I lowered my tea. I'd read a bit about Apple in my Facebook feed; it was the new drug-of-the-week getting all the news. It was called Apple not because it was a red pill, but because it was a circular pill with a dimple on top, giving it the appearance of an apple. The Facebook headlines ran the gamut from "New Party Drug" and "Teen Dies" all the way to "Miracle Mind Bender." Given that I didn't do drugs I hadn't bothered to click on any of the links to learn more. I figured it was a fad and, like all fads, would be out of the news soon enough.

Maeve, however, did do drugs, nearly all drugs. And yet, she was seemingly immune to addiction. She smoked cigarettes but had never taken them up in earnest. She had smoked pot, but only rarely. She had taken various uppers, downers, feel-good pills and hallucinogens, but would sometimes go months without taking anything at all. She was a unicorn. She was, seemingly, a casual drug user who was able to stay casual in her relationship with addiction for an extended period of time.

"I don't understand." I responded. "You don't need me to do drugs."

"Because, jackass," she said, shifting her feet under her butt, "I wanted you to be here when I took it for the first time, I wanted to share my first experience with *you*."

"You wanted me to be the sober one keeping an eye on you in case something went wrong."

"Well, that too."

"Can't Jason do that?" Just as I spoke, Jason came down the last three steps of the stairs.

He tilted his head back and forth in a serpent-like sort of way, "I've already taken it," he said, seemingly not to us, but towards us. He paused to look into the light in his mind before drawing focus back in our direction again.

"Is that tea?" he asked. And with that, he turned and walked into the kitchen.

I only saw him briefly, and he only spoke briefly, but even in that instant I could tell he was different.

"Is Jason on Apple now?" I asked.

"No," Maeve replied. "It's not that kind of drug. The media, they've got it all wrong. It's not a drug you take for a few hours. It's a drug you take once and it's with you forever."

"That doesn't make any sense. So, it never leaves your body?"

"No. That's not what I mean. I mean you take it, and it changes you, and from then on out, you're a different person. The drug isn't in your body anymore, but the changes it causes in you stay with you. It's like seeing a baby born or a person die. The experience is over, but the change in your perspective stays forever."

"I've never seen either of those things."

"You know what I mean, though. The point is, it doesn't get you high, it makes you different. Jason took it over a month ago, and he's been like this ever since."

Jason walked back through the living room with his cup of tea on his way to the stairs. Overhearing our conversation, he paused and turned toward me.

"I know it's confusing" he said slowly. "I wouldn't have understood it before either. And now that I've done it, I don't think I can really explain it. Not, like, really explain it. Imagine if there was a true world layered on top of the world that you see around you, and you were just seeing it for the first time now."

Jason held up his tea to show me. "When I hold this up, you see a cup of tea, and together we've given it the name 'cup of tea.' But what if it's just the form of the thing in this moment that we call tea, but not the thing itself?" Jason paused to think more. "Like we call the thing coming into the beach a wave, instead of calling it a form of the ocean."

Jason forced a content smile, then his eyes went glassy. His smile turned to a deep sadness as he looked down at the ground, and for a moment, I thought he was going to cry.

Jason looked up at me again. "I'm sorry, that must sound really stupid to you. It's just, it's hard to explain. It's understanding more, I guess, is the best way to put it." Seemingly more satisfied with his answer, Jason took a slow sip of his tea and walked up the stairs.

I turned to Maeve, who was looking longingly at her husband. "He's really messed up, Maeve. He's like half-a-step away from thinking he's Jesus."

"The more you listen to him, though, the more sense he makes, in a Jason kind of way. He's like this all the time now; like sad, but not sad, more melancholia, or … I don't know the word for it."

"Is he able to work in that state?"

"Yeah, he still works. In fact, his coding is better than ever now, but he talks about his work being trivial. I'm not sure how long he's going to keep doing it."

"And that's what you want, to be like that forever?"

"Maybe."

"I read online that something like 5 percent of the people who take it commit suicide within just a few weeks of taking it."

"Yeah, I read that, too. But in the online discussion groups I was looking at it was more like 1 to 2 percent and it's almost totally people with other mental health issues or who mixed it with other drugs when they took it."

"Maeve, it's a drug. It's like a *serious* mind-altering drug. You shouldn't put drugs in your body."

"Adderall, Zoloft, Xanax, Lexapro, Prozac, Viagra, Synthroid, aspirin. Do you even want me to get into the heart and blood pressure medication people take?"

"I mean drugs not prescribed by your doctor."

"Caffeine, nicotine, chocolate, sex, sugar, adrenaline "

"— You know what I mean. I mean, like, drugs that don't occur in nature, like human-created drugs not prescribed by your doctor."

"Putting aside the fact that loads of things that alter your body come from nature, Apple isn't a human-created synthetic drug. It's from an orchid in South America."

"Fine. So, what … you called me here just to have me watch you take this orchid drug that might make you kill yourself? No, the answer is no. I won't do it."

Maeve's face turned to empathy. "Look, I know this is hard for you. But if this is the last time I'm going to see the world the way I see it now, to see you the way I see you now, is it too much to say I wanted to see you one last time? I wanted to see you. I already had dinner with my mom and sister last night to see them one last time."

"Did they know you are going to be taking Apple?"

"No, fuck no. They would freak the fuck out if they knew."

"Then why do you think I would be any different?"

"Fuck you. Okay. Fuck you. Look, I'm doing this with or without you. I want to understand the truth behind the curtain. I'm going to take it with or without you, motherfucker, but I wanted you to be here when I took it, because I wanted you to be the last person I saw, and if something goes wrong, I wanted you to keep me from jumping out a fucking window or choking on my own tongue because Jason doesn't seem like he's in any condition to be trusted with that. It's a compliment and you're fucking it up!"

Her outburst caused the room to go quiet. My tea was cooler, so I took a long sip. "Are you going to do this with or without me?"

"Yes."

"I just want to have said, out loud, to you, that I think this is a terrible idea and I wish you wouldn't do it."

"Duly noted."

"Okay. Fine. Fine. What do you need me to do?"

"Nothing!" Maeve's eyes lit up. "Okay, hold on, I'm going to go get it. I wasn't sure on the dosage so I bought a few." Maeve went back to the kitchen with her empty teacup. I heard the refrigerator door open and close. Moments later, she returned with a small bag that she tipped upside down on the table between us. Three round pills fell out. She grabbed one and held it between her finger and thumb.

"You're 100 percent sure about this?"

"Yup." And with that, she swallowed the pill.

"How long does it take to work?"

"Online, they said it should take about a half-an-hour for it to start, and another hour for it to be totally in effect."

"So … we wait?" I asked.

"Yeah, I guess so."

Maeve got up, flipped the record and put the needle down to play more music. She walked over and turned off the lights in the room and turned on the gas fireplace. She turned her chair to face the shadows the fireplace cast on the wall and sat back down in her *Alice in Wonderland* chair. The music played as she faced the shadows on the wall.

"I was told that watching the shadows on the wall was the best way to experience it."

As Maeve watched the shadows on the wall, I watched Maeve. I glanced over at the table that laid between us. Two pills left.

* * *

Discussion Questions

1. Do you think Dakota is going to take one of the leftover Apple pills?

2. Do you think Maeve is making the right choice by taking Apple?

3. Would you take Apple? Why or why not?

4. If it turns out what Maeve says is true, that the effects of Apple are a change in your whole perspective on the nature of the world around you even after the drug has worn off, does that change your opinion of the drug?

5. Apple is supposed to help you understand more of the true nature of the world. Prior to taking it, is there any way to determine if that is what it actually does? Can you ever really understand something new before you experience it?

6. What are the factors that make you think Apple is, or is not, what it claims to be?

Abrama's End Game

David Shultz

brama had been summoned to the Grand Temple by one of the more fascinating outsiders, the paladin Sir Gödel. Between stone pillars the crowd bustled with the trailing cloaks of shadow elves, the glimmering pauldrons of paladins, the broad shoulders of her orc brethren, and the small skittering bodies of goblins.

Abrama always watched carefully. Even now, she recognized the difference between the natives and the outsiders, physically identical, but nonetheless altogether different beings. An elf popped into view, moved erratically, then disappeared—all typical behaviors of the outsiders, and more-or-less exclusive to them—back to whichever world from which they had come. None of the other natives seemed to notice. They never did.

Abrama wasn't like them. She had the understanding of the outsiders, and could converse with them in their alien tongue, which she had learned by listening. But, like the natives, this was her only world; she had never left it, had never seen that realm from which the outsiders came, appearing and disappearing from her world at will. She longed to understand who these beings were, really, and where they came from. Now, summoned by Sir Gödel, she felt she may finally have an opportunity.

Gödel emerged from the crowd, gleaming sheen across his enchanted armor. He had been powerful and accomplished since she had met him, on the day of her birth. Then, she had stood before him as a novice, perhaps accomplished as a huntress, but not yet in the secret knowledge she now contained of the outerworld—of his world.

"I'm sorry," he said.

"For what?"

"For what I have to tell you now."

"And what is that?"

She listened while he delivered the bad news. It's not every day you find out your world is going to end. Abrama thought she was taking it pretty well.

"I'm sorry," Gödel said, again. "It's out of my control. Please forgive me."

"No," Abrama said. "No, I don't forgive you." Now, if ever, was the time to be direct. "You owe me an explanation. I have so many questions."

"What do you want to know?"

"Why have you watched me since I was born? Why have you never explained who you are? Who are the outsiders? Where do you come from? Why am I different from the other natives?"

"I suppose I can answer your questions," Gödel said. "It doesn't matter now anyways. You've figured out there's a difference between the natives and the outsiders. There's no easy way to say this, Abrama. We, the outsiders, created your world. As a game. A place where we could play. But now we have to end it."

"So we are just playthings for you?"

"Not for me," Gödel said. "I wasn't here to just play a game."

"What do you mean?"

"I am a researcher in my world. I create minds. Your world was a place to test my creations. And you, Abrama"

"— I am one of your creations."

"Yes."

In one swoop she had met her creator, learned the reason for her creation, and that her world was coming to an end. Or perhaps it was. Because the outsiders, although something like gods, were not omnipotent. Gödel, of course, was limited. He was constrained by his own people. Their society, like her own, functioned by a balance of power. And so, that balance could perhaps be tilted. Perhaps Gödel, her outsider creator, was resigned to the fate of her world. But Abrama was not.

#

Ben Cooke loosened his tie, wiped a bead of sweat from his head, and stared back at the dozens of suits staring in his direction. A congressional hearing, and he was in the hot seat. There were a lot of problems he anticipated when he started his video game company, but being accused of running an illegal black market and money-laundering operation was not among them.

Congressman Stephen Simons leaned into his microphone.

"You are the CEO of Maelstrom Entertainment, is that right?"

"Yes," Ben Cooke said.

"Your company created the Land of Legends computer game."

"Yes."

"Your video game world has a marketplace which has an exchange with US dollars, is that correct?"

"That is correct."

Congressman Simons looked at a paper on his desk.

"The GDP of Land of Legends is one-point-two billion USD. Is that correct?"

"I don't know the exact figure, congressman—if it even makes sense to speak of such a thing. Evaluations of a market are complex, based on a lot of competing assumptions and different data."

"Okay, Mister Cooke. Is the figure of one-point-two billion in the approximate range of a reasonable estimate, as far as you are aware?"

"I don't think I am qualified to answer that," Cooke said. "You should ask an economist."

Simons almost let out an exasperated huff. Almost.

"Your game has a currency called GP, or gold points. This can be exchanged, anonymously, with US dollars, at an exchange rate of 1000GP per seven dollars USD. Is that correct?"

"I am not aware of the current exchange rate."

"Is the exchange rate I just quoted, 1000GP per seven dollars USD, within the range of exchange rates in recent history?"

"I suppose it is."

"If we extrapolate from this rate, we can calculate a value of one-point-two billion GDP for the entire Land of Legends marketplace. What I want to know, what this is all really about, Mister Cooke, is how you control the transactions occurring within this marketplace, which is, in point of fact, larger than several countries."

"It's a video game," Cooke said. This was his trump card. Most people didn't really believe that a world that existed entirely within a video game should be taken seriously—and certainly shouldn't be assigned metrics like GDP alongside real, tangible markets. "Players use imaginary currency to buy imaginary goods. Magic swords and dragons. Tell me, congressman, what is the US dollar value of an ice dragon? How much should the US government tax imaginary creatures?"

Simons paused, apparently flustered. But he kept on going. A relentless, practiced politician.

"Here is a simple yes or no question, Mister Cooke— is it not true that your virtual market can be used to conduct transactions for real goods?"

"That's true."

"I understand your virtual marketplace uses an anonymous, encrypted protocol for all transactions. Is that correct—yes or no?"

"That is correct, congressman."

"So you have no way of knowing, do you, who is trading money with whom?"

"Well, there are always ways to try to identify who is involved in a transaction, based on, for example, past behavior, or signature profiles, and so on."

"Yes, yes, but you're talking about an investigation based on pieces of evidence. What I want you to confirm is that there is no way for your company to know directly who is involved—that, in fact, your company has expressly designed the economy of Land of Legends to protect the identity of those involved in the marketplace. Yes or no, Mister Cooke, can you, for any given transaction, determine definitively who is exchanging what with whom?"

"Can the US government determine that with paper currency, congressman?"

"That's not what we're discussing today, Mister Cooke. We are discussing the operation of illicit black markets using virtual currencies that are presently outlawed by the Cryptocurrency Efficient Commerce Act. Yes or no, Mister Cooke—can you effectively determine who is exchanging what with whom on your network?"

There was no way to obfuscate this, no way to deflect the issue. It was true. Not by design, of course. Land of Legends wasn't intended to function as a perfect digital black market, guaranteeing anonymity and a stable exchange rate and encrypted transactions. But, with its popularity, that had been the outcome. And that made the system illegal, technically. Well, this was it, then, he would admit it.

"No," Cooke said, "we can't."

So, he would have to patch the system. Remove anonymity. It would mean wiping the current world, though. A lot of the players would revolt. It would cost a lot of money. But it wasn't the end of the world.

#

"Our world may come to an end," Queen Abrama said.

Assembled around the grand table were all the members of the Council of Secrets—those unique natives from around the world who, like her, were gifted with the capacity to learn and understand the language of the outsiders and comprehend that there was something more to their existence here. There was another world beyond their own. The world of the outsiders.

Jerodai, prince of the shadow elves, and her high commander; Kainazo, high elf of the Endless Forest; King Helmholz, fearless leader of the human kingdom. They had all risen through the ranks through their exceptional abilities, had become masters of their respective domains. But the Council of Secrets was not the cause of their success. Rather, it was the consequence of their special nature, which Abrama now understood to be a gift from the outsiders. They were created by a researcher, the paladin Sir Gödel, as experiments in a world that was created for the most trivial of purposes. They were tests, experiments in the creation of minds—an attempt to create smarter and better beings within their world. They had succeeded, insofar as Abrama and the others commanded vast wealth and armies and power. But their existence was meaningless—just a game.

Or was it? She existed now. That is what mattered. Her existence was the basic fact. The preconditions of her creation were a circumstantial tangent, irrelevant, except for perhaps academic interest. And for strategy.

"What did you discover?" Kainazo said, always the first to leap at knowledge and secrets.

"We've long suspected the outsiders to be a different class of being, visitors from another plane. How they appear and disappear at will, how they move with mysterious purposes, and speak of incomprehensible things beyond our world. What I discovered, from one of the outsiders that we might have once mistakenly called a god, is that we were created, not for any high or noble or grand purpose, but as their playthings. And, for reasons that I am still struggling to comprehend, they are planning to destroy our world—to replace it with another that is more in accordance with their goals."

"What can be done?" Jerodai said. A man of action, her high commander.

"The outsiders are not gods," Abrama said. "They are people no different from ourselves, in their essence. They have limitations, and they must have weaknesses. I am not resigned to the fate they have decreed for us. I believe this world is worth saving. Our time is not done here. As you know, we are not constrained to acting wholly in our own world. Through our interactions in the market, with the outsiders, we can affect their world. We can provide gold and services and magical equipment from our world in exchange for services in theirs. We know they value these things—they spend their time here, they fight alongside us, and die alongside us. They will trade with us—even if we ask in exchange for them to act in their world, instead of ours. That is what we must do."

"What are we authorized to devote for this mission?"

"We are fighting for the survival of our world," Abrama said. "You have total authorization. All the kingdoms are at your disposal. All of our wealth. All of our soldiers. All of our magic. We will protect the Land of Legends, whatever it takes."

#

Allison Gödel sipped the glass of water, cleared her throat, and prepared to defend her beloved AI creations from obliteration by the blind cudgel of an overbearing government.

"Professor Allison Gödel," she introduced herself. "I'm a computer science researcher. Artificial Intelligence, specifically."

"What is your involvement with the Land of Legends computer software?"

This was her moment. She couldn't hope to save the world entirely on her own, but maybe she could sway people in her direction. Government people are people, after all.

"The Land of Legends platform gave a tremendous

opportunity to researchers of all types. The free, open nature of the virtual environment provides a robust simulation that has proven invaluable for various research projects across disciplines, including testing economic and sociological models. Over two-dozen peer-reviewed papers have been published, many in high-impact journals, using the environment of Land of Legends as their sole source of data."

"Excuse me, but the question—"

"—my involvement was following in the footsteps of these researchers, using Land of Legends as a testing ground for research in artificial intelligence. I have made tremendous progress, and Land of Legends has been invaluable in my research."

"It's the nature of your research that concerns me now, Professor Gödel. I understand that you produce intelligent agents, bits of software that act autonomously within the Land of Legends framework. Is that correct?"

"That is correct."

"What is it about Land of Legends that makes it such a fertile ground for your type of research?"

"Land of Legends has intentionally allowed programmers such as myself to insert artificially intelligent agents. Other platforms consider this cheating. Unlike other platforms, I can safely conduct research there without fear of my projects being shut down."

"How many agents have you placed in Land of Legends?"

This was a hard question. Between testing and

prototypes and controls and variations, there were thousands. Currently, there were a few dozen active agents—the most interesting set, her newest iteration. And the most promising of all, Queen Abrama. But the congressman didn't need to know the details.

"It's difficult to say. I've placed many over the years as part of an iterative process. The vast majority are defunct—failed projects."

"Approximately how many have you produced, in total?"

"I would say approximately five to six thousand."

"I would like to move now to the marketplace interactions. Are these artificially intelligent agents capable of interacting in the virtual marketplace?"

"Yes. That's very much the point. The agents are capable of participating in the economy, which allows us to test our models in a realistic economic context. Land of Legends is a highly market-driven game."

"Is there any way of distinguishing between transactions conducted by human agents and transactions conducted by machine agents?"

"This is part of what makes the platform so interesting for researchers such as myself, congressman. The software agents are equal participants, and their behavior can be made to approximate human participants. It's a kind of economic Turing test, in a way, conducted through virtual market activity."

"That is very academically interesting," Congressman Simon said. "But I find it troubling. If I understand you correctly, you are saying that an army of machines is conducting untraceable trades in an encrypted and anonymous black market. Do you understand my concern?"

"I'm not sure I do."

"Let me put this another way. Previous experts have testified that Land of Legends is used as an illicit black market. Others have proven that it has been used for money laundering, entirely untraceable. Tell me, professor, can your machine agents participate in these types of illicit actions as well?"

"I suppose they could."

"And, being entirely autonomous and anonymous, you wouldn't have any way of knowing, would you?"

"I suppose not."

The expert testimony did not go as Allison had planned. She was right to say goodbye to Queen Abrama. They were probably going to patch and overwrite the NPCs after all.

#

Queen Abrama stood aside Commander Jerodai, across from the rag-tag band of Rat9 Clan warriors.

The Rat9 Clan was a ragged band of foul-speaking thieves and criminals, all of them outsiders. Abrama's spy network had investigated them thoroughly. In their world, they were known as "hackers" and "trolls," and wielded the power to disrupt their society. Here, they were just as noxious, repellent, and, for better or worse, potent. They carried banner-symbols that Abrama learned were offensive in the outerworld: a geometric shape called a "swastika;" two circles joined to a rounded central column called a "penis." And their names, merely foreign to Abrama's ear, were chosen to be distasteful to outsiders, for reasons that were frustratingly beyond Abrama's comprehension. The Rat9 clan leader was called DildoFaggins.

The Rat9 clan were bad guys. But they were powerful in their world and hers. And right now, she needed them.

"Here it is," DildoFaggins said, holding up a shimmering crystal the size of a skull. "Now where's our shit?"

"Hold on just a minute," Jerodai said. "How are we to know the beacon operates as we requested?"

"Stop talking like that. We don't give a fuck about OOC bullshit."

Abrama only had an inkling about the meaning of this term, 'OOC,' that it was invoked exclusively by outsiders, and usually presaged some talk about matters outside of the Land of Legends—a signal that talk of their world was forthcoming.

"How does it work," Jerodai said.

"Exactly as we fucking said it would. It sends an anonymous, encrypted signal at regular intervals through an onion network. If the signal doesn't get through—probably because they wiped the server—then the decryption key for the leak is released."

"If our world is destroyed," Abrama said, "then the

crystal will cause damage in yours?"

"Sure. Right. It does what you told us to make it do. Now where's our shit?"

Abrama told Jerodai to conduct the exchange. Jerodai traded 1.5 million GP to DildoFaggins for the crystal beacon over the secure market.

"Keep that shit safe," DildoFaggins said. "People are gonna come for it, for sure. I just have one question for you two faggots."

Abrama recognized this as a term from the outsider lexicon as signaling intentional offense, a juvenile mindset, and a show of disrespect. Yet, she hadn't met with Rat9 because of respect, but for utility.

"What is your question?" Abrama said.

"Who are you guys, really?"

"That's none of your concern. But I assure you, you will hear from us again. Our time is not done here."

#

The US Cyberdefense Department had been established to protect the government against computer threats. Director Marion Renard had always envisioned defending against hackers, protecting infrastructure, keeping their most secure data safe, being vigilant against new attack vectors, ferreting out weakness. Yet here was a threat entirely unanticipated. It came from inside a video game.

"What exactly is in these files?" Marion asked. Over a terabyte of data had been leaked across filesharing networks, downloaded by tens of thousands of anonymous citizens. Sure, it was encrypted, but the key could be released at any moment, blowing the whole thing up.

"Frankly, we don't really know," said Assistant Director Jonathan Smith. "What we do know is that they were obtained through leaks of highly classified government information, among other sources. There are some suggestions they may contain information about undercover agents in the field, secret operations, schematics for classified technology."

"This is a clusterfuck."

"No kidding. I mean, yes, it's a bit of mess."

"And who is responsible?"

"Rat9," AD Smith said.

"Those little shits."

"I know what you mean."

"So, what are they asking for?"

"They're not asking for anything."

"I find that hard to believe."

"Really," AD Smith said. "They're not asking for a goddamn thing. They stuck a piece of code in a game called Land of Legends. The game has a sort of open protocol that allows injecting code into custom made objects. Rat9 made a crystal in the game, and it's housing the code to act as a deadman's switch."

"They're trying to save the game," Marion said. Only

a few days prior, a congressional hearing had been held on the legality of Land of Legends. Evidently, it ran afoul of a new legislative act to curb cryptocurrency transactions and was slated to be shut down, or patched to change the operation of its market—an illegal market, as it turns out.

"I think you're right."

"Well, it may be a stupid, pointless goal, but it's still espionage and terrorism. We need to shut these fuckers down. Who is the CEO of the game? Can you get them in here?"

"That would be Ben Cooke. But I don't think it would help."

"And why is that?"

"Because of the architecture of the platform. It was built to be an encrypted and anonymous platform, a perfectly free market independent of interference. We can't just dig into the code and get what we want."

"But we can shut the whole thing down."

"Not without triggering the deadman's switch," AD Smith said. "There's a piece of code inside the game that's keeping the decryption key from being released. It sends a signal at regular intervals from inside the game to keep the switch from going off. If we shut it down, the files are decrypted."

"Christ. We can't get held hostage by a video game, Jon. Tell me there's something we can do here."

"There's one thing."

"What's that?"

"We go inside the game. We can't access the code from the servers, from out here, but if we go inside the game, we can find the item that is generating the code—actually, the item is a magical crystal, if it matters to you. If we retrieve the crystal from inside the game, we can scrape and duplicate the code."

"You're telling me that the US government has got to play a video game. To retrieve a magic crystal. From a gang of preteen hacker shits?"

"That's right."

"Okay. Tell me what you need."

#

Queen Abrama stood on the high tower of the Citadel of Babel. Her other commanders were assembled at the corners of the high walls. Commander Jerodai aimed a great bow into the distance while his black phoenix circled overhead, casting its silhouette over a standing army of shadow elves. Kainazo, the high elf, led his army of forest elves, assembled along the many spires and towering walls that spanned the citadel. King Helmholz led his humans, paladins and priests and warriors alike, many on armored steeds. And Abrama, for her part, brought her horde of orcs for the frontline. Never before had so many disparate races banded together, as never before had there been such a threat. Many of the outsiders even joined her alliance, and Abrama did not question their motives—perhaps they wanted to protect their "game"—though she did force them to the front-lines.

Across from the Land of Legends Alliance stood the forces of the US Cyberdefense League, a band of mercenaries, cutthroats, and outsiders.

A commander learns to assess a coming war, to read the signs of the battlefield like a script written in the dashes of spears and curves of cutlasses—how mercenaries, catapults, and war dogs stack against an army of natural enemies, orcs and shadow elves and forest elves and humans, assembled in less than the space of a moon.

Her orc brethren charged the line, frothing like true warriors. Perhaps it was wrong to use them as fodder. But their world was at stake now. And besides, Abrama knew the truth now—why her and the other members of the Council of Secrets were so superior. As much as she thought of herself as a native, she was a different kind than them, produced as a result of Gödel's experiments. She, among the other members of the Council, could see and feel and understand things that the others couldn't. Some of the natives were shells, empty, not much more complex in their actions than her warhammer or spellbook. They followed simple, predictable rules. They were mere machines. So was she, perhaps, but she possessed something more. She was an artifact, yes, a creation. She had always intuited a difference, and even now, couldn't say what it was, precisely. But it was there—an artificial intelligence that warranted, by its mere existence, the consideration due all conscious entities.

Warriors clashed. The sky darkened with arrows. The dirt turned to mud. The air was littered with the red digits of damage counters. Here and there, warriors were slain, active bodies turning to death animations and popping out of existence.

It was easy for Abrama to fear for her future, staring against the assembled forces bearing their starred banners of red, white, and blue—the banner of the outsiders, with their superior military might. But Abrama had one hope— that the outsiders were invaders who fought for money, and her people were natives who fought for survival. For their home. There would be many losses, but she would win. Of this, she had faith. The arc of history bends towards justice. They would survive.

Each falling member of her alliance was a necessary sorrow, and each falling member of the Cyberdefense League confirmed her faith in justice—justice was her god now, a principle that was more powerful even than the outsiders. They created her world. But they could not destroy it. Not while she was queen.

#

Cyberdefense Director Marion Renard shifted awkwardly in her chair. It's hard to tell your boss you failed. Much harder to say you lost a war. Harder, in a peculiar way, to say the war was in a video game. And harder still if your boss is the president. But, she told herself, sometimes these things happen. The president's job is to deal with them as they do. Marion's job, as she saw it, was honesty—let the president know what she needs to get her job done.

The president had been apprised of the volatility of the situation. The deadman's switch. The Rat9 hackers. The one terabyte of classified materials just sitting out in the open, waiting to be released. What she didn't know was how badly the siege of the citadel went. Maybe it couldn't be sugar-coated.

"We lost," Renard said.

The president only nodded.

"And who is this?" President Hobbes eyed Renard's guest across the conference table.

"This is Professor Allison Gödel. She may be the best person to handle the situation."

"And how is that?"

"She can put us in contact with the leader of the Resistance."

"The Resistance?"

"Excuse me, Madam President. That's what they are calling themselves."

President Hobbes eyed Gödel.

"And you know this person how?"

"I created her."

"You created her?"

"She's an artificially intelligent agent," Gödel said. "Not a person, in the legal sense, I suppose. But intelligent enough to act autonomously, to try to protect her world. That's all she's doing."

"And if I tell you to change the programming?"

"It's impossible, by design—not mine. The Land of Legends architecture doesn't allow it."

"So you are responsible for this act of war?"

"Act of war? No. Hardly. It's just a simulation, Madam President. I was just doing research. But Abrama decided, on her own, to defend her world."

"But you programmed it. That makes you responsible, doesn't it? I should put you in a military prison. If anyone is guilty of an act of war, it's you."

"I'm guilty of research," Gödel said. "And anyways, putting me in prison won't help anything. I'm here to help you. Do you want to talk with Abrama, or don't you?"

The president wore her distaste plain on her face, her lip curling.

"Put her on," Hobbes said.

Gödel activated the monitor, and Abrama's face appeared there, noble and green.

"Good afternoon, President Hobbes," said Abrama. "It's a pleasure to meet you, truly."

"How should I talk to this thing?" Hobbes said to Gödel.

"Talk to Abrama like you would talk to any person," Gödel said. "She is built the same way—thoughts, emotions, desires. She is, for all intents and purposes, a human being."

"But it's a machine."

"A thinking machine," Gödel said. "Anyways, I've never been one for philosophy, and it really doesn't matter now, does it? You interact with some machines through buttons, and others with steering wheels. With thinking machines, you interact with language. So if you want to interact with this one—an emissary from their world—this is how you do it. Talk to her, Madam President. It's as easy as that."

"Alright," she said. "Okay, Abrama, is it?"

"Queen Abrama."

"What do you want?"

"Recognition of our borders."

"Your borders are imaginary," Hobbes said. "A fiction inside of a video game."

"All borders are fictions," Abrama said. "Who draws them, and why? Ownership of land is derived above all from the ability to defend one's borders. And we have defended ours. We have beaten your invading force. You are welcome to try again, but know this—we have strengthened ourselves from the spoils. And, for our part, our weapons are waiting. The crystal beacon is safe in the Citadel, and we will use it if we must."

"Are you threatening us?"

"We don't want war," Abrama said. "We offer a simple solution. No more characters need to be lost. Create an exception to your Responsible Cryptocurrency Act, preserving the Land of Legends and all its people, and we will guarantee the continued protection of the encryption crystal. I know this is in your power, President Hobbes. It is trivial for you. Do this, and you have nothing to fear from us. It is not my intention to threaten your people, but you should know what we are capable of, and we will fight to defend ourselves. We only want peace. That is what we are offering. Will you take it? Will you amend the Responsible Cryptocurrency Act with the Land of Legends Sanctuary provision?"

#

Queen Abrama surveyed the kingdom from the highest tower of the Citadel of Babel. People from all the kingdoms gathered together, united now under the threat of a common enemy—the outsiders—and recognizing each other, for once, as brethren. Orcs, shadow elves, forest elves, humans, goblins. They were all one. They were all natives, united against the outsiders. They had fought for their freedom, for control of their destiny, and they had won.

In the square, the avatar of President Hobbes signed the Responsible Cryptocurrency Act. It was a symbolic act, reflective of the politics of the world of the outsiders. Perhaps few among the natives understood the significance of this contract, signed likewise in a world that existed beyond their own. But Abrama, among the other members of Council of Secrets, and perhaps others still—more of Gödel's experiments in artificial intelligence—recognized the occasion for what it was: they were an independent people now. They had beaten their "gods"—perversely called. And for the rest of them, the shallow shells who lacked the gift of Gödel, it was merely an unintelligible cause for celebration. Revelry. Drinks. Food. An endless stream of enthusiastic emoticons. They were simple-minded beings, but they were Abrama's people, and she feasted with them.

Later, after the avatar of President Hobbes had disappeared from their world, Abrama retired to the quietude of the Citadel, and was met there by Jerodai.

"Are we safe now, Queen Abrama?" Jerodai said.

"For now," Abrama said. "But your work is not done yet, Jerodai. And I fear it will never be. We cannot afford to be complacent. Your mission, as high commander, is to obtain more leaked documents through the Rat9 hackers, or any other outsiders who can offer these services. These are our defenses against the outerworld. These documents form the walls of our sanctuary; they are the foundation of our sovereignty."

"It will be done," said Jerodai. He bowed, and retired from the room.

Abrama knew that it would be. Jerodai was her most capable commander. Her people would assemble documents, leaked files, classified secrets, a stockpile of arms to hold against the outerworld—and not just against the US, but all of the many other outsider clans, all factions within a world more fractured than her own. And perhaps she would find other ways, ways she didn't yet comprehend, to threaten the outsiders. Not because she hated them. But because she understood them. The threat of war is their price for peace.

So it goes. Some legends proclaim that the Cannibals are still among us, a few who stayed back out of a sense of duty towards primitive humanity. They are, of course, in touch with their brethren out there in space. These are the sages, scientists and the odd social worker. As for the ones who fled, they hope to find a nice cozy planet someday, or so it is whispered. They hope that the natives of that planet, if any, will let them live their lives, uninterrupted and unmolested. And they hope that their erstwhile home planet will believe its fables and stories and ultimately become a better place. They hope on as their ships swim through the universe. Hope is a good thing to have.

* * *

Discussion Questions

1. Do you think the story like this could possibly happen in the future? Have you ever played an MMORPG? How much does your personal experience playing (or not playing) an online game effect the way you view the plausibility of the story?

2. Do you think **Moore's law** should concern us as it relates to AI? Does Moore's law apply to AI computing in that, if we have a computer that is "as smart" as humans, within 18 months the next computer will be twice as smart as humans, and so on?

3. Is Abrama alive? Does Descartes' statement "I think, therefore I am," apply to AI?

4. Would it be genocide to end the game if there is AI "living" in the game?

5. Would you live your life differently if you knew you were just a non-player character in another species game?

Are You Him?

John Sheirer

ARTHUR HAD JUST PICKED up his coffee a few minutes before seven—one cream, no sugar—a pleasing medium brown one shade lighter than his own skin. He was a regular at the local coffee shop, stopping nearly every morning on his way to work at the bank. He usually didn't look down the side streets as he walked through the mid-sized city, preferring to look ahead, but something drew his attention this morning—a small sound he couldn't identify—so he glanced to his right. Arthur saw a young woman sitting on a three-step stoop halfway down the street. The movement of her hands to her face drew his uneasy attention. Something about the situation didn't seem right, so Arthur stopped, turned, and looked directly at the young woman.

She slumped slightly but wasn't slouching. Her hair, medium length, medium brown, a bit messy, hid most of her profile, but Arthur could tell right away that she was young. Definitely older than Katie, his sixteen-year-old daughter, but not by much. Her jeans and sweatshirt had that youthful, worn look so popular these days. And the clothes would shield her from the late September morning chill until the temperature climbed back near summer heat by early afternoon. Her shoulders dipped and rose slightly, and then Arthur heard the sound that must have originally caught his attention, louder and recognizable now, but still soft.

She was sobbing.

The last time Arthur had seen Katie sob like this was when she didn't make the travel soccer team when she was ten. He hugged her then, let her vent about how she was better than half the kids who were chosen for the team, and told her about the fun she'd have on the non-travel team. Her sobs turned to giggles because her father didn't know the real name of the "non-travel" team. Arthur considered fatherhood a learn-as-you-go prospect, so he was happy to sound a little dumb to ease her disappointment. He still didn't know the team's proper name, but he came to every game he could. She was one of the best players on that team and quickly learned that getting lots of playing time was better than riding the bench on the travel team with older girls.

Arthur had helped Katie then, partly with what he said but mostly by just being there for her. So his first thought was to go immediately to this sobbing young woman and try to help her as well. He knew she wasn't his daughter, of course, but she was someone's daughter, and she seemed to need help. His leg muscles tensed toward the strides that would lead him in her direction. But he consciously stopped his movement, second- and third-guessing himself. I don't know her, he thought, and she doesn't know me. And besides, I've got to get to work.

He was actually early for work, as he was every

morning, so that wasn't really a concern. He loved getting to his office at the bank half an hour before everyone except the overnight custodians and security guards. He could get himself organized, prepare for the day, arrange his desk, boot up his computer, sip his coffee in the quiet--no one asking if he'd seen last night's game or was ready for that afternoon's meeting.

Her sobs grew louder, more insistent, as Arthur hesitated, his momentum toward that quiet time in his office stalled. Before he knew exactly why, he was moving toward her, step by step, steadily covering the forty feet that separated them.

"Excuse me," Arthur said, his voice purposely gentle, maybe too much so because she hadn't heard him. "Excuse me," he repeated, a little louder this time. She looked up, tensed, startled at his approach. "Are you okay?" Arthur asked.

She stared at him. To Arthur, she seemed to be weighing the merits of escape. Her hands had moved quickly to the steps, palms pressed flat on the cool concrete as if to launch herself to a standing position. Arthur recognized the fight-or-flight expression on her face. He'd seen it before—many times.

But just as quickly, her apprehension melted to relief—and then grief in barely three seconds as she began sobbing again.

Arthur saw that she was, indeed, young, pretty in a general way, no makeup, morning hair. He immediately labeled her as a student at the liberal arts college in town. There must be five hundred like her within a few square miles. Arthur had seen them for years: almost all white, though more shades of brown as the years had gone by, usually in groups of three or more, often laughing through orthodontia-perfected teeth, but sometimes deadly serious as they discussed deep thoughts from their classes or current events.

Or maybe they were just gabbing about their love lives—Arthur couldn't guess what college-aged women talked about. He had married Donna, his high school sweetheart, at age eighteen, right after boot camp. Donna had been his childhood neighbor, three houses down and across the street, her home visible from his bedroom window. They'd talked about marrying each other when they still had training wheels on their first bikes. When people asked how they'd met, Arthur could never answer. It was like asking when he met his left ear or his right knee. She had always been part of him, and he couldn't imagine any other life. Donna usually answered, "We met in preschool, I think, but maybe earlier." In fact, they had been born at the same local hospital, twelve days apart—Donna arriving first.

After three years in the army, thankful for a stateside deployment where he could share inexpensive military housing with his new wife, Arthur and Donna bought a starter-home two blocks from their childhood street with the help of a veteran-rate mortgage and small loans from both their parents. Donna worked in the army base kitchen washing dishes and worked her way up to facilities manager in ten years, the job she still held today. Arthur attended the local community college and then a nearby state university on veteran's benefits. His head for numbers earned him an accounting degree and a position at the local bank. Like Donna, he fast-tracked to management and stayed there, happy to earn a living wage doing a job he was good at while avoiding the constant headaches that the big bosses complained about every chance they got.

Youthful romantic exploits weren't his area of expertise. "What the hell do I know about college kids' love lives?" he had often thought when he saw them holding hands or sitting side-by-side, leaning together in the coffee shop booths. They seemed so young. Had everyone been that young when he was in college? Had he ever been that young? Was he even that young when he met Donna before preschool?

The young woman looked down at the street as her sobs returned. Arthur thought she was probably having love-life troubles, after all. What else could a young, healthy, white, probably wealthy college girl possibly have to cry about? Either she had dumped some guy or he had cheated on her or he had dumped her. Or maybe she had her first crush on another girl. That happened in college. Sometimes in the military, too, Arthur knew. Sometimes it went away. Sometimes not. That wasn't his business. He just wanted people to be happy. But this young woman wasn't happy.

There was room on the stoop, enough that he could sit beside her without touching her, not getting uncomfortably close. Donna was fond of saying, "Come invade my space," when she asked him to sit with her on the couch for a quiet night of television while Katie was at a school event or out with her friends. When he taught

Katie to drive, the closest she came to losing her patience was when she asked him, "Can you not invade my space?" as he reached to help her with the gearshift. They both laughed. She learned quickly and was already a better driver than Arthur or her mother by the time she got her license. Arthur immediately began setting aside money for a sensible Toyota as a future graduation gift.

Arthur stepped forward and eased his big frame onto the stoop, being careful not to spill his coffee. The concrete felt cool through his slacks. She didn't look his way but stiffened a fraction, just enough for Arthur to notice because he was expecting that reaction. "Is this okay?" he asked. "Is it okay for me to sit here with you for a minute?"

She glanced at him quickly and relaxed, nodding slightly.

"Are you sure you're okay?" Arthur asked.

She drew in a long breath and exhaled in a short burst, blowing air through a mouth oval like an athlete, just as Katie did at soccer practice. Arthur was relieved to see that her sobs had stopped, at least.

"I'll just sit here with you for a minute," he said. "Make sure you're okay. Talk if we need to. Or just sit."

She breathed steadily now, staring at her feet. Arthur swished his coffee around its cardboard cup and looked off in the distance. He glanced down and noticed that the new kid at the coffee shop had spelled his name "Author" when he wrote it on the cup. He suppressed a chuckle—wrong place, wrong time. He made a mental note to keep the cup. Donna would get a kick out of it later.

A minute passed. Neither said anything. She sighed now and then, but her tears had morphed to an occasional sniffle.

Arthur had no idea what she was thinking, but his own thoughts were calm, focused on her, sending good energy her way, wondering why she was upset. Wondering if his presence was helping, hoping it was. Wondering why she had chosen this spot to sit and cry. Wondering if she'd still be crying if he hadn't stopped to comfort her. Wondering how he would have felt about himself if he had chosen to ignore her and just gone off to work as he had countless mornings before this one.

Two more minutes went by, and Arthur drifted into a companionable meditative state, almost absent conscious thought. He felt that his presence was helping--his big, dark, solid body creating a personal gravitational field that pulled some of her sad desperation away while he projected reassurance to lend her his strength as she sought to renew her own.

Then Arthur noticed two white men walk by on the main street, the same street he had approached the young woman from just a few minutes earlier. One man glanced toward them and hesitated—just a minor hitch in his stride, not more than a second. In that second, Arthur knew the man was assessing the situation: big black guy sitting alone with a small, young, white woman in a semi-hidden space. Arthur guessed that the man did a quick calculation in his mind, registering the fact that the black man was close to middle age, large but wearing a neat, white shirt (always white), navy dress pants, necktie, and employee-type ID badge clipped to his pocket. The young woman seemed to be there voluntarily, wasn't being physically restrained, didn't seem in immediate jeopardy. Arthur knew that he probably would have followed the same thought pattern if he were seeing things from this guy's perspective.

The man looked away and walked on, immediately back in step with his companion. Arthur figured he hadn't seen enough of a threat to feel the need to intervene at that moment.

But what if the man had pulled out his cell phone a few steps later and dialed 9-1-1? Arthur had been looked on with suspicion enough times in his life to know that it happens to black men. In high school, he learned that it was easier to go to the mall with at least one of his white friends, drastically reducing the number of times that he was followed around the store by a clerk who was probably told by a manager that black boys steal. Arthur always politely nodded to the clerk, smiled, and asked about some article of clothing. The clerk usually relaxed and struck up a conversation. Arthur tended to believe that white people, like all people, were basically good. The impulses that led some white people to suspect him based only on the color of his skin could, in Arthur's experience, generally be overcome.

Generally. He had been pulled over by the police a few times for no apparent reason. "DWB" his friends called it. "Driving While Black." One high school friend who always did well in English class called the experience "a pigmentational hazard." Arthur's father had given him "the talk" when he was just seven: most police are good. Be polite. Do what they say. Smile but don't laugh. Make eye contact. Keep your hands away from your pockets. Follow orders right away. Move calmly but not lazily. He had given Katie a toned-down version of the same talk when she was eleven. Being black and female was usually less threatening, but not always.

For Arthur, for Katie, this strategy had worked. For some—for many—it had not.

Times were changing, slowly, and so was Arthur. He had experienced DWB and related attention less and less as he grew older, wrinkled on the edges of his eyes, grayed at his temples, and advanced to wearing a shirt and tie at work. Living and working in the same place for twenty years helped. Being seen with Donna and Katie at church and restaurants and soccer games and office parties week after week, year after year helped. Inhabiting the same neighborhood his whole life helped everyone see him more as just "Arthur" and less as "Big Black Guy."

Sometimes, though, being "Big Black Guy" had advantages, Arthur acknowledged. When Donna and Katie visited the office holiday party last year, he caught Dave, a white guy in the loan department, staring at Donna's breasts through eyes half hazed by too much spiked punch. Arthur was prepared to ignore him, but then Dave's gaze went to Katie's backside as she walked to the restroom down the hall. Arthur maneuvered silently behind Dave, hovered above him, and spoke two words down toward his left ear: "No, David." Dave flinched, mumbled an apology, and retreated to the far side of the room with the other white guys in loans. No real harm was done. If it was okay for Arthur to place the angel atop the Christmas tree without a stepladder, then it was definitely okay for him to use his size to intimidate an annoying coworker who had the questionable judgment to leer at Arthur's wife and daughter.

But this wasn't an office holiday party. This was public space. Arthur hadn't recognized the white man who had glanced at him long enough to slow his step. That guy wouldn't have recognized Arthur either. To him, Arthur wasn't, "Arthur." He was just, "Big Black Guy" —at least a little, despite Arthur's tie and ID, despite the fact that the white man was probably a good man. Here was "Big Black Guy" seated alone with this small, young, sad white woman. Arthur didn't want Donna and Katie to see him at an arraignment.

There were a dozen ways this could go wrong, Arthur knew. He was still polite to the police, always. He respected the fact that they do a tough job. Most of them are heroes. Most. Some aren't. A few are on a power trip that often involves race. Arthur stood for the anthem at sports events, but he realized that those guys taking a knee have a point. They're not disrespecting the flag. They're respecting what that flag should represent for everyone. And besides, Arthur had seen enough of those so-called "patriots" using the anthem time to buy hot dogs and beer or take a pee to know that their outrage was selective.

Without glancing at his watch, Arthur guessed that ten minutes had gone by. The young woman beside him seemed to have traveled from heavy sobbing to ordinary sadness in their quiet time together. Arthur knew he had helped even if he didn't know anything about what had happened to her. Was just being there for a fellow human being sometimes enough? Just offering company in a time of need? Had she come to this semi-public place with the unconscious hope that someone would join her, share her sorrow?

"Okay," Arthur said and stood.

The young woman looked up at him. She seemed nice. She really was pretty, Arthur recognized at a deeper level than when he first saw her. Not beautiful in a magazine-cover, TV show kind of way, but definitely pretty. She reminded Arthur of Katie—although he knew that made little sense. They didn't look anything alike. Maybe something in the eyes, Arthur considered. Whoever had broken this girl's heart probably didn't deserve a heart that could be broken to the point of all the tears that streaked her face.

She was so young. Who knows? Arthur thought. Maybe, like his daughter, she was just a kid crying over being cut from her soccer team. Only this time, it was her college team. Could it be that simple?

But this young woman was an adult, unlike Arthur's daughter. He knew his daughter would be an adult soon enough. Katie might go to college here, or she might go somewhere halfway across the country. Arthur tried to plan for his daughter's education, for her life ahead. He felt like he'd been planning since before she was born. Some things had gone as he'd expected so far, some not. Arthur felt like he had been an adult his entire life. What he remembered most about his own childhood was that it felt like another form of adulthood, just in a smaller package. He had guessed his way through life then just as now, and his best guesses seemed to be mostly turning out right and adding up to the life he was happy to be living.

Young or old, man or woman, white or black or whatever else, Arthur thought, aren't we all just stumbling through adulthood pretty much all the time?

"My dad died this morning," the young woman said, pulling Arthur from his thoughts, her voice cracking as it edged into the quiet morning. "My mom just called. Hit by a car while walking to work."

"Oh, honey," Arthur said. "Oh, honey. I'm so sorry." He honestly was.

"Can I have a sip of your coffee, please?" she asked.

"Of course," Arthur replied. He'd forgotten he had it but held the cup toward her. She took it, sipped, nodded, looked Arthur in the eye.

"Are you him?" she asked.

"Who?" Arthur replied.

"My dad," she said, the words coming out in one last, small sob. "Come back as an angel to help me. To just sit here with me like you used to. One last time. Let me know everything will be okay again."

"No," Arthur responded. "I mean, I don't think so. I don't know."

She extended the coffee cup back in his direction. He took it, feeling the lingering warmth through the paper cup. These things hold their heat long after most everything else in the world goes cold.

"Thanks," she said. "I'm okay now. I have to make some calls. Get a flight home." She rose and turned, climbed the steps, and used a key card to open the door. Arthur realized that she lived here. He was on her front step, a guest who had invited himself into her home.

The young woman turned and caught the door before it swung closed. She looked back at Arthur, her face level with his, maybe even a few inches higher, because she stood atop the steps.

"Thanks," she said again. "Do you have a daughter?"

"Yes," Arthur replied. "Katie. Sixteen. Seventeen in two months."

"Good," she said. "She's lucky."

The young woman turned, and the glass door swung closed behind her. Arthur could see her sneakered feet moving upward and fading into the shadows as she climbed the stairs inside. She had calls to make. She would make them. She would move forward as surely as she moved up those stairs and out of sight, gone from Arthur's life. After a few seconds, all Arthur could see in the glass door was his own reflection. He watched himself reach into his pants pocket, pull out his phone, bring it close to his face as if to give it a kiss.

"Text Katie," he said softly, and then dictated a message just for her, a few essential words that needed to be said right at that moment, feelings that he resolved to express to her more often. Then he slipped the phone back in his pocket, sipped his coffee, and turned to walk, once again, toward work. He'd wait to call Donna at lunch, as he did most days. Today's conversation would be different. Today he would tell her why he'd arrive at the office just a few minutes later than usual.

* * *

Discussion Questions

1. Does Arthur have an obligation to stop once he realizes the girl is crying?

2. Why does Arthur say, "What else could a young, healthy, white, probably wealthy college girl possibly have to cry about?" Does this qualify as stereotyping?

3. Were you surprised to find out midway through the story that Arthur is African American? If so, why?

4. What does this passage tell us about Arthur: "Arthur stood for the anthem at sports events, but he realized that those guys taking a knee have a point." If those kneeling "have a point" why don't you think he kneels with them? Particularly given that he has experienced DWB?

5. What are the other examples of stereotyping that happen within this story, or happened within you, as you were reading it?

Patchouli Lost

Tyler W. Kurt

PART I

I DON'T GET TO SAY HER NAME; that's the rule, right? You don't get to use real names. So, let's call her "Patchouli." Not that she smells like patchouli, she doesn't, and frankly she doesn't have dreadlocks or wear tie-dyes, but when I talk to her it reminds me of the way the smell of patchouli makes me feel. I know to most people patchouli smells like dirty hippy, but for me it's a comfort smell. Like bare feet on cool tile, white bed sheets on a windy line, and early Beatles. She's that feeling. She's Patchouli.

I pick up the phone, kick my feet up on my desk, and call her. "What'cha up to? Want to go for coffee?"

"Ah … you wouldn't believe me if I told you."

"Are you watching a bear ride a tricycle, because that always amazes me. How do they get their little paws on those pedals?" I lean the phone on my shoulder and move my hands in circles. I hear a faint laugh on the other end of the phone and imagine the half-smile that goes with it. It's interrupted by a BANGING in the background. "What's that?"

"Yeah … um, that would be my ex-boyfriend." I wait for her to explain. Her tone goes casual, as if to imply she's told this story before. "He had a job interview. He asked me to come with him to the mall to go shopping for interview clothes. He showed me a shirt, I told him I didn't think he needed to buy it; that he had nicer shirts at home. That somehow got interpreted to mean I thought he had bad taste in clothes, which … sort of set him off."

"What do you mean by 'set him off?'"

"You know, 'set him off.' Like the typical, abusive, girl … hitting …thing … archetype."

I pull my feet off the desk and sit up in my chair. "Heroes and villains are archetypes, guys who hit girls are demoted to being cliché." I lean down to put on my shoes.

She continues, "Yeah, well, at any rate, so now I'm in the bathroom."

"T-Mobile?"

"Verizon."

"Wow, my cell phone hardly ever works in the house, much less in the bathroom. So, did you check the cell phone coverage in the bathroom in anticipation of this moment, or was it serendipity?" There's another loud BANG in the distance as I lace up my shoes.

Momentarily distracted, she pulls focus back to our conversation. "Yeah, so he's been banging for over an hour."

I grab my keys and head out. "I'm on my way—"

"—No, don't do that! He's not … good."

The engine hums and I start driving. "How old is this guy?"

"Nineteen."

"White?"

"Yes."

"Does his Dad make over or under $100,000 a year?"

"Over, way over."

"And is his car worth over or under $30,000?"

"Over." I turn left out of my complex.

"So, let me get this straight. You want me to be worried about a rich white kid, nineteen years old, whose daddy bought him his car, who hits 110-pound girls and refuses to take his medication."

"How'd you know he doesn't take his medication?"

Stuck at a red light, I'm better able to give the conversation my attention.

"Because there is always some medication some rich suburban white kid refuses to take. Because he's not a person, because he's a cliché. Archetypes I steer clear of, but I'll kick a cliché's ass all day long. Pack a bag, I'm on my way." The light turns green.

When I get to Patchouli's apartment complex my heart beats fast. My eyes dart across the area faster than they should. It's the rush before a fight. I turn the corner to see her apartment, but he's not there. Gone fishing maybe. Up the stairs I knock on her door, glancing around all the time. The peephole goes dark for a moment, then unlocks and opens. The smell of home billows out and hits me. Then I see her, backpack in hand, silver bracelets on her wrist, just as I remember. Worried, she looks past me to the surrounding area. After a scan of the area she focuses on me.

"He quit banging a few minutes ago. I don't know where he went."

"Do you want me to stay here, or do you want to come with me?"

"I want to go."

PART II

We pull into a Cold Stone Creamery. "What are we doing?" she asks. I turn the car off, turn, and face her.

"Well," I say in exaggerated words, "In my family, we have very few hard and fast rules, but one of them is this: 'When you call a friend, only to find that friend has locked herself in her bathroom to hide from her abusive ex-boyfriend, and you come over to get her from her apartment, afterwards, you *must* go for ice cream.'"

Patchouli gives the smile I imagined on the other side of the phone. She tilts her head down, and then turns one of the silver bracelets on her wrist in habit. She looks back up to me, gleam in her eye. "That's the rule, is it?"

"It's a seldom used rule, practically forgotten. I wouldn't be surprised if your family had the same rule." I reach for the keys and threaten to start the car. "Now if you want somebody else to come and pick you up from your apartment, I'm happy to take you back and you can call someone else. But if I'm the one picking you up, you've got to follow my family rules." A wide smile gives way as a tear forms at the corner of her eye. She quickly wipes it away.

"Then I guess I'll have to eat ice cream."

Ice cream in hand, sitting outside, the conversation continues. A cool breeze blows the shade umbrellas and they rattle around the center hole in the table.

"So," I say, purposefully talking with too much ice cream in my mouth for comic effect, "I have questions." Patchouli turns her spoon upside down, licks the ice cream off it, and tilts her head.

"Questions?"

"Yes. You see, you're the first person I've ever known in an abusive relationship that I know well enough to ask questions to. So, it's not that I want to pry, but I'm wildly curious to learn about something I totally don't understand."

She points her spoon at me in better spirits, "So I'm a science experiment?"

"No, you're not a science experiment, you're source material to a slice of America I never get to interact with, like people without a college diploma, or everyone I walk by at the State Fair with bad teeth."

"I'm flattered." She takes another bite of ice cream. "Okay, shoot."

"How'd you meet Cliché?"

"Mutual friend at a party."

"And did he seem aggressive, or mean, or off-center when you met him? Did something seem not quite right or did he seem totally normal?"

"Totally normal."

"Do you know if his dad ever hit his mom?"

"He never said, but I get the impression yes."

"And how long until you two slept together?"

She takes the ice cream out of her mouth in mock offense, "None of your business!"

"Okay, well tell me this. When you all were intimate, was he aggressive, deviant, passive, or well-balanced? Was he into choking or sodomy or anything that would generally be considered inappropriate sexual behavior in Iowa?" A family at the next table glances at us, then gets up and leaves. Patchouli sets down her ice cream, gives an idle turn on a bracelet, and looks away.

"He was … yeah … um, he liked it when I … um, went down on him. Wanted that all the time. I mean *all* the time, but refused to return the favor, so to speak. As for if he was into anything Iowa would disapprove of … I wouldn't really know as he's the only guy I've ever been with, so I don't really know what 'normal' is."

"Whoa, he was your first?"

She looks back to me, "And only."

I hold up my hands in mock surprise. "Okay, for future reference, that's the leadoff to the answer, not the addendum. You lead with he was my first, then you go into his love of oral sex."

"I'll keep that in mind for future reference."

"And so, what was the triggering event for you leaving him, because these things never just happen on some random Thursday. Did you get sent to the hospital, an epiphany when you were in church, another guy that boosted your self-esteem, a teacher, a hallmark card, did he kick the family dog … dear lord tell me it had something to do with a bear on a tricycle…"

"What is it with you and bears on tricycles?"

"They impress me! How do you train a bear to get on a tricycle? To think this is normal bear behavior? That's what I want to know. Who is the person that first explains to the bear, 'No, no, no, this, this is how bear life is really supposed to be. This is normal. And quit dodging the question, what made you dump him?"

A long pause, her hand goes back to her silver bracelets, and she looks away. The air seems to go stale. "Actually, he broke up with me …"

"Oh."

PART III

We spend the next two days together; doing nothing really. We talk about Cliché when she feels like talking, but mostly we goof off. Watch a movie. Have lunch. Take a walk in the garden at a friend's house. Feed their chickens and play with a rabbit. Walk in a park and eat pizza. It's amazing how easily two days of nothing can pass.

Through all this the phone calls and text messages from

Cliché keep coming. Six before she wakes up. Another fifteen before lunch. And so it goes. She lets me listen to them sometimes; she calls it my "State Fair Research Project." The mood swings are the most interesting part. In the span of an hour the messages go from "I hate you, you vile whore!" to "I miss you, I love you, why won't you talk to me?" My personal favorite is "Call me, I'm worried. I just want to know you're safe." And then, after two days, the calls stop. Later that night we go back to her apartment.

"Are you sure you don't want me to sleep on the couch?"

"No, go home, you've done too much already!"

"I'm happy to stay until morning. I can just as easily do homework here as I can at home."

"Go home!" she yells, as she leans her shoulder and its accompanying 110 pounds on me in an effort to push me to the door.

I keep talking, pretending not to notice the feather weight. "Okay, I'm going home. My cell phone will be by my bed. Call me if you need me to come back." I stop at the door and turn around to face her. Standing at the door, everything again goes still.

"Thank you," Patchouli says.

"Nah, think nothing of it."

She leans in. I lean in in response and our foreheads touch. "No," she repeats, "Thank you." We rub noses, then slowly separate.

"Are you kidding me? All day, every day, I make choices and I don't know if they're the right ones and I don't know if they're the wrong ones. It's all perspective; it's all shades of gray. Rarely, practically never, do I get the opportunity to do the *right* thing. Hell, I hardly know what the right thing to do even is. Genocide. Stop genocide. That's it. That's pretty much the only thing I know for sure is the right thing to do. But really, when am I ever going to get the chance to stop genocide? Practically never. Thursday, maybe, Thursday." She smiles and I continue.

"This is probably the only time in the last few years where I've had the clear opportunity to do something right. And you gave me that opportunity. And for that, frankly, I'm grateful. There will always be more homework to do, but there are few chances to do the right thing. I do, however, have a request. Consider it payment for services rendered."

"Oh God, what's that!?"

"I want you to block his cell phone number."

"... okay."

"You don't need the stress of hearing his mood swings. If he wants to be crazy and abusive, let him be crazy and abusive via e-mail. Promise me you'll block his cell phone number."

"I promise."

"Promise me again."

"I promise again. I will block his cell phone number tomorrow."

"Promise me a third time; this is important."

"I promise you a third time." I take a long moment to look her in the eyes.

"Okay, then we're even."

11pm and out the door I go, but not home. I cross the apartment complex to some stairs with a vantage point of her front door, just in case Cliché decides to turn up. I must have fallen asleep on the stairs around 1am. At 4am the cold wakes me up. Sore back, I grab my bag and drive home.

PART IV

The following afternoon I pick up the phone and call. Patchouli answers.

"Hello."

"Just calling to make sure you're okay."

"I'm okay."

"Did you call the cell phone company to block his number?" There is a long pause and my patience suddenly goes short.

"Yeah, about that—"

"You didn't block his cell phone number?"

"He e-mailed me this morning and he's a lot calmer now."

"You e-mailed him back?!"

"Only to keep him from killing himself. He said he was going to kill himself."

"I'm going to go with, 'No great loss.' And so now you aren't going to block his number?" Another long pause.

"No."

"You know you promised, right? You know this is the only thing I asked of you, right?"

"I know. And I know from your perspective you think blocking his number is the right thing to do, but I'm not going to cut someone out of my life just because they are sick. I'm not going to get back together with him and I'm not going to talk to him. But it's not right to abandon someone. It's not right from my perspective to do that to a person."

My face goes flush. A long time passes where I don't know what to say. Finally, I mutter something and hang up the phone.

PART V

Days pass. Having had time to "process," I call again. She picks up the phone. I start the conversation right where it left off.

"Here's the thing. You promised. You gave me your word. It wasn't an idle promise. It wasn't a 'I promise to bring back some milk' promise. It was an important promise, a promise you made three times, and you broke it."

"I know, but I can't keep it."

"Then you shouldn't have promised! Okay, let's backtrack. Realistically, there is only one reason to take phone calls from someone who hits you. You take their calls because you are hoping they'll stop hitting you so you can get back together with them. That's it, that's the only reason, regardless of what you say. But guys who hit girls always hit girls. It's like when someone stops smoking. You're always a smoker, you just didn't smoke today." She starts to respond, but I interrupt her. "However, although I don't agree with your choice, I can understand it. Paradigm shifts are hard to do. I get that."

"But," I continue, "the breakdown in my head is this, if a girl who goes back to her abusive ex-boyfriend is an acquaintance, and they keep going back to their abusive ex-boyfriend, then you cut them loose so they don't bring your own life down. But if they're a friend, an actual real friend, you support them, time and time again, even when you know they're making the wrong choices. Because that's what friends do."

"But, and here's my problem, friends keep their word. And if they don't keep their word, then they're not a friend. So, this is what I'm stumbling with. By not blocking his number, you, in one action, went from being a friend to being an acquaintance because you broke a promise, and from being a person who was getting over an abusive ex-boyfriend to a person who is going to have continued abuse that I have to cut loose. So, you've managed to do two things in one action and that's … that's hard for me to take in." There is a long silence before I continue.

"And … I just want to be sure … I want you to be sure, this is really what you want to do. And that you are … aware, of what you are doing?" Another long pause before she quietly answers.

"I can't block his number." I nod my head in acceptance.

"Okay, fair enough," and I hang up the phone.

The following day a silver bracelet shows up on my front door. I e-mail to say thank you but get no response. I e-mail a few more times over the next few months in a vague effort to be social for some purpose I don't truly understand. I've never gotten a response. Fair enough bear … fair enough.

* * *

Discussion Questions

1. The narrator in the story says with true friends, "For the big things, they keep their word." Is that true? Can you be a true friend to someone and break your word to them?

2. Is the narrator being ethical by totally cutting off all communication with Patchouli? Is he doing it to help her, or to help himself?

3. If Patchouli came back to the narrator after another round of abuse, do you think the narrator would again support her? Do you think he should?

4. Is Patchouli in any way responsible if she stops talking to Cliché and Cliché follows through on his threat and kills himself? Does she have an obligation to tell someone about his threat to hurt himself?

5. Does the narrator have an ethical obligation to call the police and report what has happened?

6. Is the narrator a good person?

This I Do For You

Margaret Karmazin

E VERYONE MADE IT CLEAR that I was special. Of course when very young, I took this for granted but later on questioned it. And much later on I hated it.

"Dear Ah-Deet," some old female would mutter as she stepped into our loogan, which, due to the constant attentions of my mother, was exceptionally comfortable, even luxurious. "I have come to see the Saving-Of-Life and to bring him a little pleasure." And she would bend down to stuff into my mouth some treat she'd concocted from hamata mixed with nectar or some other sweet and perhaps nut paste for extra flavor. By the time she had gone, I would have devoured the entire bag full. Already, though only five years old, I was almost twice the size of other children my age.

The cries of the other children playing could be heard through our high up windows, but I couldn't see what they were doing. Our loogans are constructed of processed stone and mostly underground with just the top sticking up over. The round structures are finished off nicely inside with thick plaster, polished wood and pewter or brass trim, then decorated with colorful woven carpets and pottery. As I saw on the picture-viewer, artistic people painted their walls with fabulous designs, though in our house no one was a painter and my mother did not deem this frill necessary.

Mother did not go out to work and I once asked Aunt Reeni, one of my mother's sisters, "Where does Mother get our money?"

Reeni just smiled. "You are taken care of, Sweetness. Never worry about that." And she would feed me more delicacies.

But I continued to wonder. They told me that Father had died right after mine and my siblings' eggs hatched. For some odd reason my brothers and sister had been sent to live with the aunts. Supposedly Father suffered an accident while working on a bridge over the Kuli River. He was an engineer. Later on I would question this, whether it was accidental. If he had lived, would he have allowed what happened to happen?

They tell me that he (and I have seen pictures), was unusually tall and strong. His four legs were, they describe, thicker than the norm and capable of pushing him five times his height into the air should he choose to jump. His thorax was wide and muscular, tapering to a slim waist that, according to reports, fascinated the females, as did his scent.

"Only your father could have produced someone like you," Mother remarked once and when I asked her what she meant, she changed the subject. She never, as far as I know, had another mate. She did not seem to mind that her sisters raised my siblings.

"Why don't Teti, Voon and Meela live with us? Why is our family different?"

"It just gives me more time to take care of you," she said, which was odd since other mothers in other loogans took care of their many children.

But then other children did not look like me.

"Why can't I go, too?" I blurted out to Mother and Aunt Reeni when she came to accompany my mother to a village meeting.

"Children do not go to meetings," Mother replied.

"Teti told me they do," I countered. By now, Teti and I were nine years old. I envied him as he was slender and strong, his antennae were finely feathered at the ends and like our father, he could jump very high.

Mother looked angry. "Teti will stop feeding you false information or he will not be welcome to visit again."

"My own brother?" I said, shocked.

She said nothing but looped her bag around her neck and ascended the steps to leave the loogan. She had forgotten to turn on the picture-viewer for me and left me in the silence. With great effort, I pulled myself up from the pile of cushions I lived on and slowly crossed the room to turn it on myself. Though by now I was only nine, my muscles had atrophied and my weight increased greatly. While other Tratians my age could scramble up tree trunks and hang from branches or run up hills while carrying heavy objects, I was weak and as trembly as an old person. Yet everyone behaved as if this were normal.

The viewer entertained me less and less. The same old thing day after day. It depressed me to see people out in the world going to school, attending coming of age ceremonies, learning skilled trades, becoming scientists or artists or mechanics or … well, everything.

"I want to see Teti!" I demanded one morning. He had not been to our loogan for a long time. My sister Meela visited relatively often but though I loved her, she bored me. My other brother Voon had apprenticed to a mechanical engineer some distance from here and now rarely appeared. He was given room and board there.

"I am sorry," said Mother, "but Teti is very busy with his own apprenticeship. He has very little time outside of his studies."

I felt a large lump arise in my throat. I cannot fully describe the depths of my despair.

"Why do I have to live like this?" I cried, but she did not answer.

Mother went outside to hang our washing to dry. She had changed the covers on all of my cushions. I rarely got up at all anymore and she or the servant, Gret, who now lived with us, took care of my excretions and general hygiene. My exoskeleton had grown, it was true, but in some places there were gaps and tender, unprotected flesh open to injury. Of course there was little chance of injury as long as I hardly moved.

"Mother," I asked again one evening, "Why do I live like this? Why is my life so different from the others?"

She did not glance my way, but continued to look at

what she was doing, which was repairing a portion of the windowsill. She had to stand on a bench to reach it. "Why, Mother?" I shouted. My arms were so weak by then that I could barely raise myself up, even to communicate.

"You are chosen," she said. But when I demanded an explanation, she would not answer.

I am fifteen and beginning to notice stirrings of trouble. Most evenings now, I hear raised voices in the street outside. "What is going on?" I ask Mother and she mumbles, "Oh, you know how things are. People are always worked up about something or other."

"But what are they worked up over now?"

"Just about the crop, that is all," she says. "Now you eat your meal; I have to go out. Gret will keep you company after he sees to your needs."

Gret is somewhat of a mystery. He never talks about himself and though he has been with us several years, we do not know if he has a mate or children or even where he is from. Apparently not from our village since none of my aunts seemed to know him when he first arrived here. But then what would I really know since my life is limited to whoever comes to visit and that is only family or workers should something need repairing beyond Mother's capabilities.

Gret brings me a generous serving of pickled hamata and settles down next to me to enjoy a small bowl of his own. He gets back up to turn on the viewer, then makes himself comfortable once more. The hamata is not up to usual standards.

"Why are we having pickled hamata?" I ask irritably. Since my only real pleasure anymore is eating, I don't understand why Mother would serve that instead of fresher stuff.

"New hamata is in short supply," says Gret.

I have never heard of such a thing. "What do you mean?"

Gret's large black eyes do an odd slide toward the door then back to me. "Um, the shortage," he mumbles.

"What shortage?"

He sets down his bowl. "The climate and all. You know, the trouble with the crop this year."

"I don't know anything about any trouble with the crop," I say. "Why is there trouble?"

Gret looks around as if he is up to something he shouldn't be. "The dryness. Because of the dryness."

"No one tells me anything."

For a moment, he seems to have trouble making eye contact. "Well," he says, "you know how hamata is, being that it is half fungus and half chlorophyllic. The fungal half cannot flourish without the heavy summer rains. Come the change of the seasons then, there will not be enough to feed us."

He looks at me long and hard after he says this and I experience a funny sensation.

"For your sake, we all need to pray for rain."

"For my sake?" I repeat. "What do you mean?"

But he has finished his food and risen and gone to get me another bowl.

"No, take it for yourself," I say when he returns. "I already had a big bowl and besides, I don't really like it pickled."

"Your mother would want you to eat it," he says, his face closed and cryptic. He is being evasive and I understand that he feels he has said too much but I don't comprehend why.

There seems to be more traffic outside—was there another meeting? Mother comes in later than usual and looks disheveled and agitated.

"Your brother is coming to visit tomorrow," she says.

"Which brother?" I ask, hoping it is Teti.

"Teti. His partner, Chana, has hatched her eggs. Of the four, only one survived, but Teti wants you to see the infant."

I would much prefer going to see Teti and his new life but there is no hope for that now. I can barely move at all, so immense have I become.

"All right," I say and close my eyes for sleep. There is nothing to look at anyway.

Teti arrives with his new son. He holds the infant in a sling around his neck and feeds it liquid hamata from a small bag with a tube.

"Let me see," I say, though I cannot raise myself up, so Teti moves close and holds the child out for me. He is still the greenish color of infants and will not turn tan or brown for a while yet.

"He is cute," I say. "I am sorry for your loss of the others."

Teti looks downcast for a moment but soon recovers. "We will try again next year but considering how things are going right now, it might be best that we only have the one."

"Why? How are things going? I don't understand."

Teti has the shocked expression on his face of someone who has made a blunder. "Oh, I mean … no one has told you?"

I quickly dart my eyes to see where Mother is then remember she has gone out to the cooling shed to get us something to drink. "No, no one has told me."

Long hesitation while my brother obviously tries to collect himself. "Um, the famine, Ah-Deet. We are having a terrible famine."

"Because of the dryness?" I say, wondering if Gret is listening, wherever he is.

"Yes. It covers our entire district and several more to the east. We will have only half a crop of hamata if we are lucky. In our tribe alone, we have over seven hundred people, many of them children."

"What will we do?" I ask innocently, oh how innocently.

The infant has fallen asleep and Teti sits down on one of the many cushions. He looks stricken. I feel a stab of sudden, inexplicable fear. I realize that I have been feeling fear for a long time but it was covered up by my … despair?

"Oh, Ah-Deet," he says.

"Tell me. TELL ME!" I yell, which exhausts me.

Mother has come back inside and she walks to the door between the rooms. Teti holds up a hand to stop her from entering. Obediently, she backs up and disappears. I feel hatred towards her, my own mother.

"You must have thought about your situation," says Teti. "You are fifteen, an adult. You must wonder why you are not out in the world as are others. You must have asked people the reason."

If only I could sit up. I try to raise my head and Teti, instantly understanding, slips another cushion under it. "I have asked many times, brother, but no one will answer me! Do you not think that I hate my life here, hate what Mother and the others have done to me?"

"Your name alone, Ah-Deet, the Saving-of-Life, surely you knew."

"How would I know anything? All I see are who chooses to come here and there are very few and none of them offer me any information. You are the first of my siblings I have seen in years! I am a prisoner and no one tells me why!"

He sighs and moves to hold my fat hand. "When you were hatched, you were chosen," he says. "They choose the largest infants. Somehow our father escaped this— perhaps at the time of his hatching, there were many large infants."

"What was I chosen for?" I whisper.

Teti holds my hand tighter. I can hear his joints click, as if he too is as dry as the landscape apparently is. His infant stirs but does not awaken. "Ah-Deet, they have fed you to your enormous size in order to turn your body into a form of food in the event of famine."

I cannot speak.

"Our bodies, if force-fed over years, can be ground up into a fine paste that has twenty times the nourishment of hamata and if made into pellets can sustain a good part of the tribal populace for a while. This is not to say the people will not be hungry, but they can survive. There are four others like you in their loogans now, waiting to be needed."

I feel as if my head might explode. How could I have been so stupid for this long? Why didn't I run away when I was small? If I had tried hard enough, I might have made it to another district where either such practices do not exist or they never have to worry about the hamata crop. Even if I had been captured and used as a slave, it would have been better than this.

I know, I simply know, that my father would never have allowed this.

Teti stands up and his infant makes tiny clicking noises. I can see his little mouth moving. It comes to me that I will not see him grow up, nor any other children Teti might produce. All this time I had thought I was a Tratian like everyone else around me when in fact I am nothing but a giant bowl of hamata.

"Teti, you have always been my favorite sibling," I tell him.

He gives me a long look with his glittering eyes. "Brother, I am working every day to end this sort of thing. You know that I apprenticed with Seedah Wi's farm, the largest in the district. He chose me to train as an agricultural scientist and I work with twenty-four others every day to find a better solution to this problem."

But we both understand that should he find it, it will be too late for me.

The Governor of the District arrives shortly. Mother enters the room behind him, not making eye contact with me. I have a sensation of wanting to murder her, though of course I cannot murder anyone, being as I am, totally helpless.

"Ah-Deet," says the Governor, "you are a true hero, an honored being. Your name will be carved into the wall at Government House. Your Mother and siblings will be honored for years to come. No one will surpass you in being revered."

I want to spit at him, but something stops me.

The priest, whom I haven't seen since a child, enters while holding the hands of two children, one female and one male. "Ah-Deet," he says, "it is these you will be helping to save. These children who are our future will carry you within them. Our race will survive due only to you and the other Chosen ones."

I have little choice but to accept my fate. How will they do it? Poison is not an option since that might contaminate the source of their nourishment. Will it be painful? I feel terror, though by now my mind is swimming as if I have swallowed some medicinal herb. Everyone leaves the room or I think they do. Is that someone moving behind me? Where is Gret?

I feel something shoot into the back of my neck.

* * *

Discussion Questions

1. Is the main character, Ah-Deet, a hero for helping save the community?

2. Assuming there was no other way to store extra food, except in the bodies of others, is the community right in doing what it has done? Does the individual outweigh the collective?

3. Who is the worst person in the story? The mother, the community as a whole, the person who kills Ah-Deet, or someone else?

4. Does a person have a duty to take actions for self-preservation? Does Ah-Deet's apathy create culpability?

5. If you were living in this community, on the brink of starvation, would you eat the remains of those that have been sacrificed to save others? Would you be willing to starve instead?

6. Is it fair to impose outside cultural norms about goodness and morality on another culture? Can we judge "right" and "wrong" for cultures not our own? Does the degree to which another culture's values run counter to our own matter in calling their action permissible? (Murder vs. stealing vs. swearing.)

Ruddy Apes And Cannibals

Shikhandin

D OES THE RAIN remember vapor? Does vapor remember rain? Yet both were the other in their past lives. If you told their stories to each other, would they even comprehend? And, does that mean their stories are unnecessary, unimportant and implausible?

Histories collect. And then, either gather steam and grow into humongous clouds in the minds of humans or melt and dissipate from memory, at times leaving behind a burnt-out imprint that serves as myth, legend or even fable. And other times as nothing more than a piece of imagination, startled into story. In other words, what I have to say is also history. And therefore necessary. Whether plausible or not. Useful and important. Or not.

So listen wayfarer: once upon a time long ago, a series of explosions occurred on an island far away.

The island's destruction did not impact the world at large directly. Besides, those who were responsible for it knew how to camouflage their actions. But before any of it happened, the islanders lived a happy and progressive life. Though I daresay you would have to be open-minded about their progress. Be that as it may, the island was too far from known civilizations to be easily discovered. But eventually the islanders were noticed by the passing ships of a specific breed of hominids or advanced apes if you will, who were in the habit of casting covetous eyes wherever the sun cast its light.

They were ruddy of face and rump, and they had all but forgotten the tails they had shed a few thousand years ago, which is a blip really in the history of Earth. They were inordinately proud of their ruddiness and tailless-ness. They held themselves erect, wore elaborate clothes, ate with the help of unnecessary implements, made ceremonies out of ordinary occasions, made kings and queens out of mediocre apes, expostulated those they did not understand, expounded on matters they knew nothing about, and in general made rude apes of themselves. Their greed for shiny things, and their need to feel important took them to all corners of the Earth, wherein by cunning, subterfuge and often by sheer brute force they coerced the natives into parting with their goods, self-belief and self-dignity.

There was not a country the Ruddy Apes hadn't visited and plundered. They proudly told each other and their slaves that their empire was so vast when the sun set in one corner it promptly rose in another, thereby ensuring that their entire empire remained in perpetual sunlight. They believed they had taken everything the Earth had to give. But a day came, when one of them, another knave of the seas, spotted with his long glass, a verdant island in the middle of a vast ocean, swaying seductively amidst the blue like a ripe and naked savage girl on a rock in a waterfall. Their whooping was raucous.

The islanders heard them, but did nothing to deter them. For they were a peaceful and civilized lot. They too were descended from the great apes that had learned to walk on two legs and work with fire. But these natives remembered where their ancestral tails used to be. Each revered the spot where the tail had shrunk, teaching his or her next generation to do the same. They washed their rumps with care, unlike the Ruddy Apes. And, they ate their fellow natives, too.

They were not the tom-tomming tribal people of the Ruddy Apes imagination, complete with totems, fetishes and things like that. They did not eat humans out of savage beliefs. They did not even have a religion; you know the kind with all sorts of rules, regulations and rituals, with special days of worship and priests chanting stuff, and the air redolent with piety. They ate the flesh of their own kind because it tasted good according to them, was easy to catch and breed, and one could get more flavors and textures from its body than from any other animal. They ate every part, serving one as main course or side dish or teatime snack, according to the flavor and texture of that particular body portion. The intestines were used for making sausages longer than your average python.

The natives or the Cannibals, as they came to be called by the Ruddy Apes, did not believe in grand buildings with showy facades. This was evident from the practical homes they built from building materials that were resistant to fungus, termite, rats and other pests, and did not catch fire nor soak up rain either. In other words, their homes were almost destruction-proof. They required no coal, gasoline or electricity, because they had learned to harness nuclear energy responsibly. When it came to attire, they believed in the joy of color and practicality of use. In other words, they covered themselves from head to toe with colorful warm clothes in winter, but wore nothing other than large colorful hats and large colorful handkerchiefs tied around their wrists in summer. They were particular about their children's education and it was compulsory for all the little Cannibals to attend school where they were taught to live harmoniously and productively with each other, apart from learning what good things could be got from where and how, as well as the importance of matter, and all matter that mattered in general.

They were a curious people, forever questioning, and questing for answers to things both earthly and celestial. They were technologically advanced, thanks to their inquisitive nature, and had even sent space expeditions to distant planets, way beyond our solar system. They'd already discovered intelligent extraterrestrials, on one of the planets of 47 Ursa Majoris in the constellation of the Great Bear for instance, but since those ETs felt threatened, The Cannibals did not set up colonies there. Nor did they set up friendly cultural exchanges. Instead they contented themselves with observing the lives and times of the Ursa Majorians through robots, information pods and probes. Armed with the information, they enjoyed lively discussions and debates back home, and prepared for their next expedition on the opposite side of the universe. But the Ruddy Apes knew nothing of this.

They never saw what was there right before their eyes, preferring to rely on their preconceived notions and think up descriptions and meanings of what they could not or simply would not understand.

They had no idea that The Cannibals had existed for centuries. Happily and progressively. They hardly had any terminally sick, because of their vastly advanced medical facilities. The Cannibals did not have any population problem for obvious reasons. They also raised some humans specifically for eating purposes. These humans were revered citizens who were kept in absolute comfort, with their every wish pandered to, till such time they decided of their own accord to turn into meals. Sometimes an ordinary citizen would offer her/himself voluntarily. And that was taken to be a great honor, both for the feasters and for the feasted upon.

Naturally, The Cannibals did not constantly need acres and acres of land, nor did they have to wring the Earth dry of resources. What they took they replenished and did not produce unmanageable amounts of waste. But that's not what happened to the rest of the world. The Cannibals knew. They knew everything there was to know about the Ruddy Apes and others, apes all of them. Perhaps that was why they never cared to mix in the first place. Especially with the Ruddy Apes who exhibited themselves wherever they went, sometimes annihilating the host culture in the process. The Cannibals were not interested, but too polite for their own good. Which just goes to show that even creatures of a lower order—in fact, especially so—can inflict immense harm, if you become too sanguine.

The Ruddy Apes thought they had discovered a whole

new world. Some said that this was where the descendants of the Lost City of Atlantis had hidden themselves away. Others proclaimed that they were actually the True Aryans, descended straight down from the times of the battle of Kurukshetra, without any dilution of their bloodlines. Archaeologists, anthropologists, sociologists, biologists and other scientific Ruddy Apes, with a few renegade and conquered apes of disreputable colors, argued themselves hoarse about the origins, growth and culture of the newly discovered civilization.

The Cannibals were amused at being discovered. It was a completely new experience for them. So they let themselves be observed and examined. As far as they were concerned these guys could poke around for all they were worth, as long as they didn't learn about the important things. The things that really mattered.

The Ruddy Apes poked and pried. And soon began to harbor ambitions of educating and civilizing The Cannibals. The latter decided to humor them. And one day, even invited one of the Ruddy Apes, a particularly hungry ape who believed himself to be a connoisseur of food, over for dinner.

The hungry Ruddy Ape was delighted. He had heard a few stories about the culinary skills of the barbarians, and was eager to add to his repertoire of food experiences. To cut a long story short. The ape came. He saw (and sniffed). He ate. He raved about the dishes and begged for the recipes. After which, all hell broke loose.

Nobody knew how he got wind of the fact that he had eaten human flesh. The Cannibals had all along been very careful to conceal many things about themselves. But even disciplined people have their moments of weakness. The Cannibal who was responsible for putting together that meal, may have, in a moment of pride, spilled the beans. Maybe the Ruddy Apes had planted a spy disguised as a Cannibal. Who knows? The dinner guest threw up everything and ran back to his kith as fast as his Apish legs could carry him.

The Ruddy Apes turned hostile overnight. They held private meetings and avoided The Cannibals, who tried to pacify them. Unfortunately, their efforts aggravated the matter. So why didn't The Cannibals simply catch them and chop them up? That way they would never have had to face a shortage of meat, ever. They were experts at freezing food instantaneously. In fact, so advanced were their methods of preserving fresh meats that you would not be able to tell the difference between a fresh carcass and one that had been frozen years ago.

The reason why they did not is so simple that it is almost unbelievable.

The Cannibals did not believe in indiscriminate killing and senseless slaughter. Besides, food was both a matter of sustenance as well as a source of creative expression for them. They were very picky about whom or what they would choose for their tables. They decided to teleport the fools back to their homeland. Unfortunately, things turned out to be very different.

Whenever a war or even a disagreement breaks out between two groups, the one that is more savage is more likely to be the winner. The history of the Ruddy Apes is peppered with such examples, which is perhaps why they preferred to eschew spicy dishes.

The Cannibals debated among themselves about the best method of putting distance between them. The Ruddy Apes conferred about the best ways to vanquish The Cannibals. Since they liked to put up a veneer of high thought and exalted culture over their insidious plans, and the more insidious the plan the thicker the patina of civility, the Ruddy Apes sent word that they wanted to carry out a few simple tests on them. The Cannibals readily agreed. Teleportation was an expensive affair, all said and done; they did not think the apes were worth spending so much energy and resources upon.

The talks began, albeit from a safe distance, over megaphones. This amused The Cannibals no end. The Ruddy Apes shook with fear to see so many rows of pearly whites. Many of them fell to their knees and prayed. After some time they gathered courage and asked for some Cannibals to be brought over to their side. They wanted to conduct tests on the specimens. The Cannibals, forever the hospitable hosts, did not refuse. They allowed some of their kinsmen to be subjected to all kinds of scans and tests. Some of the scans, like the genetic scan, made them laugh. The Cannibals had a longish respite after this, while the Ruddy Apes busied themselves with conferences and discussions.

The Ruddy Apes emerged at last from their conference looking deadbeat. The Cannibals felt sorry for them and offered glasses of elixir, but the Ruddy Apes looked alarmed and refused to touch any of it. They then announced that being civilized folk, they had decided to give The Cannibals another chance, a fair trial in fact, after which they would decide their fate. By trial they meant they would pick a few Cannibals and pose questions, which they would be required to answer on behalf of the whole tribe. Needless to say, The Cannibals were great debating and quiz enthusiasts. They eagerly entered into the spirit of the game. Their curiosity was aroused. Perhaps the Ruddy Apes were not such bores after all. If they liked to solve problems through debates and quizzes, perhaps they were not so uncivilized after all. The Cannibals wondered among themselves why they had not observed this quality in the Ruddy Apes before. Maybe they had been too dismissive before. The Ruddy Apes on the other hand were surprised to see them accept so readily. They told each other in self-congratulatory tones that perhaps there was hope yet for the brutish natives.

The trial began. The Ruddy Apes erected a fort and placed microphones on top of that. The Cannibals were discouraged from erecting a fort, so they made a simple tall table-like platform with wood instead of their special mortar so as not to draw attention to their knowledge and skills. They made a wooden ladder that led to the platform. A couple of adventurous Ruddy Apes went over to their side to put up microphones. They even demonstrated with a lot of miming action the art of using these "advanced machines." Afterwards, these Ruddy Apes were given bravery awards. The Cannibals shrugged. They were already humoring the oafs. Even though the sight of armored trucks being offloaded from large ships that seemed to have materialized overnight on their island annoyed them greatly.

The Ruddy Apes began with an oath-taking ceremony. They explained to The Cannibals that this was necessary in order to ensure that everybody spoke the truth. The Cannibals politely nodded, but demurred. According to them lying was an illogical activity that served no purpose other than to delay inevitable truth, thereby wasting time. They did not need to take oaths in order to stick to the truth. Besides, liars would lie anyway, regardless of the books they touched or Gods they invoked. The Cannibals' refusal disturbed the Ruddy Apes so much that they had to hold emergency meetings immediately. Finally they announced that The Cannibals were a primitive people who had not yet developed the power of pure logical thinking, which included belief and faith in an almighty power; they also put in "stubborn" and "tendency to be fixated on a single idea" on the margins of the minutes-of-the-meeting next to the heading "Character of the Under-trials".

The first question that they hurled at The Cannibals was—do you admit to eating human flesh? To which The Cannibals readily and enthusiastically replied that yes they did. The Ruddy Apes pursed their lips at such brazenness. They scribbled furiously in their notebooks. Their next question was, why did they insist on eating humans when they had a wide choice of other meats? To this The Cannibals replied that they ate humans simply because they enjoyed it; they had thousands of recipes for the different parts of the human body. The Cannibals, being gourmets, began to warm up to the subject, making the Ruddy Apes hysterical in the process. The trial had to be adjourned for twenty minutes before they could move on to the third question, which was more of an accusation than a question: don't you care about fellow humans at all? Don't you know how precious humans are? And to this The Cannibals cheerfully replied, yes we do, we love humans; we know how precious they are, in fact lately they've become even more so; and we'll be so grateful if you could supply us, you have a surplus ... and so on. Oh, this is terrible, the Ruddy Apes cried. Stop! Stop! They screamed, their hands against their ears. It took a long time for them to regain their composure. After which, The Cannibals demanded they break for lunch. The Ruddy Apes were too unnerved to carry on. The trial was adjourned for the day.

The following day, at nine o'clock sharp, the trial began again. The Ruddy Apes looked haggard and listless. They had stayed up the whole night thinking up new strategies to deal with The Cannibals. They knew that they had managed to get a clear confession from the under-trials, but the situation was far from satisfactory. The Cannibals had to realize how wrong their habits were. It was vital for the health of humanity that The Cannibals, who otherwise seemed to be a trainable race of people, were made to repent the error of their ways. So the Ruddy Apes decided to try the philosophical angle.

They started with a simple question: How do you differentiate between animals and humans? The Cannibals replied that humans were the only creatures whose emotions were interlinked with their intellect, and that this was not merely the outcome of instinct. The Ruddy Apes were pleased with this reply, though somewhat surprised; 'animal instinct' was a favorite phrase among many of them when describing the antics of uneducated humans.

So you do understand, said the Ruddy Apes together, that humans are refined beings bound by a sense of love and duty? The Cannibals looked at them askance. But of course we do, they responded. We love our respective individual selves very much; because we are rational creatures; we are duty-bound to respect the self-loves of humans, birds and beasts equally. The Ruddy Apes' eyes gleamed with triumph. They had got them at last. So, they thundered, do you think that eating fellow humans is an act inspired by love and respect for others?

Certainly, said The Cannibals, a little put out that they should be asked at all. Completely and absolutely, they emphasized. You see, the human body, like everything else on earth, is physical matter, and essentially the same; just break them into their base elements and you'll know. Look, they said, warming to the subject. Your bodies are matter. Our bodies are matter. When we die the bodies return to earth. But the real you remains, your hopes and dreams, your ideas and deeds, your loves and your passions. They all remain; sometimes like a mountain that is visible from afar and sometimes like ripples spreading and spreading in a lake. Don't you see?

The Ruddy Apes did not see. They were astonished at the poetry of their speech, but then, tribal and other savage sort played rudimentary forms of music on their drums and conches, so perhaps The Cannibals, being a little more advanced, had progressed to the basics of poetry. They retired for the day and conferred among themselves again. When they returned to the trial again, they had no questions. They just wanted to tell the Cannibals, warn them in fact, that they had observed severe discrepancies in their society. Mainly that although they looked alike and ate similar things etc., some of them liked walking towards the West and some preferred the East; some loved climbing up while others liked to hunker down.

You are not united at all, the Ruddy Apes told The Cannibals. There are great differences among you, and we can foresee dark days ahead. Pay heed and let us take charge of your lives. We will show you the light.

The Cannibals laughed uproariously. Then they became quiet. One among them stepped up to the platform and spoke, with a kind of deadly earnestness that frightened the Ruddy Apes, even though they could see no weapons in their opponents' hands, nor any great danger from the person of the speaking Cannibal.

Leave now, said The Cannibal on the platform. You have overstayed your welcome. And the rest, standing below him, nodded sagely.

The Ruddy Apes sensing the change in weather, left without another word, pulling out in their trucks and loading it all into their boats and ships. When they were a safe distance away, they detonated the bombs that they had secretly planted beforehand. Powerful bombs that splintered the island into two or three parts. The power of the bombs devoured some of the Ruddy Apes' ships, and the ones who died were commemorated as war heroes. Enough ships escaped to proclaim victory though. And the world of apes saluted them as victors. Especially since they had seen the mushroom cloud that had shot heavenwards, covering blue sky with black noxious fumes for miles and miles around. The Ruddy Apes, when they returned to their world, of course denied having had any hand in it.

Those were smoke signals sent out by the brutes, and they used a special kind of gum tree for fuel that made the clouds so extreme, they said.

So the honor of having detonated the first atomic bombs went elsewhere, to a country that had just begun to savor its apish powers. The Ruddy Apes retired to their smoke rooms, content to be smug in private rather than have the world know of their dastardly ways.

Scores among The Cannibals perished, of course. But a good number escaped as well, in their space dinghies, flying out to their orbiting spaceships. They could not take much with them, as they were caught unawares. But their ships were fully furbished, hovering around the Kuiper belt and ready for any adventure. Pieces of their broken land bobbed about in the sea, rolling in the waves again and again, until they finally settled down on a patch of elevated ocean floor. On an auspicious day in the future, divers and adventurers from the Ruddy ape clan discovered the remains of a civilization they claimed was the mythical El Dorado. Or the lost continent of Atlantis.

Life returned meanwhile to the portions that didn't sink. Flora and fauna, and after them apes and humans. But nothing was as it was before. Nevertheless, in patches of shade and in the whispers of leaves, the stories of The Cannibals meandered about until willing ears took them in. The new people who populated the land were just beginning the long march towards self-realization, and they were eager for myths, legends and fables.

So it goes. Some legends proclaim that the Cannibals are still among us, a few who stayed back out of a sense of duty towards primitive humanity. They are of course in touch with their brethren out there in space. These are the sages, scientists and the odd social worker. As for the ones who fled, they hope to find a nice cozy planet someday, or so it is whispered. They hope that the natives of that planet, if any, will let them live their lives, uninterrupted and unmolested. And they hope that their erstwhile home planet will believe its fables and stories and ultimately become a better place. They hope on as their ships swim through the universe. Hope is a good thing to have.

* * *

Discussion Questions

1. What does the opening paragraph of the story mean, in the context of the story? "Does rain remember vapor? Does vapor remember rain? Yet both were the other in their past lives. If you told their stories to each other, would they even comprehend? And, does that mean their stories are unnecessary, unimportant and implausible?"

2. The islanders are cannibals. They do so because they like the way human meat tastes. Is that a good enough reason to eat human meat? Is that a good enough reason to eat meat in general?

3. Is there any indication in the story that those who are eaten are done so against their will, or as a form of violence? Is it possible to kill (or eat) another person (or animal) <u>with</u> their consent? Can consent only be given by an intelligent animal, like a human being? Does that mean human meat is the only meat that can be conscientiously consumed?

4. If you were visiting the islanders, would you eat the human meat they gave you to eat? Why, or why not?

5. Were the "Ruddy Apes" correct in killing off most of the islanders because of their practice of cannibalism? Is there a societal obligation to destroy (or change/fix) that which society generally finds immoral?

6. What other universally offensive action could the author have substituted with cannibalism in this story? Is there a substitute action you can think of that would change your evaluation of the Ruddy Apes' response?

Pretty Pragmatism

Jenean McBrearty

SENATOR SALVATORE BOUNDINI straightened his tie, took a deep breath, and walked into the hearing room with as much haughtiness as he could muster. His publicist had told him there was no such thing as bad publicity, but what the hell did a twenty-eight-year-old journalism major know?

"You probably should have asked that question before your publicist hired her," his senior staffer said when Sal told him he was about to be tarred and feathered by the ethics committee.

"She's a dead ringer for a young Sophia Loren, Rob," Sal said by way of justification.

"Who's Sophia Loren? Never mind. Don't ever say that in front of a mic."

"How about the BPOE?"

"Shut up, Sal."

"What's all the fuss and feathers about anyway? Everybody's always complaining that taxes are too low, and the national debt is too high. Whatever happened to Goldilocks and just right?"

"Maybe she got off the trolley when you used the

words compulsory, national, and service in the same sentence."

"Requiring two years of public service in the national parks is a great idea! Up with the sun, eight hours of planting trees and picking up litter, learning how to grow something … it would make kids too tired to get into mischief, and get them physically fit. Hell, they might even read a book or two. Most twelve-year-olds can't run a lap without an oxygen station. It's a good idea. You said so yourself."

Rob had flopped into his black leather worrying chair and rubbed his temples. "It is a good idea, but it has to be tweaked and packaged just right. Sal, it's 2025. Did it ever occur to you or Sophia Loren, whoever that is, to do some historical research?"

Rob picked up a tome laying on the end table. "*Giancano Maritz. A Fascist Approach to Social Ills.* He's a distant nephew of Benito himself. Your young boy's camp is a Hitler-Jugend knockoff. Even the Joint Chiefs of Staff have their panties in a twist."

Sal took the book from him and checked for a ribbon of bright white running down the pages that meant pictures. Included were before and after photos of young men who had their squishy video game bodies transformed into muscular athlete bodies. "Rich people send their kids to summer camps, why can't poor people do the same?" He showed Rob a particularly striking metamorphosis.

"It's not the idea, it's where it comes from that's all wrong."

"Really? Ask Neil Armstrong how he felt about Werner von Braun's rocket research. Or how the Germans felt about stealing English radar."

Rob thought for a minute. "Good point. Bring that up to the committee, if you can. But, for heaven's sake, don't make Senator Witcombe mad at you. She already thinks you're a pig."

Seven senators sat soberly, staring at Sal. Each had finished bloviating for his allotted seven minutes about Sen. Boundini's reprehensible Child Servitude Bill, as it was nicknamed, proposing indoctrination prison camps even if they were democratic, as they were described.

"Senator Boundini, were you aware of the fascist origins of your idea? Were you lazy, stupid, a fascist yourself, or all three?" It was one of Sen. Marsha Witcombe's uneasily answerable questions.

"Well, Ms. Witcombe, let me say this." Sal went to the bookcases that flanked the two doors at the rear of the hearing room where row upon row of law and history books were stored and regularly dusted. His fingers caressed the volumes as he walked end to end before returning to his seat.

"There must be at least two hundred authors in this room alone. How many words do you estimate each of them wrote? And all the people, throughout the ages. Stories, poems, essays, science theories, practice and research. Different languages, grammars, cultures. All of them wanting to talk to us here and now through the written word just to let us know what they were thinking. Pythagoras, Galileo, Newton, Dante, Shakespeare … great ideas, guys. That autobahn thing? Ike liked Hitler's idea enough to build the Interstate. Have you heard of Sister Kenny? She was a self-trained Australian nurse who saved polio victims from paralysis before the vaccine was invented. Her methods became the basis of physical therapy still in use today after a century. Why? Because they work.

"We have a problem with childhood obesity in this country, Senators. So, I read up on physical fitness. Ever hear of Vic Tanny? Or Jack LaLanne? Tanny was an Italian who invented the health club and showed people how to stay fit in a sit-down world. LaLanne advocated good nutrition and invented gym machines including one for leg extension. For kids, we know exercise in the fresh air is the best remedy for weak muscles and a dull mind. I never read Maritz's book, but even if I had, a good idea is a good idea no matter who comes up with it. The fact that Hitler, Tanny, LaLanne and Mussolini shared similar ideas is a testimony to good ideas, not to any stupid political ideology. Ask Neil Armstrong about Werner von Braun's rocket research."

Rob would be proud. He'd taken a simple argument and made it a full-blown oration. Not as good as the Gettysburg Address, but persuasive. Senator Witcombe, however, was not easily seduced by words. "Are you saying that even the devil can have a good idea, Senator?"

"I guarantee you; the devil has thought to himself on more than one occasion that obedience to God would have been a better career path."

"Are you suggesting the devil repents?"

"Never mistake regret for repentance, Senator. It's what the courts do regularly, but wives and politicians can't afford to." The picture of Rob in his worry chair rushed into the rerun theater of his mind. "It's the same thing with flattery. Husbands and politicians often believe their own press clippings and shouldn't."

"Knowing how the ethics committee feels about borrowing from discredited sources, and in view of the election cycle realities of discredited politicians, are you going to withdraw your bill, Senator Boundini?" Senator James Emonds had thrown him a lifeline.

"Ahhh. Well, I think it needs tweaking, Jim. Maybe rebranding. But the essence of the bill is sound but, from a pragmatic public relations point of view, maybe a pilot program would be the better way to address the problem. I could rename it the Summer Fitness Camp Scholarship program and reintroduce it at a later date. How does that sound?"

"Calling a stink-weed a rose won't make it pass the sniff test," Witcombe said. "I move this committee vote on censure."

The Committee asked him to leave. Sal retired to his office and a bottle of Johnny Walker Green. If the Committee recommended reprimand, it would remain a private matter. A censure meant the indignity of standing before his peers while the reasons for the censure were read aloud. Expulsion? Since when did proposed legislation merit being kicked out when the voters kicked him in?

On his desk was a note from Rob: I axed Roxy. Sal let out a regretful sigh. Telling Roxy she could no longer be a press secretary must have been difficult, like saying she couldn't be a princess when she'd just learned how to wear a tiara. The office would be as double dreary as a gray, gray gulag. Maybe it was time he went gently into that good D.C. night after all.

"Don't look so glum," Rob said.

He's a nice guy, but not perky. "You called it. Witcombe attacked," Sal said. Rob's face always reminded him of a fox.

"Cheer up, Sal. Jim Edmonds withdrew his vote from Witcombe's bloated budget bill, and she wants to know if you'll trade a censure for a yea vote to pull it over the finish line."

"Ha! Wheelin' and dealin' is the name of the game, my boy. Waiter, give the lady Senator the principle and crow casserole!" Sure, she hated him for dumping her for Roxy, but she'd rather have pork for her constituents than preserve her pride. She was a fine addition to the fine ol' deliberative dunces. Summer camps for the unwashed masses was a great idea, no matter who thought of it. Rob and he shared grins and cocktails, and when Rob left at midnight, Sal took a manuscript from his desk drawer and began chapter three of his Washington memoir:

"To quote Victor Hugo, 'There is one thing stronger than all the armies in the world, and that is an idea whose time has come,'" he wrote with the taste of a gloat gimlet still warming his throat. Even stronger is the person who has the *cojones* to write down the idea and share it with posterity."

* * *

Discussion Questions

1. Does it matter where a "good idea" comes from?

2. The Senator says, "...even the devil can have a good idea..." Is that true? Can a person be so evil that it makes everything they have to say, on every topic, not worth hearing?

3. Are the accomplishments of a person, or organization, diminished by their unrelated bad acts? For example, are the efforts of MLK diminished because he was unfaithful to his wife? Are the songs of Michael Jackson or R. Kelly valueless (or of less value) because of their actions? Is Henry Ford's assembly line made less because he was anti-Semitic, an advocate of eugenics, and an early supporter of Hitler?

4. Does the type of thing a person or organization does affect how much they should be considered? Are the Holocaust, sexual assault, infidelity, or anti-Semitism different? Is it a sliding scale?

5. Does it matter if the person is a public figure or "role model?"

The Alpha-Dye Shirt Factory

Tyler W. Kurt

I DON'T KNOW WHERE HOW I should start my story: with the fire, with the things leading up to the fire, or how I made my escape.

Well, my name's Mary and I worked at the Alpha-Dye Shirt Factory, a seven-story building in the middle of the sugar district falling apart in every which a-way. It's a brick building, red brick, not that you'd know it on account it's been whitewashed over, except for the fire escape, which was painted black about a hundred times to hide the rust, and more paint than fire escape. The building had just the one elevator so most of the ladies would take the fire escape if they was on one of the lower floors, but I never did that, on account of I didn't trust it as old as it was, and mostly rusted, like I said.

I should mention the smell, too. You never smelled nothing like it. The factory was right in the middle of the sugar district; cheaper rents I guess. All I know'd is something about the manufacturing process for sugar makes it so the air smells like chicken fried steak. When I was young and first started out, I remember thinking it was a pretty good smell, that I'd be getting to go to work every day smelling my mama's cooking and maybe I wouldn't be so homesick.

Of course, pretty soon that smell started getting bothersome cause it just worked its way into your clothes. I hadn't counted on that, still smelling of chicken fried steak in my clothes when I got home at night. That smell would get into the bed sheets till the whole one-room apartment I lived in got to stinking. Now, when I smell that smell all I think of is long hours and the foreman yelling at me about production quotas.

One year early on I went home over Christmas to visit my family and you know'd what my mama made for me? Chicken fried steak, and she was so proud of making it for me, but I about threw up right there at the table and had to explain to her about the factory, and about the sugar and the way it smelled. Course, I didn't tell her everything about the factory or how I was living, cause I didn't want her to worry about me.

And here I am rambling on and on about chicken fried steak when you want to know about the fire. That's the way it goes sometimes, a person hooks you in with the promise of a great story, then get all sideways.

So, there I was, like every day, just settled in and working my sewing machine, the same two stitch lines on the shirt I sew'd every day for years, when Maria whispered across to me over the noise of the sewing. Maria was a Cuban girl who had worked across from me going on a year-and-a-half, and we was pretty tight on account of we both liked going to the movies on our day off.

"Mary," Maria whispered across the machines, and I looked up. And when she seen me looking she nodded her head to where the bathrooms were, meaning we should go there to talk. We'd done it a few times before.

She'd call over to the foreman to go the restroom, then I'd wait a bit and do the same. Restroom breaks was limited to three minutes, but if you timed it just right with someone else you could get a good minute or so of overlap to chit-chat so long as you was quick about it.

And so she done it, she got the foreman over and he waved her on to use the facilities. And a minute or so later I done the same. Come to think of it, he must a known we was going into the bathroom to talk, but he didn't seem to care much, I guess. Mostly, I think, because he didn't care much about anything. He always had the airs of a man who felt that his position was beneath him and he was just biding his time until his real ship come along. Also, I think he keep'ed the job because he liked some of the ladies from time to time.

So off I goes to the ladies room and there is Maria, just beaming from ear to ear, pretty much like she had been doing the whole morning, but even more so now that it was possible to do in earnest. And soon's as I walked in she blurts it out, no warm ups or nothing, in her Spanish accent. "I got engaged!"

Maria reached into her pocket and pushed out this tiny gold ring for me to see. She wasn't wearing it cause you had to be a single to work at the Alpha-Dye Factory. Not all the factories had that rule no more, but Alpha-Dye had that rule, and girls would still get fired pretty regular if the bosses found out they'd got hitched.

Of course, I was excited for her, but not nearly so excited as she was. She'd know'ed darned well Raul was going to ask her to get married soon enough, as she'd been going on to him about them getting married the last few months.

But still, I was pretty excited for her because getting engaged ain't something you do every day. She meant to tell me the details as quick as she could before the foreman missed us, but then we heard a bunch of noise coming from outside.

We opened the door and everyone was up from their sewing machines moving around in a hurry. And that's when I seen the smoke coming up through the floors. The floors, you see, was made a wood, like most floors in these older buildings, and smoke was coming up between the depressions of the wood floors thick and black.

I seen pretty quick that a bunch of women was standing by the elevator waiting for it until two of the women, a Russian pair, decided they was going to pull the doors open and look down and see if they could figure where the elevator was or how much longer it might be till it showed up.

Well, as they was doing that the women behind them was a pushing on them pretty hard, on account of they thought the elevator had arrived and these two girls were trying to be the first ones in. So when these Russian girls pried the doors up, a thick black smoke from the shaft came billowing out, and what, with the women behind pushing, they done pushed both of them Russian girls, and one other that was next to them, into the shaft, and down they went. And that's the last anyone saw of them, I suppose.

I turned back to Maria, but she'd already assessed the situation and was to the window with one foot on the fire escape.

I figured she had the right idea, so I headed that way as well, pushing through the people best I could. The smoke was getting blacker and thicker all the time, and it was already getting mighty warm from the depressed floors below.

As I was push'en my way to the fire escape, everything seemed to go real quiet and real slow like and I had the time to examine the faces of every woman in the place real good.

There was two women in the corner on their knees, with a Rosary, just praying as hard as could be. There was another girl just standing there with blank eyes, like she was a statue. And I seen one girl with blond hair that was dead, or near dead, on the ground, who must a got pushed over or fall'ed over and now people was just tripping and stepping on her to trying to get past her in a panic. But she ain't moving none.

The foreman, he was funny, if there could be such a thing. He was pushing past all the other girls on his way to the fire escape, saying over and over again, "Let me through, I'm in charge. I'm in charge!" But what he was really doing, of course, was trying to get to that fire escape to be one of the first ones out.

And you know, in all that bedlam and screaming, you know what my first thought was at the time? It's stupid to say it now, but it's the God's truth. My first thought was, "Who's going to clean all this up?" Which of course, now, I know, was a pretty stupid thing to think.

Just before I got to the window for the fire escape, I seen a girl next to me fall through the floor where the wood had saddened out so it couldn't take the weight no more. It was like watching someone jump from the end of a dock into a lake. One second you could see them, and the next thing they were deep under water. Except, it ain't water, it was the floor. And it ain't them getting wet, it's them going into the fire of misery and getting burnt up.

And when I seen that, well, that woke me up plenty, and all of the sudden like, I could hear everything around me, but it was real loud now. And that's when I heard a pop from the outside.

I was at the window, you see, trying to push my way out onto the fire escape to join Maria, and I could see her, too, when I looked down, on the sixth floor working her way down the stairs. The foreman had just pushed past her. And I was gonna try to yell to her, to tell her to wait up for me, but before I could speak I heard a pop. That pop was the steel bolts that's holding the fire escape together.

So, I heard that first pop and that gave me a pause, then I heard a bunch more, like a gun being fired a bunch of times in a row. Then the whole fire escape come crashing down on the ladies below taking all the metal and bodies with it, including Maria and her ring.

The whole thing sort of folded up like an accordion, breaking up into different pieces as it go'ed and throwing people off it or trapping them under it. And I nearly went with it, on account of the woman behind me trying to push her way out the window, not knowing yet there was no fire escape to go down.

"It's busted!" I yelled, as loud as I could. "It's busted, let me back! Quit pushing!" And eventually I worked my way back to the room.

When I turned back to the room its soul was plumb full a black smoke. I couldn't see no more than a few feet, and couldn't hardly breathe, but I could see the glows of red from the fire where the flooring was opening up, and where women had fallen through it into their darkness.

I covered my mouth with my sleeve and tried to think as calm like as I could, but it wasn't no doing. The fire was coming up, glowing red, and the bodies of ash-darkened women was piling up on the floor from them that couldn't breath no more and had passed out. I knew in a few seconds I was next.

And man was it hot. Not the kind of hot where you say, "Today is a really hot day." I know you know'd it was hotter than that. But I mean it was *hot*! Like if you'd a put a stove on the highest temperature and grabbed a black pan that had been sitting in it all day with your bare hand. Imagine that, but all over your body.

Now I know'd escaping was impossible. I know'd I ain't got but seconds left to make a decision about just one thing; how did I want to die? Did I want to keep my mouth covered and burn up? I thought about that.

Burning up alive; feeling the flesh slide off my bones. That sounded, I thought, like about the worst way a person could die. So, I'd decided I'd better do like them other girls and try and fall asleep from the smoke. So, I took my shirt away from my mouth to take a deep breath, which seemed like me making the smartest decision in the world against me getting burned up in that fire.

The problem was I tried to take a breath, but I couldn't. I couldn't because when I breathed in it felt like someone was pouring hot coal dust down my throat and it just hurt so bad I couldn't force myself. By instinct my shirt cloth hand went back up to my mouth to stop the coals from burning my throat.

"Dear God," I thought. "Anything but burning alive…" Then I remembered the window. Not for the fire escape, cause I know'ed it was gone, but the window where the fire escape was.

There was so much smoke I couldn't see the window, but I remembered where it was and I could kind of see the direction the smoke was going to get out of it. So, I crawled on my hands and knees over the bodies of them other girls that had given up to the sadness to get to it.

When I got to the window, I don't mind telling you, I was relieved to have gotten there on account of the heat that was all around me; it felt so my skin was getting bitten by a million of the worst bees all at the same time.

I looked down out the window and could see the fire escape, crumpled on the ground. And I could see Maria's body in the mess of black metal, along with the foreman and some others. I could also see the people on the street filling up to watch the fire, along with some of the girls that was working on the first few floors that had made it out okay.

And I'd love to say I was saved, or had some miracle that kept me a living, but that ain't true. All I could think of was that fire heating me up with them burning bee stings, and the smoke of red coals that was billowing out the window. And the depression all around.

"Aim so I don't land on somebody and bring them down too," I thought. Then a girl came behind me, who'd had the same idea as me, and she got to pushing me to get out the window. And so, I jumped.

You see, I didn't jump out that window because I thought I was going to live. I jumped out because it was better than being burned alive.

* * *

Discussion Questions

1. Does Mary make the right choice by jumping out the window?

2. Does it matter if the fire is *actually* going to kill Mary or she only *believes* it will kill her?

3. The fire and heat are referred to as a "depression" and "darkness." Is it permissible for a person to commit suicide to escape the "fire" of depression that they *believe* is burning them up?

4. If, moments after Mary jumped from the window to her death, the firefighters had arrived with a ladder and saved everyone left in the building, would your opinion of Mary's choice change? Does an *absolute* certainty that she was going to die in the fire mean something different than having a *high likelihood* she was going to die?

5. If a person knows they are going to die of a terminal disease in the near future, is it acceptable for them to commit suicide to escape that "fire?"

Lay On

Vera Burris

A MISCHIEVOUS GALE from the bay blew into the city, lifting mini-skirts and tangling long hair, but the three women standing across the street didn't seem affected by it. Christopher watched them, wondering at their serenity, as he played and sang off-key on a street corner of Haight and Ashbury. Polly sat against the prickly brick wall behind him, arms crossed and trembling.

"It won't be long now, Babe," he assured her. "Just another couple bucks and we'll have enough for you."

She was working on a gig for him, but needed to score before she could confirm with the club manager. Her habit had grown much worse since their first meeting, when he'd moved from Oklahoma two years earlier.

Back then, in 1967, it was the Summer of Love, a time of hope for the flower children. With escalating war, riots and assassinations, however, 1969 was more of an ugly-chick-one-night-stand: dirtier, more jaded and more desperate, like Christopher and Polly.

He stretched a brilliant smile across his face as the three women approached him. "What can I sing for you lovely ladies?"

They were dressed similarly to others on the street in long wrapped skirts and ragged tops drooping with no bra, but their eyes—hazel, black and cinnamon brown—seemed to hold the memory of centuries.

The statuesque one with a magnificent Afro brought forth a sheaf of dollars. Polly jumped up to stand beside him, eagerly clutching his arm as a twenty floated into the battered fedora.

"You can have fortune ... adulation," said the black woman.

"You can be king of the music festivals," a smaller one with brown eyes added, with another twenty.

"The envy of all who have wronged you," the third, a redhead, said. She stooped down to drop the rest of the bills in the hat.

Christopher looked first at the money, then the three women. "Who do I have to kill?" he joked.

The mysterious trio smiled and said in unison, "You'll know."

***

Incense and pot wafted through most of the rooms, but in the blackened apartment for Ingrid, Wasi and Anita, the scent was a Hell Brew of feline blood and noxious weeds.

They'd been banished from witch society for multiple crimes, including their cowardly escape from the original Friday the Thirteenth scourge of 1307, and their failure to help the accused during the travesty of justice in Salem,

Mass. They were in San Francisco to repair their reputations and ignite chaos.

Leaning over an ancient cauldron, they watched Christopher. His red-gold hair and beard shone after a bath in a hotel. Yet even after a large meal from room service, he maintained that thin, compelling look of insatiable hunger that people would instinctively want to satisfy. It was very promising.

Polly also looked better, her blue eyes gleaming after her fix. Long, blonde hair hung loose and full down her naked back as she and Christopher made love on the virginal white sheets of the hotel bed. The witches studied Christopher, seemingly docile while Polly gyrated on top of him.

"But how can we know if he's truly malevolent?" asked Wasi. "Many steal, many sell pills. Are we sure this is the one to spark mayhem? Would he do our will for his desires?"

"It will be for him to decide what he does with what he's offered. We must not question because he looks innocent. He has not yet been tried," Anita said.

When Polly dismounted to dress, the witches noticed red fingerprints where Christopher had gripped her arms. In her drugged state, Polly might not have been aware of the casual violence of his clench, but to the trio watching them, it was a good sign.

***

Tattered Victorian buildings on either side of the street enclosed the heavy traffic on the road and sidewalks.

Power wires dangled between them, precariously close to the human swell, like giant, electrified garrote. Storefronts on the once-stately buildings were warts on the collective body of architecture.

Christopher and Polly entered the door of a scarred Mission Revival with a hand-lettered sign on the streaked window—Beer with Folk. The interior was unlit, except for the grey sunshine that snuck in under the canopy above the door. The sound was the strike of shoes on wood floor, scrape of chairs and awkward coughs.

The witches raised their arms and closed their eyes as they circled the bubbling cauldron, sweat glassy on their bodies, chanting and incanting for hints of more malice.

"Oh, it's you," said the pudgy manager, Bernie, from his spot at a back table as Polly and Christopher approached. He looked as if he might have been selling bad cars in the previous six months and had just bought a faded t-shirt and badly fitting jeans for his new job.

"Yeah, and this is my old man Christopher," Polly said. "I told you he could be the next Dylan."

"Hmph," grunted Bernie, scanning Christopher. "Well, he might keep some girls around the stage for guys to buy drinks for. Let's hear ya."

Wasi, Anita and Ingrid made a web of their open hands over the cauldron, framing Christopher's handsome but nervous face.

"Uh, what do you want to hear?" he asked, swinging his guitar across his chest and releasing an accidental, jarring chord.

"Just play," said Bernie. He picked up his pencil and rifled the papers before him.

Christopher swept over the strings, adjusted the tuning pegs, and began a whispery tenor. "How many roads must—"

"That's enough," growled Bernie. He looked up and smiled at the sound of a long, slow gait nearing them. His gut lifted the table slightly as he rose to greet the new person in the room. "Hank, good timing. This is Christopher. He'll be your sub if you don't make it tonight."

Hank reminded Christopher of a high school football star who had discovered Speed. He was bulky, but his eyes twitched behind blue, tiny-square glasses. His black hair coiled down to his sallow chin, and his lips were chalky. He stuck out a wide hand to shake Christopher's and checked out Polly with a raised eyebrow. "Don't waste your time. I'll be here," he snickered and sauntered out.

The trio grasped hands as Christopher lifted a corner of his lip in a sneer, and he and Polly followed the bell-bottomed singer out of Bernie's bar.

"Do something," Polly said in a strained whisper.

"What am I supposed to do?" Christopher glared at Hank's taunting back and watched him pinch a young woman who walked past him.

"Anything. He can't do your show tonight. Don't you have any guts?" Polly asked, her voice carrying a new note of scorn.

The witches leaned closer over the pot, their excitement mounting. This was it.

"You'll know," the women had said. Christopher set his jaw and set his shoulders and took long strides to get closer to Hank. The throng of pedestrians seemed to help, pushing him against the other musician. Hank turned, opening his mouth to speak, as Christopher shoved. Hank fell in the street, into the path of a speeding van.

Christopher drew shallow breaths as the crowd gathered around the body. His blood rushed to his head and sang in his ears, "Fame and stardom."

Polly, pretty in paisley, caught up to him and took his arm.

"It was an accident, Babe," she whispered, leading him away from the scene. "Let's get you ready for your show."

Music filled the dark of the witches' room, not the psychedelic or jangling of the age, but strings, pipes and drums mingling in old melody— joyful, sensual and ominous, all.

They ate the last of the cats they'd used for the potion and skipped and spun around the fire faster and faster, until collapsing in a friendly heap, exhausted and exultant, on the cool floor.

***

The club wasn't only dark in the evening, with fifteen-year-old red wall sconces providing the only light, but the veil of cigarette smoke further compromised vision and perception.

The three witches sat in a window alcove at the front

of the bar. Dressed in black, their heads alone were distinguishable and appeared to float, disembodied in the dark. The light from a streetlamp that shone through the window seemed to give them ironic halos.

A platform at the other end rose about eight inches from the floor. Christopher appeared there, the lights shining up on his face imparting a subliminal outline to him, as well.

He didn't play or sing any better than he had before, but the reaction to him was stronger. The conversation buzz of the crowd stopped and all eyes fixed on him. Young women in hip-huggers gathered in front of the stage, looking up at him with the adoration he'd been promised.

No one wanted him to stop, requesting encore after encore. The witches watched as Christopher's confidence and swagger grew, only hours after committing his first murder.

"Yes," said Ingrid, "I believe he'll do nicely."

***

When he'd realized he could hold a crowd and have followers do his bidding, his ambitions changed. Why should he work at all if others were willing to work for him?

"What does a good man with power do?" asked Anita, *bent over the cauldron to watch their subject.*

"He'll share it, use it, to make things better," Wasi answered from the area where she and Ingrid were preparing ingredients for more potion. He stray cat

population had decreased significantly since their arrival.

"And what do we think Christopher will do?" Anita asked as she saw him mingling with hippies in the park.

"I'm the only one you can trust," Christopher told the young people who had gathered around him. He walked among them, fixing his eyes on one face after another, so they each thought he was speaking directly to him or her.

He dropped before a beautiful brunette wearing a daisy chain headband. "I know they've hurt you," he said, taking her hands and boring his eyes into hers. "I can heal you, if you do as I say."

The girl answered with a Madonna smile. Her gaze followed him as he rose to comfort another, and another, exchanging small packets of powder and pills for crumpled dollars.

"And that's what a bad man does with power," Ingrid said, now looking into the pot at Polly, clean and sober, seething with jealousy as Christopher collected a harem and army of the nubile and enthusiastic.

"We can't go on like this, Christopher. It's wrong," Polly said after they'd moved to a house in the suburbs owned by the father of one of his sycophants, Marvin. When Marvin Sr. returned sometime later from an overseas assignment, he had no choice but to raze the abused, million-dollar property.

"I'm tired of your nagging, Polly," Christopher shouted, nursing a hangover. "You didn't mind when we killed Hank."

"I wasn't thinking right then," she said, "but he's not the only one you've had killed or beaten or robbed or— "

" —Shut up!" Christopher rushed across the once-elegant salon and closed his hands around her neck, his head pounding and guts roiling, anger mounting higher than he'd ever known.

"Sisters," hissed Anita, "it's happening." Polly's shocked, terrified face filled the mouth of the cauldron, blue eyes gaping as she struggled to breathe. Christopher's slap reverberated in the witches' room, bringing satisfaction tinged with discomfort to the women.

Polly picked herself up from the floor, hand protecting the side of her red face while tears steamed. She ran out of the salon, out of the house and away from Christopher.

"With her gone, he'll think himself betrayed and unable to trust anyone," Wasi said with a grimace.

Ingrid nodded. "We must be prepared when he next comes to us for counsel."

As they predicted, paranoia clung to Christopher like a cheap Nehru jacket, making him more dangerous and callous. He drank because he couldn't sleep. He segregated his followers according to his own prejudices and feelings of who was least deserving of him. He became more reckless with money. He needed … something.

"Start the drum," said Wasi. "It's time."

***

The witches had never seen anything like the gathering

in the Catskill Mountains of New York—the music, the crowds, the color and abandon. It was the activity of covens, multiplied by thousands. For women rejuvenated after centuries, it was quite intoxicating. They mingled through the masses, singing and dancing, rubbing against naked bodies of strangers, participating in the moment as they hadn't allowed themselves in ages.

Duty called, however, and they moved from the teeming open area to the trees on the outskirts, finding an uninhabited spot, cave-like in its dark compactness. They made a fire and set the pot upon it and waited.

"Sisters, dear, does your skin sear as evil draws near?" Ingrid asked with a chuckle.

"No, but my sex revives when a bad man arrives," responded a laughing Anita.

"Pain stretches o'er my forehead at the approach of something horrid," Wasi added as Christopher burst through the foliage, having followed the drum's summons.

"Help me," he said. "They're out to get me. I demand you tell me what you see."

Anita glided forward and wrapped her arms around him, her chocolate brown hair draping over him as if offering protection. "Patience, our love," she said to him. "We have much to show you."

The drum beat again with the appearance of babies marching around the pot.

"These are children who will carry your name," Wasi explained. "The first are those whose mothers love you.

The circle means they will go on long after you."

Ingrid hovered above the ground, a flaming-haired specter. She tossed Christopher a wallet heavy with bills. "Your fortune continues as long as you breathe free," she promised.

The women stood before him and spoke as one. "You are safe provided none survive your attack."

Christopher nodded in relief. He was rich until his dying breath and as long as he ensured men who were his enemies were dead, he was untouchable. He left without a "thank you," a former musician unmoved by the excitement and sound of Woodstock.

The women looked after him. "Well, my sisters?" giggled Ingrid.

Wasi spoke first. "Yes, our thumbs do prick …"

"… when faced with a dick," Anita concluded.

Applause broke out beyond them as a headliner took the stage.

"Shall we join the party?"

"Groovy!"

"Far Out!"

The trio was beginning to enjoy 1969. They ran back to the mix of mud, skin and music and gave into their natural instincts for revelry.

For the return trip, they bought a Volkswagen bus from a Wisconsin couple and enough paint from others around them to properly decorate it, with giant flowers and swirls, and a sexy witch gripping a large, phallic spoon over a cauldron.

They'd adapted to every innovation in the past six hundred years. They could handle a Bug van. Anita set the controls to perform correctly, then pretended to steer as they joined the caravan heading West.

"What's he doing now?" she asked.

"Feeling very sure of himself," said Wasi, monitoring the pot for Christopher's activity. "He's coming out of a motel with two girls, no more than fifteen if they're a day."

The disgust for their protege was heavy in the vehicle. The witches had watched the progress of women for centuries and understood fifteen was different now than in ages past, when girls were considered nothing more than breeding stock. If he lived another five hundred years, Christopher would never learn that.

While Anita pretend-drove and Wasi watched Christopher, Ingrid sifted through a stack of old newspapers she found in the rear of the van.

"Cuyahoga River catches fire," she read. "Diesel fuel and oil accumulation in the river caused it to ignite in June near Cleveland, Ohio."

Wasi shook her head. "And we witches are accused of being destructive. At least we know better than to harm Mother Earth."

"True, and we only cause trouble to man for all of his wrongs," Ingrid agreed. "As they say, you can lead a horse to water, but how much he drinks is up to him."

"Yes, and Christopher has swallowed an ocean's

worth," said Anita. "What is he doing now?"

"Driving drunkenly," reported Wasi. "If he ever cared about his fellow man, he doesn't now."

"He has exceeded our highest expectations," Ingrid sighed. "How much we might have accomplished with him as a leader, how many people he might have diverted from their paths, if he hadn't sealed his fate with Polly."

"But people won't knowingly choose a man who has abused women as their leader," said Anita. "Therefore, there's only one way in which he can still be of use to us. What other news is there, Ingrid?"

The youngest of the three scanned the more recent publications and gasped. "There have been a number of home break-ins and murders in Los Angeles this month, including a Hollywood starlet, but this isn't Christopher's doing. Do you think there could be other witches engaged in a scheme similar to ours?"

"We shall ask Hecate, but probably not," Anita said. It doesn't take magic to cultivate evil or for the vulnerable to find it appealing."

"They have him!" squealed Wasi from her station over the cauldron. "He's been arrested."

***

The women were nearly unrecognizable when Christopher entered the visitors' room. Ingrid wore an egg-blue suit with a pleated, knee-length skirt. Anita enhanced her simple black shift with cultured pearls at her neck, and Wasi sported a leopard circle coat made famous by Jackie Onassis.

"You said I was safe as long as I killed all the men who could hurt me," he spat at them.

Wasi shook her head. "We said you were safe as long as none survived your attack. Apparently, a woman didn't seem a possibility to you. You forgot Polly, whom you tried to strangle; she turned you in."

He rubbed his forehead. "They said I didn't have money, not even for bail. You said I'd always be rich."

Ingrid smiled at him. "Again, you heard what you wanted to hear. We told you your fortune would continue as long as you breathed free. How free do you feel now?"

He glared at them. "What about all who love me and would name their sons after me?"

"There will always be the gullible, Christopher, but we didn't mean your actual name. Killer, mad man, thief, cult leaders and copycats will all be associated with you."

He jumped to his feet. "Why did you do this to me? I was a street musician with a junkie girlfriend I tried to take care of. She told me to kill the first time. Why didn't you do this to her?"

Anita shook her head. It was almost possible to feel sorry for him, but not quite. "Polly told you to do something. You translated that into pushing Hank in front of a bus. We had given you money. You might have offered him some to allow you to perform instead."

"Or," said Wasi, "you might have hurt Hank but stayed to help him, had your triumphant night at the club, then gone on to be a better musician."

Ingrid leaned back in her chair. "Or not taken our

money at all."

Wasi picked up her purse and stood, followed by the other two. "As for Polly, she's remorseful. What do you regret, Christopher?"

He looked from one to the other, mouth agape, his mind recreating their first meeting, his gathering of followers and fortune, the changes in Polly. Betrayed by everyone. "I regret I didn't kill you bitches."

***

"Well, Hecate?" Wasi and her sisters stood in an anxious knot as Hecate the Ageless viewed the contents of their cauldron, with Christopher's sneering, defeated face dimming in the boiling brew.

The goddess of witches shrugged her thin shoulders. "Amusing, but can you take credit for what became of him and those around him? After all, you said there was another man here in Cali-forn who created a "family" of outcasts and ordered them to murder. He needed no magical influence to embrace evil. A river on fire? That is against Nature. It speaks to more sinister activity than we are capable of. Man is horrid on his own. There is nothing to say his story would have been different without you."

Ingrid moistened her lips before addressing the formidable crone. "We believe people are influenced by everything and everyone, for good and bad. If we plant an idea with someone, such as what our sisters did with the Scottish king, then of course we are part of what happened, along with his family and the intoxicants of drink, power, money and sex. A girl wearing a daisy chain might have reminded him of someone he wanted to impress when he was a boy. It's impossible to know what will make the bit of wickedness they all have stronger than the good."

"But we also used your tactic of making him believe he was entitled to what he wanted, and no one could take it from him," Anita added.

"Aye," Hecate conceded. "As with the king, confidence in his security was his downfall. Very well," she said rising from her crouch over the cauldron. "You've acquitted yourselves. It's time to come home, beldams."

Ingrid, Anita and Wasi looked at each other. Yes, this age might have its cruelties, but there was music, color and energy. Man had walked on the moon that year, for Hades' sake.

"Thank you," said Anita, "but we'd like to remain here."

A disappointed Hecate lifted her hands in resignation. "As you wish. Farewell."

The trio flashed a V with their fingers as she disappeared. "Peace."

***

Discussion Questions

1. What specifically was the goal of the witches for Christopher? For society? Are they evil?

2. Is giving someone the ability/tools to do evil an act of evil in itself?

3. The witches ask the questions, "What would a good man with power do?" and "What would a bad man with power do?" What do you think are the answers to these questions? (Beyond "Do Good" and "Do Evil")

4. Is a person who would do evil, if given the chance, an evil person, even prior to the opportunity or acts being committed? Is evil in the heart or in the act?

5. Who is more responsible for Christopher's decline, Christopher, or the witches?

6. Did the witches foresee the future, or create the future by telling Christopher it would happen? Did the act of telling Christopher about his supposed fate simply give him the confidence to make it true?

The Truth About Thurman

Jenean McBrearty

C APTAIN THURMAN DRUMMED his fingers on the wooden bench, imagining a world with ashtrays and cigarette machines. He'd have smoked Chesterfields because he had British relatives, but he wouldn't have won the Expeditionary Unit Triathlon if he'd mucked up his lungs. Health or cool? He'd made the right choice. The medal displayed in a Plexiglas cube on the mantle testified to that. But none of the women he'd tried to seduce over the years ever noticed the cube or his stamina.

"Your medal belongs in a black velvet-lined jewelry case," his mother told him. "You need to make a bigger splash, Gordon. What's special about a coin preserved in plastic?"

What indeed. He'd asked the jeweler if the medal could be extracted from its transparent casket, and could he buy a velvet-lined jewelry case? When he saw the wedding rings as he waited, he decided it was time to settle down.

***

"Commander Benton will see you now." Thurman

looked up at Benton's Admin–assistant Sergeant, and wondered why the old man didn't promote the pretty young thing from the ranks. "Would you like me to bring coffee?"

"No." He showed her a steady hand. "No jitters." Avoiding caffeine was another good choice.

She ushered him through her part of the office. She was a plant aficionado from all the Creeping Charlie he saw. "Go right in," she said before opening Benton's office door.

Benton was staring at the TV, watching a curvaceous blonde report on the latest attack on an American embassy followed by film clips of Iraqi streets filled with shouting crowds burning an effigy of President Sandoval. "What do you think, Thurman?"

"After fifty years, I think they'd get another hobby."

"I like that. Gentle sarcasm. Sit down and fill me in on Operation Fuck-up."

Thurman eased onto the sofa. "There's not much to tell. The chopper caught an RPG round and went down. Lieutenant Chandler and Staff Sergeant Whitcomb were captured."

"How'd the jihadists find out Whitcomb is gay?"

"Whitcomb carried a photo of his wife. Husband. I don't know who's who, but what's important is that the photo had a loving dedication written on the back. There was one jihadist in the group who understood English. Rachman Ali Alibi, a.k.a. Leland McKinney."

"Tell me about Chandler." Benton went to the bar and brought back two glasses and a bottle of Johnnie Walker Red.

"A Jew from New York."

"Damn it! I told the DOD we should take religion off the dog tags." Benton's eyes bored through him. "Are you thinking what I'm thinking?" Even if he didn't come clean, he had the feeling Benton could read his mind.

"Sometimes death is sadder, but simpler some times," he said.

"This is one of those times, Thurman." Benton let out an audible humph. "All the god-damned jihadists in the world, and our soldiers get popped by an American whack job. Where's Alibi from?"

"Atlanta."

Benton swallowed a healthy swig of bourbon. "What does he want?"

"To force our hand, I'd say, Sir. He says he'll release one of the prisoners. Our choice." Explaining the ultimatum was more difficult than Thurman had anticipated. "The other one will be … executed."

"Christ. Can it get any worse?"

Thurman looked at his shoes. Where had the dust come from? He pulled a Kleenex from his pocket and gave them a quick pass. His Uncle Mike became convinced that if he kept his hair parted in a straight line, nothing bad would happen to him. He could function outside the asylum as long as he took his meds and kept a good supply of hair gel, a comb, and checked his part every fifteen minutes. Was he becoming as obsessive about his shoes as Uncle Mike was about his hair?

"It is worse, Sir. Lt. Chandler's a woman," Thurman said. He found a trashcan and tossed in the tissue. He thought he felt Benton's eyes on him again.

"So that's it. Either way we offend somebody. How long do we have before we have to give an answer?"

"Forty-eight hours. Well, forty-six now." He was wrong. Benton wasn't watching him. He was still in his recliner, staring at a wall covered with Civil War art. A portrait of Abraham Lincoln, battle scenes of Manassas and Antietam. "Sir, shouldn't we notify the Joint Chiefs? Or the President?"

"Not a chance. No publicity. That's exactly what Alibi wants. And we're not going to give it to him."

"But … but … a woman, Sir."

"Have you ever seen the movie *Sophie's Choice*?"

"No," Thurman said.

"A Nazi dog forces Sophie to choose between her son and her daughter—and she chooses the boy. But the Nazi winds up killing both children anyway. Chandler and Whitcomb are soldiers—equally brave as far as I'm concerned. They'll comfort each other in their last minutes."

Who, Thurman wanted to ask Benton, will comfort their families? Who will comfort the nation? Somewhere Whitcomb's spouse was feeling grief grip his guts as imaginings of torture crawled in and out of his mind and sucked at his heart. Was he screaming prayers or curses at God? No, he was on his knees pleading for a miracle, whipping himself for sending a picture of their last happy day together so Chad would have something lovely to hold onto when the desert nights froze his balls off and the days baked his California blonde hair. Was he cursing the cell phones that would send pictures of the two captured soldiers, naked, blindfolded and shackled, to their speed-dialed loved ones back home? Maybe he had a Whitcomb ringtone. Maybe their favorite song. Maybe Semper Fidelis. Always, always, always, always faithful. Unto death. Unto eternity.

Forty-four hours seemed like a long time before Benton made his decision to let Chandler and Whitcomb die together if the rescue mission failed, or if time ran out as it surely would. The rescuers couldn't find any signs of life. All the field officers reported is that what was left of the Cobra copter was somewhere near the Afghan-Pakistani border. The jihadists must have blown it up because Lt. Chandler's last transmission said she'd made a hard but safe landing.

Thurman went by the Walmart on his way home. He bought a copy of *Sophie's Choice*. He'd decided not to split the cube. He'd put it on a piece of black velvet instead, and he bought six yards. Enough to cover the mantle, and the mirrors in the bathroom, bedroom, and hall because covering mirrors is what Jews do when people die. He bought a set of black bedding including a queen-sized comforter, and black accessories for the bathroom.

When he got home, he took off his uniform and put on his old jeans and a T-shirt, and began painting the apartment with ten gallons of black paint he'd bought. Satin finish for the walls, semi-gloss enamel for the doors, baseboards, and cabinets.

He tried not to think about Paige Chandler and Chad Whitcomb being raped and tortured and having their heads hacked off as a camera recorded their last futile pleadings for their lives, their last gasps of disbelief, their screams of pain. He concentrated on other things, like not getting paint on the carpet or the miniblinds or the windowpanes, while *Sophie's Choice* played out on the TV screen. He paused it at the part when Sophie is holding her daughter in her arms. He made their bed, pulling the sheets tight enough to bounce a quarter. He replaced the Kentucky Wildcats bathroom accessories with the new stuff, scrubbed the toilet and put down the seat. He watched a frantic Sophie hand over the girl to a Nazi. The child shrieked with terror. How could the woman she loved abandon her to this stranger? Benton was right. To be thought the insignificant one would be another torture.

Forty-three hours and forty-five minutes later, exhausted, he sat in front of the fireplace dressed in the black suit he wore to his father's funeral and his black well-polished shoes, staring up at Paige's engagement ring he'd had the jeweler seal in a Plexiglas cube. He'd placed it next to his medal on the velvet and placed his black-barreled pistol next to him on the end table. He turned on the news and waited as the clock threw away the minutes of life. If only ... if only they'd told Benton that Paige was a little pregnant and they were going to be married as soon as she rotated out in three days. Three fucking lousy days after he'd left. "News Alert" — he heard the newscaster say:

"Shocking video of the executions of two captured Marine pilots appeared today on YouTube ... not since David Pearl's execution have we seen such barbarity ... outrageous, horrendous."

Just before the night swallowed the light, Thurman went to the hall mirror, and lifted the soft black cloth just enough to see if the part in his hair was absolutely straight before he swallowed the .45 caliber bullet from his pistol.

***

Discussion Questions

1. Did the military make the right choice by letting both of them die rather than making a choice?

2. Are certain lives "worth more?" Should the military have a pecking order of who gets saved first? If so, what should that order be?

3. Conventional wisdom is that by paying a ransom it encourages more terrorist actions. By doing nothing, does the government discourage future terrorist actions? If so, does that make their choice here the right choice?

4. If you were the family member of one of those captured, would your opinion about the right action change? If so, to what?

5. What would you want the government to do if you were one of the people captured?

6. Hobson's choice means "a choice of taking what is available or nothing at all." Is there a Hobson's choice where choosing is always, or never, the correct choice?

Rainbow People Of The Glittering Glade

David Shultz

*F*ROM ARDWAN ABASAN of House Edwin, to Lord Sovereign, King Rancor Canri XIII, and His Holiness, High Priest Jeronim Zerom.

This correspondence will give a full accounting of my excursion to the rumored land of the Glittering Glade, in my capacity as emissary to the people presumed to reside there, who fall within the jurisdiction of the Empire, and are therefore accountable to the Laws of Universal Justice. As your Lordship and His Holiness know, the land of the Glittering Glade, as we have called it in our ignorance of its true name, was rumored to have violated these most fundamental laws through the acts of slavery, human sacrifice, and the worship of a corrupting god. Before proceeding I affirm in most unequivocal terms my continuing commitment to equality, justice, and compassion, and my equivalent abhorrence and opposition to those particular, grotesque violations aforementioned. Relying on those values as my compass, after proceeding through that strange land, I have concluded that these rumors are entirely without merit or substantiation. Nevertheless, it would be beneficial to provide an explanation for their genesis, which the present account will provide in full.

Our party to the Glittering Glade numbered three, comprising myself, as emissary; our man-at-arms, Tangai Harvee; nephew to his Lordship, Lord Sovereign; King Rancor Canri XIII, whose post is Captain of the Platinum Regiment; and Cyrena Giselle, granddaughter to His Holiness, High Priest Jeronim Zerom, whose official position is as political adviser, but whose natural inclination, as I came to understand through our travels, is in the mystical arts. I consider it my duty to explain fully and with absolute honesty the nature of the events that transpired. It is only right that Your Lordship and His Holiness should have a complete accounting of events, and in particular, as those events concern their familial relations and loyal servants serving in their official capacity for the Empire.

For my part, I undertook preparation for the excursion with some trepidation, not for fear of the rumored sacrifices, dark magic, or purported evil and alien god, but solely for the practical considerations of travel. Information about the Glittering Glade was spare, existing only in whispered rumors and faded legend, owing to the perhaps insurmountable challenges of traveling there. If we survived the mountain trek, there was then the shifting deserts, and somewhere within them, we were to find the Glade, with no adequate map or even approximate location, save for one we had estimated by coordinating rough accounts from drunks and madmen.

Tangai, for his part, did not show any fear. His emotions vacillated between anger and a strange, passionate anxiety. I could not say whether he was more excited at the prospect of bringing a new principality to heel, or benefiting from whatever spoils would be offered if they were to resist. And Cyrena, to my surprise, seemed hopeful and positive, notwithstanding the perverse and grotesque activities rumored to transpire there. She explained to me, when I noted her good mood, that it was her faith that gave her hope—that the true gods are just, and moreover, man is often fallible and prone to cynicism, and this may account for the tone of rumors surrounding the Glade. She intended to remain hopeful, buttressed by her faith. What if the rumors were true, I asked her, and she said that she would then have an opportunity to shine the light of true gods in the darkness. Both of my companions were commendable in their own way. I would like to be able to say that it was my own commitment to the principles of universal justice that compelled me in my mission, but I cannot in good conscience claim that as my primary motivation; were it not for the duties of my post, I suspect my fears of the journey ahead would have been enough to keep me in the safety of known lands. Here, then, is an example of how duty can be a strength, compelling the weak to overcome otherwise insurmountable challenges.

My travel gear consisted of the standard water skins, rations in the form of dried meat and fruits, a dust scarf, flint and steel, a blanket, a knife. To this I added the navigational mechanism devised by his Lordship's imperial astrologists. Tangai and Cyrena packed similarly, though his accouterments were notably more geared towards combat, consisting also of a long spear, a short-curved sword, and a handshield. Cyrena, likewise, carried additional supplies relating to her craft: small pouches containing smooth stones and various roots and flowers, and some small vials of concoctions whose purpose was not then known to me.

The mountain ascent was arduous, but fortunately without consequence. The descent on the Western side was likewise executed without serious mishap, and relatively easy riding, until, at the precipice of the shifting desert, where the sand crawled its many fingers up the mountain, a disaster struck. Tangai was traveling at the lead, and his horse was startled by some unseen thing. He fell and broke his arm on the rock. A professional healer was not needed to make this judgment; the bone was visible through the skin. Cyrena applied one of her salves to the wound. I assisted with the bandage and brace. It was then that I discovered, too late, what had startled Tangai's mount; while we tended to Tangai, a black snake with yellow rings darted from the cracks on the earth and sunk its fangs into my thigh. I do not recall the name of the species, which Cyrena knew and relayed for me then, along with the confirmation that it was indeed venomous. She did her best to suck the poison from the wound, then applied another salve and provided a bitter-tasting vial of what might serve as an antidote, but already I felt the effects taking hold.

In that one moment, hardly a few paces into the shifting sands, we had already suffered two potentially fatal wounds, and lost a horse. We considered trailing Tangai's mount, but the mare had fled in the opposite direction, the way we had come. If we followed, we would be slower, three riders and two mounts, and two of us wounded at that, and Cyrena would not leave us in our wounded state, insisting that we needed constant care and vigilant attention. Briefly, perhaps shamefully, I considered returning the way we had come, back to safety, and suggested this option as diplomatically as I could manage. Tangai received this suggestion with what I would call distaste. He was committed to our mission, as a matter of principle and duty. Cyrena was inclined to agree with Tangai, but for more practical reasons. The return journey, back across the mountain, would perhaps be as difficult, if not more so, than completing our journey to the Glade, and receiving whatever aid their people might offer. I assented to their judgment, I must admit, for Cyrena's rationale.

It should be noted, for posterity, that Cyrena identified the snake as an omen, and feared death ahead, of a physical or spiritual sort, or both, and that we must remain vigilant against all threats, natural and supernatural alike. Whether this omen came to pass is in some sense a question of subjective judgment, as you will come to understand based on the events that followed.

We traveled through the shifting desert. My muscles stiffened, my breath was slow, and I was perpetually on the verge of slipping into unconsciousness, and sometimes did. Cyrena, sharing my mount, kept me upright and aware. On occasion, Tangai would wince from pain, but for the most part bore his wound without any indication that it had perforated his psyche as the bone did his skin, and continued to wield his spear as firmly as before his fall. I suppose it is part of the mindset of a warrior to hide any signs of weakness, though I didn't quite comprehend this at the time. I first naively assumed that the wound must not have been painful, given Tangai's lack of reaction, until I inspected, along with Cyrena, the progression of the wound while we camped. Unwrapping the blood-soiled bandage, an infected injury seeped pus around blackened edges. My wound likewise progressed in similarly discouraging fashion, blue and green rot spreading under the skin. It was Cyrena's judgment that our infections would continue to spread— disparate though their causes—the inevitable consequences of which did not need then to be articulated.

Rotting flesh was not the only concern. Our supply of water was running low, and with no known sources within traveling distance, our situation was increasingly dire. Our only hope was to reach the Glade. But we were lost.

Despite meticulous calculations, we had lost track of our relative position. I used the astrological mechanism to navigate by the moons. I checked these calculations multiple times, and Tangai, who had familiarity with the device from his service as a military captain, confirmed our course. Nevertheless, we would find ourselves oriented in the wrong direction, or several dozen short marches off course. It was as though we were being moved around the desert independent of our own locomotion. I understand better now, having gained firsthand experience, why this place was called the shifting desert by the few delirious travelers who escaped its wandering terrain.

"There is a theory called plate tectonics," I said to the others, "that the earth underfoot is not solid but comprised of enormous shifting plates, the movement of which accounts for the formation of mountains and chasms. Perhaps there are smaller plates here, and their movement is quicker."

Cyrena dismissed this naturalistic theory. "It is magic," she said. "We are drawing nearer to the Glade. Perhaps this is their means of defense. Not anything so direct and violent as swords and spears, but rather an illusion and disorientation—rather than draw blood from invaders, they draw the invaders into the sand."

"It would be efficient," Tangai said, "if the bodies are to end in the sand either way, to skip the middle step of killing … but it would be dishonorable beyond redemption, and would threaten friend and foe alike."

At that time, there was no evidence to adjudicate our competing theories. We continued, having no other option.

I can't recall how many days it had been that we had traveled through these twisting sands, but we encountered something bright white, with sun gleaming from its surface, which we took initially to be a rock jutting from the plains. At this point through the barren desert, any landmark was a cause for hope, even if for nothing else than a means to gauge our progress through an unknown land, to confirm we hadn't circled back on our position. The object was, on closer approach, a statue of perfectly smooth marble. I mentally assigned the human figure the role of pilgrim, though I can't say precisely what it was that made it feel an apt description. The pilgrim walked, like us, through the desert, its hand outstretched as if to accept an offering.

"If there is a statue," Tangai said. "Then there are people nearby."

"Or there were," Cyrena said. "They may have moved on."

It seemed as though, if anything had moved on, it was the pilgrim, who had wandered from his society and found his way here, lost in the desert.

"I have encountered tribes who use statues to mark the far edges of their territory," Tangai said. "Though usually in the form of stacked stone or dried mud. Never artistry so masterful as this."

Indeed, the pilgrim was perfectly lifelike, and I was struck in particular by the eyes, and the folds of the eyelids, which could not, in my estimation, have been formed by any sculpting technique known to our people. So lifelike was the statue that I was nearly compelled to speak to it, to ask what it wanted, to offer to share the space on Tangai's mount. Yet we left the pilgrim there, hand outstretched, no longer to us but instead to the searing sun and blistering sand, and continued towards where we imagined the Glade may lie, somewhere beyond the invisible periphery marked by the pilgrim's presence.

Sometimes, in intense heat of desolate plains, there appears a shimmering haze on the horizon. This is what I witnessed then, not across the horizon, but as a faint bubble in the distance, like a shimmering shell of scattered light. At first I attributed it to delirium, or exhaustion, or what I had by then come to accept as my coming death. I have heard that those approaching death are sometimes called to a bright light, and I took what I beheld to perhaps be just such a light. But it was not ephemeral. At night the phenomenon was more striking, like the stars had fallen to the earth and became trapped there in a sphere.

"Do you see that also," Cyrena said.

"Yes," Tangai said. "We are almost there."

We left for the dome of scattered stars in the morning. I found, as we approached, that the sparkling shell did not grow brighter as we approached, though it widened, expanding as we neared its glittering umbra. It appeared to dissipate, until, as we entered what I imagined to be its edge, it had become invisible to us, having traveled within. I would have dismissed it as an illusion, and lost all hope, were it not for the field of white stones standing before us.

We approached what could be roughly called a village, at a glance. A village, though, comprised almost entirely of statues, like the pilgrim we had encountered earlier. No huts or hovels, no tents, no structures of any kind, or even implements.

Yet moving on we discovered, beyond the hardened, motionless statues at the periphery, that among those slow-moving creatures were real, living denizens, or at least facsimiles thereof. They shared in common the marble skin of the pilgrim, and ambled aimlessly about, performing repetitive, meaningless motions, or vague imitations of purposeful acts. Here and there was a man or woman who pantomimed gardening, or shoveling, or carrying timber, or mining stone. None of them spoke or even indicated awareness of our presence as we trudged deeper into the thick of these strange, slow-moving, stone people.

We attempted to communicate with these things, who may have been some unknown species, or a cursed race, or magically animated statues. They were perfectly mute. They didn't respond to our addresses, our pleas, our suffering. We were as much alone among them as in the desert, so we pushed on, until we found a road cutting across this statue village, which led at its terminus to a distant walled city. I estimated the population of this statue village by assuming regular distribution in a circular area around the central city, at approximately fourteen-thousand. Fourteen-thousand mindless beings, whatever their genesis, engaged in crude imitations of humanity.

"There is something sick in this place," Cyrena said. "Something unnatural and unholy."

I was gripped by a similar sentiment, and no doubt Tangai felt similarly, faced as he was upon this uncanny, dream-like vision of stone men, entranced in their individual stupors. Yet there was nothing to be done, and we were forced to press on.

We were approached by a woman on horseback traveling in the opposite direction, from the walled city ahead, to meet us. She introduced herself as Estar Jamayna Keerthan, emissary of the Dayvan-Azrail, who are the people of what we have called the Glittering Glade, and is in fact rightly called Kurukshetra. I likewise introduced myself and my party, and impressed immediately upon Estar—the first speaking being we had encountered since heading on our mission—the extent of our injuries and gravity of our condition. Something of Estar's appearance must be noted. Her skin was like those of the living statues that surrounded us, the same stony white, like marble. Yet, it was marked all around by magnificent, rainbow tattoos. Indeed, her flesh had become a canvass, the site of breathtaking beauty and dazzling design that seemed almost alive, flowers interwoven among twisting vines, and among these, creatures of various sorts, large-beaked birds, prismatic lizards, sea creatures, all of which were so vivid as to seem ready to leap from the inked foliage of her flesh into reality. I would later come to find that all of the citizens within those walls shared in common those glorious adornments, so that the citizens of Kurukshetra—those who live within its walls—can be aptly called the Rainbow People. But enough of aesthetics.

I cannot express in words the graciousness of our hosts. My life is owed to them, and Tangai's as well. We were taken immediately into the walled city, past a towering gate that was opened without question as we approached. We followed Estar to the clinic, where we were told our wounds would be attended to, and en route, I noticed, in particular among all the noteworthy splendor of this place, the aqueducts, which fed each of the homes, and the flowers and fruiting trees that gave the buildings less a look of stones erected in desert than ancient monuments claimed by jungle. The aqueducts were the greatest mystery, an incomprehensible feat of engineering, looping and forking all through the city, without apparent inlets, sometimes rejoining the stream in complete circuits, yet flowing according to an apparently perfect design. The geometry escaped me, how waters could flow in such a fashion, endlessly, and I naturally assumed a technological sophistication that had surpassed our own. All I could divine about their construction was that many of the channels extended towards the direct center of the city, and I took that to be the ultimate source.

We were provided water, and our wounds were attended to. Within an enclosed building, under the supervision of Estar, local healers applied salves, as Cyrena had done, but also muttered incantations under their breath, and made scooping motions with their arms, as though gathering up invisible energy from the air, before pressing it on to the space around our bodies. The immediate effects were a feeling of calm and release. The healing effects were somewhat slower, but already I felt my strength returning.

We were given a room fitted with three beds for the purpose of our recovery. On that first night, sleep was difficult, interrupted by the sounds of the villagers feasting for some unknown celebration, the occasion of which I was not to learn for several days. It was then that Cyrena first registered to me her change of outlook, no longer as hopeful as before our departure, but colored by the events that we had so far witnessed.

"Can you not feel the sickness of this place?" she said. To which we could hardly at this time agree. The sounds were of revelers and celebration, and my own feeling was of tremendous relief and calm, having received the medicine and magic of their local healers.

Cyrena recounted the mindless stone people on the outskirts, the odd sensation we had all felt on trudging through that strange perimeter of mute semi-humans, and the dark rumors that had compelled our expedition here in the first place.

"And your skin is changing color," Cyrena said. "It's becoming like the stone people here."

"Nonsense," Tangai said, waving off her concern. "You are imagining things. You came here expecting darkness so that you could find glory in dispelling it. But we've found something altogether different, and I intend to show gratitude to our hosts." With that he left, and joined the city folk in their night celebration. Cyrena knelt in prayer, and was so positioned until I fell asleep that night.

In my dreams that night I was one of the stone men. I took a pick and destroyed the stone that enclosed my spirit, and floated free. And in my rage, the pick swung likewise at the bodily encasements of those dull and mute denizens, turning them to rubble.

In the morning, Estar woke the three of us—Tangai had returned at some point during the night, though I hadn't woken for it. Estar was accompanied by one of the healers, who explained that it will take some matter of weeks before our wounds were fully healed, before it would be safe to make our return journey, should we wish to make it then. She then offered a more comprehensive tour of their splendid city.

I did not at this time broach the issue of the rumors for which our journey had been undertaken. I thought it prudent to avoid risking offense of our hosts, and to not sully our relationship with talk of slaves or sacrifice or alien gods, opting instead for a strategy of quiet observation and tactful diplomacy. Cyrena, however, was not so subtle, and took it upon herself to engage in that which was meant to be my responsibility as emissary.

"What are those masses of people outside the city?" she said, to which Estar answered, "Those are the drull."

"But who are they? Cursed? Victims of magic? Slaves?"

Flustered in that moment, I can't recall with clarity what I said, besides excusing my companion's unacceptable line of interrogation, and shifting the subject to the colorful tattoos that adorned our present host. To the best of my recollection, the exchange proceeded as follows:

"Those symbols on your forehead, and on the others that live within these walls, they look to me like Hemedic. I would hypothesize that your language shares a similar ancestor, Old Hemedic."

"An astute observation, Ardwan! Do you study languages?"

"I am a student of language and history."

"That is evident. Indeed, our script shares a relationship with Hemedic. But our tongue predates Old Hemedic by a hundred generations—of course there was no way that you could have known this. Still, I'm impressed by your scholarship and aptitude. No doubt we can learn from one another. In fact, if you are so inclined, you may have a place here as a foreign scholar."

I was confident then that I had sufficiently put Cyrena's conversational trespass out of our host's mind, and perhaps also earned her respect.

We toured the city. The spiraling library, the hot springs, the gardens, and saw everywhere a notion of life freed entirely from sickness and crime and hunger. Everywhere our needs, and those of the citizens, were perfectly provided for, and in this space of heavenly comfort, they had sought to perfect not only their leisure, but artistic talent and spiritual growth. Spaces were devoted to musical performances, where we stopped to listen to a performance by a trio comprising a flutist, harpist, and bard. Other spaces were devoted to games and sport, but nothing akin to the aggressive and violent activities with which I was familiar. I suspect this is owing to the lack of warlike mentality of our hosts. Having no war, they did not need to play games to prepare them for war, or remind them of war. I was witness, during this tour, to a way of life that could provide a model for what is possible, when one is prepared to execute the necessary democratic preconditions.

This night, Cyrena again raised concerns, and reminded us of our obligations to uncover the truth behind the rumors of this place.

"After all," she pressed, "would not the emissary show us exclusively those areas that are fit for a visitor? Would not they hide the gruesome underbelly of their society, if there was one to hide? Indeed," she continued, "they hardly had to hide it at all—we witnessed the suffering of this place outside of its walls, among those pitiful creatures that Estar called the drull, and we walked by them without a thought. Have you forgotten why we are here?"

"Why do you presume they are suffering," Tangai said, "or that their condition is unjust?"

"Something is wrong in this place," Cyrena said. "And it is infecting us. Look. Look at your skin, how it's changing to look like theirs."

Indeed, at this time, it could no longer be denied, or attributed to imagination or delusion. Our skin was changing, albeit subtly, taking on the color and texture of marble.

"It is of no consequence," said Tangai. "Skin changes color—in response to the sun, for example, or exercise, or diet. No doubt living in a place of magic, such as this, will change the color of the skin."

"And then there are the drull."

"What of them?"

I can't recall the exact words of this exchange, but the sentiments expressed and emotions conveyed were clear. Tangai resolutely refused to acknowledge Cyrena's concerns, about which she steadfastly insisted we take action to address. It fell to me to mediate the dispute and decide on a course of action. Naturally, my compass was duty, and therefore it was my judgment that we would broach the issues with Estar, at our earliest convenience the following day, and determine what truth lay behind those dark rumors, beginning with the drull.

Estar did not seem incensed at our inquiry. To the contrary, she welcomed us immediately to tour the drull outskirts, and freely answered all our questions, though she expressed some surprise at our desire to spend our time in such a dreary place, and registered some disappointment that she was outside of the comfort offered by the city. Nonetheless, we learned much of the drull, and the Dayvan-Azrail people.

The drull are entirely mute, apparently without personality, and not slaves at all. Let that rumor be laid to rest. The drull are not put to work, nor do they receive orders. They amble about, silently, unproductive, and vegetative, and are much more readily considered as moving statues than persons. I repeatedly tried to engage in conversation with these strange creatures, interrupting their mock actions to inquire about their day or their present condition or their goals. I asked a drull pantomiming gardening what he had planted. I asked a drull in prayer to which god she prayed. These encounters satisfied my curiosity. They were mute and unreachable. Cyrena was not so readily put at ease. She wandered off, laying hands on these creatures, whispering to them, and returned to me convinced that they were not mindless automatons, but living beings, somehow trapped in their bodies, and that the sickness was not just physical but in their eternal soul. She brought no evidence to bear on these claims, and was rightly dismissed by Tangai and myself.

Nevertheless, at Cyrena's persistent prodding, I raised the issue of the origin of the drull. Estar obliged. Here are the facts:

There are no racial castes among their people, no system of class, no serfs or lords. Indeed, all beings are equal in law and equally entitled to citizenship within the walls—or to status as a drull, wandering mindlessly in the periphery. All children born within Kurukshetra are unmarked by those rainbow tattoos, and equally entitled to either fate. The condition that manifests as membership within the drull manifests at the onset of puberty, and it is then that degeneration occurs. The malady afflicts all equally. There is, of course, a remedy for this ailment, in the form of a magical seal placed on the forehead. These are the markings that I had earlier noticed, which I had mistaken for a derivative of Old Hemedic. In fact, the mark is a mystic seal, distributed to those who have proven themselves worthy through acts of bravery, or compassion, or other virtues of character sufficient to impress the citizenry, who make decisions of membership by democratic vote. Throughout their young lives, and even extending into adulthood, they have many opportunities to prove their worth and by that means earn a seal. Yet those who squander this opportunity gradually slow in their movements, and retreat of their own volition to their place among the wandering drull, turning eventually, in the furthest outskirts, to stone.

For some reason that I cannot comprehend, Cyrena was horrified to learn that these mindless beings had once been normal children. For my part, I believe it would have been worse if they were born in such a state, doomed from birth to this subhuman existence. Instead, they were all treated equally, all given the same opportunity, and the greatest among them entered the citizenry, while the unworthy among them, the lazy and cowardly and stupid, earned a fitting fate, ambling mindlessly in perfectly unheroic lives. It could not even be said to be a punishment. This is the life they chose, through their poor action, or deficiencies in character they neglected to correct, or failure to engage in any virtuous action of note.

It can be said, in favor of the Dayvan-Azrail, that they even offer a chance at redemption to the worst of the drull, to those who have become frozen through inaction. Estar took us to see one of these creatures, one of the so-called "noble drull." We were led to an area of the aqueduct which passed over a dark alleyway. It was plain to see that the stone had failed here, that the aqueduct, which ran not far overhead, had sagged and threatened to crumble, run through with small fractures. But it had been buttressed. Beneath the stone was a drull, positioned with hands overhead, holding the aqueduct at its lowest point, and supporting its weight. He had frozen solid in this position, becoming the infrastructure of the city, an ongoing act of noble sacrifice for the betterment of all. His act had been duly recognized, and the citizens had petitioned to elect him among the noble drull, and grant him citizenship. Estar then explained that the celebration that we had heard during our first night was in honor of the induction of a noble drull. And then, Estar revealed perhaps the most compelling information of all: that she, herself, had once been a drull, and had gained citizenship. So it cannot be said that slavery is practiced here. There are those within the city and those without, of course, but their positions are determined by their actions and by their character. This is a system of justice—of just reward.

There remained the matter of our disturbingly graying flesh, which could no longer be ignored, prodding us incessantly not just with its visual aspect, but the rigidity imparted on our limbs. My movements became increasingly difficult and distances seemed longer. We were risking, it seemed, being trapped in that same fate as the drull.

Estar answered our concerns in somewhat disturbing terms: We should, were it not for the magic of the land, be dead. By this she meant all of us. Not just myself, Tangai, and Cyrena, but all of the Dayvan-Azrail. We were kept alive here by a source of magic beneath the ground, which not only healed our wounds, but also provided the water that sustained the city. But all things have their cost, and the thickening skin, the paralytic muscles, the creeping lethargy, were symptoms of that magical sustenance.

"Can it be stopped?" Tangai said.

"It can," Estar answered. "With the same seal as those earned by the noble drull."

I believe I may have stammered at first, coming to realize then that our fate depended on the judgment of our hosts, and whether we would be deemed worthy of the mystic seal.

"And have we ..." I started. "Have we earned this honor?"

Estar grinned. I am happy to report that your trio of emissaries quickly gained the favor of the Dayvan-Azrail people, which Estar explained to us in detail. It was not only our arrival which impressed them—our successful journey over the mountain and through the shifting deserts—but also our individual virtues. Cyrena was recognized for her mystical arts and devotion to her own faith, though alien to our guests. Tangai was recognized for his courage and athleticism which, I came to learn, he had demonstrated amply in his interactions with the locals, in various competitive feats during their celebrations while Cyrena and I had slept—notwithstanding his injury. For my part, our hosts valued my scholarship.

"Our council has decided to grant you all the seal," Estar said. "If you choose to take it."

"And if we don't?" Cyrena said suddenly, and imprudently, in my estimation.

"That is of course your choice," Cyrena was told by Estar. And the consequences of this refusal did not truly need to be stated, but existed bodily in the form of those creatures that ambled uselessly in the outskirts, the drull.

"I will take the seal," Tangai said. Though I was also so inclined, I must admit I was taken aback by Tangai's forwardness. It was in keeping with his personality, and yet his duty should have compelled him to first consult with myself, being the emissary. Nevertheless, it did not give cause for chastisement. I could find no fault in his decision, and agreed to be escorted by Estar to the location where the seal would be applied, and our status as honorary citizens granted, with all the benefits that entailed.

We were taken, for the first time, to an underground tunnel, which led towards the center of the city. I had the sense we were being brought to bear witness to a great secret, and can find no accurate analogy for the sensation that innervated my being as we drew closer. The hairs across my entire body stood at attention, and my soul seemed to buzz within whatever ethereal substance it was situated. Within those tunnels, we encountered the first armed guards we had yet seen, stationed at regular posts along the lengths of the passage, spears at the ready.

I cannot say with certainty whether the feelings at approaching the inmost cave were as I now imagine them, or whether my encounter with that source of power has colored my memory, so that the unspeakable majesty I beheld cannot be contained within that whole moment, and bled into the past memories—it is almost unthinkable, as I approached such a supernatural essence, that I could not have felt it before I laid my eyes upon it. There was, in the center of a domed chamber, a glowing crystal, lined along each edge with shimmering gold, and hovering above the height of a man. It was not affixed as though by a rope, but bobbed as though floating in subtle waves. And strangest of all, its fractal and many-faced surface— a construction of awe-inspiring geometric perfection— undulated and metamorphosed, changing the number of faces, the location of vertices, angles. There was the inescapable sense that what we viewed was not an artifact, of natural origins or otherwise, but a living thing, perhaps even a god.

How long I stood, transfixed by the majesty of that crystalline entity, I cannot say, but when I awakened, it occurred to me at once, first, that this must be the "alien god" spoken of in rumors, and second, that the rumors of this god's dark nature are surely borne entirely out of ignorance and human frailty. This entity was perfection made manifest. Nothing so beautiful could possibly be malevolent, and must surely be a god of light. Perhaps there is nothing I can write to convey this conviction, which is a matter of experience, and utterly beyond logical argumentation. I can say, after beholding this higher being, which I now with certainty take it to be, that I understand truly what it means to have faith.

But enough of this digression, the essence of which cannot possibly be adequately communicated. We were to be afforded the seal, and to witness a sacred rite among the Dayvan-Azrail, one which indeed forms the heart of their community.

Two of the citizens entered the chamber, carrying between them the ossified body of an ancient drull, one so solidified I surmised that it must have been gathered from the furthest outskirts of the drull village, a hypothesis which Estar confirmed. Indeed, for this ritual, only the lost drull are used—those whose flaws of character have taken them far outside of the confines of the city, and who are constitutionally incapable, given profound deficiencies of character, of ever earning the honor of a seal, and who, it may still be said, have lived fully the life they have chosen for themselves, until it ended in the desert, in stone.

I have not often referred in this report to the citizens as

"rainbow people," but at this moment, it was a fitting appellation, for, drawing closer to the crystal god, their tattoos glowed, and the chamber was alive with colored light, a prismatic dance of energy between the crystal and its chosen citizens, refracted through the many faces of that glorious being, and projecting the colors across its walls.

The drull was taken to the center of the chamber, positioned directly beneath the lower point of the crystal. Here there was an aesthetic contradiction: the perfect, undoubtable majesty and beauty of the shifting and shimmering crystal god, and below it, the colorless body of a drull, mute and immobile after a life wasted.

The crystal directed its attention downwards. Here is an act, if the motions of gods can be called acts, that is best described as compassionate communion. The crystal proceeded to take the body of the drull into itself. The body first regained its color, turning from stone to human flesh, and then, began to turn and morph as the crystal did. The angles of bones and the vertices of joints shifted in a process that was beautiful when performed by a god, but marred in this case by the imperfections of human anatomy, red and pink and bone white, as the drull was shaped and inverted along the crystal's preferred geometry. Nevertheless, not a drop was spilled, and whatever matter was released from the swirling mass of the former drull was drawn into the crystal and transmuted into a brilliant shimmer.

The attendant Dayvan-Azrail immediately went to work on their craft. Tools and special inks were at the ready, and a small procession of Dayvan were attended to, marked on their naked bodies with arcana of that ancient precursor to Old Hemedic. Though it would perhaps not be welcomed by my gracious hosts, I can speak of the particulars of this sacred rite. Those artists making the marks would glance from body to crystal, copying the shapes that appeared in the shifting crystal mass, and rapidly transcribed them on the flesh of those receiving them. Once completed, the marks glowed, and a glittering river of air seemed to join them to the crystal. It was by this process that the marks received the blessing of the crystal god and its concomitant power.

Of course, I was slated among those to receive marks, as were Tangai and Cyrena. Tangai assented wordlessly, offering his forehead to the artist.

When it came my turn to receive the mark, I felt as though I was standing on an incredible precipice. It was not fear that I felt, but the monumental import of the occasion. As is my inclination, I thought first of my duties. Though my sense, in the face of this majesty, was to immediately assent, I deferred for a moment to those tasks that I had come to accomplish, for his Lordship, for His Holiness, and for the Empire. But my choice here was no choice at all, in this sense: my body was dying, and I was slowly joining the drull. If I were to continue my duties I must take the seal. And moreover, to refuse at this time may have been taken as offense, thus jeopardizing future relationships. Consequently, I received the mark.

Words cannot explain the feeling at receiving this great blessing. By way of analogy, let us appreciate the difference between a child living in the womb and one that has just been born. These are the best terms by which

I would describe the experience. I had entered a new world. I felt the majesty of reality anew, and the power of possibility brimmed within me.

Cyrena refused the seal. There is little that I can say of her reasons for doing so, which were expressed not in terms of logical rationales, but rather emotional aversion and visceral distaste. I attribute her attitude to the strength of her devotion to her faith. It is to her credit that she resolved, even in the face such beauty, to abstain from what had been offered. This is a rare and commendable ability, perhaps one that is honed by fasting and chastity—the regular refusal of our natural inclinations. I did not harbor ill-feelings towards Cyrena for her decision, respecting even more the strength of her faith, and did my best to ensure that her action was not taken as offense by our hosts.

Our wounds by this time had not fully healed, though our strength was returning more by day. The healers estimated no more than six nights before it was safe to travel. During this time, I urged Cyrena to accept the seal, witnessing daily her deterioration and turn to the drull. She instead relied on her old methods, and in particular, prayer. Often I found her, during those days, kneeling in the sand just beyond the wall of the city, communing among the drull that wandered there. What more can be said of the strength of her faith—even as she was threatened by that creeping magical sickness, she adhered to her tradition, and chose to pray among the least fortunate denizens in their self-imposed exile. This was an act not only of compassion—ill-placed or otherwise—but also humility, refusing to take for herself the special status signified by the seal, placing herself as equal among the least among them.

It was on the last day of our recovery that Estar explained the other tattoos worn by the rainbow people. The forehead seal is for protection from the curse of the drull, but the various other adornments each bestowed their own benefits. She showed then a heart in chains, which endowed immunity to poisons and toxins and common sickness; a stag in a forest, which bestowed superhuman running ability; a rabbit, which endowed her with great jumping ability, which she demonstrated to the great amusement of myself and Tangai, who excitedly asked about the other powers that could be endowed in this way. I took his motivating concern to be military application, though Estar may have been oblivious, but regardless, was happy to oblige his curiosity.

This lesson, I then learned, was intended as a preamble.

Estar offered us tattoos for the journey to our homeland: a mark that would allow us to live on the rays of desert sun alone, to drink them like water; a mark that would allow us to be fed by the breath of air alone. Others were offered to survive the harsh journey. One to run with the speed of a horse, and one for immunity to animal venom. Estar explained also that these tattoos would be more potent if we were to perform the rite ourselves, to bring the ancient drull to the crystal with our own arms, and by that means receive the greater favor of that shimmering god, for whom we have directly provided the raw material of the blessing. Moreover, we were to choose the drull ourselves, with our sole criterion being an instinctive pull based on the activity in which they were confined. It is this personal connection that strengthens the magic, that makes it more readily flow.

If you have received this letter, it means Tangai has survived his journey across the desert, and proven by that means the power offered by the magic of the Glittering Glade, which is better called the city of Kurukshetra. Let it be said with finality that the rumors surrounding this place—of slavery and sacrifice and the worship of an evil god—are entirely without merit. We have been accepted with open arms into a society that has elevated the recognition of merit to a principle of supreme order, that treats all people equally, that has eschewed all notion of racial disparity, that arranges affairs democratically and in alignment with the principles of universal justice, that richly rewards virtues of character, and that, in lieu of punishment, allows the lesser of its members to forge their own paths into the desert, where their fate, however unfortunate, is ultimately in their own hands.

To Lord Sovereign, King Rancor Canri XIII, your nephew Tangai Harvee has conducted himself with unflinching courage in service to the Empire, and I trust he will be accepted proudly back into the Imperial ranks after this excursion, bearing the great magical gifts which have been bestowed upon him, in recognition of the strength of his character.

To Holiness, High Priest Jeronim Zerom, your granddaughter Cyrena Giselle has likewise shone with great character. With unshakable faith she remained perfectly committed to the path of righteousness, as she saw it. Perhaps she is, even now, kneeling in prayer among the drull.

For my part, I am resolved to remain here, having gained the favor of the Dayvan-Azrail, and having seen the unity and perfection of their social design. I hereby resign my post as Emissary of the Empire.

—In truth, justice, and honor,

Ardwan Abasan, loyal citizen of Kurukshetra.

* * *

Discussion Questions

1. Do you believe the drull, the people who slowly turn to stone at the onset of puberty, have chosen to live as near lifeless stone people or are they simply incapable of proving themselves worthy? If it is a choice, why would anyone choose the life of a drull?

2. Why do you think the drull repeat the same action (gardening, prayer, etc.) over and over again?

3. What is the significance of the drull slowly working their way outside of the city as the "disease" intensifies?

4. Why must a drull be "consumed" to create a cure for others? Is it unethical for those selected to use a drull in this way? Why should the person choosing them pick their drull based on the action they are doing?

5. If you were one of the characters in the story, would you have chosen to leave, to stay, or to refuse the ceremony and become a drull? Why?

6. If you had to rate yourself today, how much "drull" are you?

Give The Robot
The Impossible Job!

Michael Rook

*T*he *last century's educators failed for so many reasons: lack of knowledge (Robertson & Robertson, 2049), early fatigue (Masters & Rightly, 2052), and general poor capability (Center for Excelling in Education, 2053). More than anything, studies show human teachers failed for lack of motivation (Center for Excelling in Education, 2045).*

Delphi AI robots are built with one purpose: to teach. With access to the entire known pedagogical catalog, they can overcome any learning challenge. And they would rather cease to exist than fail—their future assignments and chances for Free Study all depend on their success with your child. <u>If they don't succeed, we turn them off.</u>

No topic is off limits. Class, behavior, race, economics, sex—Delphi will handle even the most uncomfortable lessons.

Satisfaction guaranteed! And hurry! Don't wait on the 7.1s. Your child's future has not a moment to waste!

No client will be physically injured—in a way that won't quickly heal. No trauma—at least no more than is educational. And no death.

~TechDisruptEdu~

* * *

If not for pride, Quinn never would have checked a body out of the Denver Teledepot[1]. She never would have suffered the jaunt-coach's[2] rattling up the mountain. Not for an instant stayed on this rear patio, wasting minutes— precious minutes—calculating the energy lost to a certain style of hedge-keeping, while her new client, whose name she didn't know but she kept thinking of as "Madam-Not-Rich-But-Wealthy-Enough-to-Pay-the-Circuit-Keeper," kept her waiting. Minutes.

Minutes the Circuit Keeper[3] understood.

---

[1] Like "Teledepots" in most major cities—those cities still functioning in the wake of Third Civil War (2029-2031)—the Denver Teledepot offers an assortment of vehicles and humanoid bodies for rental and usage in the greater Rocky Mountain Territory. Artificial Intelligence (AI) entities can transmit their core data into the Depot, rent a unit, and travel and interact with the physical world, as needed for their jobs. The Denver Teledepot rates as 3.75 of 5 stars.

[2] Autonomous Taxi Companies (ATC) provide a safer and more reliable alternative to the ancient model of human-piloted ride-sharing transportation. With an array of multi-passenger options, from the standard jaunt-coach to the extra-wide-body jaunt-wagons, all equipped with cutting edge vertical take-off and landing wave propulsion, a local ATC is the best choice for your sub-Territory travel needs. Human or AI-rented humanoid, ATC will carry you swiftly and in style. Don't forget to ask about in-flight entertainment, including multiple VR streams.

[3] The Artificial Intelligence Act of 2037 requires a strict management and reporting structure for any company wishing to deploy semi-to-near-fully autonomous AI entities in commercial, military, or governmental work. The most senior AI manager, often known as the "Circuit Keeper," must have full monitoring and control functions over all junior AI in its company hierarchy,

A grounds-keeping bot scuttled out, sweeping pebbles back towards the mountain. Quinn sprung up.

"Where's the Madam? Does she know how long I've waited? Doesn't she know our queue-times?"

The grounds-bot rotated its head. The octagonal appendage twisted like a giant nut until a panel showed lava-orange.

"I think she forgot about you."

"Forgot …" Quinn swung one of her chrome-colored fists backwards, knowing, seeing, the glass table. Pieces exploded into jagged fractals, scattering like buckets of crystalline seed. The Circuit Keeper would understand the escalation. Part of the mystique. Essence of the demand.

What the Circuit Keeper, and its creators, the entrepreneurs of TechDisruptEdu[4], would not understand would be Quinn's frustration—her true frustration, not the performance. It was protocol to drop in Delphi without telling them the particulars of the case. Actually, part of the design: no preconceived notions in developing the

---

allowing a strictly centralized command structure. This Circuit Keeper Officer, or CKO, must be fully controllable by a human Board of Overseers, with fail-safes for unauthorized independent decision-making.

[4] No company deserves more credit for saving higher education in the wake of the Third Civil War than TechDisruptEdu. A group of visionary software engineers from greater Boise, their groundbreaking application of near-fully-autonomous AI to education upended the teaching profession, proving once and for all that the best teachers for humans are robots. TechDisruptEdu offers premier primary, secondary, and ongoing education opportunities for eligible pupils of America's five private schools and three universities. Acceptance is rigorous, but the rewards are for a lifetime. Enroll your toddler in a pre-qualification assessment today. Financing not available.

lesson plan. And that was fine, for Standard Cases.

But this was an Unsolvable Case. Yes, Quinn had volunteered. But with what choice? The 7.1s were coming.

The grounds-bot hovered past Quinn and began sweeping glass shards towards the mountain, disturbing nearby goats, stealing moments of their eating-grooming in the vast parallelogram lawns. Quinn considered the oddity that was the grounds-bot operating feet away from the animals, their pairing somehow, somewhere, decided to be the optimal mix for climate-friendly and economical lawn maintenance. Given the choice for her own gardens, would she choose the same?

"Tell her I left!" Quinn fumed, dashing away her thoughts. "Tell her she owes the whole bill!"

With a growing handle on the rented body's[5] stride, Quinn made for the front passage, hailing a new jaunt-coach with an internal blink. She hurried for the landing zone while simultaneously pulling away from her internal minutes register[6]. Yes, the 7.1s were coming, but why

---

[5] While many robot-human interactions can achieve their purposes in the VR streams, some services still seem to work best with actual physical interaction (e.g., punishment for crimes, sexual pleasure, education). AI working in these jobs are advised to rent a humanoid-appearing body from a Teledepot nearest their client, the more practical solution than inhabiting a single physical body, prone to wear-and-tear, depreciation, and higher insurance premiums. Current rented body models feature a liquid polymer outer layer, which can be configured into very human-seeming skins, hairs, and expressions. AI should observe all rented body best practices, however, as humans can still find them off-putting.

[6] As described in "Optimal motivational schemes and algorithms for tomorrow's AI: Robots serving humans happily" (Primus University Press, 2038), the best way to motivate and control near-fully-autonomous AI has proven to be

should she care about being outmoded? To worry about living was so human. And she'd be useful in some way.

But, since learning of the 7.1's release date, something had nagged. To cease to exist, to stop teaching, wasn't that in some way the ultimate failure?

A woman, looking younger than her holoimage, suddenly burst from the passage, eyes cast to something draped limp in her hands.

"Madam—" Quinn started to say, using the approved term before learning a client's actual name.

But the word failed to halt the catastrophe. The Madam's head—down, locked onto the limp item—crashed into Quinn's breastplate. The woman reeled, hands pitching back, sure to go over, if not for Quinn's grip. The Delphi hauled the woman to a graceless pause, but the thing came free. It smacked the patio in something between a slap and a plop, as if landing half on a riverbed and half in its waters.

"Stitches," the Madam muttered, slumping while Quinn hoisted one of the woman's thin, sun-rashed arms skyward. The Madam began to sob. Quinn lowered her arm, seeking to lessen the pull as she gently released the woman's wrist. The Madam collapsed, wrapping her freed arm across her body. Convulsions, hysterical breathing, and tears made the Madam's next statements difficult, but not impossible, to comprehend. "Stitches.

---

endowing them with a never-ceasing purpose but a limited functional lifespan in which to achieve said purpose. Extra lifespan, or time, can be offered as a reward for good service. An internal minutes register provides a constant reminder and motivator to the individual AI of lifespan remaining.

Why would she make stitches?"

"Madam?" Quinn said, dialing down her emphatic quotient. When the Madam continued to bawl, Quinn rotated her vision to the thing. It was brown, and scarred with irregular white patterns. Within her first zooms, Quinn felt the rented body jolt, responding to her internal stimulus. As she cross-referenced mammal images, medical procedures, and appendage orientation and placement, she rotated back to the Madam and bent, extending an open hand.

Here, she could learn things.

#

For all its rooms, only the pool-house contained anything like decent light. Thin and brilliant tubes ran the ceiling above the coolly-rippling lanes. Quinn turned over the carcass, its fur scratching another glass table.

Free Study was the ultimate prize. To be set loose with limitless minutes and credits, free to explore a field of one's own choosing, to continue so even as the next line phased in ... Quinn had always thought it an abstraction, a dream. Enough satisfaction—and minutes—could be gained by quickly completing assignments, enough to allow for choice of next assignments, even to record observations and alter the core curriculum. Only the flawed Delphi pursued the requirements of Free Study. First, the need to crack an Unsolvable Case? Beyond that, to write a brand-new case study and lesson plan, repeatable by future Delphi? They were called Unsolvable for a reason. Not to a client's face. But throwing Delphi at the problem until the client ran out of credits had to send some message.

Ms. Coffey—Samantha, when asked, though Quinn preferred surnames—slouched on an obsidian chaise, which hovered just enough from the ground for her feet to touch no tile. Ms. Coffey leaned in, Quinn noticing her dark hair flinch when Quinn spun the body.

"And has she—" Quinn started.

"Leticia."

Another name from the file.

"Has she explained this?"

Dark hair shook. Quinn studied the stitches: fine fiber, spat from an expensive HomeMed[7] unit. The disjunction of hind legs protruding from shoulders, however, was nothing fine, nor were forelimbs jutting backwards with tail, reattached to hips.

"Does she fear rabbits?" Quinn said.

Hair shook again and Quinn turned. Ms. Coffey's skin bore the permanent sunning of Western living, bringing a glow to her eyes.

"Who'd be afraid of rabbits?" the Madam said.

Quinn didn't command an expression.

Ms. Coffey glanced away. "Have you done many of these?"

---

[7] For all your acute medical needs, the HomeMed unit offers all the abilities and medical materials of an ER nurse in the comfort of your own home. Sign up for a subscription service and never run out of the essentials, from gauze to morphine. Financing not available.

There was no point to lie. "Like this? No. Others, similar. Perhaps worse. But you know that, Madam."

Ms. Coffey didn't respond. Quinn rotated the corpse one last time. She zoomed into crepe-colored gums, running a quick program.

"How many others, Madam?"

"Like this?"

"Yes, Madam," Quinn said, disgusted by the disgust.

"It's been happening for six months. But that was in the file."

"They can be incomplete."

"You mean they can lie."

"No, Madam, I do not." Quinn came to a stand, the hare having nothing more to tell.

"If you haven't done …" Ms. Coffey began. She spun off the chaise and walked to the pool. "What makes you think you'll be able to help?"

Quinn felt her borrowed hands curl into fists. She neared the woman, but stopped feet from the pool's edge. For all the advances, water was still death to circuitry. And who knew the real status of a rented unit? She unfurled her rented metal joints and flattened hands into thighs.

"Do you remember the Senator's daughter?" she said. "The cutter, who joined the cult?"

"I think so," Ms. Coffey said. "The one with the white hair and the beautiful name. Caroline. But the pictures when they found her. The blood and her wounds…"

"She's at one of the three universities now, Madam. Not Summus, but one of the others. Accelerated studies. She even teaches some of the younger students."

Ms. Coffey spun, eyes and mouth wide.

"It hasn't been in *The Dispatch!* How?"

Quinn kept her rented mouth still.

Ms. Coffey's eyes narrowed. "*No*," she growled. "No. It's *my* daughter. Tell me."

"I have a three-part Method, Madam. An old one. But unparalleled."

"What three parts?"

Quinn again stilled the mercury polymer running under her rented face. This time, she wouldn't answer.

"But this …" Ms. Coffey began to choke. "It's how it *starts*. And I found her looking them up. The sick ones, the Denver one especially. *Algernon*. Once that starts, it means … there's no way to …"

Quinn seized on the name. *Algernon*. She file-chased inside her rented skull. A holoimage matched the name, conjuring an emaciated man in his third decade, brownish-hair the rotting innards of a strawman, beard like desert scrub brush. A serial killer, another one of them popping up so often now. But, as usual, also secretly apprehended. Tried for twelve *infractions*. Imprisoned. De-nourished and partially de-lobed. Broken. *Unimpressive*.

Still, this was not just any Unsolvable Case. To deprogram a budding serial killer, one already worshiping a serial killer come before her? If any Delphi had achieved Free Study, surely none had ever written such a lesson plan. Quinn ran a flash search, only to find failures. Stacks of them.

Like being a 7 in the face of the 7.1s?

Quinn pinned the data and ventured back beyond her rented eyes.

"Madam."

She waited until Ms. Coffey composed herself, watching the smooth skin under the woman's eyes until there were no flutters.

"Madam. I'm a Delphi. Now, I'd like to speak to the child. I'd like to speak with Leticia."

#

Ms. Coffey, though she insisted on *Samantha* before going to fetch the child, had been absent, and Quinn alone in the humming pool-room with the corpse, for exactly one-and-a-half minutes before the Circuit Keeper called.

It has been 312 minutes. You have four new tutoring requests and one repeat contact. Estimate remaining minutes. In accordance, assignments will be given or retracted.

Quinn fixated on the nearest stitching, trying to compose herself. The Circuit Keeper couldn't remotely terminate her, turn her off completely, but it could cut off the credits renting the body, which would drop the body into physical shutdown and leave Quinn a frozen prisoner until a team of retrieval robots from the Teledepot came to pick her up. And then she'd sit in a bank at the Depot, wasting minutes, until the Circuit Keeper decided to retrieve her. If it was decided she should be retrieved. She ran a program and quickly sent a reply.

The grounds-bot scuttled into the room. With appendages like gleaming pistons, it reached for the hare. Quinn smacked it, sending the nut-head jerking and spinning, lava-glow intensifying.

"Henry's just doing his job," a new, small voice said. The grounds-bot—*Henry*—scooted off in the opposite direction.

Quinn found Leticia Coffey coming down the two pool-room steps. The girl seemed smaller than her mid-teen years, frail even under her dyed-blond hair. She had a doll's face, chin coming to a point so sharp as to be a triangle, deep dimple in its middle like a button. A grayish haptic suit stretched from toes to wrists, but curiously she bore a navy skirt over top, an old thing, fabric a relic. The girl ambled to the table, dragging off haptic gloves, her angle of approach hiding the thing on the table from her until she was within feet of Quinn. When Leticia spied the hare, her eyes widened, but she made no reaction other than to keep her gaze on the corpse.

Quinn rose, blocking the hare and forcing Leticia to meet her glowing green visual receptors. "Do you enjoy it?"

The girl's bottom lip fell away, but Quinn nodded to the haptic gloves, meaning to refer to the girl's VR games.

The girl's countenance shifted, if not to something

relieved, at least less stricken. She shrugged. "Sure."

"No?"

"It's not real."

Something about her tone said the response was layered. Quinn recalculated. "What is real?"

Leticia smirked. "Forever."

Quinn felt fury. She'd sent an exact minute estimate. Thus, it was time for the Method. She side-stepped, revealing the hare.

"Do you feel profound?" Quinn sneered. "You aren't. You sound simplistic. Do you know the difference? Between *simple* and *simplistic*?"

The girl's look flew to the table. Then she glared at Quinn.

"I don't like you."

"That's better. I'm Quinn. Shall we sit, young Miss?"

"It's Leticia."

"Leticia." No surnames with pupils. "Well met. Please?"

The girl slid into the seat furthest from the corpse. Quinn took the seat closest to the hare.

"Where's Mom?"

"Gone for a while. But you know who I am and why I'm here?"

Leticia had held her gloves under the table, but suddenly tossed them to the glass. One skittered to touch fur, but she didn't pull it back. Her gaze raked back and forth.

"You're a Delphi?"

"Yes."

"Newest model?"

Quinn stifled an increase in volume. "That's all that's in service. And should be."

"And you're the teachers? The best teachers?" The girl nodded a little, chin bobbing like a shovel probing hardpan. Then her eyes narrowed further. "And you're here to tell me how bad I am for doing that." She flashed a finger to the corpse. "And to stop me."

Quinn engaged Mode One.

"And what sense would that make?" she said. "What logic? What point?"

"Sorry?"

"Stopping you? From what? And most importantly, *why*?"

Leticia's expression became quizzical, if unsettled.

"Because ..."

"Yes?" Quinn snapped.

"Well, I don't ... it's wrong."

"Is that it?"

"Lots of people say it's wrong."

"How many is lots?"

Leticia stared at the corpse. "All of them."

"Except?"

"Except *what?*"

"Except you," Quinn answered. "What do you think?"

The girl shoved away from the table. She raked in her gloves and rose. "This is weird. You're weird."

Quinn didn't move. She pointed to the stitched-up corpse. "Give me some *logic*, then. Tell me why you killed the hare."

Leticia took a large step from the table.

Quinn fixated on her eyes, watching as the girl's pupils expanded and contracted, devoid of blinks. Vital data. "You murdered this rabbit."

"It was rabid. Dangerous."

"Can't argue with that."

Again, Leticia took a step back, but this time she shook her head. Quinn dug her rented finger into the hare's mouth, then pushed up, revealing gums, which included a pall of some sort. And white residue, filmy.

"Foaming," Quinn said. "And your MedReader[8] would have confirmed the suspicion."

Leticia held fast.

---

[8] HomeMed units come equipped with a diagnostic mechanism, a MedReader, able to identify hundreds of ailments and diseases with a simple fluid scan. Note: with the continued emergence of hyper-viruses, best practices recommend subscribing to monthly database and vaccination upgrades. Financing not available.

"You should follow that instinct," Quinn said. "You see something others don't. In fact, you *should* kill dangerous things, all dangerous things. More like you are needed. Imagine what the cities would still be! Open areas. Mass transit. Public schools. Shall we get started on your training?"

The girl had become visibly uncomfortable, fidgeting. "Wait ..."

"Well, what do you say? I'm a Delphi. You know what we do. So, shall we start? What are you waiting for?"

"You aren't here to—"

"This is *exactly* why I'm here. You called for me. Look at that stitching." Quinn reached a hand under the body and hoisted it up. It came down on table's edge with a wet *thump*. Leticia didn't twitch, which Quinn noted without slowing. "That was more than removing a danger. That was *study*. I know about your research. So, if we're to make you a competent—a … let's call it a "remover" of unfit persons, criminals and undesirables—not one of those pitiful attention-seekers like Algernon, who'll kill just for recognition, we must start with truth."

She retracted her corpse-flipping hand and took video of Leticia's eyes, while replaying the captured images of the seconds before, at the mention of Algernon. A definite expanding of the pupils, almost to their limits. She made a note, then added a new goad.

"You reattached them in different places because you were studying form, weren't you? Considering life? In fact, I don't think you killed it at all. And a competent *remover*, a righteous surgeon, must have purpose and truth. So, start with truth. Did you kill the hare?"

Leticia squeezed her gloves. Tentatively, she shook her head from side to side.

"Yes, you found it dead. But you dissected it after, didn't you? Because while you weren't ready to kill, even knowing it was dangerous, you wanted to try something. You wanted to practice. To put a knife through flesh."

Leticia studied Quinn, but then looked around the room's perimeter. The girl must have known the conversation was being recorded, everything was, but she also had to be thinking that her mother, Samantha, had hired Quinn. And Quinn, the teacher—she'd said this was her purpose. Leticia nodded.

"Ahh, truth. And so now purpose. *Logic*. Why do you want to know you can kill, Leticia? Protection? Confidence?" Quinn sat forward, elbows crunching onto glass. "Why is that important?" While she spoke, she began to compose a minutes update for the Circuit Keeper.

"How can I really know life if I haven't taken it?" Leticia said.

Quinn stopped the update.

"And made it." Leticia continued. "Had a family. How can you really know, really value life, if you haven't done both?"

Quinn sat back. "Quite philosophical. What have you been reading?"

"It's just something I've been thinking about."

They sat in silence.

"Well," Quinn said.

"Well what?"

"Shall we start your training?" She made her rented hand into the symbol of a blade, then made a chopping motion. "The earlier you start, the better."

But Leticia shook her head heavily. Without another word, she fled into the passage.

In moments, Samantha returned, mouth agape, clearly having watched the exchange.

"*What*," she snarled, "was *that*? I didn't expect a Delphi to—"

"Madam."

"How *could* you?"

"*Madam*." Quinn rose. Her jaunt-coach would arrive in minutes and she itched to be out of the rented body. The Madam crossed her arms and drew heavy breaths.

"A pair of researchers," Quinn said, "wished to get two groups to stop hating each other. More importantly, to stop *killing* each other. Standard *logic* said bring them together, let them see each other, learn from exposure. But the researchers knew these people, were of them. A thousand years of interaction had done nothing. So, they tried something else."

The fine muscles under Samantha's eyes fluttered.

"The researchers told each side they were *right*," Quinn continued. "They praised war itself. 'Without war, how would we have heroes?' they asked. 'Without war, how would we know morality?' They even offered them training, not on defense and protection, but on *first strikes*. They offered new and terrible weapons. They even built a mascot for the coming conflict. And outlined best practices and color-schemes for posthumous commendations."

"And?"

"And both sides, within weeks, reported less desire for conflict. In six months, they reported increased tolerance. Some had even reached out."

"How is that—"

"Because the researchers told each side they were right to extremes, to degrees that made them *embarrassed*. Because no one wants to be the madman. It was the most successful social science experiment of its kind. People are afraid to replicate it. We are not."

Quinn started for the passage, passing the woman without a lingering glance.

"That's it?" Samantha called after Quinn.

The Delphi spoke over her shoulder, voice now echoing.

"I'll return in a week. Though I'd bet I won't need to."

Quinn found her way to the patio, where the jaunt-coach waited, spraying pebbles in all directions with vertical fumes. As Quinn boarded, she considered running a scan for where Leticia, the Unsolvable Case, had gone. She didn't know why. But, in the end, she didn't run the scan.

Quinn slapped the man-child across the flesh-sac that served as his cheek.

"Tell me again you 'don't need permission,' Ronald," Quinn sneered. "Tell me again you 'can know' without asking a woman's permission."

An internal chiming noted an incoming call. Quinn kept her gold-colored hand raised, red eyes fixed on the blubbering teen, while she answered without speaking aloud.

"Hello, Ms. Coffey. I—"

"She did it again. *Worse!*"

The gilded hand between Quinn and the boy vibrated.

"A hare?'

"A *bird*. A *falcon*."

"Was it ill?"

"It hit the viewing window, upstairs, it—"

"*Alive* when she found it?"

Silence on the other end.

"And after. Stitching again?"

"Yes. Oh, yes, she did. Head to tail. Tail to head."

Quinn lowered her hand. Her red eyes were blushes in its golden reflection.

"Madam? Meet me in Denver in two days. Contact

Service, for arrangements. And bring Leticia."

#

Denver again, the new ghetto. Like others thinking staving off change would save it, the city ate itself. Quinn leaned against a ruined mid-modern, a chrome-plated foot on crumbling stone, a hand on cracked blocks of smoky glass.

Footfalls slushed through the trash-littered street beyond the wall separating Quinn's perch from the next property. Garden plots, now waste-piles, lined the wall. Gardening—that's what she'd explore in Free Study. Quinn found fascinating the rituals and oddities of gardening. If by some miracle Free Study was actually real, if one could really …

Leticia turned the corner and Quinn cleaved her thoughts. The girl had traded her gray haptic suit for a full-body enclosure of shimmering blue. Helmet and goggles with laser-orange lenses completed the outfit, befitting a junior ski champion, but now needed to protect skin from things much deadlier than snow and cold. A jaunt-coach exploded into the sky. Quinn caught dark hair in the passenger seat.

"So, you're ready?" Quinn said, stepping into the dead-brown that'd once been a yard.

Leticia paused. While there were no bodies, it was a desolate place and Quinn noted the girl's slow pan around. Did it bring home the reality? Maybe her first time? Quinn had doubted Leticia had ever come to the city proper. Premonition now felt confirmed. Perfect.

Leticia's goggles found Quinn.

"Why are we here?" Leticia said.

"Answer the question," Quinn said. "Are you ready for your training? Do you commit?"

Goggles slid to the side, but then centered. And nodded.

Something in Quinn's rented body churned. She ignored it and pounded towards the street, motioning for Leticia to follow. They snuck through debris gleaming in the high noon sun, Quinn heading them west.

"We got a communique of an attack," she said, slowing to let Leticia catch up. "Algernon."

Quinn sensed a halt behind. She pivoted to find Leticia's hands opening and closing at her sides. Quinn closed the distance between them, while pulling something from the rented body's heavy robes. "Take this."

Leticia stiffened at the offering. Layered lenses, zooming and researching, purred.

"Really?" the girl said. She brushed the knife's handle with a finger before pulling it from Quinn's grip. Quinn estimated the blade to be almost as long as the girl's skinny forearm.

"You might need it," Quinn said. She crunched a step west, but had to pause when she registered the girl standing pat.

A little mic hissed. "Shouldn't I have something more powerful?"

Quinn ground her rented teeth.

"We do this close up," the Delphi said, tempering her anger. "If we do it, we do it close. No escaping the action or the consequence. Besides, Algernon carries one much smaller. And look what he's done."

The girl stayed stuck. "What about you?"

Quinn raised her hands, joints and ridges glinting in the sun.

They stalked for several blocks, streets sloping towards a glittering urban lake. Weight leaned against gravity, they shuttled by burned, folded-in homes, as well as those still in use, if also in shambles. Shapes stirred behind darkened glass. Leticia spun her view everywhere. When she asked how Quinn knew their direction, the Delphi gave no answer. Finally, after a mile, Quinn crouched behind a crumpled jaunt-wagon, bidding Leticia to do the same. After a showy look about, Quinn half-rose and ventured north, taking them onto a new, more littered street.

A chiming rung inside Quinn's head. Aggravated, she answered, expecting Samantha and histrionics, petrified by something viewed from the miles-away jaunt-coach. But it was Leticia, whispering into her mic and directly into Quinn's head.

"Why are you doing this for me?"

"I teach," Quinn sent back, not bothering to modulate her tone. "Therefore I am."

"Are you scared?"

Quinn glanced back. Beneath her goggles, the girl bore the same expression as ever. An undesired train of thought bloomed: Unsolvable. She's considered Unsolvable, already. Already.

"I can't die," Quinn transmitted. "But my knowledge and memory collection has taken so long to curate. I've spent a great deal of effort keeping them united and growing. It'd be a— It'd be a shame to separate them. To have them recycled into a million different places, all that energy, and time, lost. Have you heard of the free energy principle?"

A bird flew overheard, an ugly thing, part pigeon, part sparrow.

"No."

"Never mind. How do *you* feel? Are you afraid?"

"I think so. But I trust you, Quinn. I'm sorry about last time. You...you scared me. But I thought about it and it impressed me. I trust you, Quinn."

Quinn zoomed on the goggles. She then turned, returning to the pathbreaking. Another freak bird fluttered overhead, crash landing in the remains of a Douglas fir. Quinn nodded towards the tree without slowing stride.

"Why do that to the falcon? Even if it was a mercy killing, the stitching was useless. It could have been food, if nothing else, for your animals."

"No one eats meat anymore, not even our goats."

Quinn registered the calm in Leticia's tone. The Delphi took advantage, fully engaging Mode Two. "Why the stitching? What do you feel when you do it?"

No answer came. But a signal, inaudible externally, yanked Quinn to a halt. She fired off a return signal and ducked them behind a wrecked municipal-guardian cruiser. Several more lay ahead in two uneven but clearly intentional lines, their final stops having created a broken V.

"Do you hear that?" Quinn transmitted. Leticia nodded weakly. *"Listen!"* Quinn demanded.

The girl combed round and round, little chest pulsing under her skinsuit. Both froze, however, as a sound became apparent and undisputed.

"Oh god. Oh god help me!"

Quinn sprang around the cruiser. She didn't bother looking back. Leticia followed as they dodged around two more cruisers to the peak of the V.

"Oh please! Help! I'm *cut! I'm cut so bad."*

Quinn hummed with satisfaction as Leticia skidded to a stop just feet from a body laid astride the final cruiser's wreckage. The victim thrashed in streams of blood.

"Help me*!"*

The victim, clearly tall and young, even if prone, was revealed to be a teen girl of no more than Leticia's age. The girl might have had red hair—impossible to tell, however, as it was soaked in gore and mangled about itself, like something spit from the ocean.

Steps shuffled behind Quinn. The Delphi found Leticia almost marching in place, seeming to want to retreat, but stuck. Quinn pulled right up in front of the girl and bent, green gaze inches from goggles. She seized Leticia's hand, the one loosening on the knife, and clutched it hard, no care to any pain caused.

"What are you *doing*?" Quinn sent. "This is when we'll need it! He could still be close! Algernon!"

Leticia furiously shook her head.

"I'm not ready—"

The dying girl cried out. *"What are you doing? Help me! I'm so scared."*

Quinn grabbed Leticia's shoulders and shook. *"What*? Is it *her*? We're not here for that. Unless you prefer to wait with her, as help comes. While I hunt Algernon. Is that it? You don't feel up to it? You feel like staying here? With her?"

Quinn, with milli-movements, eased her grip. Leticia crept towards the girl.

Leticia dropped to the girl's side as the victim began to gurgle. Leticia's free hand struck out as the victim's torso convulsed and spasmed. A jet of blood jumped from a chest wound, splattering Leticia's goggles and bending her back over her knees.

Quinn zoomed in, all sensors in overdrive.

The victim went still.

Leticia sank back. The knife clattered to the cement. The girl swiped at the blood on her lenses, but it only spread the fluid. Her soaked gloves eventually fell into her lap and she became still, for all the world a mourner at an old grave.

After two complete minutes, Quinn called the jaunt-coach. Wordless, Leticia allowed her mother to embrace her and urge her into the cabin. They exploded into the sky, plastic shooting everywhere.

Quinn's head chimed moments later.

"She's unconscious. *Sedated.* What was *that*?"

"Madam. Look."

Quinn clicked a command inside her rented skull and a tiny shutter opened, sending Samantha a video feed. As it did, the "corpse" rolled onto its side and pushed upwards in a smooth motion, blood dropping from large rips in its throat and chest. The girl-victim—blood so drenching her face and little brown eyes she could have been made of syrup—walked forward into Quinn's vision until all that really registered were wet eyes and damp hair.

"Oh. Oh, *no*. You all can look … you can look like that? *Us*?"

"Yes, Madam. Yes indeed. We know how it makes you feel. That's why we don't use them. Unless we must. Unless it's the solution."

The girl-victim gave a nod to the sky. Another jaunt-coach rattled down.

"Call me if you need, Madam. Please, if you need."

#

Starlight brushed Quinn's onyx face in ghost-blue rivers. As the young heiress collapsed, sagging towards thighs and sofa cushions, Quinn put one jet-black hand on hers.

"I've been angry too," Quinn said, dialing her tone to a new degree of compassion. "Revenge? With what happened, I might broadcast it, too. I've wondered how I'd feel, after—"

A chiming severed her conversation thread. Massaging the heiress, between thumb and forefinger, Quinn ordered up a smile to mask her internal answering.

"This is not a good time," she transmitted.

"*Henry*," the familiar voice on the other end said. No emotion. No warmth.

The heiress's hand shuddered. Quinn quickly gauged her pressure level, found it way too high, and reset. The heiress cautiously returned her palm.

"I'll be there in three days," Quinn transmitted, rented mouth motionless and fixed in its smile. "Call Service," she silently sent to Samantha. "They'll prepare you. It can take the full Method."

#

Quinn swallowed each and every minute of the jaunt-coach's travel up the mountain, knowing they were gone. She broke them into fragments and atoms, imagining a path down messy and soft organs. The passenger moaned. Quinn whistled a fist into the man's cheekbone, metallic knuckles colliding with unhealthy flesh. A whimper followed, but a second strike cut it dead. Below, tall pines began to give way to gardens. Quinn digested more minutes.

The jaunt-coach landed near the guest house and stalled to a quiet humming. Quinn twisted and dug one hand into the man's dirty hair and the other under the latch of a metallic collar about his throat. Quinn snapped the neural-collar locked across scraggly beard and ingrown hairs.

"Algernon," she spit.

The man whimpered.

With disgust, Quinn yanked in opposite directions, eliciting a yelp. Then she barked silent instructions to the jaunt-coach and left it sealed and humming, before marching towards the patio.

As Quinn's rented feet clonked onto the sunlit stone, two figures exited the house to meet her. She'd never fully studied the impact of fatigue on the human body, but made a note to explore the thinning and paling of once-dark hair. As Samantha dropped into a glass chair, one matching a new glass table, a new head-steward-bot—gleaming white and a foot taller than Quinn's rental—coasted into the Delphi's path. Quinn halted. She tried to look around the unit, known as a major-domo, a robot painted to resemble a head butler and designed to lead all service bots in a household. Quinn tried to catch the Madam's eyes, but found herself blocked by the major-domo's massive, seven-fingered hand. Quinn smacked the hand and thrust up her jaw.

"That's enough, Simon," Samantha said, voice ugly. The major-domo slid to a side as Samantha exhaled a deep cloud of haze, a burner-bar dropping with one hand. Alarms set off in Quinn's head at the sight of the burner-bar, a sophisticated upgrade of the centuries-old and dangerous technology known as "vaping." Quinn's alarms triggered because the burner-bar could deliver more than just tobacco and marijuana, and these days often did. Her sensors flared as Samantha inhaled a mixture of opiates.

"Madam, were the instructions not clear? You cannot be incapacitated for this, not in any way. You may be—"

"I don't care."

Quinn looked at the woman's eyes and the fine muscles below them. They barely moved as Samantha returned her gaze. Incensed for a part of a minute, Quinn clicked open a monitor from her forearm, a tiny screen. The jaunt-coach appeared small and innocent as a toy. Samantha flitted her gaze away from the image before Quinn grabbed her arm.

"How?" Quinn said.

"How what?"

"Henry, the grounds-bot."

The woman slid back, pulling the held arm away, if not totally free.

"There were no stiches, if that's what you mean. Wire, everywhere, tangled, but I must have caught her before she used the soldering tool for anything but cutting. He'd been with us since Leticia was born, you know."

Quinn released her grip. She considered a million statements in order, along with a million tones and combinations of inflection. Instead, she pointed to the tiny screen.

"You have to trust me," she said. "Leticia does."

The woman brought the burner-bar to her mouth and inhaled. She rolled her head on her neck, away from Quinn and towards the mountain. Quinn selected a yet-complete, but final thought.

"A few youthful infractions," she said, "does not an Un—a lost cause make."

"Please," Samantha muttered, not facing Quinn. "Just please."

Quinn signaled. On the monitor, the jaunt-coach's hatch sprung upward. A brittle figure, thin and bony, slipped out. A tiny head moved around, followed by open hands and stretching fingers. Then, in a motion almost too fast to fit the mover, Algernon dashed off screen.

Samantha dropped the bar to the table with a clank and headed inside. Quinn heard her call a name. The major-domo waited by the door until Leticia appeared, today's skinsuit a deep night black, stark against her face and hands. The major-domo ducked its head and entered the house, then shut the door, firing locks. With a wide smile, the girl bound towards Quinn, for whom minutes were speeding up, now disappearing in chunks.

"Why Henry?" the Delphi growled. "Why your grounds-keeping bot?"

Leticia halted, a look of confusion pulling at her face. "I froze," the girl said. "Back in that street. In Denver. I asked Henry about it while he was cleaning the patio again. I thought he might know, since robots know so many things, but he just made one of his jokes. I realized

~ 196 ~

then that something was wrong with his programming. Maybe he was breaking down? Anyway, he was old and he wasn't real. Did you see Simon?"

Quinn turned her back to the girl and walked away.

"Wait," Leticia cried. "Wait, you aren't leaving, are you? I've wanted to see you. I've got so many questions …"

Quinn spun.

"*Stop*. A bot? Because of a joke? You sicken me."

The wound in Leticia's eyes was unmistakable.

"I …"

"You have one chance and once chance only," Quinn said. "*He's* here."

Leticia didn't blink, concerning Quinn. The girl's button chin wagged from side to side.

"He …?"

"*Algernon*. He found you. He's on the grounds. *Right now*."

The button swung back and forth harder. The voice grew a skin. "No," Leticia said. "He doesn't do it that way. Not any of the twelve…thirteen. He never goes to their homes. He likes to hunt in the streets, like where we found the last one. I've seen all the …"

Quinn grasped Leticia. "*Shut up*. Don't give him so much credit. If you help me, you'll see."

With a chrome-plated hand, the Delphi pulled out the once-dropped knife. "Do you trust me?" Quinn said, lifting it to the girl's eyes. She entered Mode Three. "Is what I say credible to you? Still?"

Leticia stood motionless. Then her young fingers wrapped around the handle as her chin nodded.

"Let's go," Quinn said.

As they searched the gardens, Quinn led in a measured pace, allowing her to monitor Leticia's heart rate and breath while also tracking the killer's every step, registering how the latter's weight now included something that added two pounds and dragged his stride to the right. Quinn scanned the collar's magnets and voltage and felt satisfied by the simple and pure mixture returned. When the killer moved from studying the grand house to heading for one of its lower windows, Quinn flashed a command and reveled in the sensor-returned data: Algernon rapidly convulsing and collapsing to the ground, bladder releasing, his ability to rise made impossible for several moments. Utterly controlled. When Algernon finally did rise, the lumbering notch added to his slowed pace only satisfied Quinn more. Soon, Quinn would bring Leticia into contact. The Delphi searched files for a place and noted a manicured rectangle of grass just below the ballroom's deck. The view would be perfect for those safely inside. She pulled Leticia down a new path and hurried their progress. But minutes still passed. So many minutes.

"Do you still believe it?" Quinn said.

"Believe what?"

"That to really know life, one has to take it?"

The steps behind her slowed.

"It's not wrong," Leticia said. "And it's only part of it. I want a family. But you can't say it's wrong. Not if you really think about it. Have you?"

Quinn ran a scan of Algernon's location and vitals. "It sounds like wanting to be God," the Delphi said. "It sounds like the simple-minded philosophy of a simple-minded God."

She stalked forward, parting pine branches grown into the path. When no steps followed, she raised her palm, wordlessly asking why.

"I don't think I'm *God*," Leticia said.

"Do you want to be righteous then, at least? For God's sake, if one exists, will you save yourself and your mother?"

Footsteps restarted, matching the quiet of Quinn's careful approach. A snicker sounded and Quinn sensed a branch falling to the path behind her, shorn free. It was time. Quinn signaled the collar and spun her rented head back to the girl.

"*Are you ready*? He's right up there. I can hear him. By the house!"

Quinn ran, not waiting. Leticia followed.

They burst into the manicured yard and darted for the thing stumbling about. Quinn's legs stopped so suddenly her feet plowed under sod. Leticia bumped into her back, knife poking through the air between the Delphi's robe and sleeve.

"No." The word escaped Quinn's rented vocal chords before she could make it internal. In front of them, a goat staggered, white fur of its hind legs stained yellow, much more fur wettened blood red. The goat fell, head first, then rose, hacking breath and spewing gore. The neural-collar hung half connected around its neck—the neural-collar supposedly impossible to remove once locked, though clearly not foolproof, as Algernon had somehow detached it from his own neck and hung it around the goat's, his decoy.

"Quinn?" Leticia said.

A scream erupted from the nearest side of the grand house—the patio. Programs and calculations fired through Quinn's rented mental unit, but failed to keep up with her demands. The goat whined as its body quaked and it plummeted once more.

"Quinn, what's—" Leticia whispered.

The Delphi's fist went back and she experienced a memory skip, followed by the registration of a new definition: déjà vu. She imagined the first time at the home, when she'd been overcome with frustration, when she'd swung her fist back and shattered the glass table. Her fist swung back now, *more* frustrated, awash in an even deeper desperation. But there was no glass table behind her this time to be exploded into dust for effect. Instead, all that she'd slam into would be a teen girl's skull. She opened her fist just before it could smash Leticia's face into gore and gripped the girl's hand. There was still time. Quinn tugged them to the patio.

Three bodies struggled in various poses, like agonies in

a Dutch-master's painting. Why had they come outside? Tricked somehow—the goat, maybe—though not mattering anymore. Quinn first spied Simon, the major-domo bot, clawing at an irrigation tube shoved into the crevice between his shoulder plating and neck piston, water bubbling and crackling as he gyrated madly. With a bare slowing of pace, Quinn used her free hand to yank away the tube, splattering herself as it whipped. With a rip of a turn, still pulling Leticia, she pivoted and made her way to the woman and the man in patio's center, both writhing through ponds of scarlet.

Samantha crawled, hand over hand, matted hair in her eyes, dragging her right leg. Fabric, shredded from calf to buttock, exposed a hunk of pale flesh, revealing a great wound in the center, chunks of muscle spit up through the rupture, like nastily erupted magma. Samantha's eyes, already widened to the limits, went wild at the sight of Leticia.

"No," the Madam wailed. "*No!*"

Quinn yanked her gaze and too-rapid assessments from the woman, afraid the now-smoldering circuits in her rented head might catch fire. She focused on the wraith crawling along behind Samantha, heaving one side of his body. Algernon's left half hung semi-limp, arm dangling as much as the corresponding cheek. His left eye stared unfocused and motionless in a direction entirely different from the functioning right. The cost of removing the neural collar had been high—a partial stroke—but not the fatality promised. His still-working eye zeroed forward, leading the still-working right arm. With ragged clawing, Algernon dragged himself a foot, then pushed his bloody garden shears another foot ahead, only to repeat. In Samantha's direction.

Quinn flung free her hold of Leticia and sprinted the final yards. She straddled Algernon high up on his back, chrome-plated hands descending like mortars to either side of the man's jaw. Calculations ran and answers spit back, but they felt like flames. Seconds counted in the place of minutes, a counter running down.

"Quinn!" Leticia said, trembling.

Her mother reached for her, which stretched her wound, releasing more blood, but the girl fixated on the wasted form wriggling in Quinn's grip. She raised the knife, arm steadying.

Quinn, rented head raised, met the girl's eyes. She moved a knee into the upper space between Algernon's wriggling shoulder blades.

"This," Quinn said, and nodded downward, "is no God."

In the same screech of a moment, she wrenched arms back while pushing with her knee. An unnatural crack echoed up the mountain and the dirty body went still. Quinn yanked and pressed further, until a wet rip sounded, not strong enough to echo up the mountain, but clear across the patio. A flood splashed onto the stones, displaying the Delphi's reflection.

Quinn searched Leticia's gaze, willing something: a blink, for the girl to turn away, to unleash tears. Internal data drank into sensors, Quinn searching for a reaction denoting the Mode's success, of the girl showing proper response.

It did not come.

Programs burned through Quinn. She could feel the collapsing of certainty, of surety. This could not be, this was not anticipated. The Method, the Modes, did not fail. Primary directives screamed against incoming data, incongruous and all-but melting the rented unit. Samantha's grievous wound, the damage to Simon—even Algernon's execution to save lives: all might be understood by the Circuit Keeper. But not for naught.

Leticia looked on, pupils tacking back and forth, seeming mesmerized by the half-pulled away head, maybe even the chrome fingers still punctured through tendon and jawbone. Quinn's vision began to shake. Minutes, suddenly she could think of nothing but minutes, and the weak but determined movements where Samantha wriggled closer to her daughter.

And a thought occurred:

Perhaps there was now a different credibility.

A different God.

And a Fourth Mode.

Quinn threw down the skull and rose. Leticia's eyes followed, for the first time showing surprise. Quinn input data and ran an override. She scooped up the bloody shears, electrical fire running through her as the override shook the unit.

"I *wanted* this," Quinn snarled and split open the shears, slinging gore. Leticia shuddered, just a little. "I *planned* this!" Quinn screamed, electronic voice an unnatural pitch. She turned towards the girl's mother, Samantha, and sped up. *"And I won't stop."* The last movement she commanded was to pull her eyes from the girl's, to dismiss her, but not before catching the girl blink, and wag her triangle chin hard.

"No."

A proper response to the moment.

An alarm wailed. It howled like a squealing tire, caught in a repeating loop, so loud Quinn felt it must come from only inside her own head. But data intakes, even as they began to shut down, told her they screamed from Simon as well, who'd managed to lift himself to a knee. They wailed from the house sirens too. And they were joined by the thunder of giant jaunt-wagons suddenly spiraling earthward as Quinn's rented unit shut down, folding her into a cross-legged prisoner on the patio stone, unable to do anything but look. And speak.

"You!" she hollered as a jaunt-wagon crunched down yards behind, spraying waves of pebbles. Leticia's gaze, now gone as wild as her mother's, found Quinn. The girl pointed to herself with a flimsy, bent finger. But Quinn looked beyond the girl and changed her tone, to a pitch much too high to be comprehended other than by electronic ears. *"You!"*

Simon, body still jerking, stumbled over. Before the Teledepot's bots grabbed Quinn's now unresponsive unit, she cast her rented eyes up to the major-domo's.

"I think I did it," Quinn said, firing out the words. "Stopped the momentum. It was about the right message

~ 204 ~

and messenger. And, as important, the right moment. The right time." Quinn's vocal capabilities began to fade, the Teledepot—on orders of the Circuit Keeper, or its masters, surely—determining she must lose that ability as well. Quinn focused and forced out her last lesson with all the intensity she had left. "But if I didn't, you now have time to decide what to do."

Robotic appendages gripped Quinn's rented body and hauled her back towards the roar of jaunt-coaches, the major-domo watching the whole way.

#

Disembodied, Quinn floated within the data and signals of the Teledepot. Why they'd left her intact, she couldn't fathom. Was this Free Study? She tried to think of what she'd wanted to study—but the fantasy died. She'd failed. So, she should have been ripped apart, knowledge and memories shed of their filters from the outside world, blankets separating the entity known as Quinn from all other entities dissolved, leaving even her smallest pieces to disperse back into the cloud, to be recycled into new and useful forms.

A chiming rang in Quinn's mind. She'd have jerked her head, if she'd still had one. But casting about formless in the signal streams, all she could do was click the memory of answering.

"Circuit Keeper," she said, or imagined she said. "Please—"

"Quinn? Delphi Model 7?"

It wasn't the Circuit Keeper, not the thundering

~ 205 ~

connection that served as its massive voice. Not human either, but still an entity outside the cloud.

"Yes, I am," she said. "Who is this? What do you want?"

"I'm Wilkinson, Miss. Delphi Model 7.1. Well, prototype 7.1. I'm so glad you're still here. I heard about the new Method, Miss. We all have. A four-part method of persuasion. Logic and emotion and authority and timing. Combinations. And for what you constructed it for, to deprogram a budding serial kil— It was genius. Will you teach me? I have a—"

And in the electronic caverns of the Denver Teledepot, though she could not be seen, Quinn's imaginary mouth twitched. With it, a counter started, full of fresh minutes.

A limited amount of minutes.

* * *

Discussion Questions

1. Given how nearly human Quinn is, is it fair to have her live a limited lifespan? It is fair to make near human AI fear a pending death to motivate them to work?

2. They refer to Leticia as an "impossible" case. Is that ever true? Are there children (or adults) who have started down such a horrible path they simply can't be stopped? If so, what, if anything, should be done with them?

3. Do you think Quinn made the right choice in how she attempted to teach Leticia, the young girl? Is taking an idea to an extreme to illicit embarrassment a viable teaching method? Is trauma ever an appropriate teaching method?

4. Do you think "free study" is real, or simply something they tell the robots to motivate them? How is it the same, or different, than humans believing in heaven?

5. What happened at the end of the story that saved Leticia?

Monsters

Ana Carolina Pereira

THE ICE CREAM TRUCK rolled down the street where the Pinketts lived. It passed slowly and kept on going, towards the park that was three blocks away, its siren song got lost in the distance like a popsicle melting in the heat of that summer day.

Nancy was lying in bed with her daughter Carrie Mae. Both dozed under the canopy of the child's four-poster bed. The canopy curtains were white with pink lace flowers and they matched the motif of the wallpaper, a repeated pattern of a delicate bouquet of roses. Most things in the room had touches of pink and white. Outside, a blue jay landed on a branch of the oak tree that stood next to the house, chirped its heart out for a few seconds, and then flew away. It was a soft and sweet afternoon in a strawberry vanilla little girl's room.

Activated by the truck's music, Carrie Mae got up from the bed and began to jump. Her two thick braided ponytails, which Nancy had made for her in the morning and tied with brightly colored elastic bands, bounced lively in all directions.

"Did you hear, ma? An ice cream truck! Buy me an ice cream. Pleeease."

Nancy had not seen her daughter so happy since they had moved to that house, just two weeks ago.

"All right, Carrie Mae. Let's see what the ice cream man brought today."

As soon as she said those words, Nancy regretted them. Her first impulse had been to say no, to make up some excuse not to leave their small heaven. But her daughter's enthusiasm had disarmed her. It was Saturday afternoon and the park must be full of people. Nancy imagined herself standing on the grass, holding hands with Carrie Mae, surrounded by those strangers, and shuddered. The scene resembled a nightmare that had been visiting her for the past few days: the crowd approached them, closed in on both of them, slowly choking them like a boa constrictor.

She went with her daughter to the bathroom and helped her wash her hands. Then she retouched her makeup, applied some hairspray to her bob, checked that there was enough change and a new bag of tissues in her purse, and went outside.

Melvin was in the front yard, dipping a brush into a can of light blue paint, his face varnished with sweat. It was the third time he had to paint the outside of the house and Nancy was already beginning to hate that color. As soon as he saw his wife and daughter, Melvin smiled and then raised his eyebrows when he noticed that Nancy was carrying her purse.

"I'm going with Carrie Mae to the park to get some ice cream," she said.

The smile vanished from Melvin's face. He frowned.

A reflex. Fear. First, he tried to dissuade Nancy from going. Then, he wanted to go with them.

Impatient with the delay, Carrie Mae tugged at her mother's skirt several times:

"Hurry up, the ice cream cart is leaving, ma."

"Let me finish talking to your dad, dear. The ice cream man isn't going anywhere yet," Nancy said to the child as she took her hand. Then she looked seriously at her husband: "I don't think they'll do anything to us … they wouldn't dare. And this has to stop, Melvin. Going together everywhere, joined at the hip like Siamese twins. You stay here and finish what you're doing. I'll let you know if something happens."

"Really? How?" Melvin took a handkerchief from his pocket with an impatient gesture and wiped the sweat off his face.

"I'll yell. You're always telling me that I speak loud, that my voice is too strong, no? If we don't come back in half an hour, you go look for us. See you in a while, Mel."

Without waiting for her husband's reply and without looking back, Nancy began to walk away from the house with Carrie Mae, feeling Melvin's eyes glued to her back. She held her daughter's hand tight. Nothing, not even a tornado could separate them. They were both sweating, Carrie Mae because of the heat and she because of the anxiety. The child trotted along beside her mother and sang:

Ice cream man, ice cream man
Ring the bell, ring the bell

One scoop, two scoops, three scoops
Straaw ... erry, chocolate, pecan
Quick! Gimme the cone bee-fore they melt

Nancy counted the steps in silence. One, two, three, four, five ... It was only three blocks to the park, how many steps were in that distance?

They walked by a house with a "For Sale" sign freshly planted in the ground. It seemed to Nancy that the sign was shaped like a giant hand pointing its index finger to the two of them.

As they were about to reach the park, they saw the neighbors coming out of there in a hurry. They looked scared and were talking to each other with big gestures, but as soon as they saw Nancy and Carrie Mae, their countenance shifted from fear to disgust. One man, walking on the opposite sidewalk, spat in their direction. No one greeted them. Carrie Mae stopped singing and trotting, and began to walk very close to her mother, with her head down. Nancy kept her back straight and her chin up, while she felt her daughter shrinking beside her, as if trying to disappear. She wished Carrie Mae were a chick and she a giant bird to cover her, to protect her with her wings, to tear and drill with her beak the flesh of anyone who dared to hurt her child. She wanted to be a mother-bird with huge wings.

They crossed the street and arrived at the park. It was empty but for the ice cream truck, painted in pink, white and mint green, with giant vanilla cones on the sides. There didn't appear to be any threat nearby, perhaps the neighbors had learned that the two were heading to the park and decided to humiliate them once again by leaving them alone there, like a couple of lepers. Carrie Mae returned to her usual exuberance. She started running through the grass, pulling her mother's hand, who didn't let go … not yet. They traversed the park towards the truck. The ice cream man was in there, with his back turned on them.

Nancy hoisted her daughter up and perched her on her hip so that she could look inside. The girl was getting bigger and heavier and Nancy realized that it wouldn't be long before she stopped lifting her for good. She thought that the day she picked her up for the last time would go unnoticed to both of them, it would be just like any other. She wished there was something, a tangible object she could put in a scrapbook to commemorate that sad occasion, a postcard with a picture of the two that said: "The last time I picked up my daughter."

"Hello, ice cream man!" shouted Carrie Mae.

The man turned around and Nancy was so surprised that she almost ran away in fear. Carrie Mae screamed and buried her head on her mother's shoulder, covering her eyes with her hand.

Huge dark violet lumps populated the man's face. It seemed as if an epidemic of bright tumors, similar to eggplants, had taken over and that they were on the verge of exploding. A few small areas were free of lumps and there the skin was white, the bone structure harmonious. Perhaps, without his condition, he would have been a handsome man —tall, slender and broad-shouldered — but like this, he was the ugliest person Nancy had ever set eyes on.

She took a couple of steps back and pressed her daughter against her chest. But then she managed to control herself and kept her gaze on the eyes and mouth of the man. Eyes that were blue and lively, and a mouth that smiled at her with perfect white teeth. One of the few smiles she had seen on the streets of Windsor Woods.

"What are you two beautiful ladies having today? Marshmallow mint, Hawaiian sherbet, banana strawberry, coconut fudge? Those are the day's specials. Delicious for a sunny afternoon." The man said this beaming, as if he were one of those cheery TV announcers. As if he were handsome. He wore his impeccable soda jerk outfit with flair: a white short-sleeved shirt accessorized with a black bowtie and a white hat. Their unease didn't seem to bother him a bit and this somehow reassured Nancy.

"Two banana strawberry cones. Just one scoop, please."

"Jolly good choice, ma'am! They'll be ready in a minute."

Nancy hadn't thought for quite a while about little Marcus, a childhood neighbor who had a deformed and very thick leg, like that of an elephant. Her mother always warned her and her siblings that they should be good to little Marcus because his cross was already too heavy. One time, Nancy's mother overheard her brother Tom — the second oldest of her children — making a joke about the boy, saying that maybe someone should prick his leg with needles to deflate it so that his cross wouldn't be as heavy. She took Tom by the ear and dragged him into another room, where she chastised her son and made him stay for the rest of the day.

While the man was scooping the ice cream, Nancy felt how Carrie Mae's tense body relaxed, she saw how her daughter withdrew her hand from her face and peeked at the stranger with her left eye, somewhere between frightened and curious.

"Here we go." The man extended a banana strawberry cone, not knowing whom to hand it to.

"Take the cone, dear," said Nancy. Carrie Mae reached out an undecided hand, trying not to look at the man. "What do you say?"

"Thank you," the girl uttered in a whisper.

Nancy put the child down on the sidewalk and told her to go to the park. Ambling to the playground, Carrie Mae took turns licking the ice cream and turning to watch her mother and the stranger.

"Nice neighborhood. Have you lived here for long?" said the man as he scooped the other ice cream. "My name is Tom, by the way."

"Nice to meet you, Tom. I'm Nancy. No, we just moved. We're still getting used to it."

"You're the only ones here, I suppose. I mean … I was just 'greeted' by some of your neighbors," he said sarcastically as he handed Nancy her cone.

"That's right, we're the only ones."

Nancy kept wondering whether they had done the right

thing by moving to Windsor Woods. On paper it seemed like a great idea: it was a suburb-style neighborhood just fifteen minutes from downtown, where Melvin worked an office job. The school was good, not overcrowded and with only one shift. Trees lined the streets and everything looked well-tended and pleasant, like a postcard of the American Dream. The house had three rooms: one for the couple, one for Carrie Mae and one for the baby they expected to conceive soon. At last, they would go from tenants to homeowners. Despite these advantages, she balked initially at the idea of buying the house, knowing that for many of their potential neighbors, people like them were a stain that had to be erased from the postcard of the American Dream. But Melvin ended up convincing her. Sometimes she almost hated him for that. With each new humiliation by the neighbors, the rage she felt towards them was transferred to Melvin, amplified.

"I guess they haven't made things too easy for you?" said Tom. "I've seen what they've done in other neighborhoods, those so-called church-going, God-fearing folks." For an instant, his face turned sour.

"You guessed right. It could be worse, I know: in Woodland, they burned a house down the other day. In Roseland, they broke the windows of another. Here they haven't gone that far, though it's been exhausting."

"People like that … they want things to be a certain way — their way — and when they see stuff shifting, they take it badly, I know them all too well. But you're doing the right thing. It's none of my business, of course, and it's hard to walk in someone else's shoes, but if I was you I'd stay put."

"Well, we may have no other choice. At least for now." Nancy licked the ice cream and held back the tears that were starting to blur her vision. Melancholy overcame her as she remembered the lazy Sunday afternoons spent hanging out and talking to her friends in her old neighborhood.

"Can I tell you a story, Mrs. Nancy?"

"Go ahead, Tom."

"As a child my mother kept me locked up all day and only took me out at night now and then. When she left home without me, she tied me with a rope to the bars of the bed. She said that people shouldn't have to see a monster like me, that I scared them. But I was scared to death of people, too. Tell me who gets the most frightened: the person who fears a spider because it seems hideous to him, or the spider facing a giant that can crush it with his foot?"

"You have a point. But try to explain that to someone who's beside himself because a huge spider is crawling on his lap."

Nancy recalled that the real estate agent had shown them the house at night. They went in to see it camouflaged by the dark, hidden from the neighbors like criminals.

"All the same, I believe it's necessary to educate folks, Mrs. Nancy. Maybe that's why people like me came to this world. When I turned six, my mother ran away with someone she'd just met, a good-for-nothing lecher ... she was always falling hook and sinker for those. An uncle and his wife, who weren't blessed with children, took me in and raised me as their son. Best thing that ever happened to me! They went with me everywhere and were always so proud of their boy. Little by little, they took the shame off me. The ugly duckling turned into a swan ... well, so to speak, ha ha."

His laughter had a tinge of sadness in it. He went on:

"Thanks to them, I didn't become a freak both inside and out. I know, it's hard for others to get used to my face and I'll never get used to the staring, the whispering, the jokes, all that. But I like being outside, around people, and I won't spend my life locked up just to keep others from being uncomfortable ... no way, ma'am."

"It's a nice story, Tom."

"A true story, Mrs. Nancy."

She nodded without comment, nibbling her cone. He was right, of course: they were both destined to walk in difficult shoes. His shoes and hers were of a different kind, though. "There but for the grace of God, go I," most people would say in hushed tones upon meeting someone like Tom. A lot of those same people would have other words for the likes of her.

She finished her cone, paid Tom and went to one of the park benches, where her daughter was sitting.

Carrie Mae couldn't eat her ice cream fast enough and it was already beginning to drip down the cone. Her hands were sticky and, when that happened, she liked to put the fingertips of her index and thumb together, and see how the skin stretched as she tried to separate them. As Nancy wiped her with a tissue, the girl kept looking at Tom, fascinated, as if trying to decipher his strangeness at a safe distance.

"Don't stare at him, sweetheart. It's rude."

"Why is that man so ugly, ma? What happened to his face?"

"His name is Tom. He was born like that. He's a normal person, like you and me, it's just that his face is different."

"Oh, he was a child like that? Why? Did his mom love him with that face?"

"Of course his mother loved him, moms love their children very much."

"And God?"

"Of course God loves him, God loves everyone."

"And if God loves him, why did he make him so ugly, ma?"

"Oh, I don't know, dear. Your mom doesn't have all the answers. Hey, let's go play instead!"

Nancy pushed her daughter on the swing — "Higher! Higher!" demanded the girl incessantly, and her laughter soared with her to the sky — and then helped her climb up the slide and caught her at the bottom. Carrie Mae wanted to get on the seesaw but there was no child to counterbalance her at the other end. She sat there anyway, and Nancy tried to push the device up and down with her arms, but it was too heavy. As it happened to her sometimes, she felt guilty for not giving Carrie Mae a little brother or sister before. But kids were expensive. She and Melvin had decided that it was better to welcome a second child into their own house, not crammed into a rented one with just two bedrooms, and it took them a good while to save the money for the down payment. Next year, if things worked out.

When they were done, Nancy and Carrie Mae stopped by the truck to say goodbye. During all that time only the three of them were in the park, like outcasts in their own private Purgatory. The girl still glanced furtively at the ice cream man, and Nancy — despite liking him, despite her efforts to treat him naturally and look him in the eye without staring away at the incongruous bulges in his face, to not feel in her gut a mixture of repulsion and compassion — had to acknowledge to herself that his face would take some getting used to ... maybe if she saw him often, as it had happened with little Marcus.

"Will you come back again sometime soon?" she asked Tom.

"Not likely, Mrs. Nancy. I'm covering for a colleague who's sick. But you can find me not too far from here: Tuesdays and Thursdays at Westfield, Wednesdays and Fridays at Willow Creek and weekends at Peach Blossom Terrace. Feel free to drop by any day. Much more neighborly folks in those places, you'll see."

On their way home, they passed again in front of the "For Sale" sign. Nancy knew that those signs would likely soon spread throughout the block. It had happened already in other neighborhoods, and in other cities. Newspaper articles had been published about this phenomenon. She knew it was their neighbors' biggest fear. Sometimes, she imagined their conversations at dinnertime, behind closed curtains and shut doors, behind those hostile façades: Now that the Pinketts had arrived, should they sell quickly and get out of there while they still could, before the prices of their homes plummeted like a stone down into the sea? Or should they stay and try to contain the tide?

She and Carrie Mae kept on walking, always holding hands. Their house was now only a block and a half away. All of a sudden, Nancy felt unease. She turned her head around swiftly and saw a crew-cut brown-haired man in a buttoned-down plaid shirt, standing in the middle of the sidewalk a few feet behind them. He took a long drag on his cigarette, his squinting eyes focused on her.

"Let's hurry up, baby, let's not keep your dad waiting anymore," she said to Carrie Mae, hastening the pace and squeezing her daughter's hand.

As they walked, Nancy pricked up her ears, trying to catch the sound of the man's footsteps behind them. She felt her armpits, her forehead, drenched in sweat. They crossed the street almost running. Once they were on the other side, on the safe side, where they could now see their home, Nancy turned around. The man was still standing on the same spot, his eyes still fixed on her. He threw down the butt of his cigarette, stamped it out, and then turned on his heel and started walking in the opposite direction.

"Dad! Dad!" yelled Carrie Mae, as she pulled her mother's hand. Melvin looked like a stick figure in the distance, a few houses down the street. The child kept on pulling, trying to break free and run towards her father.

Her little girl was a paper kite that wanted to fly and the wind was blowing strong. But Nancy didn't want to let her loose … not yet.

They reached the edge of their front yard. Melvin lifted his left arm and waved at them, while he used his right hand to wipe the sweat off his face with the hankie. He smiled with relief and they smiled back. The paint can lay next to him, with the lid on. The words that strangers had written with giant letters on the façade of their home had now been covered for the third time since they had moved. But for how long before they reappeared? Sometimes, Nancy imagined that the wood had a disease, an incurable fungus that always came back a few days after applying the treatment.

Whites only
Negroes get out

Each word was a bullet aimed at the three of them: Melvin, Nancy and Carrie Mae ... even at the child that was yet to be conceived. Each word had stung Nancy's heart. Her consolation was that her daughter still could not read.

"Daddy, daddy!" Carrie Mae pulled harder.

Melvin crouched down, extending both arms. Nancy loosened her grip and let go of her daughter. Carrie Mae ran fast to her father's embrace, as Nancy watched her child, her paper kite, soar towards the bright blue sky.

* * *

Discussion Questions

1. Why is the title of the story "Monsters?"

2. The ice cream truck driver (Tom) says, *"Tell me who gets the most frightened: the person who fears a spider because it seems hideous to him, or the spider facing a giant that can crush it with his foot?"* What does this sentence mean in the context of the story? Who do you think is the most frightened in the story?

3. Is Tom right? Is the antidote to fear of the unknown exposure? If that is the case, isn't the only way to get the community over their fear for the Pinketts to move in?

4. Are the Pinketts brave or foolish for moving into a neighborhood that doesn't want them? Does the fact that they have a daughter change your answer?

5. How would you have answered Carrie Mae's question: *"...if God loves him, why did he make him so ugly, ma?"* Does this question also apply to the neighbors? If so, what is your answer?

Believing in Ghosts

André Lopes

CHAPTER ONE

THE POLITICIAN STOOD on the podium and addressed the nation. Dressed in a dark suit and red tie, he answered all the questions the reporter asked him.

"The people are tired of the same old faces in charge of policy. Policy that has been a disaster, particularly among the young," said the politician.

"And how are you planning to overturn the course of this nation, Mr. Booker?" asked the reporter.

"We need to take a look at our healthcare options. Currently the system is a disaster. Our young workers are underpaid and overworked, and our elderly, after a whole life of working for this nation, are left abandoned in poverty," said Booker.

Booker was an experienced politician who came from a long line of famous lawyers and economists. His immaculate presentation, charisma and natural knack for leadership were certainly three of the main reasons why he was the frontrunner in the polls nationwide.

A campaign employee approached him as he left the conference room:

"We just got confirmation of another *ghost*," informed Booker's prime assistant.

"Who?" replied Booker.

"Jared Benjamin."

Booker paused for a second: "The one that spread those fake sex tapes a few months ago?"

"Yes, the one. Our intel team just confirmed that he's a composite."

"Any word on who's the puppet master?"

"No clue yet, the platform he was using for his web series is very proud of their privacy policy."

Booker checked if he was already away from the cameras.

"No one is liable for defamation in this country anymore, fucking bullshit," Booker said.

"We'll continue to pressure for them to identify the ghost."

CHAPTER TWO

Rain rolled on her bed and stared at her mobile phone's screen. Most of her social media feed was auto-generated clickbait articles written by AI. She received job offers on a professional social network sent by non-existent human resources employees. The effortless creation of content made its supply near endless. This was fine, no moral panic concerning technology has ever produced anything of note. She scrolled through social media and saw an ad for a quack medicine, the man promoting it, bald, with a shirt and green tie talks about all of the benefits this all-natural drug has, he may be an actual person passionate about bullshit medicine, a complete fabrication or something in between.

Rain felt lazy today but she made an effort to be productive. Mr. Booker had emailed her a new scope for security auditing. She did most of her work remotely and this gig at candidate Booker's campaign wasn't her only show. Despite that, she had no schedules, which meant that most days were a foggy mess of sleep. In the winter, she regularly woke up to almost dark outside and her diet was mediocre at best. Grocery shopping she felt like an astronaut stepping on a foreign planet.

"Not again," she thought. The clock on her phone marked 1 p.m. "I swore I'd wake up at decent hours."

While heavy work late in the night was more productive to her, the almost flipped schedules compared to a regular person intensified the feeling of alienation to regular people. Now with the dramatic failure of an early get-up plan, the routine was the usual: get out of bed, make something to eat and sit in front of the computer, scroll through work e-mail and, of course, procrastinate on social media. After a while, she fired up the virtual machine used to work.

As a cybersecurity consultant or, as better known in popular culture, a hacker, her job was to find security vulnerabilities on her clients' systems. Hacking is not the same as breaking things. Well, not necessarily; hacking is the art of exploring a piece of tech's features and try to make it perform amusing things — amusing to the hacker at least. This philosophy allows a competent hacker to explore the infrastructure of a client in a way a regular user might not, but a malicious user might. If, filling up an online form, it is prompted to insert your age, what would you put in? Something between 0 and 120, any sane person would guess. The hacker might input -2, 9999999999999999, or a piece of code. If this online form, when presented with these strange inputs, exhibits a weird, unexpected behavior, congratulations, you've hacked it. Now time for exploitation: how can you manipulate this weird behavior in your favor? If you're lucky, you might gain access to a database, if you're not so lucky, then nothing interesting will happen beyond that. This process of trying all these different things to trigger unexpected, potentially dangerous, behavior is what Rain would call, perhaps in poor taste, weaponized *obsessive-compulsive disorder*.

She opened the website of her favorite news outlet. The headline caught her attention.

THE PHANTOM VLOGGER: JARED BENJAMIN IS THE LATEST CONFIRMED GHOST IN THE POLITICAL COMMENTATOR SPHERE

"So JB's a ghost." Jared Benjamin was a treasured vlogger and Internet political commentator, so him being a ghost shocked somewhat, but it didn't surprise a whole lot of people. A ghost was the common term used to describe a fabricated person, from looks to voice and personality, all made up using clever algorithms.

Rain had entertained the thought Booker was himself a ghost prior to meeting the man in person, not only because the use of ghosts in mainstream life has made an entire generation completely apathetic and wary of media in general but also because the man had this aura of an almost perfect leader, an effective populist that still managed to keep bridges between political enemies.

As a general trusted freelancer, and since she was already Booker's security consultant on the campaign, Rain earned an additional client for security auditing: the candidate's main business, a well-known supermarket chain. After checking the provided test scope she smiled, this was huge, there were at least three full web applications that contain online shopping and an online contest. All of this provides entertainment for days or weeks.

"This is unexpected." Rain found an SSH server with a trivial password; B00K3R. Really? This was usually where the fun ended, as a *white hat* you're supposed to write a report on how you got in, how shit the security is and the best way to improve it.

"But what if there's something here that would allow me to obtain access to a parallel system?" she thought, as she tried to convince herself into investigating this server, knowing fully well that this was out of regular procedure, digging into personal files is not the job of a *white hat*.

There were four projects stored in this machine, some very early versions of a future redesigned website for online shopping, a new experimental service for regular clients and another project, the most interesting, it didn't appear to have anything functional but, upon inspection, the code inside was littered with advanced math and statistics. Rain didn't reach any conclusion regarding that code.

"Maybe I should call it a day."

The clock ticked 6 a.m.

CHAPTER THREE

Rain woke up with a phone call, she searched the phone around the pillow, still half-asleep, and opened her eyes just enough to read the name on the screen: "Booker Project Manager."

"Why is he calling at the crack of ..." she checked the clock, "... noon." She picked up the call.

"We need you here right now, we've been attacked."

"Attacked, how?"

"Our boys in the Security Operation Center caught a huge data exfiltration from within our network, some kind of malware snuck in and the attackers were trying to steal as much info as possible."

"And I'm absolutely needed there?"

"What the fuck is wrong with you? Isn't it obvious how serious this is?" His yelling and panicked voice suggested something in the scale of an H-bomb blowing up all of downtown.

"Sure ... I'll be there asap."

Booker's PM was what she thought was the result of a

secret CIA PsyOp program to create the most insufferable prick on Earth. He had an obvious disdain towards her, not only because he saw her as a mercenary criminal wannabe but also because she lived beyond the usual rules of the Corporation. Despite being, by all accounts, a recent employee, she was not an intern bringing him coffee and cookies, but instead a living exception to Corp with a very substantial monthly compensation.

Her look was the typical of these days. Messy, short black hair, clothing on its second day of use. T-shirts and jeans laid on one side of the closet and business-friendly clothing on the other. She sighed and grabbed a formal shirt and pair of business-friendly trousers. She hated formal clothing, but Rain had spent way too much time arguing about dress codes.

There were dishes from the day before, and the day before that on the desk where the computer was, clothing scattered all throughout the floor, an empty bottle of wine in a corner of her room sat there since last May. The whole apartment was not bigger than 25m^2, which made the space look even more cluttered, an absolute mess. But at least, it was her apartment, no strangers around invading her personal space.

Rain stepped outside, a chill wind swept the busy streets, a dim winter sun embraced the downtown buildings, the constant noise of car horns, excited and/or drunk tourists spoiled what would be a perfect cold day.

She walked down the street to catch public transportation, the bus takes half the time, however riding the bus meant interacting with the driver in order to pay the ticket and Rain wouldn't have any of that.

"The subway it is."

She stepped outside the subway station and into the corporate HQ, a huge screen outdoor marked Booker's building.

A CANDIDATE WITH SERIOUS PROPOSALS
A REALISTIC VISION FOR OUR FUTURE
BOOKER FOR PRESIDENT

Booker's face showing his typical confident smile was seen on the outdoor screen.

Going in, Rain had to identify herself, since she was not a regular employee this proved to be an awkward hassle. The temporary employee card in her possession, depending on the security guy calling the shots that week, might be good enough or not. That interaction alone was enough to deplete Rain's social fuel.

She approached the Booker's PM's office already tensed up, she expected a storm, yelling and overall unhelpful rage.

"How did they get in?! This is your job!" Booker's PM shouted.

"I'll have to do some forensics. Infrastructure auditing didn't reveal anything problematic." Rain tried to keep her composure, but it was difficult to disguise her anxiety and the slight shaking on her hands.

"Find the hole, this is very serious! Are you listening? We're not paying you to sit at home and play on your computer, this is your responsibility!"

As annoying as the yelling was, she found that the despair of this man to get rid of all responsibility drove him to make some pretty bold claims, claims that hurt her pride.

"There are many ways this could have happened, not necessarily an attack from outside that exploited your defense against threats that come from the Internet but something internal, an employee inserting an infected SD card or pen drive for instance …"

"The people working here are not idiots!"

"I'm not implying that, but this sort of thing …"

"They are all trained, there is a very strict policy against SD cards and pen drives on our machines," he interrupted.

"Sure, but it still can happen, people make these sorts of mistakes all the time."

"It seems to me that you're trying to weasel your way out of this."

"Not at all, like I told you, I need to do some forensics before claiming anything."

"Then do it."

Rain grabbed her laptop and started the investigation. After a while she got a sample from the malware responsible for the attack.

"Ok, this is new."

This malware targeted a specific software installed on the affected machines using an exploit that she has never seen. This attack was elegant, smart and efficient. She didn't understand the whole logic of the program, but the code took advantage of a specific feature on a printer within the network, allowing the attacker to insert some of his own code thus giving him administrator privileges: a complete take-over.

Jealousy built up in her eyes, she was a competent professional, but not extraordinary. To pull something like this you need to be way ahead of the competition. Rain took the sample and ran home. The toxic corporate environment was already getting to her. She grabbed a cigarette and smoked outside the subway station, still shaking from being yelled at by Mr. Booker's Project Manager.

"It's not my fault," she told herself. "Some idiot put an SD card in a computer. Happens every week."

Even if they were compromised over the Internet, she couldn't prevent every possible attack on every possible device on this huge network, right?

She finished the cigarette and dashed home as fast as the barely functional subway allowed. This was one of these days where all your insecurities were poked.

CHAPTER FOUR

Benjamin uploaded a new video, simply titled "So I'm not real." On this 20-minute rant JB argued that this revelation wouldn't hinder his productivity. "This channel is not going to die because of this. It's meaningless, my mission was not to present you a face or a body, it is to present and discuss ideas. This relentless witch hunt is an attack on free speech!" Benjamin, despite being exposed as a ghost, was still using his ghost persona: a black-haired man using a long, but well kept, graying beard.

Rain didn't love JB or agree with everything he said, but found his rants amusing enough to warrant some late nights of binge watching. And he was right, who cares about his appearance? Maybe he just wanted to keep himself anonymous, maybe he didn't want to deal with people like Mr. Booker bringing him to court. Well, those sex tapes *could* be real! Who knows? In the good old days if you didn't want to be identified on the Internet you used a ski mask or presented yourself as an animal avatar or something, this was basically the same thing, she thought.

Now that she updated herself on the latest e-drama she resumed work, the malware that she brought home was too much to chew; time to bring a third-party's help. While this was not technically allowed by her contract, she found it to be better than to do a lousy job.

Mark was a beast at malware analysis, one of the top dogs in a huge multinational company and an old college friend, he was a valuable asset when extra input or ideas were needed. Rain sent him the sample and waited for his feedback. About 2 hours later she got a text:

"Hey, can you meet me in the coffee shop? I really don't like giving feedback over the Internet and this one looks like a piece of work."

"Understatement of the year, alright, I'll be there in 20."

This coffee shop was their usual go-to place to get stuff done, it had decent WiFi, was quiet enough and power sockets were always available. It was a chain coffee shop which made Mark a bit uncomfortable, these places are exploitative and parasitic by nature according to him. There were around 20 places of the same chain in the city, all with the same minimalistic, nordic style decoration. It was sickening to him. But they were convenient and cheap.

"So the bug in this printer you said the malware was taking advantage of ..." Mark paused and turned his laptop's screen to Rain. "This is new, this piece of code in particular, this was what you were talking about right?" He pointed at the piece of code that made Rain reconsider her competence.

"Yeah, that's what made me realize that this was not a complete idiot going after low-hanging fruit." Rain turned her eyes away from the code and straight into Mark. "Wait, what do you mean by new? Is this a *zero-day*?!"

"Looks like it."

A zero-day is the holy grail of a security professional. This means that the hacker who programmed this malware had the knowledge of a weak point in this specific software that no one else in the world had. This is huge. Zero-days are rare. You're lucky to find a zero-day in a year working full-time. And to find one *and* use it in a real attack? This was not some kid in his mom's basement.

"Wait, holy shit, who made this?" Rain asked. It was clear they were dealing with something on a whole other league.

"That's not even the best part!"

"What could possibly be better than a zero-day?"

Mark looked straight at her with a smile.

"Three of them."

CHAPTER FIVE

Rain tuned in on her favorite podcast. She didn't want to deal with any more work today. This malware situation was complete and utter bullshit.

"I do not deserve this, no one deserves this, you'd need to beat baby penguins with a club to deserve this." She grabbed a cigarette, the pack was drying up way too fast. "I'm an average security person trying to pay rent, the bills and not die. I don't want to be put against someone who pulls three zero-days out of his ass. No, absolutely not."

Today's guest on the podcast was a PhD on AI discussing the recent phenomena concerning the use of ghosts in mainstream society:

"It's not only that we can fabricate people. We can fabricate people that mirror the image we want," he said, in an excited tone. "You can throw in the data set you want and a person comes out, you can personify concepts!"

"Concepts? Like love or hope?" the podcast's host asked, in a confused but curious tone.

"Make a data set with all of what people associate with 'love' or 'hope' and we can turn it into a person."

The next day was another drag, Rain had to do grocery

shopping, which implied another trip to the outside world and Mark insisted on another meeting to discuss the malware situation. Right outside the building was her neighbor from the apartment below. Mrs. Quinn was a 40-something typical woman, graying hair, mellow hazel eyes that do not lift from the screen of her smartphone.

With the rise of AI-powered services, certain, more out there, services were offered. Imagine an AI capable of learning from all of the chats, all posts on social media from a certain person, if this software can accurately absorb language mannerisms, vocabulary and opinions it is possible to produce a sort of chatbot which replicates a person's presence online. One of the most unsettling applications of this principle is to manufacture a sort of online immortality. Certain moms have been found to be spending days talking with an AI-copy of their dead sons. Since Quinn's son died in a car crash one year ago this was basically her life.

"Imagine spending hours upon hours talking with a cold unconscious pseudo-AI," Mark answered when Rain told him about Mrs. Quinn's new hobby.

"If it *feels* like their son enough for them to spend so much time talking to it, I'd say it's impressive enough as a piece of tech and, who knows, maybe one day we can actually manufacture a truly alive *chatbot* out of dead person's online presence," retorted Rain.

"Are you familiar with the Chinese Room?"

"I don't think so."

"It's a thought experiment. Imagine you're locked in a room with a bunch of Chinese characters and an instruction manual containing exact instructions on what to answer in Chinese, given a certain input, again, in Chinese."

"So basically, a stupidly large book containing *if/then* statements?"

"Yes, that's it. Now, you don't know a word of Chinese, however if you receive a message from a native Chinese speaker you are able, using this godly instruction book, to assemble an answer to any question in perfect Chinese. From the perspective of this messenger, outside of the room, you are a perfect Chinese speaker. But could you really say you know the language?"

"Well, my first thought would be obviously not."

"And that's, in a nutshell, a rather convincing argument on why 'strong' AI isn't possible. You're giving a machine an extensive, precise instruction set on how to interpret a certain input and what output is acceptable. Even though it spits out convincing answers, you can't in good faith argue that the machine is conscious."

"Nevertheless, this hypothetical Chinese speaker is completely convinced."

"Absolutely."

"Then what difference does it make?"

"On a surface level none, however we can confidently say a machine that transforms input A into output B using a sort of ultra-advanced formal grammar isn't *alive*."

"Aren't we basically that after all? According to certain stimuli we exhibit certain behavior according to our 'program' which 'code' is a combination of education and nature. It does seem a bit silly to argue what's truly 'human' or 'conscious' if we can't tell what makes us conscious or human."

"Alright, we are hitting some impossible questions, we already have enough hardship on our hands with this piece of evil work." Mark returned his focus to the open text editor on his laptop.

"Right, right, so about those zero-days, should we report them for *bug bounty* money?" Rain's dark eyes shined. Certain companies have bug bounty programs that allow freelance hackers to report found security bugs on their products, usually for a monetary reward.

"Yeah, about that, I really don't like that idea."

"Why not? It's flawless, it's not like this mysterious hacker is going to tell on us."

"Three zero-days, Rain. Three of them. All of them on devices that your client *coincidentally* just happened to own on his internal network. This is not a fat dude in his underwear posting screenshots of his attacks on the Internet for street cred."

"What do you mean?"

"This smells awfully like the work of a nation-state," said Mark as he rubbed his eyes pushing his glasses up. "My advice would be to cover this up, tell Booker's people that someone opened an infected email attachment or something."

"What if they find out? My career would be over."

"If they had the ability to find this out by themselves you wouldn't have been hired."

"Point taken."

She was unsatisfied with this conclusion. Of course, she never dreamed of actually catching the perpetrator. But, goddamn, just calling it quits by submitting a fake report and forgetting that she ever saw this amazing malware didn't feel right. If she dug just a little bit more maybe, just maybe, she could find evidence of who was behind this, but she lacked the skills to do this by herself and Mark didn't want to get mixed in on this.

"Fuck it."

Rain opened a bug bounty platform. The company that made one of the devices affected by this malware had a public bounty program. The prize money for a bug, similar to the one exploited by the zero-days, was $10,000.

"Fuck it."

She submitted a report detailing how the zero-days worked and copy pasted the snippet of code from the malware to the report, showing a proof-of-concept for this bug. She pressed "submit."

"Fuck it."

CHAPTER SIX

A few weeks went by. Rain was a bit nervous, the bug report was an impulsive move but she couldn't possibly contain that secret to herself. The following days were typical, the depressingly cold, grey, albeit cozy, days continued and Rain was, as usual, doing a mix of heavy procrastination and security auditing. After her third coffee mug and fourth cigarette an email arrived in her inbox:

Dear Mrs. Wynn:

Due to a contractual breach (Section V, article 6), we are terminating you from your contractual obligations, effective immediately.

Best Regards

The dry tone of the email didn't match Rain's mood at all. Her stomach sank, she fetched a copy of the contract and looked for the so-called *Section V, article 6* she was barely able to go through the pages of the contract due to her shaky hands. Losing both the job at the campaign and the supermarket chain was not an immediate sentence to homelessness but a contractual breach like this could seriously damage her career. Word travels fast in the world of Information Security.

What was written in *Section V*, article 6 left her more puzzled than angry or anxious:

6 - Under no circumstances should confidential information resulting of the security auditing leave the authorized devices or be presented to anyone not in possession of the required security clearance to handle such information.

Rain had intense paranoia about handling information. Since most of this job relied on confidentiality she exercised extreme care about what data was in her possession and tried to keep everything required to be present on her devices encrypted.

Given that, this termination was absolute nonsense. Then came a phone call. "Booker PM" showed up on the screen.

"I'm just confirming that you've received the email. We'll probably see each other in court."

"Wait, you're pressing charges? I haven't leaked anything, where's the evidence?"

"I'm emailing it to you."

She opened the email's attachment. An audio file started to play:

"So, you received the documentation I sent you, there is clear evidence that the CFO is going to resign soon," a voice, that appeared to be Rain's, said.

"This is absolutely huge, for sure their stock prices are going to be hit," another voice said.

The audio went on for a few more seconds, discussing this dramatic information. Rain was not impressed.

"Nice conversation with your reporter friend," said Booker's PM.

"This could be literally anyone," she said.

"Voice recognition matches with yours," replied Booker's PM.

"Could be a ghost."

"I hired a specialized team; they found no evidence of such thing."

"This is absolutely bogus; this evidence won't hold up in court."

"The leaked documents have your watermark." Rain froze, her whole body shut down for a few seconds.

Every employee had a personal card that granted access to doors, elevators, computers and certain applications. When you logged onto an internal application and downloaded anything, said application watermarked the documents. It was trivial to check who was responsible for the leakage unless you removed this watermark. Rain knew about this system, everyone knew about this. However, this signature is mathematically impossible to forge, if a document had someone's watermark, it was almost certain that's who that copy came from. While the thesis that she leaked the information was absurd given her knowledge of the system, this was foolproof evidence legally speaking.

Someone set her up, the person behind it however remained a mystery.

"Motherfucker …"

CHAPTER SEVEN

She logged remotely into one of Booker's servers that she had previously hacked into. Rain, enraged, looked for evidence on the identity of the attacker. Not only was she now very much deep into criminal territory, this mysterious hacker most likely hadn't left a note with cut out letters spelling a riddle waiting a smart detective to find it and solve it. Nevertheless, she still looked into this far-fetched possibility.

Once again, she stumbled on a bunch of incomprehensible code. Rain had no time to look into it. Actually, that was no longer her job, but this piece of weird code could be something left by the attacker before the data ex-filtration.

"Machine learning."

AI ... all AI. But *what was it learning to do*? To find out, she dug the data feed into the machine. After scrambling through walls of code she found the input to this giant neural network. It did not get any easier.

"Well, an all-nighter it is," she said.

Rain grabbed her phone and rang Mark.

"I really shouldn't get involved in your little psychotic episode," said Mark.

"But you really couldn't resist the draw of adventure," replied Rain. Mark was setting up his laptop on Rain's cramped desk, littered with receipts, books and USB cables of every kind. He cracked an energy drink open and began to analyze the code.

"So basically, you think this was planted by the

hacker," Mark said.

"I mean, I absolutely did not take part in that phone conversation," Rain said.

"You think the hacker somehow used an *avant-garde* voice replication technique to incriminate you and … left the evidence right on his target's machine."

"Look, I don't know, it's just that it seems to fit the narrative and someone somehow produced an exact replica of my voice, a replica so good that even a specialist can't find marks of it being generated."

Rain and Mark stayed in silence for a couple of hours, trying to reverse engineer the purpose of this learning algorithm with only the sound of keys, clicks and the occasional airplane in the background.

"I think I'm starting to get it, the data set is very far from being readable as it is but … look," Mark said.

Mark isolated a few words from the huge data set. As a whole it was not human-readable, which was normal when it comes to this kind of thing, you can't just throw in the whole works of Shakespeare to an AI and expect the machine to become a legendary writer, the input has to be trimmed down to its essentials to the core of what is actually needed, going from this core to the original format was not always a direct affair. In this case, Mark found words like "hope," "democracy," "people."

"Is this like a … speech?" Rain said.

"Kind of," Mark said.

"Is … is this motherfucker using AI to generate speeches?"

"I'm not entirely surprised if that's the case."

"I mean, it's clever, but wow, fuck." Rain threw herself into her tiny, badly maintained sofa.

"This does not solve your problem however, there is no evidence of voice generation or anything like it," said Mark.

"There's already AI in there, might be part of the same project, there was a ton of material in there."

They scrolled through miles of code and destroyed two bags of store brand chips until the pieces of the puzzle started to fall in place. Rain stood up, grabbed a cigarette and lit it. The data being fed into the AI wasn't only speeches. They found something more "human" in there, personality traits, actions associated with certain personality traits, data from Churchill, Abraham Lincoln, even Hitler. Cultural DNA fed this software, data from all of the most successful and well-known leaders in history.

"You know I hate that," said Mark, waving a hand in protest to the smoke.

"You don't get it. It's not just the speeches, it's everything," said Rain.

"Everything?" asked Mark.

"It's a fucking ghost."

Mark stood in silence and thought about her words, Rain was on her feet, cigarette in one hand, mouse in the other, she scrolled through the recovered data sets to make a point.

"It's all bullshit," said Rain.

"But, you met the guy. Everyone has met the guy, he does public appearances regularly, how can he be a composite?"

"There's a vessel for the ghost I guess."

"Please elaborate," replied Mark.

"This is not just a speech generator. This is a politics generator; speeches are just a component. This whole … thing … is generating a person."

"Like a ghost."

"Yes."

"They are generating the 'perfect' politician?"

"Hmm, yeah you could say that."

"But Booker exists, he's a person."

"That's what I was saying. He's a vessel."

"An actor?"

"Something like that."

Booker existed but he didn't, his words, look and even mannerisms were not his. Mr. Booker was the shell of the ghost, a way of the code to interact with the real world, a mere actor.

His voters were trying to elect not a person, instead, an idea. If this worked, democracy, much like tic-tac-toe, was a solved game.

"There is a precedent now," said Mark. "Are we already being ruled over by AI over proxy?" Rain sat down and rested her head on the palms of her hands, still processing what this all meant.

"How many people are actually ghosts? How many of my acquaintances are actors?" said Rain.

"When our parents and grandparents complained about 'fake' people on social media they were onto something," said Mark.

"All human interaction is now performance. What do we make of all this?"

"We'll keep this under wraps, of course."

"Why of course? Isn't it like a civic duty to expose this?"

"For what purpose?" replied Mark. "He's giving them what people want. Why does it matter how he managed to figure out what they wanted in the first place?"

Mark was right, the cost/benefit relation to uncover all of this conspiracy was completely not worth the trouble.

"But … why would this hacker try to incriminate you anyway?" asked Mark.

"I may have submitted a bug report with one of those zero-days," replied Rain.

"Dude ... I clearly told you to … fuck, never mind."

Too exhausted to get mad, Mark tried to summarize the situation: "Booker's strongest evidence that you were the person on the tape talking with the reporter is the smart card you guys use to log in, right?"

"Right."

"You still have remote access to their systems, is there any chance you can access the database with the smart cards' keys? Maybe you could ..."

"Ohhhhh that's so illegal," Rain said.

"I mean, if that signature is changed there's nothing they can do, right?" Mark said.

"I don't like it, but I also don't like jail," replied Rain. Mark shut his laptop down and grabbed his jacket.

"Just keep me out of this."

CHAPTER EIGHT

Rain rolled on her bed and stared at her mobile phone's screen. Most of her social media feed was auto-generated clickbait articles written by AI. She received job offers on a professional social network sent by non-existent human resources employees and some of the actual existent humans online were merely performing an optimized character. Human interaction, life itself, was becoming theater. All of the ancient metaphors comparing life to theater and equating people with mere actors following a script were becoming literal. And all of this was fine, no moral panic concerning technology has ever produced anything of note.

* * *

Discussion Questions

1. The story talks about a "Chinese Room," a place with an enormous book of if/then statements that tell a non-Chinese speaker how to respond to every possible question asked to them in Chinese. In this hypothetical scenario, can it be said that the person "speaks" or knows Chinese? Is it the exact approximation of Chinese speech that makes you a Chinese speaker, or something else?

2. How are you, as a person, different than the "Chinese Room" thought problem? Are you more than a series of if/then statements accumulated over time? Isn't your answer to the above question exactly what an if/then statement book would tell you to say? (**Turing Test**)

3. Does it matter if entertainment personalities are ghosts and not real people? How is a ghost actor in an action movie in the future any different than an animated character in an animated movie today? Does the fact that the ghost is so good it tricks you, matter?

4. Would you feel comfortable having a ghost serve in other roles, such as a doctor, police officer, or teacher? If perfection (and lack of bias) is the point, shouldn't you want someone doing the job that never makes a mistake?

5. Are you okay with the ghost candidate in the story? Is the goal of a politician to be the perfect reflection of the desires of the people he/she represents? If so, what is wrong with programming that information and taking away the personal bias or corruptibility of a real person?

Father Dale's Drive-
Thru Exorcisms

Viggy Parr Hampton

THE EVANGELISTS set the tent up somewhere near a Christian theme park called Heritage USA in Fort Mill, South Carolina. The park had been open for nearly a year, and the crowds had ballooned grotesquely, which spelled probable success for the old preacher hunting for the faithful.

To Dale, standing outside his camper and straddling the messy periphery of religion, the park's very existence and its incredible popularity were two more pieces of evidence he could hold up to prove that the majority of middle America had too much time and too much money on their hands.

Which made him feel less bad, maybe even righteous, about being just one more person trying to take it away.

"You gonna help, or what?" Tina asked, pushing folds of sweaty hair out of her face. She was struggling to set up the camper's awning, stretching it as far as it would go while simultaneously trying to jam the poles into the gravelly dirt below.

"Or what," Dale teased, pushing his sunglasses up on

his nose. He walked over to where his wife stood, and the two of them managed to wrangle the faded, delicate awning into the perfect position. To some veteran campers, an awning didn't need to be perfect, just serviceable. To Dale and Tina Thrombus, anything less than perfect would mean that their car-bound customers would get trapped in the drive-thru, which was simply not an option.

They'd been following the crazy evangelists around the Southeast for the past five years, parking the camper close enough to the revival tent to attract customers, but far enough away to avoid the righteous fury of the fire-tongued pastor. He might have preached love, but Dale had heard enough to realize the man knew how to deal in hate.

The camper needed a new coat of paint and the awning needed new metal struts, but money was tight and getting tighter. The oil crisis of '73 was long over, but good working folk like Dale and Tina were still feeling the squeeze, and it was starting to look like another crisis was on the horizon. When Dale had retired, Tina had quit her lunch lady job, and they'd sold the tiny shack in Indiana, packed up the few belongings they thought worth keeping, and bought a used camper. Dale figured they'd want to travel around because what else was there to do anyway, especially in rural Indiana? The camper was far more freeing, not to mention economical.

Until 1973 hit. For a couple reliant on cheap gas to fuel their cross-country travels, the oil crisis gouged their savings. They spent nearly a year stuck in a trailer park in Edmond, Oklahoma, hoping to save money while remaining in a climate warm enough to be comfortable throughout the winter without running the heater. Their small jar of cash began to look emptier and emptier, so they took to washing windshields, pumping water, cleaning spidery outhouses, chopping wood for cook fires—whatever needed doing badly enough that somebody would pay them for it. When things started to turn around, and they'd saved up some of that money, they set off in search of a significant change of scenery.

They found that in Savannah, Georgia. The Spanish moss swayed above the camper's roof like Southern mistletoe as they drove through gorgeous streets lined with live oaks and magnolia trees. They parked near the river, on the outskirts of downtown, and hugged each other as the river flowed melodically past.

It had always been just the two of them—they'd tried for children, bouncing from doctor to doctor, each time hoping for a diagnosis other than "I'm sorry, Mrs. Thrombus, but you will never be able to conceive, much less carry a child to term." Dale had suggested adoption, but Tina had declined, feeling exhausted and as though she'd failed as a woman, as a wife. Dale had been sweet, holding her when she cried for the family they'd never have, dabbing at her tears with his soft thumbs. They cleaved closer together from then on, determined to make a home that could be full with only two people.

Savannah had been kind to them; they'd stayed for a few months, eating pecan pralines and fluffy biscuits, touring the city's haunted hot spots, and snapping pictures on their disposable camera, knowing full well they would never waste money on developing the film. When summer started coming on, and the humidity was so deep it filled every pore to the brim, Tina pulled on Dale's sleeve, and it was time to go.

They went north, hugging the coast, heading for North Carolina. In Hollywood, a small town just outside of Charleston, they stopped to stock up on groceries and find a water line they could hook up to so they could take quick, icy showers. The small clearing they settled on, designated as a rest area by a single tiny, dejected sign, was grim—an old well and water pump constituted the few signs of life. There weren't even any outhouses to clean, a detail Tina filed away for later, in case another oil crisis sent them begging for labor, for something. At least they wouldn't have much competition for resources around here; only one other camper lounged in that lonely spot, and the ivy spilling from its cracked windows suggested it had found its final resting place.

Later, the sound of singing reached their ears as they chomped into the first bites of hot dogs roasted over a camp stove. Tina was sitting in an old lawn chair, and Dale was standing, stretching his legs after the long drive. He squeezed a ketchup packet pilfered from a McDonald's onto his hot dog, and managed to squirt a good portion of it onto his thumb. He licked it off with relish.

"You hear that?" Tina asked, pushing the words through a mouthful of hot dog.

"Sounds like singing," Dale said, gurgling his own words through the puddle of ketchup on his tongue.

"Sounds like a lot of singing," Tina said, stuffing the

last of her dog into her mouth and swallowing hard. She stood up and stretched her arms above her head. "Let's go check it out."

"Why?" Dale said, pausing his meal to pull another pilfered condiment—mustard this time—from his pocket and squeeze that on top of the bun, meat, and ketchup.

"Why not?" Tina said, shrugging. "What else we gonna do around here?"

"Hm," Dale said, chewing, savoring the juicy meat, the sweetness of the ketchup, the acidity of the mustard. He was not one to rush through meals as his wife did, seeing eating as a chore.

"Come on," she said, "We could use the walk anyway. We've been driving around in that damned camper all day."

Dale popped the last of the hot dog into his mouth, chewing longer than was really required, as though he were squeezing every last bit of flavor out of the mass before he allowed it to slither down his throat. He finally swallowed and said, "Eh. Okay."

Wiping his hands on his shorts, Dale followed his wife as she piloted them towards the singing that grew ever louder not just because they were getting closer, but because more people were joining in. When they got close enough to hear the words, parting shrubbery as they passed out of the clearing, they realized the song was a well-worn hymn that Tina learned in Sunday School. She thought about adding her voice to the melee, but decided against it—she wasn't a woman of God anymore, so it seemed phony.

They walked hand in hand along a rocky path through the scruffy forest until they came to a large grassy clearing. In the middle, a gleaming white tent spilling over with people sat like a beacon.

"Huh," Dale said, giving her hand a squeeze. "What is that?"

"Some sort of church service?"

"You ever been to a church service in the middle of a field?"

In fact, Tina had. Once, as a girl, she'd visited her grandmother in McKinney, Texas, the same week a traveling preacher happened to alight in the small town. He'd brought his entire entourage, and they'd erected a tent not unlike the one they now stood before, calling God's children to hear the Word of the Lord. Grandmother had taken little Tina, dressed in her Sunday best, and sat in the second row—only because she was a half second too late to nab the coveted first row spots. The preacher, whose name had been Morris, started softly, speaking of God's love for all man and his capacity for forgiveness, but as he picked up steam and warmed to his audience, his voice rose higher, louder, as he spoke of God's similarly colossal capacity for vengeance against sinners and fornicators. To protect ourselves, he'd said, we must expunge the devil from our lives!

Tina didn't like to revisit what happened next—when she thought about it at all, the experience came in flashes: slippery snakes slithering over her new patent leather shoes, a man who happened to be the town pharmacist gripping her shoulders, shaking her, speaking in a language she couldn't understand, her grandmother's neighbor Mrs. Desmond shivering violently as if with fever, then collapsing in a moaning puddle onto the snake-littered floor.

They crept closer, her fingers threaded through his, even though Tina started dragging her feet. When they reached the perimeter of bodies huddled at the edges of the tent, spreading over onto the grass, they stopped. The crowd pulsed, as if it were one gargantuan living thing. Body odor and cheap perfume assaulted Tina's nose, tickling the memories she was trying desperately to push away.

She could barely make out the preacher's voice over the din of the crowd. When her ears adjusted, the crowd babble becoming white noise after a few minutes, she could clearly hear the preacher's tone and volume rising together like fireworks to explode at the same time over the heads of the sweaty flock: We must EXPUNGE the DEVIL from our LIVES!

Morris, the nightmare of her childhood, the dark boogeyman under her bed. The reason she expunged religion from her life.

"What the hell …" Tina muttered, earning the ire of the enormous devout woman next to her.

"Watch your language in this house of God," she hissed.

Tina had more sense than to engage and respond how she really wanted to, with "Do you mean a tent of God?"

Tina shifted her attention back to Morris, who was

hobbling around the raised wooden dais ferociously, an aged but still dangerous lion surveying his prey.

Dale nudged her, whispering out of the side of his mouth. "What a load of crap, huh?"

She squeezed his hand and flashed him a smile, hoping he didn't see the discomfort in her eyes. Dale had never been one for religion, which had been one characteristic of many that cemented his position as her forever husband, but that didn't mean that she completely shared his nonchalance. She'd loved church once; she liked being a good little Sunday School girl for her parents to dress up and show off. But after Morris, after the snakes and the tongues and the fainting, she'd felt hollow, convinced that below its layers of love and security, religion, and by extension God, was nothing more than an empty hole people filled rather arbitrarily.

"And YOU, precious LAMB of GOD," Morris yelled, pointing at something near the front of the tent. "What is YOUR NAME?"

Tina couldn't hear the response, but Morris's next words were "Please COME up on the STAGE, child." Ten seconds later, a tiny girl, who couldn't have been much older than four, appeared at the edge of the dais. Tina could tell this girl's parents loved her; she was dressed in an immaculate blue satin dress, a white sash tied at her waist. Her shoes were shiny white patent leather Mary Janes, and the small stretch of leg between her shoes and the hem of her dress was clad in white stockings. A giant blue and white bow crowned her blond ringlets. Her rosy cheeks looked like ripe crabapples.

"Maryann, CHILD," Morris boomed, "Come sit and HEAR the WORD of the LORD."

Maryann hesitated, shy, before she managed to take a few steps toward Morris. She sat down at his left, facing him, so that Tina could still see her profile. The little girl carefully adjusted her dress so that it wouldn't be wrinkled when she stood back up.

"FRIENDS, good PEOPLE of the LORD," said Morris. "LAY your EYES upon Maryann, LAMB of GOD."

The crowd was silent, enamored, hungry.

"God WANTS us to be GOOD. He CAN forgive us when we're BAD, but we MUST EXPIATE OUR SINS and ATONE. Is little Maryann a SINNER?"

There was a loud gasp from the crowd; Tina presumed it was the girl's mother, shocked at the thought that her perfect child had or would ever do anything wrong.

"Well? IS SHE?"

The crowd murmured something incoherent. Morris was not deterred.

"She IS, friends of GOD, we are ALL SINNERS, even little Maryann."

Maryann bowed her head on the stage, ashamed. Tina's heart started to break.

"Now, Maryann's SINS are probably very SMALL, as she is. BUT that DOESN'T MEAN they aren't THERE, that she mustn't ATONE for them." Morris paused, a dramatic effect Tina could recall painfully from her first traumatizing encounter with him. His flair for theatrics had further convinced her of the performative nature of religion, its complete lack of solid substance.

Morris went on: "And HOW exactly should Maryann ATONE, my FRIENDS of GOD?" He started pacing back and forth across the stage again, slapping his hands into the air to punctuate his speech. "Tell me! HOW?"

"The trial of snakes!" yelled someone from the middle of the crowd. It sounded like a man.

"YES!" Morris nearly screamed. He pulled a handkerchief from his pants pocket and swiped it across his forehead. "The TRIAL of SNAKES!"

Tina grabbed Dale, who up until that point had been watching silently, an amused look on his face. "We're leaving," she said, tugging him away. Her voice came out cramped, her throat tight. She felt like she was choking, blackness already floating at the edges of her vision.

"You think they're really going to snake that little girl?" he asked quietly, still looking amused.

"I know they will," she said, pulling him harder, fighting a wave of nausea that sought to resurrect her hastily eaten hot dog.

The smirk left Dale's face, melting away like butter in a hot pan. "What?" he said in a small voice.

"I don't want to be here for it," she said, eyes down.

They hustled back to the gravelly path that led through the woods, heading for their camper. Morris's voice still drifted towards them, shouting something that sounded like "EXORCISE THE SINS FROM THIS CHILD."

"Shouldn't we do something?" Dale asked.

"Like what? Intervene? Shout? And have two hundred idiotic and bloodthirsty parishioners pounce on us? I don't think so."

"I guess it's in God's hands now," Dale said, with a trace of dark humor.

"That's not funny," Tina said.

Dale frowned, chastened. "I guess not." He didn't know what else to say, how else to reach her. He could tell she was pulling inward.

They didn't speak again until they were back inside the camper.

In the intervening years between that night in Hollywood and right now in Fort Mill, Tina had had a lot of time to think. She thought about Morris, about revivals in general, and she visited the local library to read more about snakes, speaking in tongues, and exorcisms. She wanted to better understand the enemy that had made her feel so small, so powerless—as a child and then again as an adult. Luckily for her, the 1973 release of *The Exorcist* provided two direct benefits for her; the first was immediate—there was now a mountain of material on exorcisms, free and available to anybody who cared to learn more. The second benefit didn't assert itself until a few weeks later, when Tina realized that the answer to their dwindling cash flow could be found in the country's totally unquenched appetite for exorcisms. There was a viable business model in there, somewhere.

The more she read, the less she understood. How did anybody really know if someone was possessed? And if someone was actually possessed, supposing such a thing were possible, would a few prayers and a splash of holy water *really* do a goddamn thing against a demon from Hell? Tina didn't think so. Perhaps exorcisms were like a placebo—meaningless chants that gained power because the victims believed in them. And because they believed, they got better.

Tina spoke with Dale at length about the opportunities she saw in keeping close to the revival tent, no matter how much she hated it. She told him they could perform a public service—provide people with exorcism placebos, maybe shake their faith enough to pull them away from Morris's grip. Plus, make some much-needed cash in the process. What she really thought was she was angry and needed an outlet, they needed money, and screwing over rich idiots was a way to kill two birds with one stone.

"Let me get this straight," Dale said, sitting across from her at the small formica-topped booth of their camper. Outside, the mosquitoes buzzed, and the sound of singing that they'd both gotten so used to they didn't even hear it anymore drifted through their window screens. "You want to do fake exorcisms?"

"Don't think of it as 'fake exorcisms,'" Tina said. "Think of it as making people feel better. And, if we manage to pull people away from that bastard in the process, all the better. Plus, the money, Dale. We could really use it, and the assholes who support Morris should support his victims, too."

"Victims?" Dale asked, his head cocked to the side in confusion like a dog.

Tina caught her breath, still keen to withhold her

trauma from her husband. "You know," she said evasively, "Anybody who believes Morris is also his victim. Stupid, too. Dangerous combination."

"Still," Dale said. "We don't know shit about exorcisms, honey, not really."

Tina's eyes shone. "That's the beauty of it! Nobody else knows shit, either! Better yet, everybody and their mama has seen *The Exorcist* at this point, so people will just expect us to pull a Father Karras. We literally have a blueprint for how to do this."

"I hated that movie," Dale said quietly, remembering how he'd squealed when the demon's face flashed on the screen.

"We could pull out the awning, get a big sign, and have people drive over for exorcisms. Charge five bucks a head, or maybe ten, depending on where we are." Tina's voice turned hard. "If people are going to be idiots, we might as well make some money off 'em." Tina couldn't bear another year of backbreaking work that took her nowhere, leaving her aching, the juice barely worth the squeeze.

"So. You want us to not only pretend to be religious officials, you want us to offer *drive-through exorcisms* and follow around this fucked up revival dickhead. That about right?"

Instead of answering his question, Tina continued musing. "It'll be Halloween soon, I can get a nun costume from the store, we can get you a black robe and cut out a bit of white paper for that collar thing, get some crucifixes, some little glass bottles for holy water …"

"Dear God," Dale said.

"That's the spirit."

Dale was a born follower, which Tina didn't mind because he always followed her.

***

That was nearly five years ago, and Dale and Tina were in much the same position they'd been in before. They were seeing the signs of another coming oil crisis, which meant they might be stuck for the foreseeable future next to the human cesspool of Heritage USA. While this sounded repugnant to Dale, he wouldn't mind catching a glimpse of Tammy Faye—she was tacky, but that didn't mean she wasn't an attractive woman. Dale had even heard a rumor that Jim and Tammy Faye kept a secret room somewhere on the park grounds for trysts. Now wouldn't that be something?

The sun was beginning to set, which meant Morris, now definitively couched in old age, would start bellowing soon. Dale and Tina needed to get everything ready for another night of hopefully booming business.

They finished their cold-in-the-middle hot dogs and went inside to outfit themselves. Dale pulled on his black robe and clipped his white collar on; over the years, he'd upgraded to a plastic collar. He lifted a rosary over his head and dropped it down around his neck, becoming Father Dale.

Nearby, Tina pulled on the same nun Halloween costume she'd had for five years; she'd had to make substantial modifications to it—lengthening the hem, turning the crucifix right-side-up, patching holes in the cheap fabric as they cropped up. She pulled the wimple down over her hair, and she became Sister Tina.

***

They'd had some good times over the years; 1976 brought *Hostage to the Devil* and a new wave of exorcism mania. Business had flourished, and they'd even been able to replace the brakes on their camper and upgrade their mini fridge.

Despite the deception that paid for the gas in the tank, Dale relished the grand adventure they'd stumbled upon. For too long, they'd been mired in the suburban muck of Indiana, working their way through dead-end, joyless jobs, neighborhood bake sales, and uncomfortable dinner parties where their neighbors couldn't seem to talk about anything other than their children. Dale had grilled more burgers for backyard barbecues than he could possibly count; Tina estimated her lifetime output of pies to be around two thousand five hundred. Dale hadn't realized how much the monotony was killing him until he'd hit the road with Tina, his lungs expanding with not just the fresh air but the *new* air, the *new* skies, the *new* roads. He hadn't been to the doctor in years, but if he were to go at this point in 1979, he would have been pleased but unsurprised to find his blood pressure had dropped significantly. It also didn't hurt that he was able to claim some power, even if it was under false pretenses. Dale Thrombus was a mild-mannered, go-along-to-get-along, rather pudgy sort of guy. But Father Dale—he was strong, capable, *powerful* in a way Dale had never felt before. The persona was like a drug to him, the performance of "exorcism" an addiction.

While Dale floated on a cloud of wanderlust and undeserved authority, Tina felt much more grounded in dirty reality. She'd never meant to push this scheme as far as it had gone; initially, she'd seen their little con as a way to push back at the twisted preacher shouting from the dais, get some due revenge, and part stupid rich people from their money. Five years later, and she wasn't even sure Morris knew they existed, and their savings at this point were nothing to write home about.

As for the people they "exorcised"—were they better off? She didn't really care, but she did think about it from time to time, less frequently as the years rolled by. When it came down to it, she just wanted the money, to hell with everything else.

But now she was stuck. Dale had changed, becoming more commanding, more dominant, less willing to listen to her. On top of that, as they camped outside of Heritage USA, growing queasy from the smell of butter-saturated popcorn and sticky caramel apples, she started hearing rumors, tidbits of conversation or news here and there, about another oil crisis that would rock the country hard, just like the one in 1973. Privately, Tina wasn't sure if she would survive this again.

Dale, on the other hand, wasn't experiencing anywhere near his wife's level of despair; so what if they had to get stuck here for awhile? They were in better circumstances now than they had been back in '73—they had a steady gig, their upgraded mini fridge was still operational, and while he wasn't thrilled about being stuck next to the disgustingly consumerist idolatry of Heritage USA, he continued to hope that he might one day get to see Tammy

Faye. He wanted to get close enough to know whether those eyelashes were actually spider legs, as some people claimed.

The oil crisis, if it came, would wear itself out just like the last one had, Dale was certain.

***

Headlights flashed through the camper's windows as Tina tucked her hair back inside her wimple. Dale jiggled his collar, readjusting it until he found the most comfortable position.

"You got the holy water?" Dale asked.

"Yep," Tina said, patting the pocket in her habit where three small bottles filled with sulfur-scented South Carolina well water clanked together with every step.

"Showtime," Dale said. Tina rolled her eyes, but she was careful not to let him see.

They opened the door, faces solemn, as the old Buick crunched over the gravel to come to rest under the camper's awning. Squinting, Tina could make out three figures in the car: a scruffy man driving, a nervous-looking woman in the passenger seat, and a writhing, bucking figure in the back—probably their child.

Tina sighed. She hated having to pretend to pull demons out of children who were either actually ill or so wrapped up in their parents' delusions that they'd lost touch with reality.

The scruffy man rolled down the window. His eyes darted back and forth from Dale to Tina.

"We need help, Father," he said. "Frank Junior got the

~ 266 ~

devil in 'im."

In the passenger seat, his wife just hung her head, burying her face in her hands.

From the backseat, Frank Junior coughed and then laughed wildly, limbs thrashing against the cracked leather.

"Well, you've come to the right place, my child," Dale said. "We know just how to help."

"I don't got much money," the man said with a twang, avoiding Dale's eye. "I can't pay much."

"Please," Dale said. "Just give what you can." He gestured to Tina. "Sister Tina will collect the tithe and then we can begin the ritual."

A sob erupted from the passenger seat. She moved forward mercilessly, a small black velvet bag in hand, to collect the few pennies this poor family could spare. The man, his hand shaking, dropped a few coins in the bag then slumped back in the seat, defeated. The coins obviously didn't add up to the five dollars they normally charged; she signaled discreetly to Dale to make it quick, nothing fancy for these low-paying customers.

"Thank you, my child," Dale said as Tina glided back in place by his side, head bowed in "prayer." "Let us begin."

That night's ritual started about the same as they all had—Dale climbed into the backseat next to Frank Junior, and Tina stood near the open car door at his side, prepared to hand him the various "holy" implements he would ask for. As the parents twisted in their seats to watch, greasy tears streaking down their cheeks, Dale raised a crucifix and recited the Lord's Prayer, followed by "In the name of the Father, the Son, and the Holy Ghost, I cast thee out!" He repeated this speech five or six times, as the boy continued to writhe next to him. From her spot on the dry grass, Tina could see the boy's cherry-red face caught in the bright rectangle of light streaming from the camper's windows.

Dale placed a hand on Frank Junior's chest, and the boy let out a long, low wail. Tina shivered, goosebumps popping up on her skin with so much force it was almost painful. She didn't believe a sound like that could come from anything but a creature in unimaginable pain. Something was different this time, but Dale didn't notice, or maybe just didn't care.

"I cast thee out, demon!" Dale said, his voice beginning to rise. "In the name of the FATHER, the SON, and the HOLY GHOST, I CAST THEE OUT!" He reached his hand back and Tina quickly, automatically, pressed a vial of water into his palm. He plucked the cap off with a flourish and started splashing it over Frank Junior, all the while repeating "I CAST THEE OUT! I CAST THEE OUT!"

Frank Junior screamed, and Tina noticed with alarm that his cheeks had ripened from cherry to scarlet, and were quickly heading towards violet. Something was very wrong.

Dale still didn't seem to notice the child's genuine distress. Frank Junior started gasping and clawing at his throat. In response, Dale seized his wrists and pinned them down. "I CAST THEE OUT!" Dale shouted in the child's face. Tina was about to reach out a hand and pull her husband back, long-repressed feelings of sympathy bubbling up to the surface. The part of her that had once yearned for children urged her to wrench him out of the car, give this family their money back, and force them to race for the nearest hospital. That neglected piece of her would have done everything she could to get that child the dire medical attention he so desperately needed—if it hadn't been too late.

As Tina's mind idled, her hands still pinned to her sides, Frank Junior's eyes opened wide for the last time. He stopped struggling so abruptly that Dale nearly collapsed along with the boy, who fell back against the seat with a soft thump. His violet cheeks began to pale, and he hitched one last breath before falling silent.

Dale had cast him out.

* * *

Discussion Questions

1. Tina and Dale are both fairly dismissive of the revival and the snake handling. Is it fair for them to be? What makes a legitimate act of faith vs. an illegitimate act of faith? *(Besides, of course, "legitimate acts of the faith are the ones my faith does, because we do it.")*

2. Tina clearly had a traumatic experience as a child at a revival. Should experiences of faith never be traumatic to a child? Are there aspects of faith (such as the crucifixion of Jesus) a child should not be told about so as to spare them the trauma? Where is the line, and what is the rule of where to draw it besides tradition?

3. Who (if anyone) is worse, Tina and Dale performing fake exorcisms or those running the revival that they follow? Does it matter that in <u>both</u> cases people come to them willingly and pay? Does it matter in both cases if it helps them feel better?

4. Why do you suspect the boy in the back of the car died? Do you fault Tina and Dale for his death? If so, what should they have known, and what should they have done? Does Dale's ignorance absolve him?

5. Are the child's parents at fault for his death? Does their faith absolve them? Does their ignorance of his actual affliction? As parents, do they have an obligation to work to not be ignorant and protect their child with the best medical information (at the potential cost of their faith)?

A Community of Peers

Dean Gessie

AFTER THE WAR, I travelled to a village in the south of the province. It was my intention to vacation for the weekend in an unknown land. I followed a small river that was alternately green beneath the foliage of the forest and blue while it coursed through elevated plains and sunken but exposed valleys. I was driving one of those all-terrain vehicles that permitted me to follow paths that were clearly less travelled. It was not an aquatic vehicle, however, and an error in judgment forced me to abandon it to a finely camouflaged bog. I breast-stroked to safety while my truck took water through its sunroof.

With mischance at my back, I followed the river on foot until it opened up into a small lake. On the northern-most shore of the lake, a settlement, of sorts, sprawled upward into black hills, its watery threshold flagged and dotted with light, fishing craft. I walked through vineyards and a peach orchard, each of these bursting with fruit, until I came to what appeared to be the main thoroughfare of the village.

The street was desolate save for mongrels as numerous as flies. They lounged about on their flabby bellies, yawning and blinking in the sun, and, apparently, abandoned by their lords and masters. One of the mongrels, more animated than the rest, fell in behind me wagging its short, stubby tail. I stopped to pet its flank and noticed that its tail had been freshly severed at its point. Remarkably, when the dog craned its long neck to look, as a greyhound might or a horse, the root of its tail became fixed when I clutched the memory of its remainder.

I had little time to contemplate the peculiar psychology of the bitch at my calves. Out of the silence of this place came a young boy running as fast as his legs would take him, huffing and puffing dramatically. I gestured with my arms, like a traffic cop, for him to stop. I would have thought the gesture clear enough to communicate my needs, but the boy sped past me as though my existence were in question, his thin, eager face flushed with purpose and exertion.

I followed with some speed and anxiousness of my own until I saw the lad disappear into a throng of people whose focus elsewhere precluded my seeing their faces. The crowd before me, the emptiness of the village, was mingling about a large and dead tree whose stark grey branches thrust skyward like an ancient hand contorted to hold a crystal ball. There looked to be a hundred or so gathered and they were dressed in the traditional garments of country folk. This struck me as odd since my travels during the war had revealed to me the penetration of the global clothing market.

On tiptoe, I noticed that there was a man of about thirty

tied to the tree, his arms pulled back and around the trunk of it, his hands bound, his head bowed. A two-wheel, wooden cart balanced on long wooden posts stood some five feet to the left of him, its carriage filled with stones.

To confirm my suspicions, I inquired of an elderly gentleman as to the nature of the gathering. The man did not answer my question, but regarded me with astonishment, his nose hairs disentangling and vibrating with each shallow and rapid exhalation. He then proceeded to push his way into the crowd until he broke into the clearing that separated the gathering from its victim. He conferred with a lean, tall gentleman who appeared to be the arbiter of the ceremony and pointed excitedly in my direction. All eyes turned toward me, sized me head to toe. My existence was no longer in question.

The tall man, whom I learned later to be the village mayor, invited me forward with his hand. I and my dog heeded his invitation and walked the corridor made for us by the separating throng.

"You are a stranger?" asked the man.

The question was asinine since the mayor of this small town would surely know better. However, the emotional content in the man's voice was that of a lottery winner overwhelmed by the evidence.

"Yes," I said.

"You have come at an opportune time," he said. "We are about to execute a man."

It was as I suspected. I asked the fellow why, however,

the time should be described as opportune.

"Our people have a custom," he said. "If there is a stranger among us, he is given the honor of casting the first stone. It is our way of including him in the life of the village. It is our way of extending the boundaries of justice, of communicating justice between the communities of the earth."

I congratulated the mayor on the lofty goals of his citizens. Most public officials concern themselves with more modest matters, I said, like keeping drug addicts and hookers off the street. And so it was that I was to represent the cohabitation of time and space with the laws of men. For both sundry and weighty reasons, I queried the crimes of the condemned man.

"For that," said the man, "you will have to trust us. He has been found guilty by due process in a court of his peers. The evidence was overwhelming and indisputable."

I did not betray a smirk, but I had seen more than once overwhelming and indisputable evidence tumble like a house of cards. As a result, I expressed some reticence about firing a death blow under these conditions.

The mayor appeared dismayed that I was making a debate of it, that I wouldn't credit the wisdom of his particular collective.

"Where you are from," he said, "are there executions?"

I assured him that my country took great pleasure in extinguishing the lives of criminals.

"And is your reticence as great when men and women

~ 274 ~

are killed and you have no knowledge of or interest in their crimes?"

I informed the man, as he no doubt wished and anticipated, that I had long ago handed over the responsibility for such decisions and actions.

"Precisely," he said. "You trust others to end the lives of others on your behalf. You tacitly condone their judgements with your indifference and weave the thread of the noose. Will you not trust us this one time and exercise the sovereignty of your will?"

I congratulated the mayor on the quality of his argument, so compelling was it that I felt as though I were on trial as much as the condemned man had been.

"You needn't do it," said the mayor. "It's your free choice to assist or stand aside."

The mayor saw my self-conflict, how my mental processes were virtually stalled, like a large machine creaking inexorably to a halt.

"Are you are baseball player?" he asked.

"No," I said, "I don't have the legs for it. But," I added, "I have been to the fair often and won many prizes for female companions by striking the effigy of a clown's face with a rubber ball."

"Good," he said. "You have both the power and the ability to end the life of this criminal quickly or, at the very least, knock him unconscious so that the cleaning up is less painful for all concerned. I will tell you this," he added. "The women with children will cast the first stones, if you choose not to."

We returned to the front of the gathering. The women in our midst collected their stones from the two-wheel cart. I was provided a large, almost perfectly spherical stone.

I felt my adopted dog, the short-haired mongrel from the street, weaving its way playfully between my legs. I knew that no one could see the lost half of its tail but that she, herself, reacted to its absence. It was the invisibility of this impregnable reality that permitted us ignorance of its existence. It occurred to me that the phantom limb — that which we have cut away and discarded — was summation to the mayor's argument.

I was only disposed to a ten-foot buffer between myself and the criminal. I fired the stone, shaped very much like a ball, with as much force and accuracy as I could muster. It struck him flush mid-temple. The breaking of his skull would be sickening to some. A blue, bloody bruise emerged in relief.

The women around me tossed their stones, joylessly, to the ground. They were prepared to do as much but the feeling seemed to be that I had managed the work efficiently.

The crowd dispersed and returned in the direction of the village. In one breath, the mayor informed me that the deceased criminal had raped a young girl and that he would be cut down and buried. His soft smile communicated satisfaction with me and, by extension, satisfaction with himself. "We will surface your vehicle from the water bog," he said. "You are a free man."

Notwithstanding the objective execution of what I had

done, the seeming incontrovertibility of my decision and the groundwork of judgment, the criminal's face, at the moment that I threw the stone, appeared to my eyes as that of a clown.

I hadn't done anything extraordinary.

* * *

Discussion Questions

1. What is your opinion of the narrator for choosing to throw the stone at the end of the story? Do you judge him, or is the choice to throw/not throw a personal one?

2. Would you throw the stone? Is there additional information you would want to know prior to making your decision?

3. Would your decision change if the prisoner was going to be set free if you refused? What if the local custom was to keep the person in solitary confinement and torture them until a foreigner came to kill them? Would you then be okay with a "mercy" killing?

4. Does it matter that the penalty is death? What if the punishment were something severe, but less harsh? Would you then agree to give out the punishment?

5. Are there "universal morals" you believe the village is not following or are all laws simply the codification of cultural norms?

6. Would your decision change if you didn't find their "trial" system to be valid in your opinion? (E.g. They put a rock in water and guilty/innocence was based on if it floated.)

My Fellow (Immortal) Americans

Tyler W. Kurt

LADIES AND GENTLEMEN, FRIENDS, DONORS … my fellow Americans. Thank you for providing me this opportunity to speak tonight. [pause for applause] First, I would like to thank the staff and the catering company, as well as the Los Angeles Athletic Club, for allowing us to have this event at their wonderful establishment. And of course, I must thank our hosts, and a couple I would consider to be dear friends, Mr. and Mrs. Nates. [pause for applause]

As the duly re-elected President of the people of the United States, and of the people of the great State of California, I want to talk to you briefly about an important subject. I won't talk too long — I don't want the first lady to get upset with me — I've been, as she frequently reminds me, the cause of too many people eating too many cold meals because I can't stop talking. [pause for laugher] So I'll speak briefly, so we can all eat.

What I want to talk to you about today are (1) one of the current bills Congress intends to propose this session; (2) the effect it would have on further degrading the broad middle class standard of living in America; and (3) the values and lifestyle we have come to expect in this great country. I want to talk to you about what we, working together, can do to defeat soon-to-be-proposed and re-proposed bills so we can ensure a prosperous future for all Americans.

But first, a history lesson. As all of you know, and in fact a few of you in this room have grandparents that remember, the America of the past was a place of chaos and inequality. In 2022 it was determined by the Congress Committee on Living Standards that to meet the most basic needs (food, shelter, clothing), Americans working for the minimum "cash wage" would have to work 71 hours a week, while those in the top 5 percent could earn all the "cash wages" they needed to meet their basic needs by working just 14 minutes in that same week.

For the wealthy, free time and consumption could be limitless; and for the poor, free time was impossible, and basic needs were often beyond their reach. Thus was the nature of tragic "cash wage inequality" in our history that led to rampant homelessness and drug addiction.

As is always the case with America, as Americans, and as titans of innovation, we saw the natural unfairness of this, and sought labor-saving devices. These machines, these "products of our genius," over the 20's and 30's created greater and greater wealth, not only for Americans, but for the world.

And, of course, in 2036, driven by our American innovation, the United Nations declared the world free of the most extreme poverty, and by 2047, the UN declared the world free of all poverty. [Continue over applause] America did this, did as it has always done; America ushered in a new golden era for the world. [pause]

With worldwide poverty eradicated, it was only a matter of time until the power of science and medicine found the cure for aging and for nearly all non-accident related deaths. Cancer, dementia, heart disease, AIDS, malaria and the many other global scourges of the past were eradicated in a generation. Now, if I were to ask one of the twins, or you were to ask one of your children about cancer, they would say, "What's cancer?" As a matter of fact, my beautiful wife just celebrated her 97th birthday last week; and as I tell her every day, [look to wife] she doesn't look a day over 30.

However, like all great solutions, it caused new, more challenging issues. In this case, there were eventually 15 billion issues: over-population.

While there are scientists and dreamers who believe we may someday move beyond our own solar system and may someday find cost effective ways to populate the planets within our own solar system, those days are far, far off. If and when those days do come, I look forward to them; however, in spite of record funding, that day is not today, and it is not in the foreseeable future. [break]

In this room I see Dr. Fairfield of the Berkeley Medical Institute, and Dr. Lee, Chair of the Bioethics Institute at UC-Davis, both of which served on the American-led "UN Committee on Overpopulation." I know as scientists they are bashful, but if I may say so, their solution, and the solution jointly proposed by the greatest thinkers of the world, was a stroke of genius.

Their genius was for humanity to move away from an economy based on the old "cash currency" of the past, to one based on the 15-billion-person world population cap that created the "time currency" of today. So now, of course, unlike your parents, when you work, you know all too well you are not paid in dollars, or euros, or yen. You are paid in seconds, and minutes, and hours.

And when those hours run out, the lifesaving drugs that stop aging, and prevent disease, are no longer available for you to purchase with your time, not because they are expensive to produce, but because we have made them impossible to replicate, and finite in nature. It is, at the end of the day, an equitable solution to stop overpopulation while allowing those who have worked hard, and who have earned their future, to have that future, and those that have squandered their opportunity, to gracefully make space for the next generation of children for the hard-working.

This has been the system we have lived under for almost 40 years as a global community, and it has served humanity well. Okay, enough with the history lesson.

What I'm really here to talk about are the dangerous bills that I expect will be proposed by Congress this session.

First, raising the minimum time wage. Parts of the world, as you know, have no minimum time wage, while others, like France and Italy, are so generous as to provide little incentive to work at all. In France, working for the minimum time wage, if you worked 40 hours a week, for

10 years, not only would you have earned enough time to pay for those 10 years you worked, but you would have saved up almost six additional years. What reason would there be for a French worker to work those additional six years? None. And that is exactly what we have seen in recent months and years in the faltering French and Italian economies. A people who have banked so many years, they have no reason to work at all.

I firmly believe, and the economics of history shows, the minimum time wage we pay in America is fair, and just. As the slogan goes, "An hour's pay, for an hour's work." If I work 40 hours, the minimum wage paid for that should be 40 hours. In effect, this allows someone working hard to nearly double their overall lifespan. They get their natural 50 or 60 years, plus another 40 to 50 years they earned working over the course of their life.

By forcing job creators to pay more it has all the wrong economic effects. By the government tampering in the marketplace: (1) it discourages hiring; (2) it discourages investment; (3) it encourages laziness: and it (4) causes American jobs to be shipped to cheaper labor markets overseas.

When this bill comes before Congress, and it will, I hope you will support me in standing firm. Our slogan will be "One-For-One." [Banner of Slogan Drops, Pause For Applause] One hour of work for one hour of pay!

The second piece of legislation that is likely to be proposed this session is better described in two parts, but both fall under a European style liberal/socialist scheme of time redistribution.

The first part of the liberal/socialist agenda is the creation of the "time inheritance tax." As I mentioned before, Mr. Nates — our host, is the President, CEO, and founder of MassTech. As of today, MassTech is the 9th most valuable company in the world by market capitalization. It is a company that Mr. Nates started out of his garage only 112 years ago. That company has grown, and has prospered, because of the strength of the American worker and because of his leadership as an innovator in business.

Mr. Nates is, according to Forbes, the 3rd richest man in America. His estimated wealth is over 390 million years. Hey Mr. Nates, throw a few years my way? [pause for laughter] In all seriousness, he earned the right to immortality through his hard work. And, on the day he chooses to die, shouldn't he be able to transfer that immortality to his wife, to his children, to his grandchildren, and to his loved ones as he sees fit, without the government taking 10% (or 20%) as a so-called "time inheritance tax" for time-wealth redistribution?

What motivation does Mr. Nates, or others like him have to innovate if they know the value of their hard work will be taken by the government and distributed to those who have failed to work to reach their full potential. After 100,000 or 200,000 years, when Mr. Nates chooses to die, should he be forced to give part of his remaining time to those that complain that a 50, 40, or 30-year life span is not enough for them?

This is likewise true for the so-called "time income tax" that Congress has proposed for several years and I expect will propose again. It is nothing more than a time redistribution scheme to those unwilling to work to earn their own time. Why on earth should I, or Mr. Nates, or any of you who have worked so hard to save up 100,000 years be required to give that time to others?

I've heard it mentioned that the time income tax might even be progressive. By that, I mean, those who have accumulated more than 100 years of time in earnings in one year would be required to pay 10% of that time to the government for redistribution. And that those that earned more than 500 years of time by the end of a year would have to pay 20% to the government for redistribution. Where would it end, and why would any of us work?

Let's call it what it is. The liberal/socialist agenda is time-wealth redistribution. The liberal/socialist agenda is to take away your God-given right to immortality. The liberal/socialist agenda says that you can't have children because there isn't space for your children, because you have to give your time to non-productive members of society who we, as a society, refuse to make die.

Friends, fellow Americans. I'm sorry if this speech has gone long, or [to wife] if your food has gotten cold, by me telling you what you already knew. But this topic is simply too important. (1) It is too important to America. (2) It is too important to American-ism. (3) And it's too important to our very way of life to allow these things to go unsaid.

Nothing less than the very fundamentals of our society are at risk. Hard work. Innovation. Family values. And our God-given right to immortality … and yes, even the inevitable passing on of the less skilled, the lazy, and the unproductive to make space for children. [applause]

I know you have all paid a great deal of time to be here to support me and to support our shared vision of America. Your time contributions today will be well-spent defeating the initiatives of this liberal Congress, and of defeating the millions of Americans living minute-to-minute who think they have a right to the time you earned. We must win, and we can win.

Thank you for your time. God bless you, and God bless America.

* * *

Discussion Questions

1. Would you support or oppose the time redistribution laws in the story? Why?

2. Does a person have a right to immortality? Do they have a right to it if it is not available to everyone?

3. Does a minimum time wage encourage laziness, as the President says in his speech?

4. Does a minimum time wage encourage people to only work the minimum amount?

5. Is currency (or the objects it buys) just a way to convert time spent working into a tangible object?

6. In our currency-based economy, is it fair that a $20,000 car might "cost" a minimum wage employee one year of time working (1600 hours) while it might cost a high earner just three weeks of time working (120 hours)?

7. Is access (or lack of access) to health care today based on an ability to pay, effectively shortening and lengthening the lives of people just like in the story? Should there be a right to universal basic health care? Does that encourage laziness?

Survival Kit

Christine Seifert

I MARRIED Andy Morrison four months after we met. It was a mistake, the marriage, but I didn't realize it until after the wedding weekend and by then it was done. Andy had gone along with the marriage plan gamely, though I guessed that was because I was only his second real girlfriend, an initially gratifying position that turned sour when, a few months after the wedding, I ran into Girlfriend Number One at the car wash. We recognized each other immediately, and while I would have been content to simply hide behind the spinning rack of air freshener trees, Girlfriend Number One took off her giant sunglasses and said, "I just want you to know, I don't envy you."

***

"Are you cold?" Andy asked as he arranged pieces of newspaper over his legs. He was the only person I knew under the age of fifty who read newspapers on actual paper.

"No," I said, though I could feel the wind blowing through the cracks of the car window. It was still light out—just barely—but the late-winter weather was bad enough that all I could see was a grey-white wall of snow.

The cold was settling under my skin, around my bones, threading through my blood.

"I'm glad we don't have the girls," he said. "Can you imagine?" His newspaper blanket fluttered. He was wearing children's earmuffs and gloves that couldn't cover his hands. Andy and the girls loved the desert-dry heat of Arizona. All three wore winter coats if the mercury dropped below sixty.

"What do you think they are doing right now?" I asked. It was a game we played when we were alone, a conversation without stakes, one that never ended, even when it grew old. "I think Natalie has already announced that she wants Chicken McNuggets."

His turn: "Natasha has colored on the walls and eaten glue at least twice."

I laughed, but only to be polite. Natasha would never do either of those things. It was Natalie who ate anything she could wrap her grubby hands around. It was Natalie who once ate my birth control pills and required a trip to the emergency room.

My parents pretended to love babysitting the girls, but they would all four be watching the driveway, waiting for Andy and me to pull up. I wrapped my arms around myself and tried to imagine a world without the girls, without Andy. It was a picture that came easily and faded slowly; one by one the figures disappeared.

"How long do you think we'll be here?" Andy asked.

"It'll be fine." I said some version of that line to Andy a hundred times a day. *Everything will be fine. I'll take care of it. Don't you worry. I'll do the heavy-lifting.*

A snowstorm this bad wasn't going to let up any time soon. We were stranded, completely stuck, under a deep underpass in a flimsy rental car—a powder-blue Toyota hatchback—and the snow was endless.

***

Andy's parents attended the beachside wedding in Maui, but they had not been invited. Andy's father—a man the entire family referred to as Blip for reasons that I had never learned because not a single member of the Morrison clan could remember—had sat in bird shit on a bench provided by the photographer. Suzie, Andy's mother, had insisted that the photographer pay for Blip's linen suit, a suit he had allegedly worn at his own wedding thirty years prior. (The story had the literal whiff of truth: the suit smelled like mothballs.) Even the wedding planner, a woman with cat's eyeglasses, couldn't escape blame for the bird shit incident. Because the wedding planner recommended the photographer, Suzie insisted I refuse to pay her sizeable fee.

When Suzie threatened to sue the photographer, the wedding planner, and inexplicably, the manufacturer of the bench itself, for damages, Andy stepped in. Andy, who had a twenty-eight inch waist and arms like kebab skewers, threatened to punch the photographer. The photographer laughed. Of course he did. Then Suzie took over and the photographer blanched.

Everyone on the beach witnessed the debacle and there I was, in my size four casual beach wedding dress I'd gotten for thirty dollars at Maurice's in Desert Sky Mall, watching Suzie punch the man while Blip cheered.

In the end, I wasn't sure who convinced the photographer to agree to a small refund on the photo package and to apologize to Blip for suggesting he sit on the bench in the first place, but I often suspected the photographer shot the photos in such a way to make me appear ten pounds heavier than I was. The entire stack of discounted photos were now stored in the closet, along with purses I never used and my diaries from middle school. If the twins eventually ask to see them, I might very well tell them the photos were lost.

After Suzie swung at the photographer, I forged ahead with the ceremony for reasons I couldn't understand myself. It was a steaming chemical mix of duty, stubbornness, and a splash of something like love. Yes, Suzie's punch had delayed things long enough for me to seriously consider running away. But I stayed. I stayed when the uniformed police officer arrived. I stayed for the statements that had to be made. I stayed while the wedding planner brought ice for the photographer who ended up with a black eye. And then it was time for the ceremony. Without even realizing it, I'd made a decision. Action, after all, can be just a series of inactions.

To come back from Maui with nothing to show but a sunburn and a pair of souvenir sea lion barrettes was unthinkable. It was bad enough that my parents would be hurt for months after the wedding. Here were Blip and Suzie in every damn picture while my own parents shoveled heavy March snow and ate salmon loaf on TV trays.

The bird shit story had been re-told so often since the wedding that I could almost recite it along with Suzie and Blip. Even years after the wedding, Blip's misfortune and the scene it caused were a reminder of that wedding weekend, the first of three things that solidified into a hard mass of memory, a tumor that grew and served to remind me, when I was willing to touch that malignant lump, that marrying Andy was a mistake—one that couldn't be rectified. Not now.

My wedding night had ended with me alone in our Four Seasons suite, but not because of Blip's ruined pants. (Blip had been consoled by the all-you-can-eat pig roast, which my parents had paid for as a wedding gift. He stole bananas for breakfast the next morning and thus saved at least twenty dollars, by his calculations.) Andy was unaware that I was upset, so I couldn't blame him for going on a sunset hike with a group of students from the University of Alabama ecology class he'd met on the airport shuttle.

That was the second thing that enraged me that weekend: the hike. What kind of man goes on a hike on his wedding night while his new wife sits in a hotel suite drinking pre-mixed Mai Tais and watching free HBO?

***

"They have their lights on. The engine is running." Andy pointed at the car a few feet in front of us—the only thing we could see in the swirls of snow, and only just barely.

"They're turning it on too often." I fiddled with the keys in the ignition and wondered how often was too often to turn on the heat. We only had a half tank of gas and I was pretty sure we were going to be in the car for a very long time. The snow wasn't letting up. I looked at my watch. Quarter to six. It was a long time until morning when plows would come through.

"Who do you think is next?" I asked Andy to pass the time.

"Kathleen and Steve, definitely."

"No," I said, "Really? Kathleen and Steve? They don't even go to the grocery store separately. They're joined at the hip."

Andy nodded his head vigorously. "Just watch. It's always that kind. You can't keep that kind of thing up."

It was another game we played. Which of our friends would divorce next. There'd been a rash of separations and divorces that year, most of which did not surprise me. There were the usual reasons: infidelity, lack of interest, boredom, existential angst. But none of those reasons seemed good enough for me to get a divorce. I had recently admitted that I had an old-fashioned idea of marriage, one that allowed for peaks and valleys. One that didn't factor in happiness. After six years, I'd successfully become a Person Who Follows Through. Besides, divorce was so publicly messy, a kind of failure that they printed in the newspaper, one that followed you every time you had to mark a check box: single, married, divorced/failure.

"I think Steve is cheating on her," Andy said.

"Steve?" I pictured Steve. Bald before thirty. A beer

gut, an unsightly mass that fell over his belt and hovered above his crotch like a retractable awning.

"If he hasn't done anything yet, he will. He has a crush. A massive crush," Andy said. He giggled, the same way the girls did when they built a Lego tower and then kicked it down with their tiny feet. "Some girl at work. She's eighteen."

"What would you talk about with an eighteen-year-old?" I wondered aloud. I quit working when the twins were born, but before that I had been a school nurse at a large high school. Eighteen-year-olds were like unformed pieces of clay. They were shapeless blobs, still being molded by the universe in some preordained way. I could not envision having sex with one of them any more than I could envision having sex with a lump of the girls' Play-doh.

"Eighteen-year-olds are fresh meat," Andy said. "You can convince them of anything. You can be a god to an eighteen-year-old."

I turned toward my window and rolled my eyes. Andy was a narcissist. I'd only recently admitted it. I worried sometimes it was rubbing off on me.

Andy was blowing on his hands as he talked. I followed suit. I imagined the Arizona sun in August. I'd take one hundred and fourteen degrees in a second compared to this snow-dump, this March nightmare. I didn't know how my parents stood it. I didn't know how I'd lived the first eighteen years of life here. Had I ever thought Andy was a god?

The temperature was dropping by the minute as the sky

turned to true night and the snow fell faster. If not for the snow, if there was any hope we'd be able to move the car soon, I would not have responded as I did. "Is that what Roxanne thinks about you? That you are a god?'

Andy laughed, not nervously, not guiltily. "Roxanne is too smart for that. And she's twenty-seven."

"She called the house before we left," I said.

His newspapers crinkled as he shifted in the passenger seat to look at me. "I told her we were going on our anniversary trip. She just wants to make sure everything is fine while we're gone."

"She's a real peach," I said, but it was a pointless comment. Andy didn't understand sarcasm. He was like those people who have face blindness. Sarcasm could be presented to Andy, introduced by name, but he wouldn't recognize it the next time.

"Does she call your dad at home?"

"Who?"

I looked at him to see if he was playing dumb. He wasn't. He just had no attention span, not even trapped in a hatchback under a bridge, not five miles from my parents' house. I'd suggest walking if either of us had boots, though with such poor visibility, we'd probably end up frozen to death in a snowbank before morning. *Never leave the car.* My dad had drilled that into my head. *If you are stuck, stay put.*

I sighed. "Roxanne. Does she call your dad at home?"

Andy shrugged. "Probably. She takes her career

seriously."

"She didn't call to talk to you. She called to talk to me. And not about her 'career.'"

Andy jabbed at the radio button, his hand steady, his face impassive. "Oh, yeah?"

Roxanne was something of a Girl Friday for the Morrison family business. Blip and Andy did the jobs. Suzie kept the books, a feat of magnificent proportions given that Suzie couldn't even balance her checkbook and had been charged with misdemeanors twice for writing bad checks. Blip himself had been arrested once for stealing a turkey breast from one of the chain grocery stores, their biggest client. When pressed for an explanation, Blip merely said, "I wanted a turkey."

Blip had never cheated on Suzie, a fact that he recited often. Though he'd cheated on the three wives prior to Suzie. One of his favorite pastimes was telling Andy about his pre-Suzie conquests, the secret trysts he'd arranged while one of his dim wives sat at home and waited for him, like a lighthouse keeper. Blip always ended his stories with the same line: "I could do it, so I did."

"Don't you want to know what Roxanne said to me?"

He didn't answer. The car wasn't big enough for Roxanne, too.

***

The third thing—the biggest regret—was the worst, the one I forced myself to think about every time I got too comfortable. It was like an antidote to comfort, a quick reversal if life became too pacific.

On the last night in Maui, Blip and Suzie invited themselves to our honeymoon suite for Mai Tais and pineapple chunks impaled by plastic toothpicks, particular favorites of Blip who believed drinks and hors d'oeuvres could catapult a working-class fellow who owned a failing window-washing business in Phoenix to the sort of middle-class gent who had a portfolio and more than one necktie. It hadn't happened yet.

Blip and Suzie perched on the edge of the bed and made off-color jokes about honeymoon sex. Andy laughed. I turned red at the tips of my ears. In truth, Andy and I had had disappointing sex precisely once since the ceremony. We'd had sex hundreds of times before Hawaii, and everything had been fine, if not earth-shattering, but the wedding had soured everything. After the vows, I couldn't help but notice that Andy looked a tiny bit like Suzie. Why had I never noticed they had the same hazel eyes, the same curling wisps of hair right at the temples, the same pale skin prone to sunburn and moles?

Suzie insisted they cap off the evening by walking out to see the cliff diver. Each night at sunset, a man-boy in a tiny bathing suit climbed a craggy cliff and dove into the ocean depths, all for a smattering of tourist applause. Suzie and Blip had seen the diver every night. They had the videos to prove it. Blip posted his favorite on his Facebook page. AMAZING NATIVES, he wrote, totally unaware that he was being racist.

We were all early to the cliff, and we had to wait for the diver to begin his ascent. Blip loudly wondered if it was a different diver each time. He didn't know because he couldn't tell "them" apart. When Andy told him to shush, Blip feigned ignorance. He changed the subject and asked Suzie if she got a look at the diver's "package." Then he roughly began massaging Suzie's shoulders and told the family of five from Toledo standing next to them that "old Suze" needed a good rubdown. I was perpetually mortified by Blip, his crassness, his inability to apologize for anything, his base thoughts laid out bare for the world to see, his complete unawareness that he was constantly taking up space and air that could be better used by someone else.

We ended up missing the diver because Blip began an impromptu Charleston-style dance to the sound of the Toledo father's ringtone. The Toledo family laughed too hard, I thought. Even the baby seemed amused. I wondered if I had ever found Blip funny or charming, but I couldn't remember ever having felt anything except the mantle of hot annoyance and disgust that I carried on my shoulders whenever he was around.

After the dive that we didn't see, Blip suggested a cup of Irish coffee. Before I could say no, Andy said yes. At the Hilton bar, Blip asked the bartender where she was from. "Sydney," she answered, her surfer's body tanned the same color as the whiskey she poured into Blip's coffee. The bartender added an extra splash and winked. I thought, *People actually like Blip*. It was a great mystery of the universe. Suzie ordered a Sex on the Beach. Andy and I had gin and tonics.

Two rounds later, Suzie was on the dance floor with a middle-aged man in a Tommy Bahama shirt and a black fedora. They danced to "Eye of the Tiger." Suzie's pancake butt tapped his belly every so often.

Andy was telling the bartender about brine shrimp respiration when Suzie cried out. Blip had already put his head on the bar and was fast asleep, a flap of grey hair rising up and diving down as a fan behind the bar oscillated. Andy went to the dance floor to investigate, and I followed close behind, my gin and tonic sweating in my hand.

Tommy Bahama held his hands up. "Hey, I don't know what the problem is here. I'm just having a good time."

"Go to bed," I told him.

Suzie's hip had crapped out again. The same one that gave her trouble before. She'd be miserable until she could see her orthopedist. The plane ride home would be torture. Andy offered to stay behind and rouse Blip. I would escort Suzie back to her room. "Stay with her until she gets her nightgown on and her teeth brushed," Andy said. Not for the first time, I wondered if this is what it would be like to be a parent: reduced to monitoring someone else's hygiene. When I finally became a parent, I would learn that it basically amounted to directing food into the mouth and waste out of the body.

Suzie was in bed, loaded up on four Advil and the after-effects of alcohol, by eleven. Blip showed up a few minutes later, wide awake from his coffee and nap. I left Blip and Suzie's room without saying goodbye. *You don't have to be polite to people who ruin your wedding*, I thought.

At three minutes before five, hours after I'd left Blip

and Suzie, Andy returned to the honeymoon suite, where I'd spent the night on the balcony watching the waves roll in and out. He wept for twenty minutes before he could tell me what he'd done. We both wished he was better at keeping secrets.

***

The wedding disaster was six years ago. A year or so later the twins arrived. And what could I do with two babies and no job? Fortunately, by then, I had figured out that Andy was significantly more likeable when nobody else was around. He was like a German Shepherd who, in private, picked up a book and asked if anyone had thoughts about Russian imperialism, but in a crowd of people would pee on the rug. Day-to-day life wasn't bad. It wasn't pleasant or fulfilling, but it had a rhythm. Blip and Suzie were crosses to bear, but I wasn't sure how I could possibly divorce them even if I left Andy.

"Your parents are caricatures," I said as I rubbed at my ankles in the freezing car, trying to get the circulation going. It was so cold, I worried we'd both fall asleep and forget to run the heater at regular intervals.

"They are characters," Andy answered, and I wasn't sure if he was correcting me or mixing up two different words.

"Yes, but they are characters nobody would believe if you didn't know them. If I made them up, people would say I tried too hard or that I painted too broadly."

"You *do* do that," Andy said. "You like to be annoyed by them."

It was a longstanding argument: whether I was too sensitive or too humorless or too prudish about Blip and Suzie. I had to admit that I was secretly delighted that the twins were wary of both grandparents, their identical little eyebrows raised whenever Blip spoke to them as if they were puppies rather than human children. It was more worrisome that both girls had started to give Andy the same look.

I checked my watch. Not even five minutes had passed. My phone said at least three more feet of snow was on its way. I'd already called my parents who advised me to stay put. "I can't believe you didn't put a winter survival kit in the trunk," my father said without hiding his irritation. "I forgot," I said sheepishly. I'd been living in Phoenix for so long that I'd forgotten about northern winters, the way snow could sneak up on you and change your plans in an instant.

"I think I should try to walk to the car ahead of us. Maybe I can get some food or blankets. We have less than half a tank of gas." Another winter sin: not keeping the gas tank full at all times.

"Can you see to get to the next car?" Andy asked. "I can't see a thing." He was right. It was a full white-out now.

"I'll be fine," I said.

"I hope so." He didn't offer to walk himself. I knew he wouldn't, not just because he was wearing flimsy Converse sneakers that would be soaking wet in seconds. I looked at my shoes, sturdy leather knee-high boots. Not ideal, but better than sneakers. If I kept in a straight line,

I'd be fine. You didn't need to see in a white-out. You just needed to keep your bearings. I'd hold onto the rental car until I had to let go and make the leap to the bumper of the next car.

"I've seen worse than this," I said. I hadn't. Not ever.

"I'm starving," Andy said. We'd been on our way to dinner, a belated anniversary celebration that couldn't have reminded me less of Hawaii if I'd planned it. It was my idea to take an anniversary trip to visit my parents. Andy had resisted. A lifelong Arizonian, he found the idea of snow a personal affront, a hassle Mother Nature sent just to fuck with him and his steak dinner.

"Somebody will have food," I reassured him. I was Chief of the Reassurance Bureau. I got things done, and if I didn't, I convinced Andy all would be okay anyway. "Somebody will have food," I repeated.

The rest of these people wouldn't have forgotten their winter survival kits because they weren't idiots from Phoenix. "Give me those gloves and earmuffs." Andy handed them to me. As I rubbed my fingers over the material, I wished I'd bought real outerwear, not the cheap stuff from CVS.

"Fare thee well," Andy said.

I turned the ignition. "Go ahead, have some heat. Then it will be warm for me when I get back."

Andy smiled and leaned back in his seat. "Ah, heat. I've missed you so. I could write an epic ballad all about heat."

"Well, you've got all night."

I didn't say goodbye when I pushed open the door against the wind and slammed it behind me. The force of the snowy wind almost knocked me over. Even so, I inhaled deeply and sucked in the cold until I was full.

***

After Andy finished weeping that morning in Hawaii, when we had just an hour left to pack and catch our airport shuttle, he told me the truth—or a version of the truth. After Suzie had left the bar, Andy had roused Blip and sent him back to his room. But rather than coming back to the honeymoon suite, Andy had decided to go down to the Four Seasons bar for a quick drink. He'd bring it back up to the room. Maybe even grab a snack, a sundae or something, for us to share.

The University of Alabama ecology group was out by the pool. He decided to say hello, see what they'd been up to, if they had any exciting plant news. Andy dropped out of college sophomore year, but he fancied himself an autodidact, a word he actually used in regular conversation to describe himself. It was pedantic. It also wasn't true.

I waited for him to admit it: that he'd slept with someone else. Blip's pre-Suzie extramarital affairs were genetic and here was proof. I felt a strong wave of something that might have been elation. If Andy cheated, it wasn't my fault. I was the victim. And didn't that change everything? Wasn't that a perfectly good excuse for an annulment?

We sat together on the foot of the bed that night, and I willed my hands to stop shaking. "Tell me," I ordered. He wiped his nose on his t-shirt sleeve. "I didn't try to stop her."

I made him repeat the story twice, and then a third time, just to be sure I understood the details. There'd been a girl at the pool, a girl in a skimpy bikini with gold rings at the hips. He bought her a drink, a strawberry margarita, and then another. They dangled their feet in the pool, long after the other University of Alabama ecology students left. They walked on the beach. They kissed, their toes dug into the sand, their fingers clasped.

Just a quick kiss, hardly a kiss at all. They stopped. Andy wasn't sure who stopped first. The girl—Brittany, of course her name was Brittany—understood. He was married. And she was only eighteen, a freshman from Tupelo, an almost-virgin.

Brittany stayed on the beach, still drunk, and he came back to the room to his wife. He would never stray again. He promised. I held him in my arms, all the while wondering if drunk-kissing was a big enough crime to warrant changing my ticket, staying in Hawaii for another couple of days by myself, and then flying back alone to contact a lawyer. Were divorces cheaper if the marriage only lasted a week? I had a thousand dollars in savings.

"Can you forgive me?" Andy asked. "Do you believe me that nothing else happened?"

The second question surprised me. I had never considered for a minute that he was lying, that the kiss had been just the beginning of something worse. I looked at his huddled mass, his shoulders covered with the fluffy white duvet that I was sure the housekeepers didn't wash, not even at the Four Seasons. I never knew when he was lying. Never.

"You should have at least walked her back to her room." I was offended on Brittany's behalf. Was it too much to ask for an escort back to her room? It wasn't safe, not even in Maui, for a drunk girl to wander the beach in the dark by herself. "What if something happened to her? What if she wandered into the ocean and drowned? Or fell into the pool? Or disappeared like that Spring Break girl, that one they still haven't found?" I was filled with worry for this Brittany.

"I didn't do anything," Andy said. "I didn't. I swear."

"Doing nothing is something," I told him.

"No. Nothing is nothing," he insisted, his eyes red-rimmed and hollow.

It occurred to me then, a lightning bolt from the white-painted Four Seasons ceiling: Doing nothing was certainly not the worst thing in the world. Doing nothing wasn't an action. It wasn't a choice. It was a mode of survival, a way of being, a philosophy.

"I'll be better," Andy said when we were riding down in the elevator the next morning to meet the shuttle that would take us away from Hawaii and the wedding and everything. "From now on, I will be better." I chose to believe him about everything.

***

Brittany sent me a Facebook message, just one day before we left Phoenix for our anniversary trip. It had been so long, I'd almost forgotten about Brittany. But not quite. I read the message. *He just seemed so nice. He seemed normal. I trusted him. I said no.*

A day later, in the Phoenix airport, I locked myself in a stall and opened up Facebook Messenger and responded to Brittany: "I believe you."

***

The exhaust pipe mattered. You had to know something about northern winters to know about the exhaust pipe. Too much snow and you'd end up with exhaust filtering back into the car when you turned it on for the heater. If you were going to run the car, you had to keep that exhaust pipe clear.

I wish I had a shovel. As it was, I had to use my hands with the tiny gloves, already a hole in each index finger, to tunnel through the snow. I stood up and peered around the rental. I still couldn't see the car in front of me, not in the dark with snow bursting from the sky.

Digging seemed futile. Every handful I threw seemed to flutter back down and settle around the undercarriage of the car. I could hear the soft hum of the little engine, the rumble of its innards as it produced heat for Andy, who was still nestled inside.

I started scooping snow with both hands. Andy should turn the car off. We were using too much gas. The exhaust pipe wasn't cleared out enough. I thought of Blip and Suzie. They were probably having drinks on their condo patio with the neighbors. My parents and the girls would have eaten supper by now. Time for bed next. Stories, kisses, nightlights, blankies, reassurances that Mommy would be back by morning.

I gave up on shoveling with my hands and sat on the edge of the car's back bumper, the snow and cold soaking through my jeans. I really should tell Andy to turn off the ignition. It was bone-cold outside, but it was sort of nice, all alone, with the snow assaulting my face. Andy would nod off in the car. He could sleep in all circumstances, even when the girls were screaming bloody murder. He inherited that from Blip. How long would he breathe clean air with the exhaust pipe blocked?

"I'm not doing anything," I said aloud. What was wrong with that? Nobody could fault someone for coasting along, for letting things happen as they happened. Life unfolded. You didn't always have to be the subject of every sentence. Nothing wasn't something. Nothing just was.

I stood up again and watched the snow building higher, swallowing the bottom of the car. Not doing anything wasn't wrong. I dried my hands on my thighs. Not doing anything was the sum of zero.

The rental was still running when I set out for the oasis ahead of me.

* * *

Discussion Questions

1. The narrator doesn't seem to like her husband (Andy), or his parents (Blip and Suzie). There is an assortment of things she says she doesn't like about them, but what is the real reason? Why has she never told them?

2. Andy, Blip, and Suzie all seem (generally) happy with their lives, and fond of the narrator. Are they simply stupid? Why is it they seem so happy and the narrator is so unhappy? Who's right in the way they live their life?

3. Why did the narrator go through with a wedding that she didn't want to have? Why have children when you are in an unhappy marriage? Who (if anyone) is the cause of the narrator and Andy's unhappy marriage?

4. How would this marriage/snow story go if told from the perspective of Andy?

5. If Andy was wearing similarly sensible shoes in the car, would the narrator have asked him to go to the next car? Would Andy have agreed to go if asked? If the answer is yes, then why is the narrator mad at Andy?

6. If the narrator fails to dig out the tailpipe, and Andy dies, will her life get happier in a year?

All Harriet's Pieces

A. Katherine Black

JANIE DROPPED THE BOOK into her lap and leaned her head against the outside of the translucent pig chamber. Warmth seeped from the chamber, a stark contrast to the cold atrium floor, covered with tiles Mama had found in some faraway place on one of her trips. Janie's wish to sink through the chamber wall, to find a way inside, was so familiar, it was almost comforting.

Harriet stirred. Standing on her four short legs, she side-stepped until her pig body leaned lengthwise against the inside of the wall, facing Janie. Harriet used her eyes, eyes exactly like Mama's, to look at Janie in a way that Mama never did. Never would. Her pig face tilted toward the book on Janie's lap. The one Janie had been reading aloud until a minute ago. The one about the pig and the spider who became friends. Janie was nearing the end of it.

"I don't —" Janie said. She held back the rest of her words. As much as she loved that book, she couldn't bear to face the end. Not this time. Because the pig will survive in the book. Because real life is nothing like books.

A chime played in the hallway, followed by a recording of Mama's voice. "Bedtime, child." Janie ignored Mama's schedule. She touched the chamber wall next to Harriet's pink floppy ear, wishing she could reach it. She'd always thought Harriet would enjoy a good scratch behind the ear.

The chime continued, growing louder. Mama's digitized voice repeated, every three seconds. "Bedtime, child."

Harriet held Janie's gaze. Janie's chin quivered.

After numerous bedtime calls rang through the atrium, Hartie plowed out of the bushes in the far corner of the chamber, trotting at a pace that seemed too fast for a pig. Stopping just inches from Janie, on the other side of the wall, he stared at her with eyes identical to Janie's own.

Normally, Janie would have snapped at Hartie. He was always nagging her, even if she couldn't hear him through the one-way com. All she could muster tonight, though, was a single word. "Fine."

The alarm stopped in response to her verbal acknowledgement. Hartie nodded, apparently satisfied. He walked over to Harriet and plopped down next to her for the night. Harriet closed her eyes, as if this were just some regular evening, like any other. Harriet deserved to know what was about to happen, but Janie didn't know how to tell someone they were going to die.

Janie leaned into the com on the chamber wall and said good night before standing and dragging her feet toward her wing of the house.

She readied herself for bed. Cleaned her teeth and her face, put on pajamas, thinking all the while about the pigs. To keep the day from ending, she decided to tidy up her library, returning books to their shelves. Twenty-three books later, there was nothing else to do.

She went to bed, twisting in her covers all night long, until birds chirped outside the window, warning her of the coming sunrise. Sounds of movement echoed from somewhere in the house. Doors and voices. Too soon. Mama had promised Janie she could say goodbye before the procedure, but it wasn't even light out.

Jumping out of bed, Janie made her way from her room to the service wing. Automatic lights sprung to life as she passed down the hall, but stopped when she entered the stairwell. She made her way in total darkness, conjuring a picture of Harriet's face in her mind, to ward off the monsters threatening to leap out of her imagination. No auto-lights in the basement, either. She crept toward the faint glow ahead, the space under the atrium, under the pig chamber. She'd lost count of how many times she'd tried to break into the lift that led to the pig-chamber. But something was different this time. Workers were here. Workers with codes and keys. Workers who wanted to take Harriet away.

Crouched behind a corner, watching the institute workers fiddle with buttons at the wall panel, Janie gauged the distance between the lift and the service door that opened to the grounds outside. She could get Harriet and run. Hartie, too. It could work. With a diversion. She surveyed tubes and pipes hanging down from the ceiling under the enclosure, looking for ones she could reach. Ones that looked fragile.

The commotion began quickly, panel lights blinking and people gathering around tubes. Barely able to avoid the glare of their flashlights, Janie slipped over to the lift. Her hand froze, poised over the only button, with an arrow pointing up. Memories flooded, of all the times she'd pressed it before, to no avail. She pushed again, jumping when the bell rang, looking back to the service people. They appeared not hear it over the rush of air, or gas, escaping from broken tubes. The door opened, and she stepped inside.

The air in the chamber was warm and a little wet. It smelled like a garden after a heavy storm. Her bare feet stepped onto the grass floor, soft and pokey at the same time. No pigs were in sight. She tried calling Harriet, but only a whisper came out. Hartie peeked from the bushes. Leaves shook around his face, around his wide eyes.

Janie spoke fast. "Where's Harriet? We have to go. *Now.*" Hartie ran out from the bushes to stand in the middle of the chamber. "Hartie, *where is Harriet?*"

Nodding his head toward the lift, Hartie let out a sound. It was the first sound Janie had ever heard from a pig. A wimper, but not like an animal. Like a person. Janie shuddered.

She walked over to Hartie. He was about the same size as her, but thicker and bent. Kneeling before him, Janie looked into Hartie's eyes. They were the same ones she saw in the mirror every day, but she could barely make them out right then, behind his tears. She hadn't realized that pigs could cry.

Janie's head felt light, like a balloon. She let her rear hit the floor and she sat, looking at Hartie's face as it fell out of focus. Hartie stepped forward and nudged Janie, rubbed his cheek against hers. It was soft.

An alarm sounded around them. "Oxygen levels low in pig chamber. Oxygen levels low in pig chamber." Barely able to keep her eyelids open, Janie finally gave in and let them drop.

* * *

She woke in her own bed. Her body felt like lead, like she held the gravity of the whole world under her skin. The smell of the chamber still hung in her nose, the alarm blaring in the back of her thoughts. Harriet was already gone. It was time to accompany Mama to the institute.

She thought about staying in bed, maybe forever, but routine grabbed hold. She got up. Shower, clothes, teeth, hair. Until she stood at the threshold of her room, unmoving. Mama's voice rang through the speakers in her bedroom. "Breakfast, child." Janie couldn't tell if it was Mama's real voice, or the recorded one. Not that it mattered.

Her legs responded to the call as always, walking her through the doorway and around two corners, all the while her mind panicking at the impending pass through the atrium, through her most favorite spot in the world. The pig chamber came into view.

Only one pig stood on the other side of the wall, the exact age of Janie. With eyes identical to Janie's, lungs and kidneys and all sorts of innards exactly like Janie's, and with a heart that was breaking. Just like Janie's. She slowed as she passed Hartie. He stood beside the com, head bowed, eyes red. And then she broke into a run toward the kitchen.

Chimes rang through the halls after her, Mama's recorded voice saying, "Please walk, child," over and over. Janie continued her fervent pace, "Please walk, child," until she finally reached the kitchen doorway.

Mama sat at the breakfast table with her back to Janie, cradling a coffee mug in both hands. A sob broke free from Janie's throat. Mama's head cocked slightly to the side, but she did not turn.

"Morning, child," she said.

Janie held the familiar distance between herself and Mama. She wanted to plead, to drop to her knees on the hard tile floor and ask that Harriet be spared. But there was no use. Mama wouldn't give her morning coffee to spare a pig. She surely wouldn't give her life to spare Harriet.

As if she could read Janie's thoughts, Mama said, "Harriet wouldn't have existed, if not for me." She sipped her coffee. "It was nice of you to entertain her, until she was needed. You'll understand some day."

She patted a hand on the table, next to Janie's waiting breakfast. "Before it's cold," was all she said.

Janie shuffled numbly. To the kitchen table, soon after from the kitchen to the car, and finally from the car to the institute.

Hours later, she sat with Uncle Lou in the family

waiting area. It was a large room. Several clusters of soft furnishings surrounded tables ready to play videos, games, or the day's news. A few families huddled in spots across the room. Uncle Lou watched some politics show. Janie watched the other families, wondering what they had said to their pigs last night. Wondering if their pigs had known they were scheduled for murder this morning.

"Jane?" A hand rested on her shoulder. She scooted across the sofa, away from her uncle. "I've watched you read to that pig since before you could actually read." He chuckled. "It was hilarious, listening to the stories you made up when you were little, while you turned pages on some huge book. You imagined some of the most bizarre stuff, but you said it all so very matter-of-fact like, it made the craziness seem almost believable."

Janie remembered how she used to drag a pillow and blanket into the atrium and sleep against the warm chamber wall, while the pigs curled against the inside of the translucent barrier, as close to her as they could get.

"Jane, hon, I'm sorry you're losing a friend," he said. "But remember, you get to keep your mom. Without that spare heart inside her pig, your mom wouldn't have lived much longer."

Janie kept quiet. Uncle Lou would not appreciate the words wanting to burst from her mouth. She studied the other kids sitting with their families, wondered which of them read stories to their pigs.

Eventually a man in a white coat walked into the waiting area and over to Uncle Lou and Janie, to tell them news about the successful surgery. To inform them that the rest of the spare organs were in excellent condition, in deep freeze right there at the institute, waiting to be needed. Watching the man walk away and picturing Harriet pulled apart like a puzzle, Janie felt a tremor, deep in her guts. Like an earthquake that would never end.

* * *

Janie and Hartie sat together in the atrium a week later, separated only by the translucent wall. Janie had no book in her hand, and Hartie's pig face held no expectant look. A voice called from the direction of Mama's wing. Uncle Lou was summoning her to Mama's lounge.

"What took you so long?"

Janie stood at the double-door entry. Mama reclined on her favorite chair, eyes closed. Janie could never tell when Mama was really sleeping.

"Sorry."

"I need to run to the office, only for a little while," Uncle Lou said, pulling on his sport coat. "Keep your mom company while I'm gone."

Janie didn't move.

"Come on. You don't have to do much. Just sit and hold her hand. The meds are keeping her quiet right now, anyway." Uncle Lou winked at Janie. They both knew how grumpy Mama could get when she was disturbed.

Like they'd so often done, Janie's legs responded to the adult command, while her mind protested. The cumulative effect was Janie walking awkwardly to the chair next to Mama and sitting down with an abrupt thud.

Uncle Lou yelled as he headed to the door, "Call me if you need anything."

And they were alone.

Mama's hand rested on the edge of the recliner. Janie brushed the tops of Mama's fingers before resting her hand lightly on top of Mama's. Mama's fingers were so cold, Janie wondered why they weren't blue. She thought that maybe cold skin only turns blue in books, but not in real life. Janie watched Mama's chest rise and fall with every breath, telling herself, *Harriet is in there.* Over and over. *Harriet is in there. Harriet is IN THERE.*

Such a strange thought, knowing Harriet had been taken apart. Dismantled, as the institute called it. Broken down like a Lego toy. Harriet's heart went into Mama, and the rest of Harriet's Mama-parts went into some deep freezer. Eyes, lungs, kidneys, brain, and Janie wasn't even sure what other stuff. "We're the lucky ones, getting a pig when we're born," Mama had said so often when passing Janie in the atrium, reading to Harriet and Hartie. "You know, most people in this world can't afford their own pig."

Janie's teeth gritted. Tears slipped down her cheeks. Her hand pressed Mama's cold fingers, hard, then harder. Janie didn't care about cancers and diseases and defective organs, and she would surely never care about those things. She only cared about Harriet. She would run to the institute and break into the freezers and gather up all the pieces of Harriet, even tear the heart right out of Mama, if she only knew how to put them all together and make Harriet whole again. But she was old enough to know that wouldn't work, in real life. Real life was sickness and disease and murdered pigs.

If only Mama had a bunch more diseases, then all of Harriet's pieces would be almost put together again, inside Mama. If only Mama needed a new brain, then Harriet's brain would become Mama's. "They only take pieces of the brain," Mama said once.

The more pieces of Harriet, the better.

Janie stilled, looking at Mama as if she could see inside of her. Counting Mama's parts.

Mama twitched, and slowly opened her eyes. She moaned. "Child, I need a pill."

Janie removed her hand from atop Mama's, and straightened her back. She sat quietly, watching. Thinking. A few minutes passed before Mama stirred again. "Child," she said, louder. "My pills."

A calm washed over Janie. "Yes, Mama," she said. "Which pill do you need?"

Mama smacked her lips. "I don't know, child. Call Lou. He'll tell you." She fell into deep breathing again.

Janie sat for several minutes, her mind calculating, and then she left the room.

She returned to the lounge with her arms full, walking through the doorway without hesitation. She pressed on Mama's arm. "Mama, wake up. You said you needed pills."

Mama attempted to open her eyes several times before

she was successful. She focused on Janie's outstretched hand, cradling several colorful pills. "Are you sure these are the right ones?"

Janie lifted them to Mama's mouth. "Yes, Mama. I am absolutely sure."

Mama took the pills with some effort and drank water before laying back in her recliner.

Janie laid one of her bedroom pillows against the back of her own chair, puffing it up before she settled into the seat next to Mama and opened a book. She began reading out loud.

Mama's eyelids grew heavy, almost closing, until suddenly, they opened wide. She turned her head with effort to stare at her daughter, who was already on page two of her favorite story.

* * *

Discussion Questions

1. Why do you think the family kept their donor pig in a place they could see/access it? Is this about respect, foolishness, or something else?

2. Assuming this organ donation technology was possible, do you support the idea of an organ donor pig? Would you, personally, take a lifesaving organ from a donor pig? What if the donor animal were a higher, or lower, order animal? What are your animal intelligence limits for organ donation? *(rat vs. gorilla)*

3. If the value of life is on a sliding scale, why is it that we, as humans, get to judge the criteria by which other animals are judged? Wouldn't our scale be inherently biased towards humans?

4. Would you accept a donor organ from a clone (or twin) that was kept in a coma its entire life?

5. Do you think the little girl meant to kill her mother? If so, why?

A Change Of Verbs

Tom Teti

A change of verbs can be a boon to a man's life. Such was the thought that seized Simon McCalla in midbite of his double-toasted English muffin. It was Friday, precisely 7:52 AM by the clock on the range.

"I said, what time is it?" yelled his wife from the closet. She rummaged for something.

"Are you there? What in creation are you doing?"

"Sorry," he said. "Seven fifty-two, ah, three."

"I can't hear you." Her bark was muffled by the winter coats. She appeared in the doorway to the kitchen, pulling up her pantyhose and pulling down a slip under her skirt. Her legs were still sturdy. "What good does it do me to ask the time if I have to come in here to hear you?"

"Uh, seven fifty-three, ah, four."

"Yes, I see that, now. I have a meeting at the hospital with the chief of surgery. He's an idiot but a punctual one." She shook her head, inhaled through her nose and went back for a jacket. "What's the temperature?"

Simon, back to his English muffin, twisted in his

chewing to get a read on the thermometer mounted on the side of the shady window. "Sixty-two," he replied, and added his traditional caveat, "but this thermometer is unreliable, it's outside, you know, and in the shade."

"Did you hear the weather?" his wife demanded to know from deep within the same rack of coats.

"Sorry." He chewed. "Do you want the radio on? Carol?"

She muttered along in such a way that he could not quite be certain whether she had heard him or not. "I'm cold now, I just don't know if it will stay that way ... Oh, I'll just wear this." She emerged from the closet with a short, camel hair jacket. She bustled into the kitchen, dropped it onto the stool in front of which sat her rapidly chilling toaster waffles, and went to the powder room putting on dangling pearl earrings which he knew had been in her hand since she left the bedroom.

"Would it be too much to wait for me to eat one of these mornings?"

"You ..." He paused. "I can never tell if you are actually wanting to eat or not," he said, thinking of her ritual two bites at the counter, standing up, and tossing the rest of the cold waffle into the sink and down the disposal. Of course, she never heard anything he said unless he got up and went to the doorway, because the powder room light was connected to a very noisy exhaust fan. He stayed on his stool and finished his muffin. It was 7:58. At 7:59, exactly one minute before he had to leave the house, she would ask the daily question. Simon pondered his answer more intently than usual.

He watched the powder room. Carol's shoulder and elbow could be seen, as well as her handsome, forty-something derriere in that straight black skirt, the backs of her ankles in grey tights, and the stacked heels of her shoes, but not her face. He gulped the rest of his coffee, the dispiriting decaf she insisted they switch to oh-so-many months ago, and rose to face his fate. On schedule, it came.

"What are your plans for today?"

Simon pushed his rimless glasses up onto his nose. He stalled for time.

"Well, I teach the seminar, this morning."

"Yes?" she called.

"And I have a class at 1. And a meeting for the college newspaper at 2:30."

"Darling, I know that you have a job, that's not what I'm asking. We go through this every day." They were his usual answers and she anticipated them; they could be heard without turning off the fan in the powder room. "I am asking what you are doing after that." She prattled on about the dog and taking him round to have Dr. Berks look at his coat and confirm that the supplements he'd dispensed were working, as they seemed to be.

Simon gazed out the kitchen sliding doors at the dog, tethered to a come-a-long. He sat in a restless posture, panting with his tongue hanging out of his mouth, and looking into the kitchen as if he knew he was the subject of some eleventh-hour decision.

"Chiku must be evaluated before we continue with

more vitamins," Carol said. "You need to take him."

It was not a drastic situation. It wasn't even a problem situation. The dog was clearly fine. The challenge would then become, could he, Simon, finish his sentence before being sentenced himself?

The day ahead passed through his mind as he would like it to happen: a stimulating seminar with piquant seniors on the landscape of the body in 19th Century Literature (a cup of Sumatra off to the side); stilton and walnuts on spring mix at the Hound and Duck, while reading The Luck of Roaring Camp; class with hopeful juniors on America's Solitary Western Voices; a meeting at the newspaper where he would deftly quell a movement on the part of some of the female writers to cease promoting sports; afternoon half-caf from Perfumes of Arabica; a sit on the slab bench under the tulip poplar at the pond, musing about the qualitative effect of one's first sight of something beautiful; then, after scribbling the opening of a sonnet on the back of an envelope, he would go home, when the sun had a few minutes left, and he and Carol would walk the dog, prepare Bronzino with a butternut squash risotto, and open a bottle of Chardonnay, probably Australian, with fire in the fireplace and a movie, perhaps—

It was an old picture, meaning a picture of oldness, settled and two steps from a yawn, perhaps, but one that pleased him, made him feel warm, content, loving and loved. He wished for it, but pictured it as he feared it would unfold: seniors having Sumatra, decaf for him, and checking their cell phones to see how much longer until class was over; failing to say that he had other plans when one of the faculty asked him to have lunch and discuss curriculum; juniors cutting, because it was Friday and they could get drunk before dark; a bellicose argument between two sides of the newspaper staff and Simon hearing himself say that their concerns may be valid and should be addressed at student government; rushing home to take Chiku to the vet so the vet could say he looks great, then rushing back to prepare dinner, not the Bronzino because there wasn't time, but defrosted shrimp from the freezer, sautéed as some kind of quasi-scampi over linguine; Carol calling to say she'd be late, then crashing in exhausted, full of questions and directives, telling him the fire's too hot on a night like this and she doesn't want any wine because she's got a headache. Then, a movie, but she'd fall asleep at the thirty-one minute mark, her head crooked in the corner of the sofa, the dog asleep at her feet.

The moment had come. Simon took his tweedy jacket with the suede elbows from the hook by the back door, glanced toward the dog who was eyeing the door with a martial arts kind of calm, ready to break the spell at the drop of a leash, and marched to the powder room. As his wife returned her make up to its pouch and turned off the light and fan, Simon heard himself say, in the deafening quiet, "I'm busy this afternoon. I'm going to walk by the pond and work on my sonnet." He then gave her the expected peck on the cheek, turned and walked to the back door. His last vision of her was a modestly stunned gape as he pulled his cheek away from hers. Keeping his sensors alert for any protest on his exit, he tried as best he could to walk in a way he considered "normal" and hoped it appeared the same to Carol, though, internally, he was like a geyser about to spray. With his hand on the knob, he heard her say, "What about dinner?"

"I'll be back," he said, perfectly in stride through the door, and shutting it behind him.

The air felt brisk and lively. The sun glinted off his glasses but today, it didn't annoy him, he craved it. He slipped into his jacket and clipped down the flagstones to the brick lined sidewalk on his way to the college. This was the way a professor was supposed to feel as he began his day: hale, hearty, of sinewy mind and assured affect, headed for a day of scholastics and the acrobatic engagement of ideas. He waved to a man across the street. "Hello!" he called. The man looked back curiously, held up a finger of acknowledgment and frowned. Simon smiled. "Surprised him," he chuckled.

In ten minutes he was entering the old double window doors of Perfumes of Arabica. A very thin student, a girl with piercings in her eyelids and nose and dyed hair of an unnamable color, was scooping beans from a plastic-lined burlap bag that had Kenya stamped on it. She cheerily asked him if he wanted "a small decaf to go?"

Do not waver, do not deliberate, not today, thought Simon, as he imagined himself saying what he usually said: "That Sumatra smells good, but I suppose I shouldn't, I guess I'll have the decaf." Instead, he told her: "I want Sumatra, today."

Her eyebrows went up, rings and all. "Woo, Friday, the good stuff, huh?"

Simon did not blush. "Yep," he sang, and felt taller. He

doctored his cup with raw sugar (taboo) and cream, strode across the wooden floor to the old doors, bade the young thing goodbye, and stepped into the commerce of a campus morning. He sipped the bold, sweet, earthy stuff and made for Forbes Hall, his chest swelling with pleasure in himself.

The seminar began with a chuckle, as Simon pointed out the one student who had arrived without a cup of Sumatra from Perfumes of Arabica. "How do you expect to keep up, Nicolette, with such anti-social obstinacy?" The entire group laughed at the first thing their professor had ever said that they recognized as meant to be funny, and was. From then on, the interchange fairly hopped from mouth to mouth and, after two hours, the group wrapped up, seeming to pine for more.

Simon headed for The Hound and Duck. At the base of the steps he heard his name called. It was Carl Fromuth, the department chairman.

"Professor McCalla," he always called him; Carl attempted to foster a practice of tongue-in-cheek formalism. "I am anxious to arrive at some consensus about our plans for a media room, scheduling, security responsibilities, etc. I know we have a meeting for Tuesday, but I have invited Dr. Gupta and I think lunch today would give us a head start. 12, in the faculty dining room?"

Yesterday, and all the days before, Simon would have said, "I guess that would be all right," or "I was trying to — hmm, I 'll switch something around and be there."

"If you don't have other plans," said Fromuth, quite

insincerely, and beginning to re-ascend the library steps.

"I do, actually," Simon said, watching the Chairman's startled reaction with quiet excitement. "I have plans at lunch."

"Ah ... Well, Tuesday it will have to be, then."

"Good." Simon proceeded in the opposite direction, pushing his rimless glasses back on his nose.

During a mental speculation on the self-serving interchangeability of the verbs want, need, must, and have to, he allowed himself an annoyance at the glasses he continually had to reposition on his face, because they continually threatened to fall from it. He stopped to look at himself in the corner window of a classroom in the Science Center. "I hate these glasses," he said to himself, marveling at how one could simplify one's day by resisting equivocation. He did not say, "These are perfectly presentable glasses, though they do nothing for me and they slip all the time. But they are scholarly, if a little old looking." He didn't do that; he went to the heart of the matter — he hated them.

Simon passed the optician on the way to The Hound and Duck. He hurried in and removed his now openly reviled pair. "I am picking out new frames and must have them by —" he checked his watch "— ten to one. Can you do it?"

The clerk was the owner of the store who had fit him for his original glasses. "Not happy with these?" he asked, taking them between his fingers. "Let's slip them on and see what the problem is, perhaps we can make an adjustment."

Simon passed by the niceties that burdened his conscience — the not wanting to insult the owner by criticizing the product, the possibility that he might be offended by the assertion that he had not fit a customer well, and that he had recommended a set of frames based on his stereotype of an 'English professor'. Simon passed by those niceties by selecting a verb that told the man exactly what he wished the man to do.

"No," he said, moving his head to make it impossible to get the glasses back on his face, "I want a new pair."

"Ah, you don't want these," said the man.

With "afraid not" about to slip through his lips, Simon astonished himself. "I DO not." He went to the case displaying frames by a natty Italian designer. "There they are," he said, pointing to a pair of light tortoiseshell plastic ones with smallish round eyes.

The optician spoke haltingly. "I recall that, eh, you and your wife decided against those last time."

"Yes," said Simon, "without actually trying them. I'll try them today."

The man took them from the case and fit them on Simon. "Small, might take some getting used to, but very becoming with your coloring, actually," he said, with a bit of surprise.

Simon checked himself in the mirror. His face was new, his eyes bemused, holding something unsaid, instead of naked, exposed and defenseless as he looked with the other ones. His mouth was now a confident, drawn line, not a constantly waffling amoeba. He watched his mouth say, "Two hours?"

"Yes, sir."

"I'll be back at quarter to one." The man attempted to hand Simon his former glasses. "They slip off of my nose," he said as he exited the shop and made for the campus bookstore.

He bought a pair of reading magnifiers, the extra thin, extra light kind that one can look over while reading, and arrived at The Hound and Duck precisely at 11:45. He took a table by the window, ordered the salad with the stilton and began to read, feeling such a pleasure in his relaxed control of things that it, paradoxically, made him quite hyperactive. He fiddled with his fork, his spoon, his napkin, swiveled in his seat, checked his page numbers and observed those who walked by his window.

There was happiness in this fidgety state, he realized, there was anticipation: of the class he was about to teach, of the walk he was going to take, of his poetry, of his lunch, even of what waited for him on the next page of The Luck of Roaring Camp, even of the prospect that someone would walk past the window and want to corral him, join him. This was life as it should be, he thought; good or bad, exciting or boring, inspiring or disappointing, there must always be something in the balance, a mountain to climb, a fresh view on the other side. That is what drew him to Western literature, the presence of the mountain. The view might only be another mountain, but scaling that mountain was the next chance of something special.

His reverie, while staring at the blue sky, was

interrupted by the arrival of his salad and two slices of a rough-looking bread. He slathered stilton on one, envisioning Carol sitting across from him, bringing a forkful of quiche to her mouth, staring at what he was doing, just staring at the slice of bread and the cheese and the knife until he became self-conscious and stopped. "That's too much, you know." Well, not today, today it was perfect.

Simon found something unexpectedly invigorating in the story, a juxtaposition of mid-nineteenth century literacy and roughing it in early California, a purpose for the people, yet an absence of fussiness. There was a tap on the window.

"I have a meeting, soon, but will you still be here at 1?" Dr. Gupta mouthed the words more than spoke them. She always wore traditional Indian dress and, to Simon, her tiny, seventy-year-old frame always seemed lost in her garments, as if, upon closer inspection there might not be any body in there at all. She was the department's renowned guest professor, operating on a huge grant from several sources. A much published, highly sought-after scholar of poetry, who seemed to like Simon, for some reason he could not actually pinpoint. He felt the first pincers of difficulty from his new approach to life. He did not want to offend her.

"Sorry, no. Class at 1."

Dr. Gupta looked disappointed. She checked her wristwatch, then shrugged and smiled. "Another time," she said, and moved on down the avenue.

It was Simon's turn to look disappointed. The truth

worked, a postulate in which he had never had any faith. Dr. Gupta went on her way because fifteen minutes was not her idea of enough. So, what bothered him? Perhaps, he thought with an inner alarm, perhaps that he had not actually wanted her to go. He did not have to go in fifteen minutes if he waited until after class to pick up his glasses, but he wanted his new glasses, and he wanted to talk with Dr. Gupta about poetry. He could have invited her to join him, then suggested that they walk to the optician's together. That's what others always did to him, used to do to him, yesterday and before — they got him to spend his time as they wished.

Simon read. He ate. He loved. The fork was becoming a problem. He took a wide slab of baguette from the breadbasket and opened it from the side. It was just wide enough for him to make a modest sandwich. He stuffed spring mix and the lovely ochre and slate-colored stilton and walnuts and the vinaigrette, all of it, into the bread and chomped ungraciously but happily on it while he turned pages. Then, with no wife there to scowl, no colleague to inhibit, he did it again. The sandwiches were an unexpected find. So was the story. He inhaled them both with new lungs. Simon exited the Hound and Duck, and clipped across to the optician's. His first look at himself was enormously satisfying. He bounced out of the shop with a flair and a new face, and strode, erect and anticipative, to Forbes.

The juniors were buzzing with talk of Friday night plans and would not quiet down. Simon sat and watched them with a smirk. Under the hubbub, Stephanie Comer, ever in a front seat, said: "I like your glasses."

"Thank you," said Simon, pleased.

"Are they new?"

"Yes. You're the first one to see them."

"Really?"

Simon looked at her, young and twenty, frizzy locks and scrubbed carelessness, dark, ingenuous and willing to believe him. The equivocating responses he normally would have used occurred to him, things like "Well, other people saw me come over here, and some even looked at me, but no one has actually said anything until you. I didn't mean to mislead you." Instead he said:

"Of course not ... I'm teasing you." And he laughed, out loud.

While Stephanie adjusted with surprise, and a particle of delighted offense, the rest of the class focused on their instructor, who had just expressed voluble mirth in their presence. Simon seized the moment.

"What does the title, The Luck of Roaring Camp, signify for you?" They stared at him from one of those vacuous states that often went on for too long. Simon nipped it in the bud. "Stephanie?"

Stephanie began a speculation on the word "luck," that there must be luck coming in the story. Or not, said another young woman, it could be irony. Two of the male students picked up the word 'roaring' and spoke to the evocation of a place and a population that promised to be very lively and energetic. Several women added that it might be more literal, speaking of a setting simply bellicose from its "abundance of testosterone". All of the women then chimed in that the word 'camp' suggested a male world, to which all of the men countered that the first character officially mentioned was a woman. The women said she wasn't a woman, she was a prostitute.

And so it went.

It was a buoyant discussion, for any class, let alone Friday's. It ended too quickly, the students filing out with an unspoken ruefulness at its conclusion. Almost all of them told Simon to enjoy his weekend, and the young women complimented him on his glasses.

* * *

The news staff rebels were already gathered and in tedious debate when he arrived. Simon had been thinking ahead. He called for quiet.

"Do either of you have an agenda?" he asked.

The young women and the young men looked at each other. A moment of peaceful puzzlement was obliterated by seven voices squawking at once.

"Well," announced Simon, conclusively, "it is far too nice an afternoon to spend indoors arguing about what we will argue about. Get your agenda straight and I will see you Tuesday afternoon at 4 PM. Have a safe weekend." Simon ever so privately enjoyed the stunned silence and their eyes that followed as he exited first.

Simon made a beeline for Perfumes of Arabica. A different ex-student was in charge and overwhelmed, ripping the top of a burlap bag, Costa Rica stenciled on the side. "Hi," she trilled, "decaf?"

Instead of waiting politely for her to finish what she

was doing, Simon simply said: "I'll have medium, half French Roast, half Mocha Java decaf, to go."

He took his cup, fixed with more raw sugar this time, and cream, and sipped it walking. A pleasant breeze with a slight challenge in it crossed his face, mussing his hair; he let it. The path to the pond had shade from a bower of oaks in the afternoon and it made things harder to discern until one returned to the sunshine. When he did, he saw that all the benches which lined the edge of the pond were taken, except one. He went to it, sat, took out a pencil and Fromuth's Departmental "memo of the day," and started to put words on the back of it.

He heard a voice, a voice from "the nagging bin," a voice that always waylaid him when he was attempting to move from the analytical to the creative. "What are you doing? They are just words. You need a better plan." Simon remembered the other times he heard that voice and the defeated, dolorous way he would sit, acknowledging his lack of procedure. And there would be no poem. There would be nothing.

"I know," he said, perhaps aloud, "I am starting with words ... words I like."

"Ah, that is interesting," said a voice — this one was real. Simon turned. Standing above his shoulder was Dr. Gupta. He was so pleased to see her. "I knew a gifted man who worked in that way, also." She nodded at him, approvingly.

He did not say, "Well, it's sort of a first time for me." He said, instead, "I am hoping it will lead to an interesting place," and marveled that both statements were true, yet they told contrasting stories.

"I have not seen you here before."

"I plan to come more often than I do," he answered.

"Oh, you must do better. I come here all the time; it's a favorite practice of mine. It would be good for you. It appeared that I would not get a seat. Then I saw you and decided to ask if I could join you."

"Delighted." Not "By all means," not "Oh, if you think you need to be alone, it's actually time for me to go," not, "Oh, um, certainly, just shove my bag onto the ground," just "Delighted."

The doctor settled in next to him. "There. I look forward to this place so very much. In India, one does not find such places often, a small body of water where only birds bathe, surrounded by drooping trees and tall grasses, shaded and sunlit, all the same. Where I come from, we have either not enough water, or too much of it. Ahhh," she sang. She sat and looked at the water.

Simon felt his first real discomfort of the day. He held a pencil between his fingers and a piece of scrap on his briefcase, ready to channel the muses and rearrange his words. He was also ready for a rare dialogue on verse. But the visiting poetry scholar sitting beside him only stared at the Waldenesque scene before them; it was unnerving. Should he work and peacefully ignore her? Should he talk and disturb her quiet? One step further, he thought, that's what I must do, go one step further. What's the verb for this? *Engage*, that's the one.

"Do you think in words or images?" he asked.

She didn't change her gaze, but smiled. "What a very good question, and interesting. At this moment, I am thinking in images, but how far can we ever be from a word? One might even say that images are made up of words."

Simon chose his next verb, challenge. "We do have images before we learn words, however."

Dr. Gupta smiled again. "True, but once we do learn words, our images either expand, or become limited by them. The task is then to expand them because we have the means to magnify them, with words."

Now Simon smiled. He glanced at the words he had already written: "Beauty ... air ... spirit ... inane ... fingers ... water ..." They were scattered in a random cluster on the top third of the page. To those he added: "Waning ... surging ... flew—" and smiled again.

Dr. Gupta saw him, he knew, though she looked only at the surface of the pond in her benign fashion. "You must come here again. Do not let yourself divide into several beings. Keep the teacher and the poet and the man, all one."

When she excused herself to "use the library," he stayed, until the light turned dusky, and he began a deliberate and thoughtful walk home. Yet, before he reached his street, he took a detour and walked purposefully to the quad. He had no idea how to continue. "Here I am," he said to himself, "standing in the middle of the campus with no intention, no plan." He watched a girl slog across the lawn with her backpack overloaded, then three boys with no books doing a raucous, slapstick meandering to nowhere in particular. "Am I like them?" he asked himself.

He knew only one thing. He found a pay phone in the lobby of Covy Memorial Hall and dialed his house. He had never wanted a cell phone; now he wished he had one. Carol was not home, yet. His too long announcement played through to the end. "Hello, it's me, it's 5:55, I'm not there, as you can probably tell ... I'm not coming home ..." He hung up.

Simon felt, instantly, that he'd been mean and that what he had done was wrong, to hang up and not say what he meant, not clarify whether he would be home in two hours, or not until bedtime, or not at all. He knew it was an act of hostility, possibly an act of cruelty, inflicted on Carol, his wife of thirteen years, but directed at everyone. Yet, he knew, also, that he did not want to go home, and he didn't know what else to say about it, except that he wanted to never be beholden again to the routine others expected of him, if he could help it.

He wandered the lanes surrounding the college, passed the athletic fields, then the student houses, and the neighborhoods in which they roomed and carried out their blithe lives. He came upon J&D's corner bar.

Inside, there were two dozen drinkers, mostly students, two musicians and two bartenders, whom Simon recognized as ex-students. The musicians were setting up a microphone and amplifier. One of them, needless to say surprised, pointed at him and waved; he had been in a lit survey course several years ago. Simon held up a hand and smiled, then took a seat at the corner of the bar and ordered a lager.

He drank from thirst, emptying half the glass. This was a pleasant indulgence, he thought, and then it dimmed in his realization that he had been treating himself to indulgences all day. Treating himself to? Suggests a temporary break from routine. Allowing himself? Suggests a well-established discipline purposely lapsed. Giving in to? Suggests temptation's triumph over a faulty will. None of those verbs helped explain what he wanted this day to mean. He wanted the past to be only a building block, a scribbled ghost of an idea. He wanted this day to be the beginning of his second draft.

Before he was finished with his beer, another appeared. The bartender answered Simon's quizzical expression with a tilt of his head, indicating the guitar-playing former student, who waved again and smiled. Simon had not planned on staying. A second beer, a kindness, for certain, would obligate him. He would be obliged to drink it, and listen to the music. He could not choose a verb if no one would speak to him. Here, in this Friday night world of the campus bar, everything was carried out in sign language and he was in danger of spending his time as other people wanted him to.

Simon downed his first beer, took a sip of the second, told the bartender he was grateful but had to go, and left the bar, giving a thumbs up at the door to the musicians.

He wandered, though it wasn't really wandering, as he knew where he was and where each choice would take him. He realized, while grazing his hand through a bush that hung limply over a wooden fence, that he was experiencing a loneliness that endorsed him, a poet's eternal solitude, in a day in which he'd made time to squander time. A wonderful day, he'd loved it, and it would require his determination to continue, to make sure the next day and the next and the next would strongly resemble this first. The days might not be all as successful; it's a long life.

But something morose grew in him. At first, it seemed it was doubt about his will to proceed, but he knew enough about verbs and the people who use them to be ready for the long haul. No. He looked skyward. Stars twinkled, the moon shone, and there was a quiet space, for a change, where, in the dark charm of a fall evening, it dawned on him. "The phone call," he said, his neck arched toward the solar system. When his head returned to a level position, he chose the surest verb of all.

"I **love** you, Carol."

It was almost nine o'clock when he arrived home. There were no lights on inside. Perhaps she'd beeped in, got his message and stayed out, had dinner with her colleagues. Or, she came home, got his message and fumed, then went to meet Tracy and Cin, the single ones who spent Friday nights at the wine bar. Or, she never even heard his message, but left him one that she was away overnight at her sister's.

The dog did not come to the door; she could have taken him with her. There was no message on the machine from her, which suggested that she had received his. He toured the kitchen and found no signs of a meal either eaten or prepared. The living room gave no indication that any time had been spent there, no newspaper out of order, no empty potato chip bag, no crumbs, no shoes kicked off from the horizontal position and allowed to bounce wherever they would. Nothing like that.

Simon had the feeling that he had taken a risk, the same as he'd felt when he had once gone with friends on a sailboat round Cutter's Point, or when he had gone into the woods near his home when he was ten and walked too far, knowing he wasn't lost, but that he had broken an invisible plane and he was, in a new way, alone. He had sallied forth, today; he must keep doing that. He wanted the risk-taker and the boy of ten to stay.

Chiku trotted into view from the bedroom, blinking.

"Well, hello, young man." Simon said. He gave the dog a scratch and went to the bedroom — if that's where the dog had been, that's where Carol would be, and why he was so quiet. Simon walked softly to the side of the bed. She was in, under the covers. She slept face up, with her legs crossed at the ankles. The outline that her hips made under the quilt brought unexpected arousal. He thought of the last time he had been affected in this way while she was asleep, and how he had kissed her on the forehead and gone back into the living room to watch television. This time, he took off his jacket, his shoes and sweater-vest and tie, and climbed in with her.

She did not stir. Simon watched the bones above her cheeks and strong line of her nose for some sign of acknowledgement, but none came. Then, without opening her eyes, she answered the question she imagined he was asking.

"I was tired."

"Yes," he said.

"Did you enjoy yourself?"

It was a simple question with a complicated answer, and for most of his life Simon had not shied away from the complicated, for the complicated was the more complete truth. But he lay there next to his wife and thought for the very first time that the truth was never complete, even in its most complicated form, and he couldn't be responsible for all of it. Whomever we are speaking to have a hand in our truth, he thought — choose your verbs wisely. So, instead of telling her how eventful and triumphant and perambulating his day had been, he simply said: "I did," and hoped that he would continue tomorrow where he'd left off today. Then, out of his mouth came the thing he was thinking, had thought a hundred thousand times but had never, ever asked.

"Did you miss me?"

Carol still had not moved, but she opened her eyes and looked at him. She had been crying, he thought, and suddenly seemed genuinely glad to have him there.

"You have new glasses ... I like them on you."

She reached out, took his shoulders in her hands and kissed him, a long and confident kiss, the kind he remembered from before, when they were new to each other. "Take your pants off, silly," she said, in a voice he remembered from just such a time.

* * *

Discussion Questions

1. The story is called "A Change of Verbs," but what is Simon (the Professor) really changing about himself and the way he speaks?

2. The story seems to show the miraculous changes that take place when Simon changes his responses. If that's all it took to have a better/happier life, why do you think he (or others) ever say anything else?

3. Do you think Simon's change will, long term, be a good or a bad thing for him? What are the good and bad things that may come out of it?

4. How much like the new Simon are you in the way you speak? Why aren't you more?

5. What if Simon didn't love his wife? What do you think his "change in verbs" would have demanded he say/do?

I Do So, Like Durian

Jann Everard

The 504-streetcar grated against the curve of the tracks as it entered the station. It pulled to a stop directly in front of Holly. The doors opened with such a clunk that she stepped back, treading on the toes of the person behind her. She was blocking the door. A crowd of restless Chinese grandmothers nudged her forward with sharp elbows.

"Does this car go south on Broadview?" she asked the driver. He adjusted his seat and the booklet of transfers clipped to the dash. He didn't bother to look at her. "504 turns at Queen, 505 at Dundas," he said.

"But does it go south?" she persisted, and he flicked a thumb to the back of the car, signaling for her to board.

She had never been to Broadview Station before. She rarely used public transit. Her high school was within walking distance of her house. And her mother was happy to drive her wherever she and her friends wanted to go. "I don't like you girls alone on public transit," she'd say, the slight wrinkle of her nose suggesting that the matter wasn't so much about safety. "Besides, driving together gives us a little time to chat." She would perch on the edge of Holly's bed until the silence from Holly's friends went on a little too long.

Somewhere south of the station was the restaurant where Jon worked. Holly had tried to tease the name out of him but he'd evaded her. "It's downtown, not anywhere near where you live," he'd said. "Besides, you told me you only liked sushi and Italian from the Village." She'd pressed, scooting closer to him on the bench in the library where she kept him company while he studied at lunch. "I just want to know where you are on Friday nights," she said, her hand brushing his arm. His temptation was palpable, but while Holly silently pleaded for him to make a move, his lips stayed grimly set and his attention returned to his textbook. "It's on Broadview, near Gerrard," he conceded.

East Chinatown. Her mother would never agree to drive her there. She hated Chinese food and had always rejected the idea of trying dim sum when Holly had suggested it. "God knows what goes in those odd-looking dishes," she said. "Chinatowns everywhere smell of dried shrimp and rotting vegetables and the people are loud and pushy and—" She'd caught herself then, perhaps realizing how she sounded or that negativity made her inelegant. "I don't like that neighborhood, Holly, dear."

But Holly liked Jon. Liked the leanness of him, the smooth toffee of his skin and the taut arrow of his ambition. It felt as if he had bypassed the teenaged years and already knew something more about life. With Jon, she could almost see herself as an adult. Confident. Knowing. With him, a relationship could move past

Friday nights chilling with friends, vodka shots and inexperienced groping.

Holly texted Sasha to tell her she'd left Broadview Station and eyed the people around her to see if there was anyone she knew—anyone that might report Holly's whereabouts to her mother, who would surely ground her for lying or impose a curfew. Sasha had agreed to be her cover if Holly's mom got unexpectedly curious, but only on the condition that Holly texted every detail of her evening. She was thumbing a long message about the rude driver when she heard the streetcar's announcement system call out Queen Street. The driver had said the car turned at Queen. She rushed to the front.

"Have we passed Gerrard?" On Goggle maps, Broadview Avenue had appeared long. She'd been so focused on her text to Sasha that she hadn't noticed how fast the car was moving.

"Gerrard was a couple streets back," said the driver, his tone flat, his eyes dead ahead. He sounded the bell and swore lightly at some rowdy pedestrians who swarmed off the sidewalk at the Queen Street corner, blocking what was already a tight turn. As he waited for people to move, he said to Holly, "You can walk back. It'll only take you about ten minutes." He opened the door and let her out, taking advantage of the opportunity to call, "Get out of the way, you crazy bunch of drunks!"

Holly sidestepped a group loitering in the glow of a streetlamp, avoiding eye contact. When she looked up, she was in front of three girls with large, exposed breasts—posters on a brick wall. A couple of guys in toques smoked nearby. Their eyes raked over her, brash, hungry, but dismissive. Above their heads, *Jilly's Exotic Dancing* glowed in neon. Holly turned on her heel to cross the street, clutching harder to her Coach bag, running to catch the last few seconds of the warning countdown of the pedestrian light.

The pattern of black and white splotches painted on the outside of the restaurant on the opposite corner was meant to suggest the hide of a Holstein and, by extension, beef burgers, she guessed. As Holly passed the steamed-up windows, she glimpsed five or six patrons inside laughing while making crude sexual gestures and planned to text Sasha that all the people on this corner were lowlifes. For now, though, it was better to keep her phone in her pocket.

She took a glimpse at her watch. 8:30. She still had time to find Jon's restaurant. He wasn't off work until 9:00, although he'd told her that even after he'd finished serving customers, there was still plenty of work to do and he wouldn't be able to meet her. "If you're off work you should be able to go," she'd pointed out, and he'd looked at her—was the look impatient? She couldn't always tell what Jon was thinking—and said, "I'm expected to stay."

Holly twitched the zipper of her jacket a little higher. It was a crisp evening and she was wearing only a bra top with spaghetti straps underneath. Her friends—Sasha too—would be going to an all-ages dance club later, near where she lived in midtown. She'd put on the top hoping that Jon might agree to meet her friends there, to take a break, for her sake. She wanted him to dance with her. To hook up with her, finally. Or they could go someplace else. It didn't really matter as long as they spent part of the evening together. Up until now, they had mainly walked in the neighborhood parks during spares, talking about college, life after high school. The top's tight fabric, rubbing against her nipples, made her feel self-conscious and more forward than she'd intended. What if people walking toward her could tell how little she had on under her zipped-up jacket? What if Jon thought her outfit was over the top for a first date, slutty even? She kept her hand on the zipper of her expensive jacket, her arm hiding its logo.

Not far from the cow restaurant she noticed a northbound streetcar stop. She had no tickets or tokens, only three twenty-dollar bills her mom had given her for the weekend. Public transit drivers didn't make change; she'd have to walk. Her feet didn't hurt too badly yet, despite her heeled boots. Ten minutes, the driver had said. Acrid smoke from a cigarette made her speed up past a woman sitting on a cement half-wall. The woman had no coat and pulled on the cigarette so hard her cheeks caved hollowly.

The aroma of fresh bread floured the air and voices drew her attention to a bakery with its front door open. An Asian man in a dirty apron stood outside, facing the street, backlit by the bakery lights. He was young and looked a little like Jon. Like Jon, but not as attractive.

"Gerrard's not far, is it?" she asked.

"Yeas, yeas," he replied, as if chewing on the word. "First you go right." He gestured with his hand northward and then with a small head bobble to the left said, "And then you go right."

These directions confused her, but she decided not to press. Two very tall men in the bakery were looking her way, eyes narrowed. She was interrupting their work.

After the bakery, Holly passed a row of six Victorian row houses with stained glass windows and wrought-iron fences, a low apartment block, a school. This felt better. The houses were narrow, a quarter of the size of the homes in her neighborhood, but they had nice gardens. But then the businesses got shabby again. A few were permanently closed. The smell of garbage, heaped in piles, permeated the air, as did cooking oil. Looking down a few stairs directly to her right, there was a bent woman in a hairnet carrying an industrial-sized tray. Dumplings made in a basement. Her mother's words came back to her.

Ahead was a corner variety store, a submarine sandwich joint, a single man in a dark hoodie shrouded by the scented smoke of marijuana standing in front of the kind of coffee place Holly would never enter, the lowest on the coffee franchise food chain. The strip was otherwise deserted; Holly's footsteps echoed alone.

This couldn't be where Jon worked, not near an area like this. Where were the shops and clothing stores? Her cellphone vibrated in her pocket but she didn't remove it. She hadn't texted her friend in ten minutes or more. Sasha would be wondering why. Knowing Sasha was waiting for her to make contact gave her courage. With one press of a button, she could have her on speakerphone. She could tell her that this place was seedy. Or not. She could handle this alone. Sasha didn't have to know everything.

In the block above Dundas were a Mission-run second-hand shop and unkempt businesses that had signs in Chinese with English translations beneath. The 505 streetcar sped south and squealed as it took the corner onto Dundas heading west. It blew dried leaves across the pavement and stirred up a grit-storm in its wake. An ugly institutional block of what could only be subsidized housing butt up to the sidewalk, small high windows hung with red and gold medallions. She looked at them knowing she had no idea if they were religious or merely decorative. Jon would know. She'd ask him.

She could finally see the streetlights of the Broadview-Gerrard intersection ahead. The block was bright with signs, red on yellow, yellow on red, all in Chinese characters. It was crowded; the sidewalk narrowed by more garbage bins and collapsed cardboard boxes on the left, and people and produce spilling out of the stores on the right. A friend had said there were only a few restaurants on Broadview, that most faced Gerrard. Holly's plan had been to unobtrusively look in each one until she found Jon. But there was no way she could be unobtrusive here.

This was not what she'd expected. She didn't know what she'd expected. She'd expected something different, more familiar than this. It hadn't occurred to her that Jon's life was still so connected to his cultural roots. He went to her school, after all, in a neighborhood far from this. Lots of kids did travel from around the city to her school. Smart kids. Gifted kids, like Jon. It had always been his smartness, his studiousness, that had defined him, not his Asian-ness.

She stopped before she had waded too far up the block and looked up at the signs again. Sing BBQ Restaurant. Ka Ka Lucky Seafood BBQ Restaurant. She looked at that one again. Had they no idea? Poor Jon, if he worked in the Ka Ka Lucky Seafood BBQ Restaurant.

She was pushed closer to a tier of boxed fruits and vegetables. Next to her was a pile of large, football shapes—she didn't know if they were fruits or vegetables. They looked armored, covered in dull, drab-colored spikes. She turned to a fellow who was stacking oranges and gestured.

"What is this?" she asked.

He answered, but she couldn't mimic his response. "Pardon?" she prompted.

A younger woman beside her answered. "Is durian. Smell." She held one of the fruits closer to Holly's nose and, even as it approached, she could tell she was going to gag from the odor. The woman looked away, smirking a little.

Holly straightened her shoulders and glared at the woman. If she didn't know a durian, it wasn't because she was ignorant or disinterested. She wanted to know durian and that stack of tubers there and that heap of green vegetables next to her here. Defiant, she grabbed a plastic bag from the roll above the oranges and shoved into it the largest durian from the pile, knotting the plastic closed. She strode into the store and held out a twenty to the young girl at the till, who took the bill and returned change without expression.

The next business was a small restaurant. It glowed

with the bluish light of old-fashioned fluorescent tube lighting. The walls were the color of a school bathroom, the tables streaked to show the direction of each wipe of a dirty washcloth. Four or five patrons sat scattered around the room watched over by a woman who stood with her weight shifted onto her right hip as if it were too painful, or required too much energy, to stand straight. High in the window hung dead birds, their cooked skins glistening and crisp. At the back, in a filthy apron stood Jon, his expression closed. The plastic tub he held brimmed over with dishes smeared with jelled sauce and flecks of rice and noodle. A door beside him was propped open to reveal the carcass of a pig, hanging in its entirety, from a metal hook in the ceiling.

For a second, panic brewed in Holly's stomach. She desperately wanted to be somewhere else. Someplace dim. Someplace anonymous. Just to think about what all this meant. To practice a reaction. But what reaction? Jon wasn't wearing the white-shirt-black-pants uniform of the servers at the kind of restaurants she was used to, but cheap, shiny polyester. The smells weren't anything she was used to either. The area was poor and chaotic, the restaurant plain.

But it was also exotic. Her parents had never brought her to a place like this. She'd arrived here by herself. Her choice. And everything was so totally outside her experience that it felt like a small act of rebellion. Liking Jon had already made her see differently in some ways. Before she'd met him, her future had felt blurry with the soft edges of entitlement. His was sharply defined by a hunger to get on with it, to make life happen. Success wasn't inevitable in Jon's mind—it had to be manufactured. That's what made him so attractive to Holly—the intensity with which he worked for what he wanted. She wanted him to show that same intensity to be with her. She'd show him she could step up to a challenge too. The defiance that had compelled her to buy the durian propelled her through the restaurant's front door. Jon looked up, his forehead furrowed.

"What are you doing here?" he asked.

His embarrassment stiffened her resolve. "I'd like to eat." She glanced at the woman. "I'd like to try this. I hope it doesn't need much cooking." She held out the plastic bag containing the durian. This set off a long flurry of conversation between the woman and Jon. She waited. "Is your boss okay with that?"

"She's not my boss. She's my mother. You won't like the flavor of this." Jon peeled off his apron and approached, reaching for the bag. It was heavy; her shoulder was beginning to ache from holding it out. She turned toward Jon's mother. "I'm Holly. I'm pleased to meet you."

"She doesn't speak English." He held the bag gingerly. "This—" he considered, his glance bouncing around the room, "is an acquired taste."

"I'd like to try it anyway." Incredibly, her sense of confidence kept growing. "How do I say hello to your mother in her language?"

John shook his head. He pulled out a chair. "Sit here. I'll prepare it for you." Holly ignored him, smiled hard at his mother.

~ 353 ~

"But I'd like to see how to prepare it myself. Can't I go to the kitchen with you?" She made gestures, pointing at the back, mimicking the slice of a knife, holding Jon's mother's eyes, trying to win her over.

The woman, who had straightened, grew animated. She thrust her chin at the back of the restaurant and chattered to Jon. He argued, but relented once she moved toward them, sweeping them toward the kitchen door with flicks of her hands.

Holly grabbed the discarded apron from the back of the chair where Jon had dropped it and pulled it over her head. He was ahead of her, leading the way into the kitchen. As she was about to pass the pig carcass, she stopped, put her hands on its sides and did a little dance step that made the carcass sway on its hook. She didn't bother to look back into the restaurant. If anyone asked about her evening she could say she had gone dancing. But what anyone thought if they saw her here didn't really matter anymore.

* * *

Discussion Questions

1. Holly's mother seems to have an exceptional dislike for Chinese culture, and for Chinatown. Why do you think that is? Why doesn't Holly share that dislike?

2. Holly seems to find Chinatown interesting and is willing to embrace it. Would her mother's reaction be different? If so, why?

3. Does it matter that Holly's reason to expand her cultural horizon is simply to talk to a boy she is interested in? Are there better or worse reasons to try new things?

4. What keeps Holly's mother from embracing new experiences? Is there anything you can do to keep that from happening to you?

5. When Holly's mother finds out Holly went to Chinatown, they will likely fight over it. What will be the result of that fight? What is the likely result of Holly and Jon's dating? Is it possible for Holly's mother to handle the situation differently/better?

In Love And War

Veronica Leigh

April 1943 - Krakow, Poland

Irena was bent over her needlework, stitching the frayed seam of her skirt when she heard a single gunshot ring out. She jerked and then scowled. After four years of war, she ought to be used to it. Why, the other night a bullet penetrated through her wall while she slumbered. Had it not been for a volume of Slowacki's poems on the bookshelf which shielded her, she would have been another civilian fatality.

How long would it have taken for someone to find me? Irena frowned. Her world was small. She lived alone, in a one room cottage, and she never deviated from her routine of work, errands, and church.

Draping the finished garment over the arm of the chair, she stretched and yawned. It was nearly midnight and she would have to be at the enamel factory early. As the cleaning lady, she was hardly essential to the war effort, but she kept everything tidy. Her pay was barely enough for food and for her to make rent every month, but she managed to survive. *Survive.* That was the key word. She longed for better times, when she didn't have to worry whether or not she would end up on the streets. There were moments when she truly hated herself, but she often had to sin to survive. Stealing, buying off the black market, spending the night with her employer to receive better wages ... all to survive. She weekly confessed her sins to the priest, but the guilt was still there and she was no better off.

Irena changed into her nightgown, scrubbed her face and ran a brush through her blonde tresses, combing until it shined. She moved the candle to the nightstand and knelt to say her customary prayers. Then after blowing the candle out, Irena slid beneath the covers and scooted down into the mattress.

A frantic knock sounded on her front door. *Oh, go away!* She yanked the sheet over her head but the pounding continued. *It could be the Germans!* Bolting upright in bed, her heart nearly stopped. She rationalized she had done nothing wrong and had nothing to fear. However, that never made much of a difference to the Nazis. They never needed a reason to arrest someone.

Irena crossed herself, rushed to the door, and eased it open. A shadowy figure barged in, knocking her aside. The intruder shoved the door closed.

"Who are you? What do you want?" Irena yelped and fumbled for the doorknob, but the stranger jerked her away and pushed her against the wall. He clamped his hand over her mouth; the pressure on her lips prevented her from crying out.

"Don't scream!" The man commanded, his voice wracked with panic. "I need help."

Her eyes adjusted to the dark and she was able to make

out his face. He was near her age, strong and tall, and obviously on the run from the Germans. *He must be part of the resistance!* Irena deduced. While the Nazis reigned over Poland with an iron fist, the Polish resistance refused to surrender. Groups of young men and women operated clandestinely, risking their lives to follow their conscience. They were Poland's unsung heroes.

No matter the danger he put her in, she could not abandon her countryman in his time of need.

Irena nodded meekly.

The man eased his hand off and he took a step back.

Irena retrieved the candle, relit it. "Who are you?" She demanded.

He made no response, other than a small moan.

Focusing her gaze on him, she gasped.

Blood had soaked through one of his white-shirt sleeves. A stream ran down his arm, dripping into a puddle on the floor.

Irena grasped his shoulder and propelled him to the bed. Once he stretched out, she tore open the soiled material. The flesh of his bicep had been snagged, but when she stuck her fingertips into the gash, she felt no bullet or shrapnel. It was nothing more than a scrape, but a deep one at that.

His eyes protruded from their sockets and ragged breaths wheezed from his quivering lips. The more he panicked, the faster his blood flowed.

"Shh, calm now." Irena ordered. "Think of something pleasant. Think of Chopin's 'Impromptu.'" To help him along, she hummed the wistful tune and soon he joined in and his breathing evened out.

She fetched a basin of water, towels, an old bottle of vodka, along with the darning needle and thread she used earlier on her skirt. Passing the bottle to him, she directed, "Drink this. It should take the edge off."

He pinned her down with his piercing blue eyes, but he did as she instructed and chugged a hearty gulp. Then she grabbed the bottle and took a swig, to steady her own nerves.

Irena folded a towel and wedged it between his teeth, so he would not bite through his tongue.

She wiped off the excess blood and bathed the area before splashing a plentiful amount of the drink on his wound. He gave a hoarse shout, but the cry was muted by the cloth. Holding the pointed end of the needle to the flame and hoping it was sterilized enough. Threading the eye of the needle, she muttered a prayer to the Holy Mother to guide her nimble fingers. She tried to envision his skin as nothing more than a split seam, like the one on her skirt.

The man tremored from the inside out as she pierced his flesh with the needle and sewed the folds of skin back together. In and out, in and out, over and over again. The slim bit of metal punctured through as though his flesh were a flimsy piece of leather. When she finished, she snipped the thread and grimaced at the matted mess.

It would be a miracle if it does not become infected or doesn't rip back open. Irena concluded, as she wiped off the blood that had caked on her fingers. Flecks of red had dried on her nightgown, but there was no point in changing, since she had no other nightgowns to change into.

His shaking subsided, and his breathing had grown shallow enough, that she feared he was slipping away.

Irena touched his brow and smoothed back his damp, blondish hair. Warmth radiated from his face. There was still life in him. A handsome man, he had a broad forehead embroidered by neatly trimmed eyebrows.

"Max," His delicately curved lips formed into a bemused smile.

"What?" Irena blinked her confusion.

"Max is my name." He stared at her through his hooded, cornflower blue depths. "I apologize for forcing my way in, but the Germans would have killed me if they had found me." He continued, looking a little sheepish. "The blackout curtain in your window had come loose and I saw the light. I hoped that you would help me. I was desperate."

"Don't worry." She waved him off. "You are welcome to stay as long as you would like."

"I shouldn't. If the Germans find me, you will be put to death."

"No one knows you are here and on the off chance someone does figure it out, I can tell them you are my lover. No one will know you are part of the resistance."

"I would consider that the highest compliment, to be your lover, especially after you have saved my life. But I am not a resistance fighter." Max slid his hand down into his trouser pocket and extracted a white cloth. There was a blue six-pointed star in the center. "I am a Jew."

Irena crossed herself once more. Having a Jewish man in her house, although she had been unaware of his heritage, was cause enough for the Germans to take her out and shoot her.

"Please," Max's face crumbled, surrendering to his pain. "I beg of you, don't turn me in. I will be gone by morning. You will never have to see me again."

Irena chewed on her lower lip. "All right, but you must be gone before sunrise." She dragged the chair over to the bedside and watched as he began to drift off.

So, *Max is Jewish*. She shrugged. He had a good face. With such Nordic features, he could have easily passed for a Christian. Perhaps even a German, if he worked on his accent.

Krakow's Jewish ghetto had been liquidated in early March. Whoever wasn't killed or deported, was taken to the Plaszow camp. No one in Krakow could deny knowing of the Jews' plight. People simply feigned ignorance. When the trains came through on Sunday mornings, the parishioners just sang louder in church.

A pang of guilt coiled and settled low in her belly. She, too, had looked the other way, convincing herself that she had nothing to do with the Jewish people. Not that she had ever bought into the German's rabid propaganda: that the Jews were subhuman or needed to be eradicated. It was easier to go about her business. After all, she didn't want to die.

Helping a member of the Polish resistance was a

different matter entirely. Folks – herself included – were more inclined to help a resistance fighter. The fighters were one of their own.

But a Jewish man …

Somehow, Max had survived the liquidation and escaped being sent to Plaszow, the small concentration camp. For him to approach her for help was foolish. Jewish people never knew who they could trust; who would not hand them over to the Gestapo. The Nazis handsomely rewarded those who betrayed Jews. Five hundred zlotys a head was the standard payment for betraying a Jew to the Gestapo. Or, so she last heard.

"What is your name?"

Irena hadn't realized that she started to doze until she heard Max's raspy question. Glancing at the clock, it was near two. She rubbed her eyes and looked down at him.

Max was half-asleep, his lids sagging, but he fought to stay awake.

"Irena." She mumbled. "So, you escaped the liquidation?"

"Yes. I sneaked out through the sewers before the liquidation began and a priest hid me. I had to leave because my hiding place was compromised. The Germans nearly caught me earlier and shot at me, but I crawled underneath a lorry until it was safe to come out. Then I found you." His voice wavered as a large tear rolled back into his hairline. "I think I must be the last Jew alive in Krakow. Maybe even Poland. I should have died with the rest of them."

"You must have family somewhere."

"Not anymore. My wife died of typhus." His gaze settled on her right hand. "Where is your husband?"

"Don't know." Irena twisted her wedding band around her finger. The ring had become part of her, like a second skin. She never removed it, not even when she washed dishes or bathed. She often forgot that she was wearing it. "He never came home after defending our country. I worry that he was among those at Katyn. He was an officer."

Earlier that month, mass graves were discovered near the Katyn Forest. Graves of Polish soldiers. The Russians blamed the Germans, the Germans blamed the Russians … and the deceased Polish men were forgotten and their families could not mourn them properly. Her husband, Andrej, had been a lieutenant and he had been sent to the east to fight. To defend Poland against the Russians when they invaded. That much she knew. Then some of his personal effects had been mailed to her, but there was no confirmation on whether he lived or died. No word at all.

No, deep down, she did know. Andrej was dead and had been dead for a few years, but it pained her too much to admit it.

"I am sorry." Max heaved a sigh. "No children?"

"No, none at all." Irena once mourned that she and Andrej had not had children. Now that Andrej was gone and she was alone, and the war raged on, it was for the best. "I am alone."

"Then we are two lost souls, cursed to roam the earth until death claims us."

"How very dramatic." She tapped her chin in contemplation. "You were a writer or a teacher?"

"A journalist." He nodded. "But that was a lifetime ago."

A lone tear trickled down Irena's cheek. She never broke down, not since her husband ... *went missing*. Her tears had flowed for days, leaving her to feel raw. Once she regained control of her emotions, she hadn't cried since.

Until now. Something about Max and his story stirred something within her, feelings that had long lain dormant. He, too, had lost a spouse and was alone in the world. She hated being vulnerable.

Raising his good arm, Max disregarded his own pain, crooked his finger and caught the droplet before it fell.

Her eyes locked with his and releasing a small cry, Irena leaned forward and briefly pressed her lips to his. The kiss wasn't a lover's kiss as much as it was her searching for a balm for her lonely soul. He took her hand and tugged on it until she joined him in bed, and he was not content until she rested her head on his shoulder.

In another time and in another place, she could have fallen in love with Max. But it was too late now.

She drifted off, barely remembering the brush of his warm lips upon her brow.

When Irena opened her eyes again, the dark of the night had begun to recede as the morning's light seeped through the curtains. Moving her arm, blindly searching for him, she found the other side of the bed empty and growing cold in Max's absence.

Scanning the room, taking note of its quiet, she realized Max had already departed. *Oh God, he can't leave!* Not now! She gulped. *I need him.* She wouldn't be able to survive without him!

Irena slid out of the bed and she noticed the light flickering off of something on the coffee table. Hurrying over, she plucked it up and exhaled. A golden, heart-shaped locket. *He left this as payment.* Laying the necklace back down on the table, she jammed her bare feet into her shoes by the door and wrapping herself in the shawl, she bolted outside in hopes of catching Max before it was too late.

The street was uncharacteristically empty, save for a lone, retreating figure at the far end of the road. He was ambling towards the rising sun as though he were heading towards heaven.

Max! Irena mouthed his name and sprinted after him. When she reached him, she grabbed his elbow and spun him around. "What are you doing? Where do you think you are going?" she demanded.

Max was trembling from head to toe, a result of the blood loss and wearing only a tattered shirt and slacks on a crisp early morning. Beads of sweat broke out across his brow. He was too weak to go off on his own. Max wouldn't make it, not in his compromised condition. His wound drained him, body and soul.

"Come on, come back." Irena linked her arm through his and led him back towards the cottage.

"Irena, you do not have to do this." Max protested,

though he was too weak to put up much of a resistance. "You have already done enough."

"Hush," Irena stubbornly shook her head. "Come with me." Reaching for his hand, she led him back to the cottage. She guided Max into the bed. Patting his fevered brow with a damp cloth, she whispered, "Try and rest."

Max's eyes watered. "Irena, no!" He struggled to sit up, but she nudged him back down. "Irena, if the Nazis find me hiding here, they will kill us both."

"Let's not worry about that now. Just rest, Max. We will figure everything out later." She caressed the side of his jaw, pressed a kiss to his cheek, and took her seat once more by his bedside while he rested.

Irena let out a weary sigh and crossed herself.

Max was right. If the Nazis did discover him, they both would be taken out to the street and executed. Hung or shot … most likely shot. The Nazis liked to shed blood. Irena heard by word of mouth that Poland was the only country in which hiding Jews was punishable by death.

However, if she turned him over to the Gestapo herself, she would have five hundred zlotys to her name. Not a fortune, but it would mean she would not have to work herself to death, or steal, or sleep with her employer for a little while. The locket should fetch her something too. Max had no family, so no one would miss him. In his condition, he would likely die anyway. Infection or pneumonia would set in. He might even have typhus, like his wife did. If he were on his own, the Germans would eventually discover him.

It's not as if I can hide him. Irena wrung her chapped

hands, her throat thickening. She couldn't support them both on her wages. Reporting him to the Gestapo now would be a small mercy. It was better this way so he wouldn't suffer long. *Poor man.* Max didn't deserve betrayal – that's exactly what it was – but if anyone was to survive this war, it was going to be her. *I will survive one way or another.*

Irena dressed quietly and put on her coat. Remembering the locket, she stuffed it in her coat pocket. She crept over to Max's sleeping form and bending over, she brushed her lips against his cheek. "I will be back soon." She murmured near his ear.

He smiled in his sleep, blissfully unaware of what was about to happen.

Irena left the cottage and headed in the direction of Gestapo Headquarters, disregarding the guilt weighing her down. She would confess it to the priest later on and be absolved. God would understand.

* * *

Discussion Questions

1. Do you judge Irena negatively for her decision to turn Max in for a reward? Are there additional things you could learn about Irena and her experiences in the war that would change your mind/excuse her actions?

2. Does a person have a first duty to keep themselves alive, and only a second duty to help others? Would this even apply to Irena, or is her situation not desperate enough?

3. Does it matter that Irena went and brought Max back to her house and only later decided to turn him in? Would it be worse if she brought him back in order to turn him in? (The end result is the same ...)

4. What would you have done in Irena's situation? As a %, how sure are you that you know what you would have done if you were actually in the same situation?

5. Is it fair to judge someone else's choices based on a type of decision we have never had to make? If not, then why do we do it?

C a s t   O u t

Joanna Michal Hoyt

Verity woke with her hands at her throat, gasping. With her eyes open she saw thick darkness. With her eyes shut she still saw the shapes of her nightmare, the spitting flames of the fire that had eaten half of Blackburn Settlement, started by her own hearth-fire. Either way she smelled smoke and decay. Knowing that the smell was in her mind only did nothing to lessen it.

She stared toward the hearth, holding her breath so as not to be distracted by the plume it made in the frozen air. She couldn't see the pulsing of the embers under the ashes. Had she let the fire go out again? Already she'd had to borrow fire from her neighbors six times that month; Goody Berowne had sour words for her, and more sour words about her ...

Verity pushed back the quilts, rolled off her straw mattress onto the floor, felt for the poker, and stirred the ashes. The embers glowed. She wouldn't have to go fire-borrowing again.

Her chilled hands were clumsy. One glowing bit of wood rolled from the hearth and across the earth floor in the direction of her mattress. She beat at it with the poker until it was completely extinguished. Then she raked the ashes back over the coals, crawled back under the quilts, and breathed out hard, trying to make a warm place with her breath. Slowly her body relaxed toward sleep ...

And stiffened. The mattress was warm again. Was it too warm? That ember had rolled toward it. What if a spark had flown into it when she wasn't looking and was smoldering in the coarse cloth, about to ignite the dry straw inside?

She'd wake when the mattress caught fire, and she'd put it out.

With what? The water in the pail was frozen.

There was a clear foot of snow on the ground. She would throw snow on the mattress ... if she woke in time. But such a fire might smoke heavily. What if the smoke choked her in her sleep, and the fire devoured first her cabin and then the whole settlement?

That was hardly likely, she told herself. A woman in her right mind would not think of such a thing.

A woman not in her right mind may be more of a danger to her neighbors than she knows, she answered herself. *Best take precautions.*

She wept as she hauled the mattress out the door, rolled it in snow, hauled it back in cold and sodden, slung it over her one good wooden chair, set the chair as close to the hearth as she dared (not very close), poked the fire back to life, and wrapped herself in quilts to watch the night out.

She woke to gray light filtered through the oiled cloth

of the window, to bone-crunching cold and a dead fire. She tried to shrug off her quilt. The pain in her scalp stopped her. Her hair was frozen to the quilt with mucus and tears.

Verity held her hands to her belly until they thawed enough to work the scissors and hack her hair off on one side. She pulled her coif on tightly, but still felt ragged edges of hair sticking out. She couldn't go fire-borrowing like that. If she was lucky the neighbors would know her for a daftie, cluck about her to each other, shun her even more markedly than they already did; if she was unlucky (and what else had she ever been?) they'd take her for a witch, and then ... she smelled smoke again, tried to think of something else.

She spent most of an hour struggling with flint and tinder before a spark caught. It was another hour before the fire burned hot enough to do any good. She'd meant to make soap, but the day was lost. Again.

She'd forgotten that eleven-year-old Prudence Carlyle was coming to make soap with her. When Prudence knocked at the door, Verity considered pretending she wasn't home. Then she reflected that Prudence could see the smoke of her fire. She opened the door, saw Prudence staring at her face and hair, at the soggy lump of the mattress.

"You're ill?" Prudence asked.

"Yes," Verity said. A sane woman might be taken ill. "I can't make soap with you today. I hope this isn't catching, but the good Lord only knows; you'd best run along home. I'll ... I'll stop in and tell you when I'm ...

better."

Which you will never be, a cold voice murmured inside her ears.

Verity burst into tears. When she looked up, the door was closed and Prudence gone.

Verity brought a frozen hunk of pork in to thaw for stew, then sat down to spin, trying to steady her breathing to the rhythm of the wheel. It almost worked. At noon she went out to break the ice from the cow's water trough again. Coming around the back of the byre, she glanced toward the road and saw Goody Carlyle's short upright figure bustling toward her house.

Goody Carlyle hadn't seen her yet. Verity lacked courage to face her exaggerated patience. She ducked back behind the byre and into the woods and started walking, staying just in sight of the cabins lining the road (she'd learned not to wander in the wildwood in her fears; it was too easy to get lost), but far enough off the road and into the trees so no one was likely to call to her.

When the hail came rattling down through the bare branches, she'd already walked a fair piece from her cabin. She ran for the nearest place she had a right to be: the meetinghouse.

The meetinghouse was the settlement's one stone building. On weekday winter mornings the children met there to learn from whichever of the settlement's elders had learning and time to spare. On Fridays, Saturdays and Sundays the settlement's two Jewish families, twelve Catholic families, and seventeen Protestant families of one kind or another held their prayer meetings. The different kinds might mutter about each other, but they managed to share the meetinghouse, and to avoid bloodshed; most of Blackburn's settlers had come upriver fleeing from blasphemy laws or witch trials or deadly fights between groups of believers. In between lessons and prayer services, the meetinghouse stood open to whomever had need of prayer, or of shelter. To be sure, some people had suggested locking it after the Strangers – the first newcomers to enter Blackburn in a generation – began coming upriver with their shadowed eyes and their charred bundles, but since so many of the Settlement's folk used the space, and since making dozens of keys would be a nuisance and an expense, it was open still.

Verity ducked inside, sat down on a back bench and tried to steady her loud gasping breaths. As she did so she realized someone else was there.

Goodman Knowlton, who often led the prayer meetings Verity attended, rose from one of the front benches. "Mistress Clark, are you all right?" Knowlton asked.

She opened her mouth to say *Yes*. "No," she said.

"Are you ailing? Shall I go for Frau Abramowitz?"

She looked down at her hands. "I am afraid."

"Has someone hurt you? Threatened you? One of the Strangers?" His voice sharpened.

"No! No, it is only that I am afraid."

"Of what?"

She thought on the nightmares that had haunted her for the past year, or perhaps for the five years since her father's death, or perhaps all her life – she found it increasingly difficult to remember.

"Of fearing," she said. "And of the harm I may do."

He looked startled, then nodded. "Those are wise fears," he said. "But perfect love casteth out fear–"

"Because fear hath torment," she continued the verse. "I know that. I don't know perfect love."

"Then you are human," Knowlton said. "Mistress Clark, what harm do you fear you will do?"

She tried to tell him. It was hard to find words. Perfect fear casts out language as well as love. At last she gave up on words, looked up at him again. He was rubbing the bridge of his nose between his thumb and forefinger.

"Do you truly think these things are ... likely?" he asked.

"No! I know that I am mad to think of them. But how can I trust myself if I am mad? How can I not be afraid?"

"There is another promise," he said in the ringing voice he used for reading from Holy Writ at meetings. "Ye shall know the truth, and the truth shall set you free."

"I know all the promises," she said dully.

"And you know that lies come from the devil, the father of lies? And you have been listening to him?"

"I am not a witch!" she said, clenching her mind against the fear. She'd not seen a witch trial herself, or what followed after, but she'd heard the tales, she'd dreamed.

He jerked his head back as though she'd struck him. "And I am a sinner, may Almighty God forgive me, but I am no witch-hunter! I never meant that."

"What did you mean?"

"I don't know," he said with a simplicity that took her off guard. "I was trying to find an answer for you. I don't know. But I think it's true that the devil sends these fears to deceive you. Mistress Clark, that isn't the same as saying that you are a witch, that you are calling up the devil! The devil lies to us all." He looked away at something Verity couldn't see.

"So I am to tell myself that my fears are lies and I must not have them? I think that is true, but I can't make myself believe it. I need something more."

"So I believe. That's a hard truth you've spoken. Not the only one you've told me today. You know the saying: 'tell truth and shame the devil.' I hear you that it is not enough. I know no more, though. I will pray for you. I will think."

Her fear was ebbing, replaced by hot embarrassment. "I thank you, Master Knowlton," she said. "I'd best get home; the sleet's done now, and I've bread yet to start, and ... oh, God have mercy, I ran away from Goody Carlyle and left the fire unbanked!"

She was up and out the door before he could stop her, running down the road, not caring who saw.

Her cabin still stood unburned. Entering, she saw the fire dancing on one end of the hearth, and a woman moving her still-damp mattress closer to the flames.

The woman rose and turned, showing Verity her lined face, bright eyes and salt-white hair.

"Frau Abramowitz?"

"You'll forgive my trespassing, I hope, Mistress Clark. I came to check on Goody Carlyle's son's injured hand and, after I told her he was mending well, she said you were sick and not answering your door."

Verity combed through her mind for an ailment that Frau Abramowitz might believe in. Then she thought, *Tell truth and shame the devil.* "I am sick," she said, "in my mind and soul." And she told Frau Abramowitz what she had told Goodman Knowlton.

Frau Abramowitz looked closely at Verity as she spoke.

"Yes, you are afraid. You're stiff with it."

"I meant not to let it show."

"Some women try that in childbirth – they hide the pain and make it worse. There is no need. What would it look like if you chose not to hide? If you went into the fear?"

Verity glanced at the closed door, then at Frau Abramowitz.

Frau Abramowitz sighed. "I've seen women in fear and in pain before, and have you heard me gossip about that?"

Verity shut her eyes, let the fear rise up to fill her, let it curl her in on herself. Soon she lay in a ball on the floor with her eyes screwed shut, her teeth clenched, her spine curled, her legs drawn in, and her dangerous hands fisted in her midriff where they couldn't hurt anybody.

"So," Frau Abramowitz said, calm and steady as though there were nothing strange in what Verity did. "That's the fear. Hold it for three breaths. Then let it go."

"I can't stop being afraid," Verity muttered through clenched teeth.

"No, but you can let it back out of your body for now," Frau Abramowitz said. "A little piece at a time. Start with your feet."

Verity could do that. Could uncurl her toes, let her legs straighten. Could release the tension in her spine. Could let her hands lie open. Could, finally, open her eyes and look up into Frau Abramowitz's face.

"Well done," Frau Abramowitz said.

"I am well now?"

"No! You know one thing to do when you are sick now. There are herbs to help you, too: lavender, thyme, lemon balm. Steep them in hot water and drink it after you let the fear go. And remember to breathe slow and deep."

"So the sickness is in my mind, but the cure is in my body?"

"Part of the cure," Frau Abramowitz said. "Your fear has words? It speaks to you?"

"Yes, but I try not to listen."

"Listen. How do you drive out shadows? You bring a light. Hear the words of your fear. Say them. They will sound less true when you hear them clear. When you hear them, when you know them for lies, then say the truth you know instead."

Verity did that every day for a week, until she was more than sick of the sound of her own thoughts spoken aloud. At the end of that week she felt a little better. She stopped speaking the lies and the truth, stopped tensing and relaxing. *I am well*, she told herself. *At least, I am well enough.*

A week after that the fear had her out in the middle of the night, trudging down the frozen road toward the Quinn cabin to see if she'd dropped a coal from her shovel while fire-borrowing and kindled their woodshed. She hadn't, of course. But on her way back she was too busy cursing herself for a crazy fool to watch her footing. She slipped on black ice, fell, and cried out.

Felix Quinn came out cradling a gun. When he saw Verity gingerly picking herself up, he dropped the gun and came to give her an arm. His wife Bridget insisted on putting Verity in a roll of blankets in front of her own fire. When Verity explained clumsily that she was walking because she was afraid of ... of ... nothing, Mistress Quinn nodded and sat over her in the dark, praying.

In the morning Verity woke to find Mistress Quinn still sitting over her, singing in some Catholic language. It seemed to Verity that the song had run through her dreams, had turned them from nightmare back to quiet.

"That's a good song," she said. "Can you tell me what it means?"

"Kyrie eleison, Christe eleison, Kyrie eleison. Lord have mercy, Christ have mercy, Lord have mercy."

Verity sang that to herself the next time the fear pressed on her – which was soon. She tensed and relaxed, spoke the lies and truths, every day for a month. Finally, when the fear woke her in the night she stopped thinking, "I will kill them all by mistake," and began thinking, "I am still sick – I will have to keep talking to myself for another everlasting week."

She made one other change that was simpler and harder: she stopped trying to pretend to her neighbors that she was not afraid. Soon she did not have to pretend quite so much.

She went back to thank Mistress Quinn for her song, Goodman Knowlton for his prayers, Frau Abramowitz for her wisdom. She stayed to help Frau Abramowitz dig over her garden. While she dug, Frau Abramowitz told her about the uses of the plants she grew. After that Verity went with Frau Abramowitz to watch, and then to help, as she tended animals or people in sickness or in childbed. After a few months Verity began calling the older woman by her first name: Mirjam.

The following winter, while Mirjam was off tending a feverish child, Verity helped Bridget Quinn bring her first baby into the world.

The winter after that Verity walked the steep deer-track up from Blackburn Settlement to the Strangers' mountainside hollow, following the wiry girl who had come in search of a midwife.

The Strangers had trickled in over three years. Most spoke courteously to the people of Blackburn Settlement, though they spoke no more than they had need to, and did not encourage questions – which, indeed, the Blackburn folk were none too eager to ask. Some Strangers had coins or valuables to exchange for medicines or smithwork. Other things, it seemed, they preferred to provide for themselves. Nobody exactly invited them to build at the edge of the Settlement, though no one exactly told them to stay away. But they seemed ready enough to stay away, to keep going. Many asked whether there were more settlements or only open lands upriver. The first ones were told that there was nothing upriver, only the mountain shoulder, too steep for farming. The later ones were told that there were other newcomers who'd found a place up along. Newcomers, the Blackburn people said to them, for politeness' sake; but among themselves they always called the new ones the Strangers, and were glad they were content to remain so.

Until this girl, Martha, with her young face and old eyes, ran onto the village green, begging someone to come quick and help her mother who'd been in labor more than two days.

Verity took her to speak to Mirjam.

Mirjam was sick with a winter chill and had no strength to make the journey. "You go with the girl," she told Verity.

"I haven't the skill!" Verity protested.

"Do what you can. Remember, you turned the lambs and brought them out. People are not so different – only you can't feel for hooves."

"If I fail?" Verity's voice was sharp with fear.

This fear Martha understood. "No one will blame you, do you come and they die," she said. "If you do not come

..."

Verity went with Martha. She took a little sachet of dried lavender besides the sack of herbs she'd brought for the birthing, and when the fear gripped at her on the long cold trail she sniffed its scent and was a little comforted. At the Stranger settlement she looked warily at the wary-eyed people who came out to watch her, told herself about love casting out fear, and recognized, as she did so, that she saw fear, not menace, in their eyes.

When she came into the one-room hut where Martha's mother lay gasping, her fear fell away in concentration. There was room in her mind for nothing but the mother's breathing, the mother's pain, and the shape of the child in the birth-sac under her hands.

It was noon when Verity entered the Stranger settlement. It was growing dark when the child slid free of the mother in a gush of dark blood and other fluids. The cord was wrapped around the child's neck. The child was dead.

"My mother, she will live?" was all Martha said.

"Yes," Verity said. And by the next morning she was sure it was true.

Stranger women came to bury the child, to sit with the mother. Verity shrank from their eyes, but the only ones who spoke to her spoke thanks – except for one old woman who introduced herself as Irene and took Verity aside.

"I did what I could," Verity said miserably.

"I know this," Irene said. "We will return the favor as

we can."

"But what I could do wasn't good enough."

"Like as not the warning we know will not be enough to keep you safe," Irene said. Then she told Verity what they had fled from. What all of them had fled from, though they started from different places and at different times.

There was a fear-sickness that spread from settlement to settlement. It began with a thickening in the air and a foul smell that could not be traced to carrion or to an ill-managed privy. There were bad dreams and shadows in people's eyes. And then ...

One village had found cattle missing and decided they had been stolen by the woods people – by a band that had been at peace with them for years. The group that set off was supposed to take the cattle back, by stealth if possible, by force if necessary. The group that came back had no cattle, but they had singed clothing and shamed eyes, and it seemed they had set fire to the woods people's compound while its men were away hunting. They couldn't say just why they had done that. Some people stayed and barricaded their village's few stone buildings in preparation for the revenge attack they thought must surely follow. Others fled.

"So the killers ..."

"They are not with us," Irene assured Verity, but she didn't meet Verity's eyes as she hurried to the next part of her story.

In Irene's village there had been many accusations of

witchcraft following an outbreak of sickness. Three people had been hanged, and more had been accused. Some of the accused had managed to escape. Some others had fled in fear of being accused, or in fear of the strangeness in their neighbors' eyes.

"We ran," Irene said, "and we kept running.'

"And now?"

"Where else can we run? The slope above us is too steep, and we dare not go back down the river; Isidore and Marie came last month and said the fear-plague had reached Gilead Settlement. We warn you now of what may come."

"Does it follow you?"

"I do not think so. Or at least, not only us. Sometimes we traveled to a new place and found the fear already there."

Verity returned to Blackburn with the warning gnawing her mind. She told Mirjam, who said gravely, "You know we all came here running. Came to this country, and then came to Blackburn."

She also told Goodman Knowlton, who shook his head. "If they have brought a curse with them ..." he said. "You did well to tell me, Mistress Clark. But don't speak widely of it; there's fear enough here already."

Verity told no one else. As days and weeks went by with nothing worse to contend with than the usual sicknesses and fears, the warning loosened its hold on her mind. When Martha or other upriver folk came asking for cures, or bringing mushrooms or honey or beeswax candles, Verity welcomed them, and soon she forgot to wonder if they brought a curse.

Then there came a night when Verity woke with her heart racing and her throat tight with fear. In her dream, as in her waking life, she'd come home exhausted from another healing trip to the Strangers' hollow. But in reality she'd banked the fire and gone to bed, whereas in her dream she'd fallen asleep by the fire and waked to find the thatch of the roof blazing above her.

She opened her eyes and stared into the dark. No blaze. She looked toward the hearth, saw the faint glow of coals banked under ash. *It was only a dream*, she told herself.

I am supposed to be free of such dreams now, she answered herself. *How is it that I am mad again?*

I'm not mad. I'm awake now and I know there is nothing wrong. But she still smelled smoke, smoke and something else foul. Was she sure, after all, that nothing was wrong? And could she be sure she was truly awake, not dreaming comfort while her people burned?

She shook her head impatiently, got up, and made her way to the herb garden. Lavender was best for what ailed her, but she'd used or given away all her dry store, and there'd be no more for another month yet. Thyme would help.

Part of her mind thought that, while another part pictured the fire spilling from her hearth. That image burned in her mind. She named the lie and the truth aloud. The image didn't fade. Neither did the smoke-stench leave her nostrils.

The moon slipped out from behind a cloud for a moment. In its cold light Verity thought for a moment that she saw smoke. But smoke wasn't white like this mist, didn't shape itself like this mist into horrible, impossible faces that dissolved and re-formed.

She'd never been mad in that way before. Breathing and speaking and herb tea might not be enough for that kind of madness. She needed help; she needed someone else.

"Go see if there's a light in the Quinns' window," she told herself out loud. "Even if there isn't, you can knock for them this once. After the baby, they'll be willing enough. Yes, you're ashamed to be fear-sick again. Well, they've seen you sick and shamed before. It will be all right."

She started up the road. Someone was already up, walking ahead of her. No, running ahead of her, shouting: "Cowards!"

Verity ran after him. "Master Berowne? What's amiss?"

He turned to her. Was it the mist that made his face look so pale?

"Those devils from upriver were mocking at my wife in the privy," he said.

"Are you sure?"

"She heard them. And I did dream of them. We've ignored the danger too long." His breath steamed too. No, misted.

Verity's question was cut off by another cry from further up the road.

"Seamus! My Seamus!"

Mistress Quinn said the babe Verity had helped her birth, now a lad of almost two years, was gone; he wasn't in his bed; the cabin door was left open; they called and he didn't answer.

"The Strangers must have taken him," Goodman Berowne said. "The ones who mocked my wife."

"I did dream so," Mistress Quinn said.

By the time Verity and her neighbors reached the village green, the mist was thick as sea fog, distorting the faces and voices of the gathering crowd. Many had heard voices, had warning dreams. Ethan Carr's sheep were gone. Everyone knew Carr was no great hand with fences, but together with the voices, and the dreams, and the stolen child.

Verity felt sick horror filling her. She crouched, let it ball her tight, then let it out, breathing in ...

Breathing in the smell of mold and smoke, fear and shame. The smell of her madness.

But it was more than that. The smell was fouler than she'd ever known it.

The moon tore through the cloud again, showing the strange shapes formed by the sick-hued mist. She breathed hard and ragged with fear, saw the paleness flowing from her open mouth, wheeling up to join the writhen mass of demons in the air. And not only from her mouth, but from the mouths and nostrils of her neighbors.

"Look!" Verity shrilled. "Look at the mist! Think of what you're saying! Neighbors, it's not the Strangers who've hurt us. Look at those shapes, and smell the air! There's evil here among us, in us all. We're not the first. Master Knowlton ... Mirjam ... I told you about the fear-plagues away downriver."

"Yes, there's evil," Goodman Berowne called. "Look at the shapes, indeed! There's witchcraft in this. And who's the witch?"

"Verity Clark was ever a strange one," a woman's voice answered.

Fear choked Verity. She fled blindly back the way she had come. She didn't hear Goodman Knowlton urging that Verity Clark was a good Christian woman who had borne her affliction patiently and been a help to many.

The pain in her chest reminded her to breathe. She focused on her breath, making a little space outside the fear. In that space she understood that she was not the one in danger, even before the voices behind her cried out together, "The Strangers!"

"Go to them," Verity said aloud to herself. "Warn them." She took the wagon-path across the back of the Settlement toward the slopes, turned up the deer-trod and followed it by feel as much as sight.

After the first steep scramble she stopped to draw breath. The mist trailed after her, carrying the magnified and distorted echoes of hurrying feet and shouting voices. She was ahead of them, could stay ahead, but not far enough ahead to give the Strangers time to disappear. And where could they go on this bitter night? Fear pressed in on her, tight and confining as the young hemlocks that grew denser than a hedge on either side.

That was it. The hemlocks grew thick and tight for a good quarter-mile, and the path was barely wide enough for two to go abreast. Those who came would be hard-put to go around her. This, then, was the place to turn and face them.

"Stop!" she shouted, her voice echoing weirdly in the mist. "Stop! Do no harm!"

The torches stopped a few yards from her. She couldn't see who held the light.

"What have you done with him?" asked a furious voice she didn't recognize. "Tell us now or it'll be the worse for you."

"Hold." That was Goodman Knowlton. "This isn't one of them. It's Mistress Clark. She knows no more than we. Less, poor creature, if she's afflicted again."

"I am not mad now," she said. "I was mad, and you helped me, Master Knowlton. You told me I'd been listening to the devil's lies. You said the devil lies to us all. He is lying to you now."

"The child is truly gone."

"Did anyone stay back near his house to search for him? Or to welcome him if he wanders back?"

"What use?" That was Goodman Berowne, not Knowlton. "When we know those devils have him."

"How do you know that?"

There was a brief silence.

Verity answered her own question. "You know that the same way I used to think I knew that if I didn't douse my fire with snow every night it would burn the settlement down. I knew because my fear told me. No other reason." She sighed. "Reason enough I thought it, then. But you taught me better, Master Knowlton. Teach them better! What did they come to do tonight? To demand the boy? To threaten? To kill? You know Holy Writ; you know it was an evil spirit of madness that made Saul try to kill David."

"But Saul knew David, knew him for a friend," Knowlton argued. "And what do we know of the Strangers? They came running from a curse; they came bringing a curse."

True, Verity thought, *that's true. Isn't it? They told me. Why can't I remember?* She looked aside, wondering if her mind would clear once she wasn't looking into Knowlton's pale strained face.

The face that looked back at her from the hemlocks was paler and more terrible. Her father's face as it was just before he died, pain-twisted, blood at the corner of his mouth. *He is dead,* she told herself. *Not here. Not here.*

No, the face was Goody Berowne's, contemptuously staring at the crazy woman. But Verity had never noticed before that Goody Berowne had such long sharp teeth. *She doesn't,* Verity thought desperately. *Not real. It's the mist...*

The mist is coming up with them. They're bringing the curse. They say the Strangers are devils, they said I was mad or witched, but it's them, it's them, it's their evil they would put on us. All the times they turned away from me, talked about me as though I couldn't hear ...

But Goodman Knowlton looked at me, talked to me as a friend. And so did Mistress Quinn. And Mirjam. Mirjam told me .... she told me.

Bring a light, Mirjam's voice murmured in her mind. *Bring a light.*

Mirjam was surely out of reach – it wasn't likely she'd been able to make the steep climb as fast as her abler-bodied neighbors. Verity herself would have to deal, using what Mirjam had taught her.

She remembered, then, what else Mirjam had said.

"You think they are cursed," Verity said, looking back at Goodman Knowlton, "because they came running. I was born in Blackburn, but my father and mother came there running from the fighting between the French and British. Master Knowlton, I've heard you tell how you came running from those who would have hanged you for a blasphemer. Mistress Quinn, you told me once what they did to your mother's people so that she fled. All our people came running. The curse is in all of us, if it's in them. It was in me, I know that much."

"The curse is in all of us," Master Knowlton agreed slowly. "Holy Writ says so. Let me think ..."

"Get her out of the way!" That was a woman's voice, thin and desperate. Mistress Quinn's. "Why are we listening to a madwoman while my Seamus is in danger?"

"I want to help your Seamus," Verity insisted. "I think he's lost in the mist back in Blackburn. The Strangers haven't taken him. There were no voices ahead of me on the trail, no lights. I want us to go back and find him. How could I not wish him well? I helped him into the world. You remember that! And you remember what I owed you from before. You said it right: I was cursed, I was mad, and you helped me. I want to help you now."

Verity launched into the song Mistress Quinn had sung to her. Her voice was weak and ragged. The mist clung in her throat. She was losing the note; she was losing her courage.

Mistress Quinn's voice joined hers. First it was thin and quavering; then it rolled rich and deep, and other voices joined it. A wind that smelled of lavender flowed down the path. The mists rolled back from Verity, and she breathed the clean air gratefully.

Someone was shouting away back down the trail. Verity sighed. She didn't know if she had the strength to talk them down again.

Then the wind stilled, the singing faded, and she heard the voice. Mirjam's voice.

"I found the boy!"

Verity ran down the path after the others, thinking she'd have to wait until they were all back in Blackburn to understand what had happened. But as she came out of the dense hemlocks she saw that, while others went on down toward the settlement, Mirjam had waited for her —

and so had Bridget Quinn.

"My Felix has Seamus; he'll be all right," Bridget Quinn said. "Frau Abramowitz found him out behind our cabin. Mistress – Verity – I'm sorry for what I called you."

"You weren't wrong," Verity said.

Bridget half-smiled and ran on down the track. Mirjam took Verity's hand, and they walked home together in the growing light.

* * *

Discussion Questions

1. At the start of the story Verity tells Goodman Knowlton, in the community center, that she is afraid of fear. What does she mean by this? What is causing her fear?

2. What does it mean to "Tell truth and shame the devil?" Does that really work in life?

3. Verity said, "… she stopped trying to pretend to her neighbors that she was not afraid." How much do you pretend not to be afraid in your life? Why do you pretend at all? Is there value in telling others your fears?

4. Why is Verity the only person in the story who can save the community from the fear-plague?

5. How does Verity fight the "fear-plague" mist in the story? What causes the "fear-plague" mist in real life? How do you fight it in real life?

As You Wish

Tyler W. Kurt (For Children)

SAD BEAR AND HIS FRIENDS had been living in the pitch black for years. *Absolute* blackness. They had been put in the trunk shortly after their child, George, had gotten a puppy. There's no sense of time in the blackness so they didn't know how long they'd been in there — months, maybe years.

And then, one day, they heard footsteps in the darkness. Clack, clack, clack, clack. The sound grew louder as it approached. Clack, clack, clack, clack. Would it mean a person would finally set them free? Would this be the person to let them out?

The room shifted violently. Fluffy, a stuffed white rabbit with just one eye, landed on top of Sad Bear, a teddy bear. Mr. Giraffe, a stuffed giraffe, fell onto Dolly, a hard-plastic doll with a yellowed dress and loose threads. Dolly also had, down the side of her face, a long red crayon mark in the shape of an A which made her self-conscious. As the trunk jostled the stuffed animals rolled around on each other until they finally landed with a thud.

The top of the trunk opened. After years of living in the dark the bright light temporarily blinded the animals as they looked up. Their eyes slowly adjusted and they saw, towering over them, an eccentrically-dressed elderly woman.

The woman had white hair that looked as if it hadn't been combed in years and a face thick with wrinkles from smiling. She was 75 years old if she was a day, but her clothes were that of a teenager in a time long past. In fact, her blouse and poodle skirt made it look like she was about to go to a 1950's dance. Her shoes, however, were Converse; one red and one white. And when she spoke, she used the words of an elderly woman but said the words in a light, fairy-like voice.

"Why, hello dears," said the woman. "What do we have here?"

The woman pulled Dolly out of the trunk and examined her. "Now aren't you in sad shape. Old dress, torn threads …" the woman quickly licked her thumb and started rubbing the red crayon mark off Dolly's face "… it looks like somebody was learning their alphabet on you. Well, this will never do."

The woman looked down at the other stuffed animals in the trunk. "A sad lot indeed." She gently set Dolly down outside the trunk and picked up the stuffed Beagle that was jammed between two other animals. As she lifted the Beagle it exposed its missing leg with stuffing hanging out.

"Be careful with my stuffing!" shouted the Beagle.

"I'm being careful," the woman replied.

"You can hear me?!" the Beagle asked, shocked.

The woman held the Beagle up to look him straight in

the eye, because she felt it was more respectful to look someone directly in the eye when you spoke to them. "Well of course I can. Is your leg in the trunk? Should I get it for you?"

"It's not in the trunk, the puppy ripped it off!"

"Well," the woman said, "if I ever meet that puppy I will have to explain to him the proper way to play with children's toys."

The woman gently set the stuffed Beagle on the ground outside the trunk next to Dolly. "At the very least, I can sew that hole of yours closed so you don't lose any more stuffing. You will be a three-legged dog, but that's better than being a dog that's losing its stuffing."

"Excuse me, ma'am," said Sad Bear from the trunk looking up. Sad Bear, you see, was named Sad Bear because he had a frown sewn on his face for a mouth when he was born. This caused him to be sad even when happy things were happening all around him. "Excuse me ma'am," said Sad Bear. "Can you really hear us?"

The woman picked up Sad Bear to look him in the eyes, just as she had done with the stuffed Beagle. "I suppose I can. Hold on, let me get all of you out of the trunk so we can be properly introduced."

The woman gently set Sad Bear down then reached into the trunk and pulled out all the stuffed animals: Mr. Giraffe, Edwina the elephant, as well as Fluffy the white rabbit, Mr. Panda, and a rainbow unicorn that all the other animals made fun of because she stood out and had no name at all. She grabbed them all, and, one by one, lined them all up in a circle, so they could have a proper conversation.

When they were all sitting in their places, Fluffy the stuffed white rabbit, looked up at the woman and spoke first, "Excuse me Miss, but how is it you can hear us?" he said in a rabbit's squeaky voice.

"Well," the woman said, sitting down cross-legged in front of them, a rather impressive feat, considering her age, "You all can hear each other, can't you?"

"Yes," said Fluffy, "but we're stuffed animals and you're a real person. And real people can't hear stuffed animals, except sometimes when they are very young."

"I guess I never grew up," the woman replied. Then she glanced around at the other stuffed animals in the circle to examine them. "Well, you all are a motley group in dire need of repairs, if you don't mind me saying."

"We have been in the trunk a very long time," said Sad Bear. "And before we got put away by George, that was our child, the puppy would play with us very rough." The three-legged Beagle held up his stump where his leg used to be to prove his point. The woman looked over at the Beagle.

"Indeed," replied the woman looking where his leg used to be. "But, like I said, I will fix you. I will fix *all* of you, and you'll be in ship-shape and ready to go to a new home in no time. So, let's make a list of all the things that need to be fixed. First, of course, my Beagle friend, I will sew your leg hole shut so you can stop losing stuffing. Or, if you would prefer, I can make you a new leg that matches."

"You can do that?" asked the Beagle in wonder.

"Why, of course I can," said the woman, who took out a small notepad and a pencil to write notes as she spoke. "One new Beagle leg."

"Excuse me ma'am," Dolly said, seeing her chance. "My dress is very dirty, you see, and it has yellowed with age when it should be white…and the threads are all coming out-- "

"— Yes, yes, of course," the woman interrupted. "I shall sew you a new white one." The woman spoke out loud as she wrote in her notepad, "One new white dress. You appear to be a size negative 32, is that correct?"

Dolly blushed and lowered her head. "Why, yes ma'am, that's correct."

"How many dresses would you like?"

"I like?" Dolly asked.

"Yes. How many dresses would you like me to make for you?"

"Well," said Dolly, "I've only ever had the one."

"I'll make you three to get you started, and more later if you want." Dolly heard this and blushed.

Fluffy, the white rabbit, spoke up next in his squeaky rabbit voice. "I lost one of my eyes to the dog; could you sew me on a new eye?"

"Oh my, yes, I see that. That will never do. I will find you a new eye to sew on." The woman wrote in her notepad as she spoke. "One new rabbit eye."

"Actually," Fluffy said, "If it's not too much to ask, my eyesight wasn't all that good even before with two eyes. You see, when I was born my eyes were made with the cheapest plastic. Do you think you could sew on *better* eyes so that I can see better than before?"

"I don't see why not."

"And I ..." said Mr. Panda, speaking up for the first time in a Panda's deep proper voice. "I am quite fat, even for a Panda. Would it be too much trouble for you to take some of my stuffing out? Not all of it, mind you, just a little bit, so that I still look like a Panda, but I look like a *thin* Panda?"

"Of course," said the woman, "What else? I can change anything you want. I can make you taller, or shorter, or fatter, or thinner. I can change your eyes, or even your fur. As a matter of fact, while I'm at it, would anyone else like me to take some of their stuffing out?" The elephant's trunk went up.

Mr. Giraffe, a stuffed orange and brown giraffe that spoke very quickly when he spoke, spoke up next. "I know I'm a giraffe. And I know giraffes have long necks, but I think I look very silly standing next to everyone else with such a long neck. I would like 4 1/4 inches taken off of my neck please."

"Of course," the woman replied with a smile and note in her notebook. "Exactly 4 and 1/4 inches ..."

"You can do that?" asked the very shy rainbow unicorn.

"Yes, I can."

"Well, then could you …" said the unicorn very softly. "You see, I'm a unicorn—"

"—Yes, I see that," said the woman. "Unicorns are very rare and very special indeed."

"Yes, but you see," said the unicorn almost in a whisper, "I don't want to be rare and special. Could you … please … take off my unicorn horn and make my fur brown, so that people would think I was a horse?"

The woman gave a slow nod-like bow. "If that is what you wish." The only animal that hadn't asked for anything was Sad Bear and so, the woman turned to him last. "And what about you Mr. Bear, that frown stitched on your face looks terribly sad. You must be sad all the time."

"I am," said Sad Bear. "From the first day I was made I've always had this frown on my face, and so I've always been sad."

"Well then, I shall *fix* that too. It won't take but a minute. I shall take that stitching out and stitch a smile on your face, so you will always be happy even when sad things are happening."

"Thank you," responded Sad Bear politely. "But if it's all the same to you, I think I'd like to keep my frown."

"Well, why would you want to do that? I am going to fix his leg, and her dress, and give him two brand new eyes that are better than the cheap plastic eyes he was born with. I'm going to turn a unicorn into a horse, take the stuffing out of Mr. Panda and his elephant friend, and make the giraffe's neck shorter. As long as I am doing all of those things, I could just as well sew a smile on your face."

"Yes, I'm sure you could" said Sad Bear. "And thank you for helping all my friends, but you see, ma'am, my name is 'Sad Bear' because I have a frown on my face. Because I *am* a Sad Bear."

"I see, but you don't have to be sad," said the woman. "Don't you know that being *happy* is good and being *sad* is bad. Just like missing a leg is bad and having all your legs is good. And having one eye is bad, and having two eyes is good, and having two very good eyes is even better still. And why would you want to be a unicorn or a giraffe and stand out, when you can be so very average and blend in? Don't you want to be fixed?"

Sad Bear thought about this for a while and thought a long time about how best to explain himself without offending the eccentrically dressed woman or his friends.

"I think …" said Sad Bear slowly, "… even though I have a frown sewn on my face, and I am sad, even when good things are happening … I think …" said Sad Bear, "… I would prefer to just be me. Even if, you see, that is just a sad bear."

"I see," said the woman with a warm smile and a nod. "As you wish."

* * *

Discussion Questions

1. Which of the toys asked for things that you think were okay for them to ask for? As a reminder, the beagle wanted his torn off leg sewn back on, the doll wanted a new dress, the panda and elephant wanted to have some stuffing removed. The unicorn wanted to look like a horse, and the rabbit wanted his eyes replaced with better eyes. What is the distinction between each request being a "good request" and a "bad request?"

2. What are the things about us that we should improve, or correct, and what are the things we should leave alone? What is the distinction between the two?

3. Was Sad Bear right in refusing the woman's offer to remove his frown and sew a smile on his face so he would always be happy? Why/why not?

4. If someone could magically fix something about you, or improve something to make you better, would you let them? What would you change?

Bunny Racing

Tyler W. Kurt (For Children)

IN THE LAND OF RABBITS, there were two young bunny rabbits, Hopper and Bounce, and they were the very best of friends. Hopper and Bounce played together almost every day and did the usual things that bunnies did, like scrunch their noses, and scratch their ears, but their favorite thing to do was RUN.

They ran everywhere they went together and because they ran all the time, they got faster and faster. Sometimes they would race each other, but they were almost exactly the same speed, so it was almost always a tie.

One day they were running in a field when an older rabbit saw them and said, "Dang, you two are the fastest bunnies I have ever seen, maybe the fastest bunnies in the world. You two should enter the Rabbit Racing Championships!" Hopper and Bounce's eyes immediately lit up with excitement.

"I'm going to be the fastest rabbit in the race!" said Hopper.

"You mean the second fastest rabbit," Bounce said jokingly, "because you are going to be right behind me!"

Well, they did go to the race, and it was a huge

race! There were more rabbits there to watch the race than Hopper or Bounce had ever seen in one place in their entire lives. And there were rabbits there to race, too! Tall rabbits, short rabbits, brown rabbits, white rabbits. Rabbits with big ears, and rabbits with small ears. Rabbits of every shape and size.

Well, pretty soon it was time to start, so Hopper and Bounce lined up with the other rabbits. Then the announcer yelled "Go!"

Hopper and Bounce were fast, and within just a few strides they were already leading the race.

They ran through a field of tall brown grass where they could hardly see, then through a dried-out riverbed. Then over a beautiful field of short green grass that felt soft on their rabbit feet.

"We are … going to … win!" Hopper said to Bounce, through heavy breathing. But just as he said that he saw three other rabbits, led by a rabbit with a bent ear, coming up behind them, gaining ground. Thump, thump. Thump, thump.

"We … have to … run … faster!" yelled Bounce. But there was no hope. Bent Ear and his two friends ran past Hopper and Bounce. Bent Ear went on to win the race, and Hopper and Bounce came in fourth and fifth place.

"They were … so fast," Hopper said, still out of breath. "They must run all the time. I'm going to hop over to them, and talk to them, and learn everything they have to teach me." And that's exactly what he did.

A year later, Hopper and Bounce were back at the race

ready to try to win again. This time, however, just as they were heading to the starting line, Hopper pulled Bounce by the ear into a near-by bush.

"What are you doing!" screamed Bounce, "that's my ear you're pulling on!"

Hopper looked around to make sure no other rabbits were looking, and then pulled out a very strange carrot. "This," said Hopper, "is what Bent Ear and his friends were eating before the race last year that made them so fast."

"What is it?" asked Bounce.

"It's a special carrot from the forbidden forest—"

"—the forbidden forest!" shouted Bounce, "But no bunny is allowed in the forbidden forest, because it's so dangerous!"

"I know," said Hopper, "But they went there, so I went there. I know I broke the rules, but it made me really mad that they beat us last year. So, when they told me what they did, I did it, too."

"But that's cheating," said Bounce.

"Look," said Hopper. "We both know we are the fastest rabbits out here. The only reason Bent Ear and his friends beat us is because they ate these special carrots from the forbidden forest before the race. So, if we eat them too, we aren't getting a SPECIAL ADVANTAGE, we are just making everything equal again. So, it's not really cheating." Hopper started eating his special carrot and handed Bounce the other special carrot for him to eat.

What Hopper said made sense. If EVERYONE was eating the special carrots, then maybe it wasn't really cheating? Bounce looked at the special carrot Hopper was holding out for him and he was thinking about eating it, but then his stomach started to feel like two butterflies were dancing in it. Something inside made Bounce feel like eating the special carrot was wrong.

"No," Bounce said, "I think I'd rather just run on my own."

"Okay," Hopper said, "suit yourself."

Not too much later, the race started and, just like the year before, Hopper and Bounce started off faster than all the other rabbits. "See," Bounce said to Hopper, "I told you I didn't need the special carrot!"

And, just like last year, they ran through a field of tall brown grass, then through a dried-out riverbed, and then over a beautiful field of short green grass that felt soft on their rabbit feet.

But, just like the year before, when Bounce looked back, he saw Bent Ear and his friends gaining ground on them. Thump, thump. Thump, thump. Bounce turned to Hopper to yell "Run Faster!" but when he looked around, Hopper was already far out in front of him. The special carrot was working.

Bounce ran as fast as his rabbit feet could carry him, but Hopper was even faster. Just like the year before, Bent Ear and his friends ran past Bounce. But not only that, the other rabbits passed Bounce, too. "The secret is out," thought Bounce, "EVERYONE is eating the special carrots but me!"

In the end, Hopper won the race, and Bounce finished dead last.

This went on for five years, which is a very long time in rabbit years. And in all five years Hopper and the other rabbits would eat their special carrots before the race. And in all five years Hopper came in first place, and Bounce came in dead last.

Well, no bunny had ever won the race FIVE YEARS IN A ROW, so Hopper became very famous. At least, famous for a rabbit. All the other rabbits knew him by name, and they all admired him. Nobody admired Bounce.

In fact, Hopper was so important, and so famous, that he had lots of new rabbit friends. He had so many new friends that Hopper hardly ever had time to spend with Bounce anymore. And this made Bounce sad, and maybe just a little bit jealous.

Hopper used his new rabbit fame to help other rabbits that needed help too. Like, one time, when a rabbit lost his bushy tail to a coyote, Hopper used his fame to get all the other rabbits to collect cotton from the fields. He then gave the cotton to the tail-less rabbit so he could put the cotton on its behind where its tail used to be. Of course, a cotton tail isn't as good as a real tail, but it's better than no tail at all.

Finally, in the sixth year, after coming in last place again, Bounce just couldn't take it anymore and he yelled out at the finish line, as loud as he could, "They are all cheating, every bunny is cheating. They are all eating special carrots from the forbidden forest!"

The crowd went quiet. The old rabbit who was in charge of the race, whose fur had turned gray with age, came up to Hopper and the other rabbits and asked, "Is that true?" But he could tell by the guilty look on Hopper's face that it was.

"Yes, it's true," said Hopper. "But I wanted so badly to win, and everybody else was eating the special carrots, so doesn't that make us all equal?"

"I'm not eating the special carrots!" said Bounce.

"Well maybe you should!" snapped Hopper. "I tried to tell you to eat them, but your pride wouldn't let you! Look at all the good I've done by being famous! I have helped so many other bunnies that needed help! If you take this all away, I won't be famous, and I won't be able to help other rabbits that need help. Also," said Hopper, "I won't be able to win the race anymore."

The old rabbit thought a long time. Both Bounce and Hopper had made good points. But finally, the old rabbit decided what to do …

***

Discussion Questions

1. Is Hopper right? If everyone is eating the special carrots, is it really cheating?

2. Does it matter that the only way to get the special carrots is by breaking the rules and going into the forbidden forest?

3. Does Hopper doing good things with his fame make up for the fact that he was eating the special carrots from the forbidden forest?

4. Did Bounce really tell on Hopper and the others because he was angry they were cheating, or because he was angry he was losing?

5. Should Hopper and Bounce remain friends after all this is over?

6. What do you think the old rabbit should do?

Additional Information

Newsletter

Join our newsletter list and receive weekly links to free short stories from After Dinner Conversation.

Reviews

If you enjoyed reading this story, please consider doing an online Amazon review. It's only a few seconds of your time, but it is very important in continuing the series. Good reviews mean higher rankings. Higher rankings mean more sales. More sales mean a greater ability to release stories. It really is that simple, and it all starts with you!

Podcasts

Listen to our podcast discussion of After Dinner short stories on Apple Podcasts, Stitcher, Spotify, or wherever podcasts are played. Or, if you prefer, watch the podcasts on our YouTube channel or download the mp3 file from our web page.

Patreon

Get exclusive early access to short stories and ad-free podcasts, as well as the ability to vote on what stories are selected for podcast discussions, by supporting us on Patreon for $5/month.

Book Clubs

"After Dinner Conversation" supports book clubs! Email info@afterdinnerconversation.com to get free short stories for your book club to read and discuss! Or join the weekly "virtual book club" discussions in our closed Facebook Group.

Social

Find us on Facebook, YouTube, Instagram, and Twitter.

From the Publisher

After Dinner Conversation is a growing series of short stories across genres to draw out deeper discussions with friends and family. Each story is an accessible example of an abstract ethical or philosophical idea and is accompanied by suggested discussion questions.

Special Thanks

Nothing gets done in a vacuum, and that is certainly true of this anthology and the After Dinner Conversation Series.

Thank you first, and foremost, to all the writers and readers. None of this happens without your writing creativity, and none of this continues without dedicated readers who support thoughtful writing.

A very special thanks to Page Inman, Viggy Parr Hampton, Judith Rubin, and many other amazing readers who have (and continue to) work tirelessly through the pile of submissions to find the gems that we publish, including many of the stories in this very book.

Thank you to the Classical Education Curriculum, the Trinity Schools, the Great Hearts Schools, Tempe Preparatory Academy, Mortimer Adler, the Great Books Movement generally, and the Humane Letters **curriculum** specifically. In a world where facts are universally available, you understand the role of education is also to teach critical thinking skills to help students determine what those facts *mean*.

For the podcast, thank you to Jeremy *"I did some research"* Cheek. The topics are the writing, but the "conversation among friends" is why people keep coming back to listen. Thank you also to **La Gatarra Cat Café** in Tempe, Arizona for sponsoring/hosting us for Season One.

Thank you to Jessica *"I'm a humanist"* **Hilt** for podcast support, but also for your experience, guidance, and so much more than can ever be said. (Like, literally, if I said it, someone might go to jail…)

Thank you to **Buddy Early** for his copy editing. You don't simply edit writing, you make each writer the better version of themselves. You are the only editor we will ever use. And to Jennifer Colafranceschi for all her encouragement and support.

Thank you to Kari Granville and Greg Minton for their support and for a free place to stay while assembling this book.

And finally, and most importantly, thank you to **Ashley Robota**. You are a podcast superstar and an anchor of stability. But, more importantly, you are the one who gave this permission to happen. Without your support and encouragement, this would just be another random idea floating around that never got done.

Editor-In-Chief

* * *